Praise for
AN IRAQI IN PARIS

"A touching novel-cum-autobiography about days of sex and
movies, politics and poverty, on the 1980s Left Bank. It's an Arabic
answer to Miller's *Tropic of Cancer* – occasionally shocking; always
witty and humane. Also included is his delightful memoir of an
Iraqi childhood."
Boyd Tonkin, The Independent, London

"It is difficult to find another book in Arabic like *An Iraqi in Paris*.
Samuel writes because he plays with life. It reminds us of Henry
Miller; the power of life and the power of story-telling."
Abbas Beydoun, As-Safir newspaper, Beirut

"As Shimon observes in Paris, the misery of the homeless is like
Scheherezade in that it creates endless fantasies in order to escape
from the present situation: the story sequence, the cinema and the
imagination alike provide the internal resources with which
humanity can face despair. Powerful book."
Jane Jakeman, Times Literary Supplement, London

"This is one of the gems of autobiographical writings in the
modern period, I read the book with much pain, but also with a
great sense of pleasure derived from the intelligent sarcasm and
absurdity, both of which are at the heart of this dual
autobiography."
Abdo Wazen, Al-Hayat newspaper, London/Beirut

"Shimon's bare style, denuded of artifice, makes reading *An Iraqi
in Paris* a true adventure, the style giving the book an immediacy
that compensates for the strangeness of the main character and the
unlikelihood of the events that he lives through, events that are,
nevertheless, real. This combination of a realist style with content
more akin to the adventures of Sindbad helps to make *An Iraqi in
Paris* a modern Arab fable, sustaining the moral such a fable
requires: follow your dreams and you will succeed."
Hanna Ziadeh, Al-Ahram Weekly, Cairo

"It is a manifesto of tolerance. It is a text more like the taste of wine: sweet and sour, biting, exhilarating, strong and flowing. Such a novel gives the saga of Iraqi (and Arab) exile a literary value we have been waiting for for such a long time."
Yussef Bazzi, Al-Mustaqbal newspaper, Beirut

"A Modern-Day Odysseus on the Way to Hollywood. A thrilling film, full of love and humour, kindness and humanity, dreams and illusions, a film now written as an autobiographical novel which we will read with delight and admiration."
Fadhil al-Azzawi, www.qantara.de, Berlin

"Throughout this careening, fast-paced, episodic narrative Shimon never loses his poignant touch for humor, he consistently folds the absurdity of political violence into the intimacy of human relations."
Kaelen Wilson-Goldie, Daily Star, Beirut

"Pedlar, traveller, militant, refugee, literary authority? Above all, perhaps, this personable Iraqi is a movie buff, a kind of frustrated filmmaker. It would be hard to follow the chronological life course of so non-linear a man. Suffice to say that 10 years since settling in London – where his name has become synonymous with both *Banipal*, the English language's best known journal of Arabic literature, and kikah.com, the vastly popular 'website for Arab and international cultures' – Shimon's hard-won sense of fulfilment belies dreams unrealised . . ."
Youssef Rakha, Al-Ahram Weekly, Cairo

"The story of a whole generation of Arabs, whose life was destroyed by the stupid ideologies that controlled Arab politics."
Amir Taheri, Asharq al-Awsat newspaper, London

"A cinematographic odyssey. At once amusing and touching, Samuel Shimon lets his gaze travel with a camera's precision."
Le monde des livres, Paris

"Samuel Shimon is the most enchanting of interlocutors writing with a clarity which shifts from comedy to the tragic, but always deeply human."
Alison Croggon

AN IRAQI IN PARIS

AUTOBIOGRAPHICAL NOVEL

BY

SAMUEL SHIMON

Translated from the Arabic
by
Piers Amodia and Christina Phillips
with the author

Banipal Books

First published in Arabic in 2005
by Manshurat al-Jamal as *Iraqi fi Barees*

First edition in English translation
published by Banipal Books, 2005
Second edition in English published by
Bloomsbury Qatar Foundation Publishing, 2010

This third edition, with revised translation,
published by Banipal Books, 2016
British Library Cataloguing-in-Publication Data:
a catalogue record for this book is available in the British Library
ISBN 978-0-9574424-8-1

Banipal Books
1 Gough Square, London EC4A 3DE
www.banipal.co.uk

Set in Bembo
Printed and bound
by Lightning Source

To the memory of
Gorgiya Brikha Hermiz, my mother,
who died in Damascus on 27 February 2015
and is buried there

ABOUT THE AUTHOR

Samuel Shimon was born into a poor Assyrian family in Iraq in 1956. He left his country in 1979 to go to Hollywood and become a film-maker, travelling via Damascus, Amman, Beirut, Nicosia, Cairo and Tunis. In 1985 he settled in Paris as a refugee. He began writing autobiographical short stories in 1979, and poetry in 1985. In Paris his small press, Editions Gilgamesh, published a number of volumes of poetry and fiction by Arab authors including two collections of his own poetry. In 1996 he moved to London, where he has lived ever since. In 1998 he co-founded *Banipal*, the renowned international magazine of contemporary Arab literature in English translation. He is also the founder and editor of the popular literary website in Arabic www.kikah.com, and in 2013, of *Kikah* magazine for international literature in Arabic. He and his wife Margaret Obank edited *A Crack in the Wall* (2000), poems by sixty Arab poets from the last twenty years of the 20th Century, and he was also editor of *Beirut39: New Writing from the Arab World* (2010). His second novel *Underwear Under War* will come out soon. A profile in the *Frankfurter Allgemeine Zeitung* in 2003 described him as "the Initiator" and "a tireless missionary for literary matters".

CONTENTS

A NOTE

California, January 2004

'You see, I got to America before you did,' my mother declared laughing, as she watched me getting out of my uncle's car. 'You killed us with your Hollywood! It's here, just a stone's throw away.'

As I approached her, I noticed she had become very old. It was our first meeting after more than twenty-five years. I was still gazing at her as she continued, 'Do you know how to drive? Take one of your uncle's cars and just go there!'

My mother took advantage of the chaos that engulfed Iraq after the US invasion in 2003 when it became possible to leave the country, and decided to visit her sister who had lived in Modesto, California, since 1973. I, too, took this opportunity to go and see my mother.

'Oh my Shmuel,' she cried, and she hugged me and started to cry. Suddenly she looked at me, with tears streaming down her face: 'What's happened to your nose, is it still growing?' she laughed.

I laughed too, and kissing her head and pointing at her feet, I said, 'Look at your socks, Mother! You've had holes like those in your socks since I was a child!'

'Where have you been all these years, son?'

Before I could respond, she added, 'You know, Shmuel, just a few moments after we named you, I grew very sad and told myself that with such a name we were placing too much on the shoulders of this baby!'

9

The dream is endangered
friends laugh at my dreams
while I am afraid of dying
don't kill me
listen to me
I'm the runaway from museums
I'm the Assyrian boy

PART ONE

The Road to Hollywood

Baghdad, 1979
One morning in January, I woke up and immediately looked up at the clock hanging in the hall to see that it was nearly six o'clock. That was good because the bus that would take me from Baghdad to Damascus wasn't leaving until half past nine. I had packed my little shoulder bag before going to bed the night before.

I looked at my family. They were still asleep in the large room that we used as a bedroom at night and a living room during the day. They slept in their day clothes on the threadbare mattresses spread out on the damp cement floor. My mother was sleeping in the middle of the room, and beside her were my two little sisters Nahrain and Mary. On the far side of the room, Robin and John were sleeping next to one another, and my father slept on a heap of old clothes in a corner at the back, while Teddy and Samson were on the two long wooden benches in the hall.

I lay down next to my mother and kissed her head, whispering in her ear, 'Mum, Mum, Mum. Wake up, Mum! You're usually awake at this time, why not today? Please wake up! I'm leaving soon, and you might never see me again.'

'Have you gone crazy?' my mother whispered back. 'Where are you going, my son?'

'To Hollywood,' I replied. 'Have you forgotten all my dreams, Mum?'

'He's going to Hollywood!' she uttered in a low mocking voice and closed her eyes again.

'Yes, Mum, to Hollywood,' I said loudly. 'Why won't you believe me?' She didn't answer.

I drew close to Mary, kissed her and whispered in her ear, 'Good morning, Mary . . . Hello!' But she didn't stir.

'Oh! I have to go to school,' I then heard Nahrain say. I rushed to her and kissed her face and neck.

'Nahrain, I'm travelling to America now.'

Beautiful Nahrain smiled at me and said, 'Let me go and wash my face.'

I kissed her face, telling her it was cleaner than the water. Then I looked again at sleeping Mary's face. My God, how I loved her. I used to tell her: 'When I become a film director, I'll make you the star of my movies.'

'When will you get to America?' Nahrain asked.

'In a month, perhaps two,' I said.

At that, my mother said, 'You fool, you'll be back in two or three days.' I threw myself at her and kissed her repeatedly.

'Impossible, impossible, Mum. I'll never come back, no matter what. Believe me. Please, Mum, kiss me before I leave. That's all I ask of you.'

My mother opened her eyes and said, 'Bring your head closer, crazy boy,' before kissing me.

Then I turned to my father and kissed him. He opened his eyes and smiled. I gestured to him, slicing through the air with my hand while blowing breath out of my mouth, then pointing with my right index finger to my chest and then to the ground. My father understood I was telling him I was going.

He smiled, climbed out of his bed, and went to the bathroom, to return moments later having washed his face and combed his hair straight back in order to look elegant for the goodbyes. I gave him a big hug, then watched him go back, sit on his bed and gaze at me for a long time with a smile on his face.

At last, I put my little bag on my shoulder, blew my father a kiss in the air and left home.

Before the bus left Baghdad, a worker from the transport company came up to my window, put his head through and, pointing to three ladies sitting in front of me, said, 'What a lucky guy you are! You're travelling with three foxes.'

I looked at the women, their sweet perfume sweeping up my nostrils. I whispered innocently to the man sitting beside me wearing a keffiyeh, 'God bless you, Haj. What does he mean by foxes?'

'He means prostitutes, my son,' he replied quickly. Then in a loud voice, as if he wanted the three women to hear, he added, 'They also call them artistes.'

As the bus passed through Fallujah, I remembered that as little boys, my friends and I used to steal the copper lines on which the women hung out their washing, and then we'd come to Fallujah to sell it.

A quarter of an hour later, the bus was running alongside a chain of mountains and hills overlooking al-Habbaniyah. I put my head out the window to look at my birthplace. The sun shone brightly and its rays reflected strongly on the surface of the water of al-Habbaniyah river. How I hated that river! I'll never forget the day the whole of al-Habbaniyah was saddened at sunset to hear the news of Alexi's drowning in that river. His friends said, 'We waited a long time for him but he didn't come out.' They were punished severely by their parents. He was sixteen years old when I heard my mother saying, 'Poor boy, he wanted to become a priest!' The other women of the city agreed that God had taken Alexi because he was a 'handsome, polite and upright boy'.

And when Jalil the Bear heard what the women had said, he took some stones and smashed the shop window of the Bata shoe shop, shouting at the top of his voice, 'I'm evil, I'm evil.' He was dragged by his ear to the police station and repeatedly told the chief of police, 'I'm not good and not upright. I don't want God to take me to Him!' The police chief laughed and let him go.

The bus went through al-Ramadi, where I had lived for some years. After that I slept, and was awoken only by the noise of the passengers when we stopped at the inspection post on the Iraqi–Syrian border. The bus driver asked us to get out so that our suitcases could be inspected and our passports stamped. When this was done, everyone got back on the bus except for the three ladies, for whom we then waited more than two hours.

The passengers started protesting, and the man sitting beside me said, 'These foxes are strange. They look for clients even at the border!'

'It's not what you think, Haj,' the driver remarked.

When the ladies came back, they were in bad shape and remained silent until they entered Syrian territory. Then they told us that they had been held against their will and abused by the Iraqi policemen, who had given them a choice of either paying a bribe or being raped.

'We paid them a large amount in dollars,' they said, 'but they still molested us.'

'They're highway robbers, not policemen,' one of them said in a Lebanese dialect.

'I'll never return to this country of evil murderers,' said the one with the Egyptian dialect.

The Haj retorted angrily, 'Please, there ought to be limits to what you're allowed to say.'

'What limits?' the Lebanese woman asked. 'Don't you see how brutally they treat passengers? You should have come to our defence.'

'Me? Defend you? Defend foxes?' the man asked nervously.

The three women laughed and wondered, 'Foxes! What does he mean by foxes?'

14

Looking at me, the man said, 'Tell them, my son. Tell them what I mean.'

I turned to them and said shyly, 'He means prostitutes.'

The three women laughed and said in unison, 'That's even better!'

Arriving safely in Damascus, I spent two days as a tourist before starting to look for a job. I saw an advertisement on the door of a building that read 'A car insurance company on the fifth floor is looking for a typist in Arabic'. I smiled as I hopped into the elevator. The 'company' consisted only of a manager, who was in his mid-sixties. Somewhat resentfully, he informed me his secretary was on maternity leave and about to give birth. He made me sit a test, which I passed.

One week into my stay in Damascus, two Syrian policemen came to my room at the hotel and asked me to accompany them. I was placed in a cold, damp room for several hours before two investigators interrogated me.

One of them asked: 'What are you doing here in Damascus?'

'I've come here to work, then I'm going on to East Beirut where there are many churches who help Iraqi Christians emigrate to America. My goal is to get to America to work in the movies.'

'Why did you come from a rich country to work in a poor one?' the other asked. 'Syrians go to your country to work – are you sure you haven't come here for other purposes?'

'I've dreamed of this journey for many years,' I explained, 'and after I finished my military service, I decided to travel anyway, even though I didn't have enough money. I wanted to feel that my trip to America was possible, that it could happen.'

Smacking me on the neck, one of them scoffed, 'Could happen, huh?'

'Yes. I'm telling you the truth. What do you want from me?' I pleaded.

The other policeman hit me, saying, 'You dare ask us a question, dog?'

Then I heard his partner say, 'Let him be. Abdel Adheem is coming, he'll know how to teach him some manners.'

A short while later, a thick-set man entered the room. He carried a wooden stick, attached to a base, with little shards of glass sticking out of it. He placed it on the floor and said, 'Last week, there was a stupid man here who didn't confess until half this glass-studded stick was up his backside, so I advise you not to be stupid.'

Hardly able to believe what he was saying to me, I asked, 'Why are you doing all this? Believe me, sir, I've not done any harm to anyone. I swear to God. And I'm ready to leave this country immediately.'

'Well, well,' the man said as he took his leather belt off his trousers and to my shock began violently whipping me. I fell to the floor while he continued beating me with the belt and kicking me with his boots.

'Why are you beating me when I've done nothing to any of you?' I yelled.

As he continued to torture me, I cursed them, saying, 'You're all disgusting, you're dogs. I'll report you to my country's embassy.'

I put my head down as far as I could between my legs until he grew tired of hitting me. I heard him spit on me and then leave. I remained in that position until I could feel daylight infiltrating the room and I opened my eyes. Then an investigator came in – but perhaps that was the following day – and asked me to sit on a chair. Which I did. A high-ranking officer came in, looked at me, and said, 'Stand up!' When I did, he told me to take off my trousers. So I did. Then he asked me to take off my underwear. So I did.

The officer turned to the investigator and said, 'He's not an Iraqi Jew.'

They released me when they realised I wasn't 'a Jewish spy'! As the officer patted me on the shoulder, he spoke of 'the conspiracies of American imperialism and Zionism, and of their agents in the region working to destroy Syria,' etc., etc. It would be better if I changed my name, he suggested.

I left the building, without having been given any water or food for more than fifty hours. I went directly to the hotel and told the receptionist I was leaving the country that same day.

'But now that you're safely out of prison, you can stay in the country and work. That's the end of it. You've passed the test,' he said jokingly.

I took a shower and went to the insurance 'company' where I had worked for a few days, to tell the manager what had happened.

He began to tremble, dragged me by the hand and pushed me out of the office, shouting, 'I don't want to see you here again.' But I wouldn't leave until he'd paid me my wages for the days I had worked.

I went immediately to the service taxi* station and took a seat in a taxi heading to East Beirut, which is a little over an hour from Damascus. When we arrived, I was the last passenger left in the vehicle. So the driver asked, 'Where do you want to get out, buddy?'

'I don't know,' I replied.

'Fine,' he said, 'if you don't know, we are now in the Ashrafieh neighbourhood in East Beirut, and the journey ends here.'

After wandering around the area for a short while, I went to a nearby hotel, the Hotel Alexandre, where the clerk asked for my passport and fifty-five Lebanese pounds. I paid for a room I would never sleep in and went out for a walk. I passed by the Church of the Virgin Mary and found a stationery shop where I bought a notebook and pen. After an hour of walking, I noticed I was in a narrow lane leading to the sea. Suddenly I heard rockets exploding. When I looked at the city in the distance, I could see rockets destroying buildings. I decided to return to the hotel.

* A shared taxi ride that can accommodate up to five passengers

On the way back, a military jeep approached me and I saw a fist aiming for my face. When I regained consciousness, I was lying in a darkened room and could hear the loud roar of the sea as though I was in a boat. I put my hand on my stomach, feeling intensely hungry. After some moments I tried to calm myself by telling myself I'd been grabbed by Phalangists. They're a Christian militia. I'll tell them I'm an Assyrian and have come to East Beirut wanting to emigrate to America through one of the Christian aid societies, and then they'll set me free.'

Hours later, a bald man arrived and asked irritably, 'Did you see the rockets of the Palestinians and Syrians? They hit their targets exactly. Do you know why? It's because there are spies who feed them information.'

'They are vile people,' I commented.

He looked at me, smiling, 'Who are vile people?'

'The spies,' I replied.

He struck me violently, 'Son of a bitch,' he said, 'if spies are vile people, why do you work for them?'

He then went at me, pummelling me with blows as I repeated, 'You've got it wrong, I'm an Assyrian and want to go to America.'

The man was frenzied and hysterical in the way he punched and kicked and swore at me. And somehow, all the while, I was thinking how strange, how funny they seemed to me, these swear words in Lebanese dialect that I was hearing for the first time.

'You all come here with different stories,' the man said.

Minutes later, another person arrived and asked, 'Pierre, do you need any help?' And this man began to hit me with a heavy club. His blows hurt terribly, and I began to weep and curse them with the worst words I knew.

On the same day, a third person arrived. He was handsome and well-dressed, and very much like the heroes of the Lebanese television series we used to see on Iraqi TV. He began asking me about my stay in Damascus, so I told him that I had been tortured there.

He laughed and said, 'You were subjected to torture . . . or was it training?' He then lit up a cigarette that had a very unpleasant smell and that I later learned was called Gitanes.

I told him the story of my coming to East Beirut in order to travel on to America.

He said, 'Those Christian societies that you thought would help you were closed in 1976, a year after the beginning of the civil war.' He advised me to tell the truth because otherwise he could not guarantee what would happen to me.

Then a boy about fourteen years old came in and brought me a bottle of water and a sandwich, which, despite my hunger, I ate with difficulty due to my injuries. I later learned that this was a popular type of sandwich among the Lebanese and the Palestinians, and that it was called a *zaatar manaqish*. In East Beirut it didn't take long to realise how naïve I had been, as the Christian Phalangist militiamen, who – I thought – would treat me kindly, made me feel that, compared with their treatment, my arrest in Damascus had been a comedy. The Phalangists vented their intense hatred for their enemies, the Syrians and Palestinians, on me.

On the third day, a young man came to me and said calmly, 'Get up, son of a bitch, and come with me.' He was about twenty-five years old and wore jeans and a white shirt, the same thing I was wearing. We walked along a narrow alley.

The bald man passed us by and said, as he rushed to get into a military car, 'Tony, don't waste much time on him.'

'Do we have time to waste?' the young man answered, before turning to me and jeering, 'Did you hear him, mister? Do you know what he means? He's my superior and he is telling me to throw you into the sea.'

So I repeated my story to him, pleading, 'May God bless you, Tony. Believe me, I'm innocent and know nothing about the war or Lebanon.'

He kicked me in the backside, ordering me, 'Walk in front of me, you disgusting man. You've ruined our country.'

At the end of the narrow alley, we stopped at a wide concrete wall next to the sea. Fondling his gun as he looked out at the sea, Tony said, 'I'll give you one last chance. If you tell me why you've come here, I promise I'll intervene in your favour and release you. Think hard. You have five minutes.'

He sat on the sea wall, took out his blue packet of Gitanes and began to smoke. 'You have to tell me everything,' he added, 'before I finish smoking my cigarette.'

Understanding the severe gravity of the situation, I said calmly, 'Please listen to me carefully, Tony. I'm from a poor Assyrian family and I've always dreamed of travelling to America in order to work in film. Believe me, Tony, I don't work with any political or non-political organisation. I'm telling the truth, Tony.'

He threw his cigarette into the sea and put his gun to my temple.

'If you kill me, Tony,' I said innocently, 'many people will be sad.'

'Nobody will be sad at the death of a lousy bum working as a professional spy.'

'I want to make movies. I'm not a spy!'

'You terrorist bastard! You know what "movies" means? You're not here to put a bomb in a church or a children's school? What do you know about "movies", you son of a bitch?'

'I know everything. I'm not like you and your friends, killing and smoking Gitanes.'

I felt his gun touching my temple. I closed my eyes and could hear my heart thumping. After several moments of silence, Tony said, 'Do you know Godard? Do you know someone called Jean-Luc Godard?'

I wanted to shake my head to tell him no, but I didn't dare in case it made his gun go off and fire a bullet into my head, so I said it in a low voice.

He asked again, 'Haven't you heard of the Nouvelle Vague?'

'No,' I replied.

20

'Son of a bitch,' he shouted, 'how do you want me to believe that you dream of working in film when you don't even know Jean-Luc Godard and haven't heard of the Nouvelle Vague? Huh? I've given you another chance and you've failed again.'

At that moment, I shouted out, 'I know everything about John Ford, about John Wayne, about Henry Fonda, James Stewart, Gary Cooper, Maureen O'Hara. I know Katherine Hepburn, I know Roy Rogers, the King of Cowboys, I know Victor Mature, Ava Gardner, Gregory Peck, Alan Ladd, Vera Miles, Randolph Scott, Clark Gable, D. W. Griffith. I know everything about Marlon Brando, I know Marilyn Monroe, Olivia de Havilland, I know Richard Widmark, Jane Russell, Robert Mitchum, Audrey Hepburn. I know Rock Hudson, James Dean, I know Gene Tierney, I know Clint Eastwood, Paul Newman, I know Rod Taylor, I know Lee Marvin, Humphrey Bogart, Bob Hope, Errol Flynn, Joan Crawford, I know Dean Martin, I know everything about Norman Wisdom, everything about Charlie Chaplin, everything about Montgomery Clift, I even know King Kong and Frankenstein. When I stopped, I heard Tony laughing. I opened my eyes to see he had returned his handgun to its place under his belt.

'Listen, Cowboy!' he said. 'Let it be known that Hollywood cinema is weak compared with the films of the Nouvelle Vague.'

Unable to believe what was happening, I went along with him, 'Maybe.'

At that moment, I remembered Kiryakos, who taught me everything about film-making when I was a child; he had asked me once, 'If someone asked you, "Who is the best scriptwriter in the world?" what would you answer?'

'OK, let me think a little,' I had replied.

Kiryakos had laughed and commented, 'This doesn't need any thinking about. It is God. Yes, God is the greatest scriptwriter. He created this movie in which we all live.'

In the taxi from East Beirut back to Damascus, I was sitting in the back enjoying the beautiful scenery when I looked up at the sky and whispered, 'But Kiryakos never told me You liked happy endings in the Hollywood style.'

We arrived at the service taxi station in Damascus early that evening, and I immediately decided to travel to Amman because Jordan had a border with Syria, not far from Damascus, and I could enter without a visa. We arrived in Amman at about ten o'clock and it was cold. I was hungry, so I went downtown and bought a sandwich, then walked along King Faisal Street. Although I didn't have enough money, I checked into the first hotel I came to – the Atlas Hotel.

In the morning, I packed all my belongings into my bag and left it at the reception desk, explaining that I was going to the bank. I walked for hours around the streets until I saw a cheerful young man selling tea at the entrance to a building; he occupied a small alcove by the steps and made tea to sell to the employees of the shops and businesses in the area. I told the young man that I wanted some tea but had used almost all my money on the hotel. He laughed and shook his head sympathetically. After he had made me a tea, he offered me a Marlboro and asked if I was hungry.

'I'm dying of hunger,' I said.

'Sit down,' he said. 'You seem to be from a decent family.'

He turned to his little brother who was helping him and said, 'Mohammad, go and bring a plate of hummus with minced meat for our friend. '

Later Tawfiq, who was Palestinian, gave me half a dinar and said, 'Keep in touch.'

I bought a packet of cigarettes and yet another notebook just for the sake of it, then I walked to the Roman amphitheatre and lay down on its steps until the evening. I tried to think of the misfortunes that had befallen me. It was hard for me to grasp what had happened and I often felt I was living in a movie, not in real life. I spent the entire second day on the streets, and the following morning I went back to Tawfiq.

'Have you found a job?' he asked.

'I haven't looked for a job, Tawfiq. I spent all yesterday thinking.'

He laughed, 'No problem. Thinking is useful sometimes.' Turning to his little brother, he said, 'Today we must feed our guest a cheese omelette.'

And we all laughed. At noon Tawfiq gave me a Jordanian newspaper and said, 'It has a lot of job ads.'

In fact it did, and I found one from an advertising company that needed a typist. I immediately went to the company's office and was met by a man who seemed very kind. He told me he had advertised the typist's position on behalf of another company who had now found someone for the job. Then he gave me a kind look and asked whether I had financial problems.

'Yes,' I said.

He told me that he needed a typist in his own office but could not pay a decent wage. So we agreed on a small payment, and he said I could sleep in the office until my situation improved. I accepted at once. He gave me a small advance and I went to the Atlas Hotel to fetch my bag. Wajih al-Najjar, the company manager, was a lawyer and a well-known novelist in Jordan. On the walls of his office hung the literary prizes he had received. And so I began to work in the advertising company. About 90 percent of my daily work was typing clichéd obituaries. They didn't vary except for the name of the deceased and the person or tribe who offered condolences. From the first day, I did my job perfectly well, and in a few moments could write the obituaries myself:

In the name of God, the Compassionate, the Merciful. The tribe of so-and-so, their kinsmen, and their relatives announce with deep sorrow the death of Haj Mohammad Mahmoud Abdullah, may God forgive him, who passed away into God's mercy on

Friday on such-and-such a date. Condolences will be accepted at the home of his son Ahmad in Jabal al-Nadhif, to the right of the Islamic Bank, opposite the Post Office, at the last stop of the service taxi line. We are God's own and to Him we return.

Each day I typed more than a hundred such announcements. At one point I thought that if Jordanians kept dying at this rate, the country would soon be empty.

Wajih al-Najjar used to come to the office at noon every day, and I would bring him a plate of hummus and *ful* for lunch and a few bottles of beer. We talked about work a little, and then he left the office and I went back to work. When I had free time, I wrote stories. One day I took a short story entitled 'Late Awakening' to the cultural editor of *Al-Dustour* daily newspaper. He immediately decided to publish it and told me, 'You're a scriptwriter, boy.'

'Late Awakening' was the story of a man who talked constantly about his desire to work in film; one day, when he was sitting in the Roman amphitheatre in Amman, he realised he was fifty years old and had not yet practised the art of film; shocked by this realisation, he suffered a heart attack and died. When Wajih al-Najjar read the story he asked me, 'Is this a prophecy of what will happen to you in the future?'

Apart from the routine work at the office, Wajih al-Najjar sometimes sent me to take newspapers and magazines to a Palestinian leader called Abdel Jawad Saleh, whom I later learned had been Mayor of the Palestinian town of al-Bireh, but had been expelled from Israel to Jordan, and who was a member of the Executive Committee of the Palestine Liberation Organisation. In two months, my situation improved and I began to publish my short stories in newspapers and thought of writing a script for a full-length movie to be called *Nostalgia for the English Time.*

One day at noon, as Wajih al-Najjar and I were having lunch, four or five policemen burst into the office with handguns pointed at our faces. One of them struck Wajih al-Najjar and dragged him outdoors and the others began searching the office. One of them approached me and punched me so hard I was thrown to the floor. He then asked if I was Palestinian and I said, 'I'm Iraqi.' Again, he struck me violently and gestured with his head to two of his men, who led me to a Mercedes car.

I later found myself in a prison cell in the building of the Jordanian Secret Police, the Mukhabarat, where I was tortured in a manner I cannot describe, only that compared with the Jordanians the torture of the Phalangists was nothing. They asked me about the Palestinian group I was working with, and who was the head of the cell I belonged to. With every question came kicks and punches from all directions.

I answered, half-conscious, 'I don't know anyone, by God. Believe me, I know no group and no person heading a cell. I was walking in the street and saw an advertisement in a newspaper about a job vacancy so I went to that company. You can check it out by looking at *Al-Rai* newspaper.'

Three men beat me without stopping and I could no longer tell where the punches or kicks were coming from. One poured scalding water on me, and another said, 'You criminals! You want to destroy the royal government!'

I screamed, 'By God, I'm a royalist and my family liked King Faisal II in Iraq.'

One of them laughed and punched me on the nose, saying, 'You coward, you've become a royalist after one punch.'

Next, spitting in my face, someone screamed at me, 'You're not leaving until you confess, you son of a bitch.'

At that, I screamed back in his face, 'Your own mother is a bitch. My mother is the best of all mothers.'

He put his foot on my neck and I felt myself swallowing pieces of my broken teeth. When they finally left me, I was unable to move any part of my body, and lay on the floor and slept for I don't know how long. When I awoke I cried out and asked for food and something to drink, but no one came, and it seems I lost consciousness again.

When I came to, I found that I had been taken to a large hall, where I was surrounded by three fair-haired and extremely beautiful young women, who were stitching the wounds in my face and dressing my injuries. One of them smoked a cigarette and put the Marlboro packet back in the front pocket of her jeans. Later I learned they were from the Circassian community.

Then one of those who had tortured me came and said, 'You're lucky, you son of a bitch. We're going to set you free today.'

When they did, I found out that they had decided to hand me over to the Iraqi government. However at the last moment something had happened and the decision had been rescinded. The Mukhabarat was satisfied with expelling me from Jordan within twenty-four hours. It turned out that Wajih al-Najjar was a leader in one of the leftist organisations against the Jordanian regime, and that his wife had contacted the Jordanian Minister of the Interior on my behalf, who was an old friend of her husband before becoming a minister. I also learned that I was indeed very lucky since the Director of the Jordanian Secret Police, Ghazi Arabiyyat, who had my file and who was, I was told, 'a real butcher', had been killed in a car accident that morning on his return from a security meeting in one of the Arab Gulf countries. As a result, my file was turned over by the Directorate of Security to the office of the Minister of Interior, who cancelled the decision to hand me over to the Iraqi government.

After leaving prison, I met Wajih al-Najjar's wife, who informed me that her husband would remain behind bars for a long time because he had been imprisoned several times before. She told me he had once published an article in a daily newspaper in which he showed that the expenses of Jordan's royal family were greater than the budget of the state itself. She then gave me a cheque for eighty Jordanian dinars and I went to the bank to cash it. It was sunset and I was told that bank services had stopped for the day.

I screamed that I was being expelled from the country, and had been tortured by the Mukhabarat and so on.

The bank manager came out and said, 'Well, well! We'll cash the cheque for you. OK? Just calm down!'

I went directly to Abdel Jawad Saleh, the Palestinian leader, who advised me to go to West Beirut, which was controlled by the PLO, and gave me a special letter of recommendation to a man called Arabi Awwad. I paid a last visit to my friend Tawfiq and said goodbye.

I took a service taxi to Damascus, but didn't stay for more than two hours, during which time I bought myself a new pair of shoes and a black leather jacket, which was fashionable back then. I then took the service taxi to Beirut and said to the driver this time, 'I want to go to West Beirut.'

'Get in,' he said.

'West Beirut with the Palestinians,' I repeated.

'Climb in, brother,' he said. In less than two hours I was in West Beirut, in an area under the control of the Palestinian forces. It was called 'The Fakihani Republic', and I asked for a person known as Comrade Arabi Awwad. I was told he was the leader of the Jordanian Communist Party, and they sent me to his office on Afif Tibi Street. He welcomed me and asked the people working with him to take care of me. They put me up temporarily at the home of a man who worked as an announcer on Radio Palestine and who had gone to Tehran to cover the outbreak of the Iranian Revolution; the fall of the Shah's regime, and the beginning of the rule of the clerics led by Khomeini from exile.

A few days later, I started working for the press and information centre of the Democratic Front for the Liberation of Palestine, whose headquarters were in the heart of Fakihani. My job there was to listen to the Arabic news on Radio Israel and report on the main topics of its broadcasts. I found the job very boring, so I recorded onto a cassette all the news reports from half past seven in the morning till five o'clock in the afternoon; then

I selected the important news and typed it onto stencils, from which I made up an evening bulletin that I published and named *The Observer's Bulletin of Radio Israel.* In the beginning, I duplicated twenty-five copies of the bulletin, but demand for it rose and, in a few months, my bulletin became more important than the bulletin of the Palestinian News Agency WAFA, (the principal organ of the PLO) where the Palestinian, Syrian, Iraqi, Egyptian and Sudanese workers outnumbered the pages of *One Thousand and One Nights.*

In addition to the bulletin, I became the manager of administrative affairs at the press and information centre, to which was later added the duty of executive producer of *Al-Hurriyya* magazine, the main publication of the organisation. Furthermore, I fell in love with a very pretty young Lebanese woman. She was the main reason I had a wonderful time in West Beirut. Yet, in spite of all the jobs I was doing, I still didn't have a real home. I slept on the balcony on the eighth floor of the Central Information building. Every evening, I bought several cans of Heineken, lay down on a blanket spread out on the balcony floor and drank until I fell asleep. When armed clashes broke out between the various Palestinian groups, I took my bedding from the balcony back into the room, afraid of the stray bullets that often came that way.

During that period, I got to know François, a young Frenchman who worked as a male nurse. He used to come to our archive every day at noon to read *Le Monde* and *Le Nouvel Observateur,* both of which we received regularly. One day, I went with François to Candles restaurant, next to Beirut Arab University. We ordered two plates of *ful* and falafel, and of course some bottles of Heineken. An armed man entered, put the barrel of his machine gun to my temple, and started screaming at me, 'You dirty, vile, loathsome scum . . .', yelling at me over and over with all the insults in the dictionary while he pushed the barrel of his Kalashnikov at my head.

The other customers in the restaurant looked at us as though we were part of a movie.

Calmly I said to the man, 'Why are you attacking me, comrade, when I've done nothing to you?'

'I'm no comrade of yours, creep,' he snarled.

'You're hurting me, brother, comrade,' I said. 'Take your weapon away from my head and let's talk things over.'

'If you knew the meaning of pain, you coward,' he yelled, 'you would not hurt the feelings of others and subject their honour to gossip.'

I looked to François as though seeking his help. 'Comrade Sammy is a good comrade,' François said in Arabic.

'I know you,' the armed man said. 'You're a kind French doctor. Don't defend this creep.'

'What have you done to him?' François asked me in English.

'Nothing, believe me,' I replied.

The man shoved the barrel of his machine gun at my temple again, and shouted, 'Do you deny you raped my young sister?'

When I heard him preparing to fire his gun and saying at the same time 'Your head is going to explode', I immediately cut in, 'I don't know what there is in my head for you to explode. When I was arrested by the Phalangists, they wanted to make my head explode too. And here I am facing the same fate from the Palestinians. Why does all this happen to me? I'm a kind and helpful young man.'

In a much quieter voice the armed man asked, 'Were you really arrested by the Phalangists?'

'Yes,' I answered.

At that, he took his weapon away from my head and said, 'I think I've made a mistake.'

And he began to kiss my head, repeating, 'Forgive me, comrade.'

We invited him to sit with us and ordered some food and drink for him. He was forty years old and seemed happy as he drank the Heineken down in two gulps. Realising my 'friend' was a heavy drinker armed with an automatic gun, we paid the bill and left the restaurant.

A short time later, I went to live in a small rented room in Fakihani, in a building that we used to call 'the Sheraton of the Democratic Front'. During that time I spent the nights thinking of the movies and in my imagination pictures of my family floated before me; I hadn't contacted them since my departure. It pained me to see my plan to travel to America slip away and become almost impossible.

One morning I decided to end my stay in Beirut. So I went to broach the subject with Dr Mukhtar, the head of the press and information centre, and started by saying, 'Comrade, I left Iraq with the intention of travelling to America to make movies.'

He immediately sneered, 'America! Why are you thinking of travelling to that ugly imperialist country?' And he started giving me a boring lecture about imperialism and colonialism and the liberation movements of the world . . .

I repeated, 'I've nothing to do with politics, comrade. I did my military service for my country and I've worked with you for three years now. Please help me to go.' I continued repeating this request almost daily, but Dr Mukhtar always smiled and replied, 'We'll see, we'll see.'

But what terrible luck I had! The first week I was planning to escape, the Fakihani massacre took place.

On the morning of Friday 17 July 1981, I had just left my room when François came walking up the street, and said he'd stop by that evening.

I said, 'Fine, I'll prepare some food and drinks.'

He took fifteen Lebanese pounds out of his pocket and said, laughing, 'Bring us a bottle of Napoleon cognac so we can get drunk tonight.'

Israeli fighter planes flying over Beirut had become a familiar sight for us and that's why we paid no attention to them as they flew overhead at that precise moment. But hardly had François said goodbye with his beautiful smile and gone a few steps than the planes dropped their bombs on Fakihani and blew the residential neighbourhood to hell.

A sunny day plunged into darkness.

We waited for more than an hour before the wind took away the smoke of the explosions and implosions, and the dust of the buildings, where we found hundreds of dead people – men, women and children.

François had been one of the first among them. Eventually his body was taken to France for burial. I postponed my trip for some time until we could get over the Fakihani massacre.

Later, when I had finally given up trying to retrieve my passport from the organisation, I bought a Lebanese travel document used by Palestinian refugees to travel to Cyprus. These were not expensive.

On arrival, I started working for one of the Libyan-funded Arab magazines published in Nicosia. I worked in their archives at first. Then I published articles on film. I went to Egypt several times, spending two or three months there each visit, following the activities of the film studios and conducting interviews with male and female stars of Egyptian movies.

When my travel document expired, I travelled to Tunis and obtained a letter of recommendation from the office of Yasser Arafat and used it to go to Aden, which was the capital of the Republic of Yemen at that time. Democratic Yemen was ruled back then by a Marxist party sympathetic to the Palestinians, and to Iraqis hostile to the regime of Saddam Hussein. Since I didn't belong to any political organisation, I wasn't met by anyone at the airport and spent the first day sleeping on the beach. In Aden I sold my camera, my cassette recorder, my shirts and my new trousers. Every day for a whole week, I went to the office of the President of the Republic until I succeeded in meeting the man I was searching for. He was an adviser to the president, and took me in his car to a tourist hotel, The Chalets, where many Russian technical experts were staying at the time. Three years later this adviser would be shot dead, killed in a coup d'état at the Presidential Palace.

Within a few days of our meeting, I was given a Yemeni passport and returned to Nicosia, but the magazine made excuses not to take me back. At that time, a war had broken out between the forces of Yasser Arafat and Palestinian dissidents, who were supported by the Libyan and Syrian regimes. Arafat encountered fierce resistance and once held off a siege.

I'd heard from the office of the Palestinian Liberation Organisation in Nicosia that there were physicians from Norway or Denmark who had come with many bags of blood plasma donated to the wounded Palestinians in the hospitals of Tripoli in north Lebanon. They asked if I was ready to accompany them and I said yes. In the evening, I was drinking gin and tonic at the Coach Pub with the bar's owner, my Cypriot friend Nikos, and I told him that I would be going to a place I might not return from.

Nikos smiled and said, 'Are you going to North Lebanon?'

'Yes,' I replied.

He shook his head and said, 'For you, everything is like the movies.'

That evening I felt a sudden longing to speak to my family. I had the telephone number of our neighbour, Hajja Umm Ahmad, so I called them and spoke to my mother, who told me they thought something bad had happened to me in Beirut. I asked her to let me speak with my father and she laughed and said, 'You're still crazy, my son.'

A few moments later, I heard his voice, 'Aa aa aa aa ho ho aa aa aa ho ho ha ha ha.'

I answered him, laughing, 'I understand you, father. Yes, I love you too. Believe me, I've forgotten nothing and I'll never forget. Soon I'll realise our dreams.'

He replied, 'Aa aa aa aa ho ho aa aa aa ho ho ha ha ha.'

So I replied in his own language, 'Aa aa aa aa aa ha ha ha o oh oh hah ho ha ha aa aa aa.'

Tears were flowing down my face when Nikos stretched his hand out and cut off the telephone conversation.

On the way to Tripoli, Lebanon, our little ship, which had set off from Larnaca, was tossed up and down by giant waves. I remember one of the physicians looking at me and saying, 'You look like a sailor.' This made me happy because I felt I could perhaps be an actor one day. We were still at sea when the captain came and told us we'd come through the danger. He meant we had escaped the danger of being hijacked by the Israelis, who had seized several ships at that time. Before reaching the port of Tripoli, we could see rockets falling, off in the distance, on the Palestinian refugee camps supporting Arafat.

The Scandinavian blood plasma was delivered immediately to the Palestinian and Lebanese hospitals. As for me, I went to look for my friend Khalil Salman, who had become an assistant to Arafat and Abu Jihad. Khalil Salman put me up in a beautiful apartment in the district of Zahiriyya.

In the evening, one of Abu Jihad's assistants came to me. His name was Ismail and he was a handsome young man and extremely kind. He said to me, 'I don't live here but I have the key.' Then he smiled and said, 'You should be happy I'm here, because I have a lot of *lahmajoon* pizzas.'

I later learned that Ismail slept in different apartments for reasons of security (in less than two years he would be assassinated in Rome).

When I woke in the morning, I walked into the sitting room wearing only my underwear and was surprised to see Yasser Arafat and Abu Jihad arguing frantically about the ongoing battles. I said good morning to them and they returned the greeting, but I felt embarrassed. When I went into the kitchen, I found a group of bodyguards drinking tea and smoking voraciously. After Yasser Arafat, Abu Jihad and the bodyguards left, I noticed bits of glass on the carpet, the glass top of the table was broken and there were some blood stains. The next day, I saw a photo of Yasser Arafat in the newspapers with his hand bandaged, so I surmised he had broken the glass tabletop with his fist.

After many days of raging battles, the forces of the Palestinian dissidents supported by Syria and Libya were advancing steadily. News came of French intervention to get Arafat and his forces out of the Lebanese city of Tripoli, and take them to Tunis. Arafat issued a decree to withdraw all the funds under his control from the Lebanese banks, and Khalil Salman distributed large amounts of Lebanese pounds to a number of Arab and Lebanese journalists who had come from many places and were supporters of Arafat. When I told Khalil Salman that I wanted to go back to Nicosia, he gave me a small leather shoulder bag containing Lebanese pounds.

I rented a small boat with two other travellers and returned to Nicosia in Cyprus. At the Cyprus Popular Bank, I exchanged the Lebanese pounds for more than five thousand Cypriot pounds. I went back to spending my evenings at the Coach Pub, and at the end of every night I went to discotheques like the Galaxy and the Scorpion. In the latter I met a young Dutch woman who said she knew a place that served a wonderful breakfast, but whose name she had forgotten.

'You can't believe how delicious the breakfast is there,' she added.

So I went with her; it was five o'clock in the morning. I discovered that the breakfast she spoke of was called pacha, and I said to her, laughing, 'It's a popular Iraqi meal, usually eaten at dawn by workers and soldiers. In fact, *pacha* is originally Turkish, not Cypriot.'

She then suggested that we spend a few days in a beautiful little village called Ayia Napa.

After that, I left for Tunis, where I rented a house in the Sidi Bou Said neighbourhood overlooking the sea. I lived a life of bars and restaurants, and I became infatuated with a young Tunisian woman.

When I had spent all my money, I contacted my friend Khalil Salman and he made me a correspondent of his magazine *Al-Bilad*, of which he was editor-in-chief in Cyprus. During that time, my friend the poet Mustapha al-Haddad was encouraging me to leave the country, so I applied first at the British embassy for a visa but my application was refused. When I applied at the French embassy for a visa to go to Paris, I was informed that approval by the Ministry of Interior would take a long time. I applied anyhow and prepared myself for a long wait.

As the days went by, I began to feel I was lost. My dreams of film-making came back to tempt me at night and I could no longer sleep. I began to drink more alcohol, and did not hesitate to drink *boukha* in the mornings. My relationship with my friend Zahra came to an end, because her brother, who had been a drug dealer when he was in Sweden but became a religious fundamentalist on his return to Tunisia, threatened to kill her if she continued to meet 'that Iraqi infidel', as he called me.

One day during Christmas, I was walking in the souq in the capital and in the front window of a barber's shop I saw a picture of a man circumcising a little boy. I stopped for a moment and thought of how many times in my life I'd been asked if I was circumcised or not: on the street, at school, during my military service, and in many of the Arab cities I visited later, they would ask me that very same question. When I told them no, they used to laugh at me and then they'd explain the importance and benefits of circumcision. They would always talk about the topic with such zeal and enthusiasm that I often began to think that many of the Arab world's problems were linked to my penis! I entered the shop and said to the barber, 'There's a twelve-year-old boy living with me in Sidi Bou Said. What do you think of coming with me to circumcise him? I will pay your fee, and the taxi too.'

The man picked up his bag of instruments and came with me.

When we reached my home, I said to him, 'Hajji, there is no twelve-year-old child. I am the young man I spoke to you about. I am twenty-eight years old and I want to be circumcised.'

The barber paused for a moment, then took out a cigarette from his pocket and said, 'No objection. I remember I circumcised a young Frenchman who was thirty years old and I've never heard of him since.'

He started to circumcise me without an anaesthetic and I helped him. Although the operation was very painful I looked at him as though he was cutting off a part of somebody else's body, not mine. Sometimes I wondered, was I so ruined psychologically?

When the barber finished his job, he said, smiling, 'God has now permitted faith to enter your heart.' Lighting a cigarette, he added, 'I'm happy that you've become a Muslim by my hand.'

I looked at him for a moment and said spontaneously, without considering the consequences of my words, 'Why not say I've become a Jew? Jews are circumcised too, you know!'

The man was not at all pleased with my remark and said in a gruff voice, 'Give me my fee, please.'

I pointed to the pocket of my jeans hanging on the door. He brought the jeans to me and I paid him what he asked for and he left sadly.

For the next two days, I remained lying on the floor, trying to restrain my pain and hunger. I remembered my father who used to strike his left forefinger with his right one, then squeeze his nose as though he was blowing it, meaning those with their dicks cut were dirty people. What would my father say about me now if he knew what I had done?

At noon on the third day after the 'operation' I heard someone knock on my door. I shouted, 'Enter. The door is open.'

In came Hanan, my Algerian friend who had begun giving me some lessons in French. I told Hanan what had happened and she rocked with laughter. She went immediately and bought a roast chicken and a bottle of red wine, and returned still laughing. My friends, Khamis and al–Ayouni, visited me after her, and as soon as they learned what had happened they burst out laughing too.

Al–Ayouni said to me, 'I know you're crazy. You've done this to ridicule everything!'

Two days later, one of the waiters at al–Nadhoor restaurant near my home came to tell me a clerk at the French embassy had telephoned. My visa was ready and I could collect it any time I wanted. That evening I walked to the pharmacy in the middle of Sidi Bou Said and bought some tranquillisers. The next day, I went to my friend Khalil Salman, who gave me about three thousand dollars.

So I travelled to Paris. I met and befriended a young French woman, Valérie. I would take her to the movies and entertain her with stories of my childhood and my love of movies. After each evening's show I would see her back to her apartment and then return to my hotel.

One day she told me, 'You can stay here.'

When I excused myself, she looked at me strangely. The same thing happened during the following days, and Valérie noticed I was avoiding touching her. Every time I thought of telling her that I was still suffering from my recent operation, my courage failed. Because of my great stupidity, I preferred to keep out of her sight for some days.

When I felt that my health was better, I bought a bouquet of flowers and went to her apartment. I knocked on the door and it was opened by a young African guy. I said I was looking for Valérie and he said she was taking a shower. I said I was an old friend of hers and he said he was her new friend and that he was from the Ivory Coast. I gave him the flowers and said I would pass by to greet Valérie another day. The young man laughed and closed the door.

★ ★ ★

In Paris, at the French Office for the Protection of Refugees and Stateless Persons (OFPRA), I recounted, more than once, all that had happened to me since I left Baghdad. The agent in the department for refugees was listening and writing.

Finally he smiled and stood up from his chair holding my papers.

'Are you sure he was from the Ivory Coast?'

'Who?'

'The young man who stole your girlfriend.'

'I think so. Is that important for my asylum application?'

'No, no,' said the man, laughing, 'I just wanted to know.'

PART TWO

An Iraqi in Paris

Only the autumn leaf fallen asleep
under the raindrops
knows my thirst

1

France, January 1985

From the very beginning of my stay at Le Rocheton Centre for Refugees, 70 kilometres outside Paris, I convinced myself that it was just the sort of charming place I needed to write the script I had wanted so long to write. Indeed, within a few weeks I had written several scenes of a script I was calling *Nostalgia for the English Time*, the story of a small Iraqi village at the end of the fifties after the British had left.

I shared a large clean room with Rahim, a refugee from Afghanistan, and I was lucky my typewriter was manual since Rahim's love story with an Ethiopian refugee – a woman with a big sexual appetite as it happened – forced me out of the room two or three times a day. Whenever Rahim wanted to sleep with her he asked me to leave for a while. I would take my typewriter and go off and work somewhere in the centre's big garden. I often went deep into the woodland, and sometimes felt I was really a refugee in Rahim's place, not in France.

'She wants to do it, not me, believe me!' Rahim would say, smiling bashfully.

Each time I came across the Ethiopian girl in the corridor leading to my room she'd boldly, 'How's the writing going?

When are you going to finish the script so we can read it?' Once she said, 'All night I can hear the sound of your typewriter coming through my window, tak, tak, tak. You have to take a break.'

I was on the verge of replying, 'My dear, why don't you take a little break? You go tak, tak, tak three times a day in my room and you're still not satisfied!' But I said nothing.

Many of the male refugees had liaisons with the girls. The Hungarian guy, who insulted 'the Russians' at every opportunity, never left the room of the lazy blonde Polish girl. I don't know how I ever visited her room – it was like a garbage bin, filled with the nauseating stench of Gitanes cigarettes. Then there was the Turk Kamal, who found a way to have a relationship with Marina, a plump Russian widow who often urged Kamal to attack 'the Pig', her name for the pot-bellied fair-haired Hungarian. Meanwhile, you would see Johnny, the South African, playing table tennis all day with Zeinab, an Iranian. I don't know whether or not their relationship went beyond ping pong.

With us also was a group of Sri Lankan refugees who were very kind and generous. They always cooked their own special food, despite the hostel providing us with three meals a day. The smell of coriander made us feel as though we were living in the kitchen of an Indian restaurant, not a large building above whose entrance was inscribed 'Le Château'. Here also I might call myself 'lucky', for when Rahim 'expelled' me from the room in the evenings I took shelter with the Sri Lankans, who would place various delicious dishes in front of me. They always welcomed me with a laugh, remarking, 'That Ethiopian girl is a tough young lady!'

Though the Sri Lankans occupied seven rooms in Le Château, whichever door I knocked on, they were always all in there together. I never understood how they did this, even thinking for a time they had knocked down the walls between the rooms. When I asked my friend Langam about this he laughed. 'Is this what that awful wine you drink does to you?' he said. 'No one knows what goes on behind the walls of the Sri Lankans!'

Langam would speak to me with his hands in his pockets. He had adopted this habit when he started work at a French restaurant which he described as 'without question, the best restaurant

in Paris. The movie stars you talk about all the time go there.'
Once, when we were talking in English, as we usually did, I asked
him the name of the restaurant and where it was.

'*Ce n'est pas loin de l'église de la Madeleine,*' he replied.

I nearly burst out laughing. Many of the refugees had given up
learning French because of Langam.

He used to waste everybody's time with his futile discussions
with the teacher, Fatima, who was originally from Algeria. She
would ask him to read the personal pronouns *vous* and *nous* and
Langam would pronounce them *vooz* and *nooz*, the correct pro-
nunciation being *vou* and *nou*. When she covered the letter 's' with
her hand he pronounced it properly as *vou*, but when she
removed her hand he would say *vooz* again. This would go on for
several minutes while we grew bored and our thoughts turned to
slipping out for a cigarette. The teacher would instruct him to
ignore the letter 's', but he always replied obstinately, 'But it's not
logical. There is an "s".'

One day the teacher wrote 'where' on the blackboard and told
him to read it. He read it correctly. 'But you didn't pronounce the
letter "h",' the teacher joked. Putting his hands on his hips,
Langam said, 'See, she doesn't know French and now she's trying
to corrupt the English language too!'

When we got up to leave the class he stood by the door and
insisted we listen to this story: 'Yesterday, after buying a few essen-
tials, I asked the shopkeeper how much it all cost. He told me ...
Sorry, I've forgotten what he said.'

Then he turned to the teacher, 'Excuse me, how do you say
"ninety" in French?'

'*Quatre-vingt-dix,*' the teacher replied.

'*Quatre-vingt-dix*!' Langham started to laugh, 'If you translate
that into English it is four twenties and ten.' He clapped his hands.
'Where's the sense in that?'

One day, while we were playing ping pong, Fatima said,
'Langam's reasoning is quite natural. He's just defending himself

against something new. I'm sure that before long he'll be speaking French.'

And she was right.

Rahim sat on the pavement, shaded by large thorn bushes. 'You're very strange,' he said, panting. 'We've been walking for two hours and you don't seem at all tired.'

I was dressed in sports clothes and, looking straight ahead, I said, 'I spent my childhood as a street vendor, I could probably walk to Paris now without stopping.'

'What did you sell?' Rahim put his hands behind his head and looked at me.

'In summer I sold ice cream, and in winter I sold sandwiches and sometimes sweets made from dates that we called simsimiyya, I looked at Rahim and asked him, 'Do you want me to tell you some stories about my feet?'

'Yes please,' said Rahim.

'Every day I used to push my handcart from the girls' school to the boys' school, then around the streets, and in the evening I'd park it in front of the movie house. In winter I died of cold and in summer the sun scorched my head and melted the asphalt on the road. The wheels of my handcart often sank into the asphalt and I had to use all my strength to pull them out. My toes slipped out of my plastic sandals into the melting tar, but my feet stayed firm to keep the cart moving forward. In the evening my mother used to wet a bit of cloth with petrol to get rid of the tar that was stuck to the toes of my little feet. And when I played football, the mouths of my friends would gape open as they watched every ball I kicked, whether with my right or left foot, fire like a rocket towards the goal. One day, when they asked me to take a penalty kick, I stared straight at the ball and then gave it a hard kick. The goalkeeper threw himself into the air and the crowd went dizzy twisting and turning to find where the ball had disappeared to. Everybody was astonished when they discovered it stuck to the end of my toes.'

'You're going to kill me with laugher,' said Rahim stretching out on the dusty pavement.

We were on the main road between Moulin and Fontainebleau, chatting away and taking no notice of the cars going past.

'Rahim, listen to this! One afternoon as I was wheeling my handcart around, I saw Shapira (which means "beautiful" in Assyrian) on the sports field training for the district athletics championships. I left the cart and went to talk to him. "Do you see that rock, Shapira?" I asked. He nodded. "Come on," I said. "Let's see if either of us can move it." Shapira was eighteen at the time and I was ten. He laughed and began trying to move the rock with all his strength. He almost burst before managing to budge it a few centimetres. When my turn came I planted my toes in the ground and pushed the rock effortlessly. "How did you do that?" Shapira asked in amazement. "Look at the ground. Tell me, what do you see?" I said. "I don't see anything except some small holes," he replied. "Those are my toe-prints," I told him. Shapira shook his head, dumbfounded.

'Before I left I told him, "Listen Shapira, fasten one end of a thick rope round a tractor tyre and tie the other end round your waist. Drag the tyre around everywhere with you and don't stop doing it until the day of the championships. You'll see the difference." I was selling sandwiches outside the movie house one evening when Shapira came by and told me he'd won three medals.'

One evening, I left the room to Rahim and his Ethiopian girl-friend and went to smoke a cigarette outside Le Château. I saw Maya, from Sri Lanka, coming along carrying her little baby.

'How many times have they thrown you out?!' Maya laughed.

'Maya, you little devil!' I said.

'My grandmother once said that love affairs are like fine per-fumes. You put them in your bedroom and your neighbours get to smell them.'

'Nice,' I said, and began to play with the baby. 'Look at his eyes. He has such beautiful eyes. They're like two fancy windows.'

'Unfortunately they're windows without a house,' she replied sorrowfully.

It was 6.30 p.m. I told her I was going to have a beer in the bar before the bell rang for supper. There I saw Marina and her boyfriend Kamal drinking Bloody Marys.

'Do you want one?' Marina asked.

'No, I came for a beer,' I replied.

A few minutes later Marina looked right and left. 'That Hungarian pig,' she said, 'I saw him stealing a tube of mustard from the canteen this afternoon. I'd love to squirt it up his nose.'

'Forget him. He's just a poor guy. Don't waste your time on him,' Kamal said, before turning to me. 'Have you finished your book yet?'

Before I could respond a girl came up and greeted us and sat down.

'This is Katie,' said Marina. 'She's from the United States. We met this afternoon.'

Katie told us she had been staying in Aix-en-Provence for a month, and that she would be staying at Le Rocheton for a week as part of her training in catering and hospitality. Kamal asked me again whether I'd finished my book. 'I'm writing a script, not a book,' I told him.

'What's the difference?' asked Kamal, taking another sip of his Bloody Mary.

'Scripts are for movies,' Marina said.

'What's your script about?' asked Katie.

'I'm sorry,' I answered a little uncomfortably, 'I've talked about this so many times, especially with Marina and Kamal.'

'Fine,' Katie said. 'I'll get two more bottles of beer.' She looked around. 'Come on. Let's go and sit there under that picture.' She pointed to a big picture of Victor Hugo under which was written 'Don't forget, he too was once a refugee'. We headed for the restaurant when we heard the bell for supper.

In the days that followed, whenever I met Katie she'd joke with me, 'When are you going to tell me the story of your script?' until she came to my room one day and announced she'd be leaving in two days' time. She suggested we go for a picnic in the woods. 'And there we can talk about whatever we like.'

'It was afternoon and the boy was playing dominoes with his father, a deaf-mute baker. The father got up suddenly and took two beers out of the fridge. He signalled to his son to follow him and they went and sat by the railway track near the house. The boy pointed to the ground with his right index finger, then moved his outstretched hand right then left ('What are we doing here?'). The father raised his left index finger and pressed it under his left eye ('You'll see'). He smiled and clinked bottles with his son to say "Cheers".

'At the precise moment that the boy heard the whistle of an approaching train he saw his father reach into his pocket with his right hand and pull out a dirham coin. He placed it on his left palm and began to turn it over for his son to see. He pointed to the two sides of the coin, the picture and the inscription. The father went and laid the dirham on the rail, and returned whistling, like someone expecting a surprise. They were drinking their beers as the train sped by in front of them. The boy watched as his father searched for the dirham. When he found it he placed it in his left hand and poured some beer over it, then stretched out his clenched hand towards the boy, opened it and blew a raspberry. The boy saw the dirham had been transformed into a smooth piece of metal with neither picture nor inscription to be seen. The father took a sip from his beer. With his right index finger he prodded his son hard on his chest, pointed to the metal and then to the ground. The boy understood what his father was telling him: "If you stay in this country you'll end up like this dirham." Then the father tossed the flattened coin high into the

47

air and broke into loud laughter.'

We were eating mozzarella and tomato sandwiches and drinking Chianti wine, lying on the woollen blanket we had spread out not far from our picnic fire.

'Did that really happen?' Katie asked.

'Yes,' I nodded.

'It's a nice story,' she said, 'I like it,' and asked for a cigarette. She put it in her mouth and lit it straight from the fire.

'You're beautiful, Katie,' I said, gazing at her.

'Thank you,' she smiled. I drew closer and tried to kiss her.

'No,' she said. 'I'm engaged and will be meeting my fiancé in Lisbon in a week's time.'

I felt a bit awkward.

'I'm sorry,' Katie said.

I said nothing. I stretched out on my back and stared up at the sky.

'What are you thinking?' she asked.

'Nothing.'

She threw away her cigarette and stretched out next to me. She began to stroke my face. 'I love your nose,' she said softly. 'You have a lovely nose.'

'What?' I asked, astonished.

'Yes. You have a very nice nose,' she smiled and nodded in confirmation.

'I love Chianti,' I said.

'And I love Chianti with mozzarella,' Katie said.

That evening, after we'd finished the Chianti and mozzarella, Katie stretched out next to me. I wrapped my arms around her and whispered 'God Bless America' in her ear.

'Why do you say that?' she laughed.

I explained, 'That boy I was telling you about earlier. Well, when he was fifteen he came across an ad in the Arabic *Reader's Digest* and hid it away somewhere for many years. He used to dream of having $2,000 one day, and of travelling to Switzerland to have plastic surgery in Geneva. Tonight that boy has discovered the question is much simpler, it only needed a bottle of Chianti, a few slices of mozzarella and a nice American girl for him to throw the ad in the bin and forget the hang-up about his big nose once and for all.'

'I love what you're telling me,' said Katie, trying to move away from the fire. I whispered in her ear, asking if she wanted me to take off her tight jeans, and she looked into my eyes and nodded, smiling.

Her panties were white with a big picture of an old-style aeroplane on the front. As I put my head between her white thighs I noticed the plane looked exactly like the one that pursued Cary Grant in the Hitchcock movie *North by Northwest*. I kissed the aeroplane and felt for a moment it was still flying.

Rahim was busy with his Persian–French medical dictionary. He had studied medicine in Afghanistan and was in his final year when he had to flee to Pakistan, and from there to Iran, where he stayed for a while, although he described it to me as being 'far worse than life in Afghanistan. Ah, if you have seen how these mullahs destroyed that beautiful country.'

Suddenly he turned to me and, closing his dictionary, said, 'For a week you haven't been typing like you usually do.' He crossed the room and stood at the big window looking out over the centre's garden. 'You must be stressed. Does it have anything to do with the departure of the American girl?'

'You're right, Rahim, I am stressed, and not only because of Katie, but because my life here is so quiet and boring.'

Rahim was somewhat bewildered. 'Don't let Satan play on your soul,' he said, then quickly smiling, 'Come on, man, think about your script. Think about that. Everything will be all right.' He came over to me and patted me on the shoulder in a friendly way. 'This evening I'm treating you to a few bottles of beer.'

At that moment, Maya knocked on the door to tell me there

was a call for me from Paris. I went out to the telephone in the corridor, where I heard the voice of Mustafa telling me, in his habitually rapid gabble, 'Take the train and come quickly. I'm in Paris for one week. Leave the peasants and come to the city!'

2

'Keep your distance from Arabs if you want to be successful in this city.' I had heard this friendly advice from several Arab intellectuals I met when I first arrived in Paris; even the famous Arab poet Adams told me when I met him for the first time, 'You will get nothing from Arabs, only a headache, keep away from them – as much as you can.' I remember Mustafa himself told me the same thing when he bade me farewell in Tunis, 'I know Paris. I've been there several times and I've had difficult experiences with Arabs, believe me!'

But Mustafa contradicted himself, as did most Arab intellectuals in Paris. They give this 'friendly advice', but you see them always together, everywhere together. Mustafa, for instance, whose knowledge of Paris and its streets and cafés is unmatched, agreed to meet me at Café de Cluny, although he knew very well that Café de Cluny was like a headquarters for Arab writers and journalists. I had been there just three or four times before, and yet already I'd become acquainted with several Arab journalists, poets and artists – like Shamil, Abdelwahab, Nabil and Riadh, Salem and others. But I agreed with Riadh that Café de Cluny was one of the best cafés in Paris. It was a large building situated at the point where the two great boulevards of Saint-German and Saint-Michel meet.

Once I went up to the second floor bar, having just bought my

Erika typewriter from the Duriez shop nearby that day. Riadh was in the café, working on a translation of poems by Saint-John Perse. He glanced up and said, 'Look at that man!' I turned round to look at the man sitting at the window overlooking Boulevard Saint-Germain. 'Oh! It's Samuel Beckett!' I exclaimed.

'Yes, and he always sits in the same place,' said Riadh, adding, 'You see, the customers on the upstairs floor are much better than those downstairs.' It was clear that Riadh was alluding to the Arab journalists who usually gathered on the ground floor.

The moment Mustafa saw me he laughed and shouted, 'Come here, you Assyrian-escaped-from-the-museums!' And he hugged me.

'What are you doing in Paris?' I asked him quite spontaneously.

Mustafa looked at me for a moment and said with a smile, 'This is an insult, not a question!'

'Why do you say that?'

'Because an Iraqi is not allowed to ask a Tunisian what he's doing in Paris. The right question is "What is an *Iraqi* doing in Paris?" Never ask a North African intellectual what he's doing in Paris!'

'Well, get me a visa to America and I will leave Paris to you, my friend,' I joked.

Mustafa started scrutinising me closely, 'Look at you! In just a short time you've become healthy and handsome. In Tunis you looked like someone with bilharzia.'

'Did you summon me to Paris to mock me, Mustafa?'

'Not at all. I came from Tunis to arrange your life here.'

'You came to arrange my life, Mustafa, or to destroy it?'

'I want to save you from your life of monotony and turn you into a legend!'

We came out of the Denfert Rochereau metro station and walked along Boulevard Saint-Jacques. 'First, I will show you Uncle Salih's bar. It's a very small, popular place. You'll love it,' said

Mustafa, and as we turned into Rue de la Tombe Issoire, where the bar was, he continued, 'Uncle Salih is a very kind-hearted Algerian. He came to work in Paris before your mother expelled you into this world to disturb us with your hallucinations about the movies.' We laughed.

I loved Uncle Salih from the first moment I met him, and Mustafa introduced me to his girlfriend Martine in such flattering words, 'Th is is my friend, the Assyrian god who escaped from the hell of Mesopotamia and the Arabian Peninsula and wants to become a cowboy!'

We all laughed.

'Mustafa has told me a lot about you,' Martine said.

'He told me a lot about you, too, when I met him in Nicosia years ago,' I told her.

Martine looked at Mustafa, 'Have we known each other all that time?' And they laughed and kissed each other. Mustafa started reading poetry in French, and Martine put her head against his chest as he idly ran his fingers through her hair.

'Don't worry, you'll learn French very soon and discover how alluring this language is,' he said, looking at me, before getting up to bring us another carafe of red wine.

Mustafa was in love with Martine. I remember visiting him at his home in Tunis and him saying, 'I can't live alone any more. I think about her all the time.'

When I asked him, 'Why don't you try to settle in Paris?' Mustafa had given me an ironic smile and answered, 'I am an independent man, and in love with a student! The Arab intellectual can only live in Paris for two reasons: seeking political asylum like you, or working for one of the Arab magazines based in Paris or London – you know, those magazines that belong to Saudi Arabia and Gaddafi and Saddam Hussein. And I am, as you know, merely a poor and independent poet. I don't want to fall into the trap of producing propaganda for those dictatorial regimes. Is it not bad enough that I've fallen in love with a beautiful French woman?' he concluded, joking.

Mustafa poured the wine, then clinked glasses with Martine and kissed her. As he loved to play the clown, he started telling funny tales about the things he and I used to get up to, suddenly turning to look me straight in the eye: 'What was it your mother said to you when she looked into your eyes?'

'I don't remember, I don't know what you're talking about,' I answered, embarrassed in front of Martine.

'Oh, you've become a shy guy all of a sudden, huh?' said Mustafa, cackling with laughter. He put his arm around Martine. 'He told me once his mother looked into his eyes when he was a little boy and told him, "You have beautiful eyes, like the eyes of a prostitute".' We all laughed. And Mustafa didn't stop until two in the morning, when he fell asleep on Martine's lap. Then we all went to the university campus in Rue Dareau, a few metres' walk from Uncle Salih's bar, to Martine's room.

The next day, Mustafa told me he had an appointment with some friends, and suggested meeting at four o'clock. We were in Place du Châtelet. 'Can you find a way to while away the time until then?'

'I'll find myself a nice bar,' I said.

Mustafa looked at me: 'I told you I came to arrange your life. I don't want to hear about bars every time we meet. I suggest you go and spend a few hours in the Centre Pompidou.'

'What's that?'

We walked for five minutes and then Mustafa pointed to a huge, modern building. 'This is the Centre Pompidou, I'm sure you'll like it.'

As Mustafa left me, he didn't realise that he'd just given me the most valuable present of my whole life. The Centre Pompidou was an incredible mine from which I extracted all that I had been deprived of during my twenty-eight years. That afternoon I became captivated as I walked between the shelves in the library, with books on literature, movies, music and art, dictionaries, even cookery books capturing my attention.

'I'd love to be imprisoned here,' I said to myself, as I sat on the floor leafing through several books at a time about making movies, writing scripts, about the lives and memories of actors, directors and film-makers.

3

The rays of the evening sun still shone red on Carrefour de l'Odéon, where I was drinking beer at the Café Danton and from time to time thinking I should go and catch a train to Moulin. I didn't want to go back to that quiet garden. I got out my pen and started writing a few notes in Arabic about my two days with Mustafa in Paris.

'It's been ages since I've seen anyone writing Arabic,' said the thin man standing next to me ordering hot milk. I looked at him and smiled. He smiled back. His eyes were sunk deep in his face and he looked like he was suffering from something.

He told me he was Syrian and that his name was Ziad. He used to be a journalist but had given it up because 'the press in the Arab world is like a brothel'. He announced that his motto in life was 'to distance myself from Arabs and stay away from them as much as possible'.

'I, on the other hand, have given up the entire Middle East,' I said enthusiastically. I invited him to have a glass of beer but he said the doctor had forbidden him to drink coffee and alcohol. 'I only drink champagne on special occasions,' he added.

After a while I told him I had to go to Gare de Lyon to catch the train for Moulin, where I lived.

'Moulin?' he said contemptuously. 'How can you live there?'

'I have no choice, Ziad,' I said, and began explaining my circumstances.

He stared at me for a minute. 'Would you like to live in Paris?' he asked. And before I could respond he added, 'I have a studio in Rue de Babylone. Come and live there!'

'Rue de Babylone?' I exclaimed.

'Yes. Rue de Babylone.'

'It's my dream to live in a street called Babylon,' I said happily. Then, after a moment's pause: 'But what about the rent?'

'No problem,' replied Ziad, shaking his head. 'Do what Parisians do. Work and pay rent.' He smiled and added, 'I'm going to have a beer this evening on your account. Get me one, will you?' I got him a glass of beer, then another and another until there were no more trains and Ziad proposed I go with him to his place in Rue de Babylone.

The studio was on the fifth floor and was so clean it looked as though it had never been lived in. Ziad explained how things worked, and gave me a set of keys. 'If I were you I'd go in the morning and fetch your belongings,' he said, looking into my eyes.

'I'll do just that, my friend,' I replied, and sat on the bed.

'Do you have 200 francs on you?' asked Ziad. 'I'm not sure if I have enough for the taxi.'

'No problem.' I jumped up eagerly and gave him 200 francs.

★ ★ ★

The director of Le Rocheton Centre told me I was the first person ever to leave the centre before having to. Usually, refugees asked to extend their stay by one or two months in order to arrange their affairs before finally leaving. She put some official documents in front of me. 'After you sign these papers, monsieur, you will have no right to return here. Is that clear?'

'Yes, madame.'

'We will pay you 1,500 francs, your allowance for the next three months, and I wish you every success.'

'Where did you say the studio was?' Marie, the nice fat secretary, asked me.

'Rue de Babylone, Marie.'

'You're lucky. You'll be shopping every day at the Bon Marché, eh?'

When I saw Rahim he looked rather dejected. I told him, joking, 'You should be happy I'm leaving, Rahim,' before hugging him and saying, 'Now you have all the time you want to fuck your Ethiopian girl!'

'Do you know who's going to replace you?' said Rahim.

'Don't tell me – your Ethiopian girl!' I said cheerfully.

'Our Hungarian friend!' said Rahim glumly. 'As if it wasn't enough to be missing you, they've added this punishment.'

'You're right. He's a real punishment. All you can do is make an alliance with our Russian friend Marina!' That was the advice I gave him before leaving Le Rocheton.

When Ziad saw my typewriter he told me I would be able to type all night if I wanted. 'Nobody lives on the fifth or sixth floors. What do you type on this typewriter?'

I didn't know how to answer. 'Actually, I'm not yet sure if I'm writing a film script or a novel,' I said. 'It's about my father.'

'Is your father that important?' he asked, half leaning against the open door. He looked a bit troubled. 'Do you think the story of your father will bring you money?'

'I'm really only thinking about art, not money, at the present time,' I said.

He took a tissue out of his pocket and shouted while blowing his nose, 'Sorry. I didn't get that. What did you say?'

'Of course,' I said.

'Of course what? I don't get you.'

I sensed he wasn't quite normal and that I was getting entangled in something, so I said, 'Of course it's going to bring me loads of money.'

'We'll see!' He smiled and went on, 'Money rules the world. Don't imagine everyone is as nice as me.'

'Excuse me, Ziad. May I ask where you live?'

'With my girlfriend . . . She's a princess,' he replied, as if it was the most normal thing in the world.

'Is she from Saudi Arabia?'

He looked at me with a mocking smile. 'What's with you? Do I look like someone who associates with Saudi princesses? My girlfriend is a French princess,' he added, smirking. 'She lives in a villa on the river at Neuilly-sur-Seine. I'll take you with me one of these days.'

Shaking my head, I put my typewriter on the table. 'Would you like a can of beer?' I asked, making my way to the fridge.

'Yes please,' he answered. 'You appear to be a well-organised young man.' He smiled as he took the can from me.

'Yes, I did some shopping this morning at the Bon Marché.'

He took a few steps and stopped at the corner near the bed. 'Look,' he said pointing to a neat stack of French magazines. 'Here are some copies of *Pointe de Vue*. This magazine represents the views of the royalist "movement" in France. Have a look at them. You'll see how beautiful these royalists are.'

'I'm a royalist,' I enthused.

'Slow down!' Ziad replied. 'My girlfriend may be a princess but I have always kept my personal relationships and political beliefs separate. I've always supported the French Revolution.'

'I think monarchies are the best form of leadership for Arab countries,' I told him, heading for the fridge to fetch another can of beer.

'Perhaps. Sorry, but I'm afraid I'll have to leave you to drink on your own,' said Ziad. At the door he paused and turned. 'Do you have 200 francs?' he asked.

'Of course,' I replied, and handed him some notes. He left. I knew I now had no more than 900 francs left.

I spent a long time leafing through a copy of *Pointe de Vue*, fascinated by the photographs of princesses and countesses at their luxurious parties. A picture of one woman in particular struck me. She was pale with rosy cheeks, and plump like one of Renoir's bathers. I left the magazine open on the bed and went off to the Café Danton for a few glasses of beer. It was midnight when I returned and I was astonished to find Ziad sitting on the bed. I had intended to spend the night writing. I was confused and didn't know what to do.

'It's not nice of you to enter the studio when I'm not here,' I told him after an awkward silence.

'I wanted to make sure everything was fine,' he said, exhaling his cigarette smoke at the floor.

He began turning the pages of the copy of *Pointe de Vue* until he came to the picture of the young girl that had caught my attention earlier. He put the picture in front of me. 'Can you tell me why you chose to leave the picture of this girl open on your bed?' he said. 'I know why. I didn't think you were that kind of guy. That's Princess Juliette. She concerns me personally,' he shouted.

'What are you talking about? Eh? Are you crazy, Ziad? If I'd known you were like this, I'd never have left Le Rocheton and got into this mess. Give me a week and I'll be out of here.'

He lit another cigarette and went and sat back down on the bed. 'Can you warm me some milk, please? It's not polite of you to call me crazy. I'm like a big brother to you.' He got up and stood in the middle of the studio. 'Don't be angry with me. No need for the milk.' He turned to leave, and once again said, 'By the way, do you have 200 francs?'

'Oh, I'm sorry! I don't have any just now. I can give it to you tomorrow!'

Next day, I was drinking in the Café Danton when Ziad came in. He looked miserable, and his unshaven face made him appear even more wretched. I felt embarrassed by him. Some people at the bar were staring at him.

'Can I give you a hundred francs now so you can go home and relax?' I asked him, remembering that last night he had asked me for money.

'Why? Does my being here disturb you?'

'Not at all. You're in a café, not my house.'

'Yes, that's true. Your house is in Rue de Babylone, isn't it?'

I told him, joking, 'Dear Ziad, I will leave your studio next week, and I will pay you as much as you want. And we can remain friends.'

'Are you waiting for someone?'

In fact I wasn't waiting for anybody, but I answered, 'Yes, I'm waiting for a girl. We're going to go see a movie.'

'You've become Parisian that quickly? You've started giving appointments to girls already. What a brilliant guy!' He smiled, adding, 'Quick, give me the hundred francs before you spend it.'

As I gave him the money, he looked into my eyes and said, '*Bonne chance, monsieur,*' and left.

It was about 3 am when I got back to Rue de Babylone and approached my building. I saw my typewriter and my bag thrown onto the pavement. I checked through everything, and my folder of papers, my script, was missing. I was on the point of going straight up to the studio, but was in two minds. I decided it would not be a good idea to be in Ziad's studio if he was there and looking for a fight. All I wanted from him was my folder of papers. So I rang the bell to speak to him through the entry phone.

'If you don't go away I'll call the police,' he shouted.

'Well, if you don't, I'll call them myself.'

'Wait there a moment,' he said, 'I'm coming down.'

'I want the folder with my papers in,' I said when he came out.

'I want the rent for the days you stayed in the studio,' he said, trying to close the door. I rushed towards it and said, 'I'm not going anywhere until you bring me my papers.'

'What papers?' he said, trying to push me away from the door.

'My folder of papers, you thief,' I said glaring into his fearful-looking eyes in their hollow sockets.

'You vile Iraqi, I'm not a thief!' he shouted, and with a sudden lunge, punched me in the face and pushed me so I fell backwards onto the ground. Then he closed the door. Blood poured from my nose. I took a T-shirt from my bag to stem the bleeding. I rang the bell and kept ringing it until Ziad appeared at the entrance and threw my folder of papers into the street shouting, 'Whatever made me get mixed up with you? I swore I'd cut off all ties with Arabs. They don't like anything, only misery.'

'You're sick, Ziad! You're sick and need to see a doctor!' I shouted at the top of my voice, not realising that this phrase would be the end of him.

He began banging his head against the door repeatedly. 'I'm not sick, you son of a bitch! I'm not sick, you son of a bitch!' He was wearing a white vest and green boxer shorts, which made him look very skinny indeed.

I ran a few metres up the road and stopped with my typewriter and my bag in front of Hotel Lutetia. That very moment a van drew up beside me and a man of about fifty years of age got out, beaming broadly. '*Bonjour*, young man.'

'*Bonjour, monsieur.*' I tried to sound happy.

He opened his van door and said, 'Take this fresh *pain au chocolat*, young man.' He reminded me of my father when I was a small boy and went to see him in the bakery. 'You are very kind, monsieur,' I said as I took the *pain au chocolat* from him.

He took the tray and carried it into the hotel. The moment he came back he shouted to me, 'Don't be sad, it's dawn. People can become sad in the afternoon but not at dawn, young man. The whole day is in front of you. And I can tell you a little story.'

'*S'il vous plaît, monsieur!*'

'My father was captured by the Nazis exactly where you are standing now. He was trying to plant a bomb in the hotel when it was the headquarters of the Gestapo in France during the war. And look at me now, the son of that hero, bringing *pains au chocolat* and croissants here every morning!' He started guffawing as he took out another tray from the van and carried it into the hotel.

'No, monsieur, I'm not sad,' I said to him as he was finishing his delivery, 'I have been thrown out of the apartment I was staying in and need some time to decide what to do.'

'That's very easy,' he laughed, 'It is still dawn, young man. Go and put your things in Austerlitz Station. The metro from here is direct,' and he pointed to the steps of Sévres Babylon metro station. 'Paris is the city of compassion.'

That was most important and quite unexpected friendly advice.

At Austerlitz Station I found I could not only leave my belongings, but also have a shower and a wash, which were both very important for me in the mornings. I made the decision to throw away some of my clothes and books, and even got rid of some of my photos. I did everything instinctively – took a shower, changed my clothes, and put my bag and typewriter in the station locker. It was as if it was normal for me. Then I went to the Centre Pompidou.

That night was my first night in Paris without a place to stay. I stopped and lit a cigarette and at that moment felt at peace with myself and thought, should I protest about my grim past? I just wanted to be far from it, to lose it and to be lost. I didn't want anything from my past. I wanted a new life. I walked from street to street until the light of day, singing a poem I'd written to myself:

> *Blessed is he who has touched my body,*
> *Blessed the earth that my feet have trod,*
> *Blessed is he who knows my name,*
> *Blessed is he who has caught my eye,*
> *Blessed, blessed.*
> *Blessed he who has breathed my flowers,*

Blessed he whom my trees have shaded,
Blessed he who has taken my love,
Blessed he who has stolen my youth,
Blessed, blessed.
Blessed he who has led me astray.

4

In fact the 'keep away from Arabs . . .' advice wasn't always good advice, for my friends — intellectuals, journalists and otherwise — were good to me. I used to visit them from time to time and stay at their homes for a night or more. And also borrow a few francs from them (which I still haven't returned).

'They are nice to you because they regard you as homeless,' Riadh said to me once when we were sitting in Café de Cluny.

'But I'm not homeless, Riadh,' I answered, somewhat resentfully.

'Sorry, Sammy, I don't mean to hurt you but this is what they call people who live on the streets.'

'I don't live on the streets, Riadh. I simply refuse to have a home, at least not at the moment. If I wanted to have a home I could easily have one.' I knew, as I answered, that what I was saying was untrue. Well, I could have a home but I would first have to give up my ideas.

'When you have a home, a car and a beautiful wife you will see how these "kind" people will turn on you,' he said.

'Then let us leave this subject until I do have a home and a beautiful wife,' I answered, laughing.

But Riadh never entirely gave up that conversation. Another time he told me, as we met in the same café, 'Those journalists who show solidarity with you are in fact only trying to appease the guilt they feel working for newspapers owned by dictatorial Arab regimes.' Then he added, hugging me affectionately, 'Don't be angry with me, my friend, if you didn't exist, those journalists would create someone just like you.'

Riadh liked me but was annoyed to see me in the company of certain people. While he was waiting for his girlfriend Véronique in a café in Place de la Sorbonne he would ask, 'How can you bear talking to that donkey who praises a dictator like Gaddafi?' or 'I was shocked when I saw you with that Saudi agent'. Each time I would explain that I wasn't responsible for the attitudes of others, but he would deride that idea and say, 'You're too kind-hearted.'

Although I aspired to a life without a home − like a child who enjoys giving more and more line to his kite to see how far it will fly − I also felt the need to be in a place with a kitchen, a bathroom, shelves of books and other people. And that could easily be arranged. A phone call was all that was needed for me to go from cardboard spread on the floor of a car park to a warm bed in the house of any one of my friends, all of whom would welcome me in an instant, even if my being there was inconvenient.

I once called Mamdouh, who worked as a presenter at one of the well-known Paris-based Arab radio stations. He told me that he had to meet a young Tunisian singer at a Lebanese restaurant in the Champs-Elysées, and added, 'I don't mind at all if you'd like to join us.'

So I did so immediately. It was the first time I had been to one of those Lebanese restaurants famous for their singing and dancing and often to be found in basements due to the very loud Arab music they played. Mamdouh introduced me to Fawziyah, who at first sight struck me as being as artificial as the atmosphere of the restaurant, which I didn't like at all. I wondered how some of my friends could spend their nights in such places, and with some of them it was every night.

At five in the morning, as I got into the car with Mamdouh and his friend, and whispered to him, in my embarrassment, to kindly drop me at the entrance of the nearest metro station, he looked at me, his eyes flashing, and said, 'How could you think, even for a second, that I would leave you in this cold, you idiot?'

While Fawziyah was in the bathroom, Mamdouh came to me with a smile on his face and placed an old typewriter in front of me, saying, 'Just keep typing something, anything, while I'm in the bedroom with Fawziyah – she's shy.'

I kept typing until daybreak, and the sound of the typewriter mingled with Fawziyah's moaning, which was so loud I had to hammer harder and harder on the keys. I didn't stop until Mamdouh stuck his head around the door and said, 'Please stop typing, we need to sleep.'

Later I read an interview with Fawziyah in a magazine in which she talked about her life: 'I was born into a conservative family that regards singing as a shameful profession, but thanks to my talent, patience and hard work I have been able to make them accept my love of music and singing and, finally, thanks to God, I have started receiving everyone's encouragement.'

As for Shamil, I visited his house more than anyone else's. For one thing, I liked his lifestyle, and he was closer to me than all the others. He had written his Master's dissertation on James Joyce and had a doctorate in film studies. I used to sit without moving for days at a time in front of his shelves of books, just reading. And it was through him that I got to know many of the world's writers and film-makers, whom he interviewed for the magazine where he worked.

Shamil liked North African women, and was very skilled in chatting-up techniques. Although he had a car, he sometimes preferred to take the metro, especially if he was going to one of those stations that are crowded with Arab women, like Place de la République or Barbès. We would be standing in the train when suddenly Shamil would jump out, shouting, 'Wait for me at the next station!' before disappearing among the passengers.

Then he'd show up at the next station with a girl whom he'd introduce to me with a theatrical flourish. 'Can you imagine, Sammy, my friend, how lucky I've been today? I've had the honour of meeting Miss Malika from dear Morocco.'

Later he would say for her benefit, 'I'm tired of French women and their complexes, just as I'm tired of bachelor life', before uttering his final patter: 'It seems God wants to me to live with a woman who shares the same culture and religion as me.'

Shamil used to give me a few francs to go and have a few beers in the café near his house. When I arrived back at his place, he had finished having sex, and the poor girl would be in the kitchen, preparing one of the delights of Moroccan cuisine to prove she was a good housewife too.

'At last I have found a decent woman who will spare me the horrors of bad restaurant food and the horrors of pork,' he would remark loudly.

Such stories happened to Shamil at least twice a week. It was perfectly normal, almost routine. My presence also became part of the scene that Shamil refused to give up. But when he found that sending me to wait in the café while he had sex was becoming expensive, he started telling the girls he brought home, 'Sammy is not just my friend, he's my brother.' He would take them into the bedroom and I would lie down and read a book on the sofa in the sitting room next to the bathroom. The girls would come out of the bedroom wearing Shamil's dressing gown (God knows how many girls wore that dressing gown) and go to the bathroom. Little by little they got used to my presence, and made a quick dash past me, naked, to the bathroom. In the end, they weren't embarrassed to stand before me, covering their pussies with their hands and asking me what the book I was reading was all about.

There came a time when I decided to stop visiting my friends' houses once and for all, and at all costs, not only to avoid embarrassing incidents but because I had become a kind of voyeur, spying on their private lives in spite of myself. My Tunisian friend Ramadan had invited me to stay at his place for a few weeks after persuading his wife to welcome me. I took my stuff and went home with him to Porte de la Chapelle. A week later, as I was working on my typewriter, I heard shouts and cries in the bedroom, but did not pay any heed to it as I had often noticed my friend arguing with his wife, especially when they prepared food together in the kitchen.

But that morning my friend's wife stormed into my room and angrily told me, 'Please leave this house at once.' I immediately grabbed my suitcase and my typewriter, and as I left the house, she told me, 'For seventeen years my husband has been eating with me. But yesterday he went with you for a hamburger. God knows where you will take him next time.'

I would not be telling a lie if I said that when I met Ramadan less than a year later, he was divorced and working as a manager for the Burger King branch at Place de Clichy. I visited him from time to time, and he always invited me over for a few beers at Café Wipler opposite his work.

I once tried to convince him to return to his ex-wife. 'Not for the moment at least, especially since Rue Pigalle is only a step away from here,' he replied with a smile, and I noticed a copy of Henry Miller's *Jours tranquils à Clichy*★ on the table.

My Algerian friend Mourad, a maths teacher, insisted on inviting me back to his home every time we ended up drinking until very late.

'And what about the hotel room I've already paid for?' I would say.

He would answer, laughing, 'I know how you look if you have a hotel room to go to.' So I would go with him and spend a nice evening with him and his wife Khadija, who was very friendly

★ *Quiet Days in Clichy*

towards me.

'Sammy, wait a minute, I'm going to make you a sandwich. I bought some *jambon de Paris* especially for you,' she would say in the morning as I was about to leave.

But later on, I started avoiding Mourad's invitations. His brother Abdelaziz had come from Marseilles to stay with him and the brothers often argued on account of me. Abdelaziz was a Muslim extremist who wore his beard long and kept his white cap on even when he was at home.

'I don't see what's so special about this infidel, for you to be bringing him into our life,' he said.

'This is my house, brother, not yours,' answered Mourad, winking at me as I sat next to Khadija, smoking a cigarette.

Abdelaziz started pacing up and down the corridor, muttering into his beard. We knew he was annoyed by my presence.

'He comes here to spy on us,' he said once.

Mourad turned to his brother, shouting, 'Why don't you go to your room and leave us in peace? Why can't you be fair? When you arrived here, you said you wanted to stay with me for a while until you sorted yourself out.'

'Are you kicking me out, Mourad?'

'No, I'm not. But if you don't feel comfortable being around my friends then go and find yourself another place to stay.'

'You should be ashamed of what you're saying,' said Abdelaziz.

'I'm sorry, Mourad,' I said, 'I think I should leave.'

'If you leave this place I'll never talk to you again,' Mourad said to me, and then to his brother: 'We are brothers and we are Algerians and we have the same fucking heads! But I swear to God that if you ever interfere in my personal life again, you'll see what I will do to you.'

'Are you threatening me, Mourad?'

'Do not insult my friend in my home. That is what I want you to understand, and if you don't like it you can take your things and leave tomorrow. That's all I'm saying to you.'

Khadija smiled and looked proudly at her husband, while Abdelaziz went to his room and closed the door behind him.

Then there was Joseph, my Syrian painter friend with his big heart. I called him at eight o'clock in the morning once. I told him I needed him for a very important task. 'Where are you?' he asked. 'In Place du Châtelet,' I told him.

'There are four cafés there, one is the Sarah Bernhardt,' he said. 'Wait for me there.'

'Do you know Robert De Niro?' I asked Joseph, when we were sitting down.

'Of course!' he replied, drinking his coffee.

'Listen, Joseph. I've seen many of Robert De Niro's movies and I spent all yesterday in the Centre Pompidou reading up about him in books, articles, magazines, biographies and picture books and I made a thorough study of his career. He's forty-three years old and has done really remarkable work. Remember *Taxi Driver*, *The Deer Hunter*, *Raging Bull*, *Once Upon a Time in America*, even *The King of Comedy* is good, I liked it, it was different.'

'Excellent!' Joseph said, shaking his head appreciatively.

'For that, dear Joseph, I hope you can help me by painting a portrait of De Niro looking sixty years old.'

'Why do you want him to be sixty?'

'Well, you remember I told you I'm writing a script which is set in the fifties and sixties about . . .'

'About your father, the deaf-mute baker who loves the Queen of England?'

'Exactly. I discovered from this research about De Niro that he is the only person who could play the role of the deaf-mute baker.'

Joseph smiled and said, 'I don't want to dampen your enthusiasm, but as you well know, you'll need two or three years to finish the script, another five years to find finance, and you can add another year or more for the studios to prepare casting and shooting. By that time De Niro will be not far off the age you want him to be painted now.'

'OK then, make him seventy.'

'Right!' said Joseph, 'At your service, my friend.'

'Come on, Joseph. This portrait will be a historic work, don't you think?'

'I will do exactly as you wish.'

I looked at him and said, 'Can you lend me a hundred francs, Joseph?'

When he said 'Of course' I immediately caught the waiter's eye and asked for a pastis.

As for my Moroccan friend Mahdi al-Tanjawi★, he used to talk to me for hours about his happy life with his Syrian fiancée, a girl from Aleppo – it was 'the alliance of Tangiers and Aleppo', as he loved to repeat.

One evening, I was sitting on a bench facing the Duriez shop on Boulevard Saint-Germain when al-Tanjawi took me by surprise. 'At last I've got you! Today I'm going to make you drink till you drop,' he joked, pretending he was trying to strangle me, 'Come on, let's go and have a drink.'

We went into the nearby Café Boulmiche and al-Tanjawi told me he had made all the wedding arrangements. We clinked glasses and celebrated. When his fiancée Rasha arrived he invited us to eat seafood at Le Procope restaurant in Rue de l'Ancienne Comédie, where I had always hoped to eat one day. Our evening lasted until dawn, and I went back with them to their place.

The next weekend, at eleven o'clock in the evening, I was a few steps away from my 'bed' at Austerlitz Station when suddenly I heard a voice inside me asking, 'What are you doing here in this cold?'

I remembered my friend Sadiq and immediately took the train to Villeneuve-le-Roi in the suburbs of Paris. I had difficulty finding the address as I had been there before only by car. At three in

★ Al-Tanjawi means 'the person from Tangiers'

69

the morning I found it. Sadiq lived in one of those buildings owned by the municipality, whose front entrance is usually broken and open, so I went directly to his apartment on the third floor and knocked on the door, quite unsuspecting what was about to happen. When the door opened, I found myself face to face with the girl from Aleppo, the fiancée of al-Tanjawi who had gone to Morocco to tell his parents about his wedding arrangements. And just as Rasha had kissed me goodbye a few days earlier, she welcomed me in the same way.

We remained silent for a few moments, then she said, 'Sadiq drank too much tonight.' We smiled at each other and she went back into the bedroom. I threw myself down on the sofa in the sitting room, and in the morning all three of us had breakfast together.

A year after their marriage, my friend al-Tanjawi invited me for a drink with the same enthusiasm as before and told me he had divorced his wife from Aleppo, 'I betrayed her so often that I had a guilty conscience. I had to divorce her so that she could find someone who would be faithful to her and respect her.'

I nodded as I sipped my Chardonnay that July afternoon, thinking of what Shamil had once said to me: 'Without illusion, life would be a real hell.'

5

It was not only difficult, but also very tiring living without a house, on the streets, and so I made an effort to get my own place. I had casually mentioned to a few friends how tricky it was to find a place. Soon, a friend who was living in Epinay-sous-Sénart told me that his French neighbour let out rooms. He would talk to her about me, but I would have to find a job so I could pay the rent. In two days I found a job through the Interim temping agency as a painter and decorator with a group of Turkish guys. So I went to live at Madame Pauline's house, and I don't know whether it was good or bad luck that on the same day I arrived a young guy from Cameroon also took a room there. He was studying engineering and at the same time working for the municipality.

After a few hours of arriving at Madame Pauline's house, my Cameroonian friend somehow noticed that I had only one pair of shoes.

It seemed he wanted to be sure of it for he asked me, 'I notice you only have one pair of shoes. Am I right, my brother?'

I looked at him on my way to the kitchen. 'Yes, that's right.'

My friend stopped, as if he was thinking of something important, and said, 'Does that mean Arabs don't like shoes?' And he followed me into the kitchen. 'Why don't Arabs like shoes?' he asked.

'I don't know,' I answered with a smile and started cooking.

That evening my friend the Cameroonian knocked on my door. 'Sorry, I can't sleep, can I take one of your beers from the fridge?'

'Of course, help yourself,' I answered.

The next day he came again. 'I'm very sorry, my friend, I've used some of your onions, and can I take some black pepper too?' The next time: 'I've taken some of your rice.' And the next time: 'Oh, my friend, I took some of your tomatoes and cucumbers.' That time he looked at me and blurted out, 'But I still don't know why Arabs don't like shoes.'

'Believe me, I don't know either,' I answered him, laughing.

'Good morning, my friend the Iraqi,' he said as he came back from his morning cleaning job.

'Good morning, my friend the Cameroonian.'

'I would be grateful if you would give me a cigarette.' Before I could give him one, he added, 'Sorry, yesterday I wanted to ask you if I could take some of your spaghetti, but it seems you went to bed early, so I allowed myself to take some.'

I handed him a cigarette and gave him a light.

'Merci,' he said, and looked quizzically at me. 'This morning when I was leaving the house, I saw your shoes near the door. They looked tired and I said to myself, "I really do want to know why Arabs don't like shoes".'

One day I went into the garden and saw my friend polishing six pairs of shoes – black, white and brown. He laughed and said, 'These shoes are the mark of civilisation, don't you think?'

I nodded, smiling. 'I'm making coffee for myself and Madame Pauline. Do you want some?'

'You are magnificent, my brother.'

I gave him a big mug of coffee and said, 'Do you really want to know why Arabs don't like shoes?'

'Oh, yes please. I'm very eager to know why Arabs don't like shoes.'

'Because they like beer, onions, rice, tomatoes, spaghetti, cigarettes, cucumbers and black pepper.' And I added, in spite of myself, 'and they don't have a complex about shoes.'

From that moment my friend the Cameroonian stopped talking to me, did not even greet me when we passed each other in the house. The next day he deliberately made a lot of noise in the corridor to show me he had been shopping. I opened my door and saw him carrying bags of groceries. 'Sorry about the noise. I'm just back from the supermarket,' he said.

That was the only time I ever saw that he had been shopping. After a few days I heard Madame Pauline complaining that some of her groceries had disappeared from the kitchen. 'I can't find the packet of rice.' Then: 'I'm sure I bought a packet of spaghetti'. Then: 'Have either of you seen my beetroot? It's not in the fridge.' Every day she had questions like these.

'Can you explain to me, Mr Film Director, how these things

can disappear from the kitchen?'

'I'm sorry, madame. I don't touch anything that doesn't belong to me,' I answered.

'Can you, Mr Engineer, explain how my things have disappeared from here?'

'I'm really sorry, madame. I don't go near your stuff at all.'

After that, Madame Pauline took an aspirin and went to her room, shaking her head. A few days later, when she saw us together in the kitchen, she declared in a very angry voice,

'Listen here, you two! I can't take this any more! My bedroom is open. My jewellery is everywhere and nothing has been stolen. How can the thieving be only from the kitchen? I want to know exactly what is going on in this house!'

The Cameroonian, who spoke fluent French, defended himself, saying, 'Madame Pauline, I leave at dawn every day to sweep the streets. Then I come back here to relax a little, and then I go to the university. If I wanted to be a thief, it would be very easy. I can go and work with the gangs that are all over Paris instead of cleaning the streets of Epinay-sous-Sénart.'

'You, Mr Film Director, what's your opinion on the disappearance of my spaghetti, my black pepper, rice, onions, my sugar and coffee?'

I looked at her, thinking of what to say to her when she said, half in English, 'Speak English, *pas de problème*.'

'Madame, these things are not important for me, believe me.'

'There have been wars over such things.'

'I know, madame. I have seen many movies about that.'

'You only know how to speak about movies? Why don't you write something about the thefts from my kitchen, eh?' And she left in a rage.

The next morning, there was a note under my door telling me to leave the house as soon as possible. In the afternoon my Cameroonian friend came and asked me if I had had a letter from her. I nodded.

'French women are psychos,' he complained. 'When they don't find someone to fuck them, they imagine thefts from their kitchen! Do you think, my brother, that we need her onions, her rice and her black pepper?'

6

I don't want to say 'suddenly I decided' to shave off my moustache. It just happened quite naturally. I was in the shower at Austerlitz Station and was shaving in front of the mirror when I found myself shaving off my moustache for the first time in my life. I didn't know that with this act I was putting myself in a bizarre situation, one that I did not need as I already had enough problems. The 'problem' started the minute I left the shower room. The Serbian lady who looked after the washroom started laughing at me strangely. It seemed she couldn't control herself. 'Are you laughing at me, madame?' I asked her, surprised. She carried on laughing, 'Pardon, monsieur! You surprised me. I thought Monsieur Aldo Maccione was here taking a shower!'

'Aldo Maccione?' I said, and looked at my face in the big mirror behind her.

'Don't you know? You look exactly like him,' she said, and burst out laughing again.

'Oh, Aldo! Aldo Maccione makes stupid movies, madame, while I want to make very serious and tragic dramas.'

'Monsieur, Aldo Maccione is very popular here.'

The Serbian lady was absolutely right. Wherever I went, people stared at me and smiled. I even heard laughter. In the streets, in the metro, in the cafés, I was under observation.

I was sitting in a metro carriage when a mother and her young daughter standing by the door started staring at me. The mother whispered, 'Maybe, I'm not quite sure.' The daughter whispered back, 'Yes, *Maman*. It's him.' 'I think you're right,' the mother said. '*Oui, Maman, c'est lui*!' When the train stopped and they got out, the young girl smiled at me and shouted, '*Au revoir*, Aldo! *Au revoir*, Aldo!' and waved. All the other passengers turned and stared at me. I couldn't believe it, and as soon as the next stop came, I jumped out.

When I told Mourad about this, he said, as he tried to control his laughter, 'You have two solutions – grow your moustache again, or hold an Arabic newspaper up in front of you when you're on the metro.' Before I could reply he added, 'By the way, you don't need to buy a paper every day. You can use the same one as no one will realise you're reading old news!'

So that's what I did, and it worked for a few days. With two pages of an Arabic newspaper covering my face not a single passenger looked at me. On the contrary, I was looking at them to see if they were looking at me. One day, however, I was quietly reading my week-old newspaper when a young African came and sat beside me.

'Are you Muslim, my brother?' he asked in French.

'No,' I replied.

'Then how come you're reading an Arabic paper?'

'The Arabic language existed before Islam, *monsieur*,' I answered gravely.

He gave a wry, nervous laugh, '*Monsieur*, it is the language of the Qur'an.'

'That's correct,' I said. 'Where is the problem?'

He smiled stupidly. 'It's shameful to say you're not a Muslim when you're reading the language of the Qur'an.' He moved to sit opposite me, and kept giving me angry looks.

I left the train at the next stop, saying to myself, 'I will be clever next time!'

Another day, another African came and sat beside me, who said he was from Senegal and asked me in French, 'Where are you from, my brother?'

'From Iraq,' I answered.

He smiled and asked, 'Are you Muslim, my brother?'

'Yes!' I told him, adding quickly, 'but I don't speak French.'

He said to me in English, 'We are Muslims. We are great people.'

I nodded and said, 'Yes, we are,' and went back to reading my paper.

'My brother, can you spare me ten francs?'

'Why don't you go to the Mosque de Paris?' I asked him.

'No money in the Mosque de Paris!' he answered me with a big smile.

I told him as I folded my newspaper, 'Me no money either!' and I left the train.

The first rubbish bin I saw I got rid of the Arabic paper. To be Aldo Maccione was much easier – and nicer, I said to myself, without knowing what surprise was in store for me. That evening, I went and took a drink in my corner of the Café Danton and I heard one waiter say to another, 'Look, Marcello Mastroianni is outside.' I turned to look and saw Marcello Mastroianni walking past the café. I watched him through the window and he looked back as though he knew me. He nodded his head in greeting as if he knew me. I rushed out after him and told him how much I admired him. He smiled and said, 'Hah! Aldo Maccione!'

7

It was a sunny day and many young people were sitting in the open space in front of the Centre Pompidou. I was walking along oblivious to everything when I bumped into the poet Adams. He was wearing a grey trilby and carrying his pipe and some French newspapers. I was delighted to see him. Immediately he said, 'Let's walk a little around this lovely place!' But he stopped suddenly and turned to me, 'When I met you just now you were looking so sad.'

'I wasn't sad, I was miles away in a very melancholy story that I had just finished reading in the Centre Pompidou.'

'A story by whom?'

'Scott Fitzgerald. It's a story called "Babylon Revisited". I read it twice.'

Adams stood for a while, thoughtful. 'A beautiful title,' he remarked, adding, 'It is a great thing when someone reads a literary text and interacts with it.

I was seized with excitement as I stood with this poet whom I admired. 'Two days ago I saw a Japanese movie about love and sex and nature.'

'Interesting subjects for me,' Adams replied.

'The hero of the movie was so obsessed with nature that he developed an aversion to both his wife and his mistress, and went off wandering in the forest, making love with the trees. In the end, he killed every member of his family and then committed suicide!'

'He's a madman,' said Adams. 'Is there anything more beautiful in the universe than the body of a woman?'

Adams had decided to live in France permanently and was giving some lectures at the College de France. The French newspapers were writing that he was a strong candidate for the Nobel Prize for Literature that year (and he was to remain on the list of nominees for several years more).

'What part of Paris do you live in?' he asked me.

'In all of Paris!' I said, laughing. I was without a house after being deceived by a friend, I explained, and told him the old story of the studio in Rue de Babylone.

Adams shook his head and said, 'Didn't I tell you when I met you the first time that you'll never get anything from Arabs except headaches?' After a moment's silence, he asked me, 'Do you have a profession?'

'I can type – and in Arabic, of course.'

'Excellent!' he declared, and busied himself with filling his pipe and lighting it. 'I'm looking for someone to type up the manuscript of my new book, which is huge. Let's go up to my apartment and talk about it.'

We went up to the small apartment he had in Rue de Venise, facing the Centre Pompidou. 'Do you want ice?' he asked, pouring two glasses of whisky.

'No thanks,' I answered.

'Me neither, I prefer whisky without ice, especially in the afternoon.'

As we began to discuss the typing of his work, he said that he couldn't pay me more than eight francs per page. He suggested giving me an advance of 2,000 francs so that I could go to a hotel 'at least for two weeks'.

'Isn't that a reasonable solution?'

'Very reasonable. I will never forget this good turn.'

'Don't think about it. You're a good person.'

We arranged to meet the next day at the same place so that I could take the manuscript, and from that day we became friends. Over the following years I was to type many of his books and he was to help me financially – even without me having to type anything.

I spent more than an hour in Boulevard Voltaire looking for a suitable hotel, as well as in Rue Oberkampf and Avenue Parmentier. Although I was very tired from carrying my bag and typewriter, I was determined to continue my search for a place to stay. Finding myself back in Place de la République, I had to ask myself what this suitable hotel was that I was looking for. The prices of most cheap hotels ranged from eighty to a hundred francs for one night.

I went into Café Parametre and had a couple of beers, and then walked down Avenue de la République. After an hour I arrived at Place Gambetta. I put my belongings on the ground, feeling that finally I had found what I was looking for. In two or three minutes I was checking into a room on the second floor of Hotel Pyrenées – and I paid for ten days in advance.

'This room should cost more than 110 francs,' I said to myself as I looked out of my window overlooking the Père Lachaise Cemetery, which, as the sun set, was covered by a veil of crimson and orange.

From the moment I had walked through the gates of Père Lachaise a voice within me had said, 'If the Centre Pompidou is your mine of culture and arts, then today you have discovered here the garden of your soul.' It was half past nine in the morning when I entered Père Lachaise, and not until the gates closed at six o'clock in the evening could I drag myself away. It was as if I was attracted by a magnet the entire time I was wandering along the paths and alleys, between the graves and the tombs, reading with exhilaration and emotion the names of the dead and the inscriptions on their headstones. This magnetic attraction didn't leave me until the sun began to set.

Over four days I got to know every part of the cemetery and could walk everywhere without a map. I knew where most of the tombs of famous artists, writers and philosophers were. I was able to say to tourists, 'Here lies Maria Callas, behind her to the right Sadegh Hedayat, next to him Marcel Proust. Go to the left, you will find Isadora Duncan, behind her Simone Signoret (Yves Montand had not yet joined her). Go to the right and you will find Guillaume Apollinaire. Go up, and there's Delacroix, and in front of him you'll find Gerard de Nerval, and facing him Balzac. Go straight up again to Bizet, take a right to my friend Georges Méliès, then continue up to Yilmaz Guney. After that, go to the left and down to Jules Romains, and you'll find Chopin.

Continue down to Jim Morrison. Then you'll find Auguste Comte and Parmentier (I always remembered him after learning that he brought the potato to France from Latin America). To the right you will find Molière, beside him La Fontaine, walk on a little to Sarah Bernhardt, continue walking to the left and immediately down, to Modigliani, and you will find Edith Piaf too. Near to her, Paul Eluard. Walk a little, and you will see Gertrude Stein. Before you leave the garden of Père Lachaise, stand and ponder over the tomb of Oscar Wilde, with the winged woman.'

By the time I finished typing Adams's manuscript, I was missing Saint-Germain; I had been away for five days. From time to time I looked out of the window at the falling rain and kept postponing going out. Hearing the sound of a car, I hurried to the window to see a taxi stopped at the taxi rank directly below me, so I put my jacket on and quickly went down.

'Sorry, I'm waiting for someone,' the driver said, smoking his cigarette. 'Here he comes, here comes my client running,' he said, pointing to the gates of Père Lachaise.

But I didn't see anyone, there was only the rain, and I don't remember whether it was silver- or gold-coloured that night as it fell in the light of the street lamps.

I looked at the taxi driver mystified, and he smiled. 'My client is sitting beside me now, *monsieur*,' he said, as he started the engine and drove off.

I returned to the hotel and checked the clock in the lobby. It was a quarter to ten. I went straight to the Moroccan grocer's next door. I bought a bottle of red wine, a tin of chickpeas and a tin of Kraft cheese and went back up to my room. I don't know what time it was when the sound of a car engine woke me. It seemed to be near my bed. The bottle of wine was empty, and so was the can of chickpeas, but the Kraft cheese remained untouched.

I went to the window. I saw the taxi driver standing in the rain looking up at me. The moment he saw me he half-turned to the cemetery gates and waved, and I could see his lips moving as if he was saying '*Au revoir*! *Au revoir*!' He glanced quickly up at me before getting into his taxi.

The next afternoon I was coming out of Père Lachaise on my way to Place Gambetta when I saw the driver leaning against his taxi.

He came across to me smiling. '*Bonjour, monsieur.*'

'*Bonjour, monsieur.*'

'You don't want a taxi now, do you? I'm free.'

'No thank you, *monsieur*,' I answered smiling and continued on my way.

'*Monsieur*, don't think you are the only one looking for a taxi at night,' the taxi driver said as he caught up with me. 'Père Lachaise is also a hotel. Most of my clients live there, and they also need a taxi at night. They are so kind, they sit beside me quietly while I drive them through the streets of Paris before bringing them back here.'

I looked at the driver and told him, laughing, 'But I didn't see anybody in your taxi yesterday.'

'You can't see them because you're not the taxi driver,' he answered.

'Anyway,' I said, 'thank you, *monsieur*, I am very thirsty and I want to go to a café.'

'Oh, *monsieur*, wait a little. I've just remembered now. How strange this life is! It's full of astonishing coincidences. Imagine, the client who was with me yesterday, who is a very nice young man, he told me he knows you. Isn't this an astonishing coincidence?'

I took a cigarette and lit it, and looked at the taxi driver in amazement.

He continued, but now in a sad tone, 'Maybe he's pretending to know you, *monsieur*. He told me he has been looking up at your window every night for the last five nights. He heard the sound of your typewriter and was surprised that you still type so fast. He said you helped him write his name in Arabic on your typewriter years ago.

'He said you gave him a pullover covered with mountains, a sun and two lovers in a small boat near a house shaded by a tall palm tree. He said that when you got a room for the first time in your life he bought you wallpaper decorated with fish and flowers and naked ladies reclining on the beach under the shade of palm trees, in Honolulu or Tahiti.

'He said he used to call you "Zee Liar" because he liked you. He said you were the only one he told about his love for a girl who had abandoned him and was the reason why he left his country, returning to it only as a dead man. He told me he is sad now because you are in Paris and you don't visit him.'

'François?' I uttered, tears pouring down my cheeks. 'You are telling me about my beautiful friend François who was killed in Beirut. I didn't know he was here in Paris. I swear to God, I did not know that.'

There was a beautiful Palestinian girl who used to work with us. 'Please tell François I love him,' she said to me once. 'Oh God, he looks like Alain Delon.' And when I told François, he looked up from his copy of *Le Monde* and laughed, 'Zee Liar'. After that he always called me 'Zee Liar'.

I used to say to him, 'I'm not lying to you. She loves you.' And he would jump on me and put his hands around my neck and pretend to strangle me, saying over and over 'Zee Liar'.

After François was killed, the Palestinian girl found a study grant somewhere and disappeared.

'Bring us a bottle of Napoleon,' he told me that morning in July 1981 as he was handing me fifteen Lebanese pounds, not knowing that Israeli fighter planes were ready to disgorge their tons of bombs. 'I'll come to your room and get drunk tonight, Zee Liar,' he said smiling, and left.

Only a few steps and the apocalypse started.

I remember that when I first got to know François I had asked him straight away, 'Can you tell me something about the Nouvelle Vague? That day he laughed and reeled off the names of numerous directors and films. 'You're François Truffaut,' I joked with him. 'And you are Jean-Luc Godard!' he answered. And we laughed.

François was not his real name, just a nickname the Palestinians had given him.

How could I find out his real name, and then find his grave in Père Lachaise?

Before the Moroccan grocer's shop closed I went down and bought a bottle of Napoleon and spent the whole night with my memories of François. I suddenly remembered that I had a photograph taken of me when I was working in Beirut, three days after the Fakihani massacre in which François was killed. In the photo I am sitting behind my desk. I knew there were two posters on the wall behind me then – one was for a number of Fakihani victims and the other was just for François. Quickly I pulled a big nylon bag out of my luggage – it was where I kept all my photographs. I found the photo but there was only one centimetre showing from the bottom of the poster, which was brown with a few illegible words in white.

Next morning I borrowed a magnifying glass from the hotel reception and I could just make out the words written in Arabic – Nicolas Royer 'François'.

The clerk at the information desk in Père Lachaise didn't take long to search her records. After only a few moments, she found his grave on the map.

Nicolas Guillaume Royer 1956 Paris – 1981 Beirut

I found these words inscribed on François's gravestone, which wasn't far from Maria Callas, Sadegh Heyadat and Marcel Proust. Since that day I have never stopped visiting my friend. I cleaned his gravestone and put flowers on it. I stretched out on the bench near him and thought about the wonderful times we had spent together.

8

As I was coming down from the upstairs floor of Café de Cluny I saw Abdelwahab sitting in his usual place downstairs, thumbing through some books that he had apparently just bought. Abdelwahab found political books baffling in general, but particularly the biographies of politicians. I had often seen him leafing through books on Samora Machel, Sukarno, Mikhail Gorbachov, Ben Gurion, Benazir Bhutto and others. What he really adored were memoirs of spies and heads of intelligence services. Abdelwahab was a successful journalist, and I was one of those who admired his articles – he wrote political analysis in a story-telling fashion. He paid excessive attention to his appearance, boasting that he only ever dressed in Armani, Cerruti and Lacoste. He was impetuous, hot-tempered, and sometimes you got the feeling he was looking to pick a fight.

I was sitting in Café Mandarin with Faiza one day when he saw us and came and sat with us. I introduced him as a wellknown journalist and introduced Faiza as a gifted painter. He immediately said to her, 'There are some painters without talent who should be in jail.'

'Faiza is studying architecture too,' I told him.

'What an opportunity!' he said, looking at her. 'May I ask you a question?'

'Of course. Please do,' said Faiza politely.

'In your opinion, how many kilograms of TNT would we need

84

to bring the Eiffel Tower to the ground?'

Faiza looked at me, shocked, then took the bill from under her coffee cup.

'I'm sorry,' she said, 'I can't continue this conversation.' She went looking for the waiter without giving me her usual farewell kiss.

'These Arab girls always pretend to be so sensitive,' said Abdelwahab in a surly tone.

'Actually, Faiza *is* sensitive. My brother, couldn't you have found something else to ask her?'

'Have you fucked her?' Abdelwahab asked me, abruptly changing the subject.

'No. We're just friends.'

True, Faiza was beautiful, but I was still struck by the fact that all my friends asked me this question. Whenever any of them saw me with her, it was 'Have you fucked her?' Even our great poet Adams asked me, maybe two or three times – 'Do you fuck that lovely girl?'

'Sit down. I'll buy you a glass of Carlsberg,' Abdelwahab said.

'I haven't seen you in ages,' I said, 'Where have you been?'

'I've been visiting a few countries in Africa and then I travelled to Cairo.' He sipped his coffee and added, 'I met some Arab intellectuals in Cairo. They live miserable lives and I discovered that they never buy new books at all.' He went on to speak at great length about political life in the Arab world, describing it finally as 'decadent'.

'Are you hungry?' he asked suddenly.

'Yes,' I replied.

It was six in the evening. 'Let's go to Chez Hamadi,' he suggested, 'it's owned by a Tunisian Jew so the food is really good.' Then he added, 'Good Arab restaurants in Paris are usually owned by North African Jews.' His mouth twisted in scorn, 'But Lebanese restaurants, they're a big con. Their food is all chickpeas, beans, falafel and grilled meat stolen from Turkish cuisine. Don't you agree that Lebanese restaurant owners are a bunch of charlatans?' he asked.

I nodded.

Before entering Rue de la Harpe on our way to the restaurant he suddenly said, 'Wait here for me. Don't move.'

He hurried into the McDonald's at the end of the street and returned a few minutes later escorting a slim brown-skinned girl in her twenties. She said her name was Layla, and Abdelwahab introduced me as 'Sammy, an Iraqi film-maker'.

He suggested we do some shopping in one of the supermarkets and spend the evening at his house.

'Sammy's a great cook,' he said.

Layla was up for it and said, 'Would you like me to go and get my younger sister Suhair? She only lives a short walk from here, near Place de la Sorbonne.'

'Fantastic idea,' said Abdelwahab.

He fell in love with Suhair at first sight. She was blonde, plump, petite and no more than twenty years old.

'Leave the small round one for me,' he whispered while we were still on the street. 'I know how to deal with this type.'

Abdelwahab put on some dance music and opened a bottle of red wine. Layla began to dance. When she tried to get Abdelwahab to dance with her he laughed and said, 'I'm no good at dancing except with a girl like this.' He took Suhair by the hand and began dancing with her. Little by little he edged her into the bedroom.

I heard Suhair say 'I'm hungry', and he answered, 'We can eat afterwards.'

'You're after my sister too, aren't you?' said Layla, sitting down on the sofa.

'That's not true,' I replied. Then added, 'Excuse me, I'll be back in a minute.'

Passing Abdelwahab's open bedroom door on my way to the bathroom, I saw Suhair on her knees giving him a blow job. I was shocked to see he had his leather belt in his hand and was hitting her.

When I went back into the sitting room I found Layla had taken off her jeans and was smoking a cigarette. I sat down next to her.

'Didn't I say you're after my sister?' she smiled, putting the cigarette out.

'What makes you say that?' I said.

I reached over and took off her panties. She came and sat in my arms.

We were having sex when Abdelwahab came in and said angrily, 'Layla! Why didn't you tell me your sister was a virgin?'

Still on me, and moving rapidly up and down, Layla replied, 'What can I do? You chose my sister and I chose your friend. Each of us has acted freely.'

'OK! You, a Muslim girl, talk about freedom of choice! Do you know you're fucking a Jew?'

'Look! I'm on top of him, not the other way around,' she panted, going faster and faster. She looked at me, her bright eyes accentuated by the heavy black kohl around them, and said, 'But you're not against the Palestinians?' Before I could answer her, she shouted, reaching her orgasm, '*C'est trop tard, c'est trop tard*!'

Abdelwahab flew into a rage. 'Get out of my house now!' he shouted angrily. 'Get out! All of you! I don't want you here a minute longer.' He picked up the belongings of the two girls and threw them out into the corridor.

It was three in the morning when we found ourselves back on the street. Suhair laughed.

'Is he really a journalist?' she asked.

I nodded. We found a taxi and Layla got out at Rue Monge. 'I live here with my mother,' she told us. Suhair and I continued on to Boulevard Saint-Michel.

'Come up to my room with me until the metro starts,' said Suhair.

'Don't worry,' I said. 'I'll just walk. My apartment isn't far from here.'

Suhair laughed. 'You don't have an apartment. The journalist told me everything.'

We climbed the wooden staircase leading up to her small chambre de bonne on the seventh floor.

'Yes. It's true. I'm homeless,' I told her.

'What did you do for a living before?'

'I was a journalist.'

'How did you end up on the streets then?'

'Don't you think it would have been silly to remain a journalist all my life?'

Panting from walking up the stairs, Suhair replied, 'You're right. Well, I'm not a virgin, and Layla isn't my sister, either.'

★ ★ ★

Less than a month later, Abdelwahab and I bumped into each other on the Champs-Elysées and he said how sorry he was for what had happened that night. He insisted on buying me a drink. It was eight in the evening and we were in Café Le Paris. I didn't like this café as a number of its regulars were Arab journalists who worked with the intelligence services of Arab governments and their embassies in Paris. At least, this is what Arab intellectuals based in Paris were always repeating to me. I recall asking Abdelwahab once about a certain Arab journalist. 'He works with DST!' he said, French intelligence as he later explained. That day I had laughed and said, 'Me, I'm with SDF!'

We were standing at the bar. Abdelwahab ordered a glass of Carlsberg for me and then pushed a few notes into my pocket.

'Here's a hundred francs,' he said. 'Drink whatever you want but don't be angry with me. I have to sit on my own. I met a Lebanese lady today who's a consultant to a number of Gulf companies. She's gone to put her car in the garage at Place de Port

Maillot because she's travelling to Dubai tomorrow morning.' Before going to sit in the corner he pinched my cheek affectionately. 'Who knows? Maybe she'll come home with me tonight.'

Even from where I was sitting at the bar I could see that the consultant was very beautiful. She spoke the whole time while Abdelwahab just smiled and listened. I decided to leave since I didn't want to spend all my money in that café, but Abdelwahab called me over and introduced me to his consultant friend, saying, 'My friend is a bohemian writer.'

The lady, who was indeed beautiful, smiled and shook my hand. 'He doesn't look like a Bohemian.' Then, teasing Abdelwahab, she added, 'My dear, don't try to hide it. I know he's your personal bodyguard.'

At that Abdelwahab's eyes lit up. The 'bodyguard' idea delighted him and he seized my hand. 'Where can we buy good champagne at this time of night?' he asked.

'The Charles de Gaulle-Étoile drugstore,' I replied.

He winked at me and whispered, 'Stay with us.'

That evening the consultant took four cigarettes from me. One when we were still chatting in Café Le Paris. A second when Abdelwahab went to buy the bottle of champagne from the drugstore. A third when we were drinking the champagne in his apartment, and a fourth when I was lying on the brown leather sofa and she came in and stood naked by my head. She took a cigarette from the box lying on the table, lit it and smiled. 'Are you finding it hard to sleep?'

I didn't know how to answer, especially as I was trying hard to keep my eyes off her pussy which was shaved a certain way just like the women's in porn magazines. She took a drag on her cigarette, exhaled the smoke with force and went back into Abdelwahab's bedroom.

In the morning, Abdelwahab told me proudly that he had risen early and called a taxi to take her to Charles de Gaulle airport. He sipped his coffee and, rubbing his balls, said, 'Never in my entire life have I fucked a woman like I fucked her last night.'

'Did she take money from you?' I asked.

He looked at me uncomfortably. 'I thought you were a civilised Assyrian, not like the Arabs. Are you trying to put me down with your idiotic question? Are you trying to say that lady was a prostitute?'

'I'm sorry, Abdelwahab. That wasn't what I meant.'

'What did you mean then?'

'OK, my friend. It was jealousy,' I said to please him.

'Nothing has destroyed the Arabs more than their jealousy of each other,' he said, rubbing his balls on his way into the bathroom.

Abdelwahab proposed cooking some macaroni with beef and potatoes. On our way to the supermarket he said he was going to tell me something very important. 'Till now, no one except two presidents and two states, Arab and African, know about it.' As we walked past a bank, Abdelwahab withdrew 1,000 francs from the ATM. 'Put this in your pocket,' he said. On our way back to the house he laughed, 'How are things, my dear bodyguard?' He raised his sunglasses. 'You won't be sleeping on the streets any more. I'm going to give your life some real purpose.' And he put his sunglasses back on. 'Do you believe Arab ministers are more intelligent than you?' He suddenly brought up his Lebanese lady friend. 'Yes. I gave her 2,000 francs to buy herself a gift. Maybe I'll need her as my economic adviser one day!' And he said to me kindly, 'I'm sorry. I should have looked on your question as one of concern for me.'

'She took four cigarettes from me. Do you know what they call that in French?' I joked.

'What?' he asked.

'She smokes CDA!'

'That's new! What does it mean?'

'*Cigarettes des autres*! Someone who smokes other people's cigarettes.'

Less than 48 hours after sleeping with his 'consultant' Abdelwahab complained to me of pain in his dick. We were in Café de Cluny.

'Maybe you put too much harissa on the macaroni,' I said.

'No! No,' he replied in agony, 'harissa only burns your arse.'

'Come on!' I said, 'let's go to the toilet.'

We went immediately to the toilet upstairs and found his dick was inflamed and smelled awful.

'Listen, *monsieur*. You have to tell the woman you slept with to see her doctor urgently,' the doctor told Abdelwahab, and added, 'She is a dangerous lady. She knew beforehand what she was doing.'

'I am now not just your bodyguard but your personal nurse, sir,' I said to Abdelwahab, laughing as I gave him an injection in his backside.

'What's your opinion of Mustafa al-Haddad?' Abdelwahab asked me as we were drinking our Carlsbergs in a far corner of Café Flore.

After returning from his recent trip 'to Africa', which had lasted nearly three weeks, Abdelwahab had avoided the Champs-Elysées cafés: the Paris, the Deauville and the Madrigal.

'There's no privacy in those cafés,' he said.

Once I asked him why he hadn't gone to Café Le Fouquet. 'It's spacious and you can talk freely there.'

He looked at me. 'Le Fouquet?' he said scornfully. 'That place is schizophrenic. A few movie stars go there in the evening, while Kuwaiti, Saudi and Qatari men nest there all day long. You can see them sitting, mouths gaping open like birds in a cemetery.'

'Mustafa al-Haddad? He's a very talented poet and one of my best friends,' I replied.

'You don't think he's a chatterbox?' Abdelwahab asked.

'He's clever and talented, that's why he talks a lot about poetry and philosophy.'

'He's my friend too. But I'm afraid of his tongue sometimes.'

'Why are you afraid of his tongue? He's only staying in Paris for two more weeks, then he's going back to Tunis.'

'Precisely. Therefore, I want to sort out a few things with him before he goes.'

'Abdelwahab, you've been hinting at something for a while. I don't understand you. Is there something you want to tell me but don't trust me enough to say?'

'On the contrary,' Abdelwahab replied, 'I trust you completely. But I want to raise the subject with both of you present.'

'Mustafa spends his evenings in the cafés around the Sorbonne these days,' I said, finishing off my beer.

'If we find him, I'll invite you both to a fancy French restaurant,' said Abdelwahab.

We looked in every café around the Sorbonne but couldn't find Mustafa, so we went to sit in one of the cafés he frequented on Rue Champollion. I asked the waiter whether Mustafa had been in that day. 'He's in Monte Carlo,' came the answer.

'What's the poor wretch doing in Monte Carlo?' enquired Abdelwahab. 'Do you know when he'll be back?'

The waiter laughed and, continuing to dry glasses, said, 'You misunderstand me, *monsieur*. He is in the Hotel Monte Carlo,' and gestured to the hotel opposite. We laughed.

Abdelwahab went to the bathroom and Mustafa al-Haddad whispered, 'We're in the best restaurant in Saint-Germain. Listen to me. Abdelwahab is from my country and I know him well. If he didn't desperately need us for something he wouldn't have brought us to this restaurant.'

Mustafa was still whispering in my ear when Abdelwahab came back smiling. 'Why don't you talk in a normal voice so we can hear you, Mustafa?'

'What's up, Abdelwahab? Do you want me to say out loud that I masturbated on my girlfriend's breasts this morning? Does that have anything to do with you?' As Mustafa raised his wine glass to his mouth I noticed his hand was shaking. Those two had a turbulent friendship, and more than once things had ended in a fistfight. So Mustafa wouldn't be surprised if Abdelwahab suddenly went for him.

'You may be a real devil, but I like you, Mustafa!' Abdelwahab told him, and looked at me.

Later, we were drinking Hennessey in his apartment when he surprised us by announcing, 'You'll be the Minister of Education, Mustafa.'

Then he turned to me. 'And you, Sammy! You'll be Minister of Culture. Never mind your Iraqi roots, we'll follow the example of the Cuban Revolution!'

Mustafa looked at me in astonishment.

Abdelwahab went on: 'We've bought fifteen ambulances which will arrive in the country next month. Likewise, we have half a million dollars cash already there.'

'Why don't you explain the whole thing to us in detail, Abdelwahab?' asked Mustafa.

'I'm working on plans for a peaceful revolution in our country.'

'You mean a coup d'état?' asked Mustafa.

'Pretty much,' Abdelwahab replied. He took the bottle of Hennessey and sat down next to Mustafa. He filled his glass and said, 'Mustafa, you're one of the most intelligent people I have come across. But look at your situation. You've reached the age of forty and are still a burden on your parents. What for? How long will this group of criminals plunder our country's resources while the people drown in poverty, hunger and disease? I don't want to hurt anyone but I have a dream of a better future for my country.'

'OK. Who's behind the coup?' asked Mustafa.

'Me, you and Sammy,' answered Abdelwahab.

'Will we stage it from Paris?'

'My dear Mustafa, we will stage the coup from within the

country,' said Abdelwahab. 'I'll be over there soon. Sammy will go before me. He'll be provided with the latest state-of-the-art video camera. He'll play the role of journalist and document the revolution. The whole operation won't take more than twelve hours. Everything will be executed peacefully and without shedding a drop of blood.'

'What is the plan exactly?' asked Mustafa.

'Listen, Mustafa! Our country is being governed by a doddering fool.'

'I asked about the plan,' said Mustafa.

'Nothing could be simpler,' said Abdelwahab. 'But pay attention, Mustafa. I swear I'll kill you if anyone hears about it.'

'If you don't trust me why didn't you leave me relaxing in my hotel?'

'Don't try and make problems. I like you, Mustafa, you know that. But sometimes I feel you're trying to provoke me.'

'If you really want to be a leader of a revolution why do you get so steamed up by a friend?'

'OK, OK!' Abdelwahab turned and kissed Mustafa's head.

'Dear comrade (suddenly we were 'comrades'), the plan is extremely simple. The ambulances will head to the presidential palace and surround it. Thirty-five revolutionaries will take part in the attack, all wearing medical uniforms and equipped with machine guns and RPG-7s, although I am sure we won't need them. I'd also like you to know that we have the green light from neighbouring countries and from the embassies of some Western nations.'

'Does Gaddafi have a hand in this operation?' asked Mustafa.

'Only financially. I've met him three times and we agreed to maintain our independence from each other in decision-making.'

'You know full well, Abdelwahab, that I regard that man as a big dictator,' said Mustafa angrily.

'I agree he's a dictator, but we need him for the first few months.'

'When will the operation begin?' I asked.

'Before the end of this year,' replied Abdelwahab.

'All right, I'm in,' said Mustafa. 'Even if you lied to me about the ministry things.'

'The decision has been made, *Monsieur le Ministre*!' said Abdelwahab, hugging and kissing him.

We laughed until dawn, each of us oblivious to the fact that other people were already drawing up plans for the very same thing – to remove that doddering old man. And they executed their coup d'état one day that winter, and that day, when the news of the coup reached him, Abdelwahab was sitting in Café Cluny. He was sad, so sad, not because some officers in his country had carried out the coup before him, but because a few hours earlier he had been in Centre Pompidou watching a documentary about the Cuban Revolution and taking a lot of important notes. From that day onwards, Abdelwahab couldn't relax unless he was arguing with someone.

One evening we came out of La Périgourdine on Place Saint Michel. There were four of us – Abdelwahab, Khalaf, Nabil and myself. We agreed to go to dinner together, and Abdelwahab suggested a popular Arab restaurant nearby.

Khalaf, who was consul at his country's embassy at the time, said, 'I know the place. It's awful. The owners are Muslim fundamentalists and won't serve wine.'

'Since when have you refused to go to a restaurant because it doesn't serve wine, sir?' scoffed Abdelwahab.

'*Depuis toujours*!' answered Khalaf, smiling, and he put his hand on my shoulder. 'Our handsome vagabond! Find us a good restaurant that will serve us fine French wine!'

'A French or Arabic one?' I asked.

'*Français*,' said Khalaf.

I sensed Abdelwahab was beginning to boil up inside. He was looking rather uneasy. Eventually he said sarcastically, 'Of course, we North Africans are strangers to French civilisation and the

Bedouins of the Sahara are now connoisseurs of French wine. All this, thanks to the oil wells.'

'That's not a decent way to speak to me, Abdelwahab,' said Khalaf.

'How would you like me to speak to you, Mr Consul,' Abdelwahab jeered.

'Politely, please,' said Khalaf.

'I'm more polite than you,' replied Abdelwahab.

'In that case, excuse me. I'm not prepared to stoop to this level,' said Khalaf, turning to take his leave of us.

'Fuck your mother and the mother of the Bedouin,' shouted Abdelwahab, seething with rage. He was trembling.

I was stunned by what he said and didn't recover from the shock until I saw Khalaf land a violent blow on him. He punched Abdelwahab to the ground and began tearing into him like an eagle at its prey.

'No one insults my mother, you piece of filth!' cried Khalaf, using all his might to throttle Abdelwahab.

I don't know where I got the strength from to pull Khalaf off Abdelwahab, who lay there on the ground, gasping for air.

'If you hadn't intervened I would have killed him and gone to prison for the rest of my life,' Khalaf told me later.

Meanwhile, Abdelwahab kept repeating to everyone he met, 'The Assyrian dog was with Khalaf against me.'

I heard he was only waiting until his health recovered to settle his score with me. One Christmas Day he did just that. He found me standing at the bar of Le Relais Odéon. 'You betrayed me when you sided with that despicable Gulf Arab,' he said, asking for a cup of coffee.

'Bullshit!' I replied. 'I saved your life.'

'You're a drunk. How could you save me?'

'Thank you,' I said, and left the café, unaware that he was following me.

I found Mohammed al-Qaroui and some of his French friends

in a very nice café on Rue Monsieur Le Prince. They invited me to spend the evening with them. There was a girl with us singing Serge Gainsbourg's '*Je suis venu te dire que je m'en vais*' and Mohammed sang along with her. Just then I saw Abdelwahab standing at the bar talking to the waiter, who placed a bottle of Carlsberg in front of him. Abdelwahab considered Carlsberg beer to be the best.

After a little while, Abdelwahab approached our table and in front of everyone said to me, 'You're a despicable and highly suspicious character. No one knows how you support yourself! But I'm going to expose you! I'll reveal your dealings with the intelligence services. Who knows? Perhaps we'll find out you work for Mossad, you low-life creep!'

He went on insulting me relentlessly, despite Mohammed al-Qaroui's attempts to calm him down.

In the end I was forced to say, 'You're just a fucking coward, Abdelwahab. You can only beat women.'

He hurled his bottle of Carlsberg at me and it hit me on the head. He fled the café and I ran out after him like a madman. Blood gushed from my head as I ran from street to street, café to café, staring into the faces of the customers and searching all the toilets. I spent the whole night carrying a heavy stick. Fury filled my heart as I searched for Abdelwahab, who didn't dare enter the Latin Quarter for weeks afterwards, not until he sent someone to me to act as a mediator. I agreed to a truce on condition he paid me 3,000 francs.

When we met in Café Cluny he reminded me he had lent me some money earlier.

'But don't forget, Abdelwahab,' I said, 'at the time I was Minister of Culture in your "government".'

And we laughed.

It was a cold afternoon when I left the cinema after seeing *The Glass Menagerie*. I didn't know that Paul Newman, whom I loved as an actor, was going to surprise me with his skill in making such a movie — tremendous on all levels. I loved its pure melancholy. I was about to enter the Café Le Relais Odéon when I noticed the clock beside Danton's statue. It was 4.30 p.m. I ran quickly to the Odéon post office where I had my poste restante. There was only one letter, with six Iraqi stamps, all portraying Saddam Hussein.

I read:

> *My dear brother,*
> *We received your beautiful card that you sent from Cannes when you attended the film festival there. I am very sorry to tell you that our dear father is dead, and that for the last three years he has been in the hands of Jesus and the Virgin Mary. Mum asks if you have started working in the movies. We all pray that you will realise your dreams.*
> > *Your faithful brother,*
> > *Teddy*

I looked at the letter for a while before quietly tearing it up, putting it in the rubbish bin in the post office and going out onto Boulevard Saint-Germain. I saw only life without sound, and people walking hurriedly, with small short steps, exactly as in the silent movies.

I drank two beers in Café Le Relais Odéon and then walked along Boulevard Saint-Germain, looking for Jean-Claude Ming. I saw Fabian sitting on the ground, leaning against the railings of the Church of Saint-German des Prés. He looked elegant as usual. In front of him on the ground was his upturned hat with some coins in it, and beside it a piece of card that said, 'I am seeking a job as a cook or a private chauffeur.'

'Have you seen Ming today, Fabian?'

'I haven't seen him for days. I think he went to stay with that fellow, you know him, that rich guy who exploits him, letting him sleep in his house for a few days and making him do paintings for him.'

I nodded.

'By the way, I saw you speaking with Marcello Mastroianni the other day. You know he's my grandmother's neighbour in Place Saint-Sulpice?'

I nodded.

'Are you sad?'

'Fabian, earlier today I received news that my father is dead.'

'I'm very sorry,' Fabian said. 'Please take some francs from the hat and go and have a drink. I know you've got nothing. Don't be shy. We have to support each other. Take all the francs, if you like. You know I'm not a beggar. How old was your father?'

'I don't know.'

'My grandmother is ninety-nine now.'

Fabian once told me that his grandmother was leaving her apartment in Place Saint-Sulpice to him in her will, and each time I met him he told me, 'My grandmother is ninety-seven' or 'My grandmother is ninety-eight', and now another year . . .

I put my hand in the hat and asked Fabian, 'Can I take 30 francs?'

'Take as much as you like,' he said.

'I'll take just 40 francs.'

'Go and drink. God will help you.'

I crossed the boulevard and went into Café Saint-Claude and asked for a pastis. After a while the owner, Madame Beatrice, who always sat in her cigarette kiosk beside the bar, came over to me. 'Your friend Ming hasn't been around for a while.' She looked into my eyes. 'Are you sad?'

'*Oui, madame.*' And then I told her my father was dead.

Madame Beatrice looked at me, 'I'm sorry! Wasn't it you who told me a few weeks ago that your father had died?'

'No, no, madame. That was Fareed,' I said.

'Oh, that Kurdish painter who hanged himself.'

'Yes, madame.'

Fareed was the only artist on Boulevard Saint-German who painted in oils. His paintings were always the same uniform blue – the sky and the sea merging – with just a single boat. Each painting differed only slightly – the small boat in one painting might be on the right, while in another on the left, or on the horizon, or up close, looming out of the canvas. Fareed had received French citizenship just the year before and had gone to visit his parents in Turkey after many years away. About two weeks earlier, all of us had been shocked to discover he had committed suicide. He had hanged himself in his room.

Uncle Salih left the bar and came over to hug me and say how sorry he was. Although I used to drink only beer or wine mostly, this time Uncle Salih poured me a double Black Label and patted me on the shoulder, saying, 'We have a good couscous today!'

From the bar I looked aimlessly through the front entrance to the pavement of Rue de la Tombe Issoire, and there was Samuel Beckett standing looking towards me. Uncle Salih was busy washing glasses and going in and out of the kitchen while Samuel Beckett remained there motionless, looking either at me or at the bar. I felt confused and didn't know what to do. When Uncle Salih returned he looked to the street and shouted out cheerfully and waved, '*Bonsoir, cher monsieur! Ça va bien?*'

Samuel Beckett nodded, and smiled and waved back, and continued on his way. After a few steps he turned to the left, along a street which, a year or so later after he died, would be named Allée Samuel Beckett.

Uncle Salih told me he had known 'that nice man' for many years. 'He always stops there and doesn't move until he has greeted me.' Uncle Salih shook his head. 'Yes, he's a nice man.'

A few months earlier I had accompanied Shamil on a visit to the Spanish playwright Fernando Arrabal's home in Paris for an interview for an Arab magazine. Arrabal had given me a hard look when he heard my name. After the interview he went off somewhere in his huge apartment, whose walls and ceilings were covered in original paintings, all works by friends such as Picasso and Salvador Dalí. Some of the paintings on the ceiling in the big living room depicted a flying angel with Arrabal's face and a small body with a pink penis about a metre long. When he came back, he was carrying a copy of one of his early books. He wrote some words in it and gave to me, saying, 'I want you to have this book. Please keep it, don't sell it.' He must have felt my surprise and emotion, and explained that his son was called Samuel, 'maybe the only one in Spain', and that he had named him after 'my dear friend Samuel Beckett who was with me when my son was born'.

That night I stayed in Uncle Salih's until two o'clock. I drank a lot and ate a nice couscous, and I cried a lot and wrote a poem to my father.

> *Bonjour, Jean Valjean, bonjour, Jean Valjean.* He opened his eyes and felt only the pain of a monstrous hangover. The darkness of the early hours of the morning still lingered over the fifth arrondissement of Paris. He glanced at the doors of the Panthéon and saw a tall spectre with a thick beard enter and close the doors behind him. He had been too tired the night before to make his usual journey from Place de Panthéon, down the Rue de la Montagne Sainte-Geneviève, to Rue des Ecoles, to Rue du Cardinal Lemoine and after onto Quai de la Tournelle and Quai Saint-Bernard to end up at Austerlitz Station, where he slept most nights. He noticed a police car

approaching the Panthéon and was immediately awake and leaning back against the cemetery railings, shuffling through his folder of papers, his pillow. He was afraid of the police, as refugees like him were not permitted to sleep on the streets. The policemen glanced at him as they passed by in their car. He thanked the voice that had woken him from his sleep, '*Bonjour, Jean Valjean*', and said to himself, 'who else can take pity on the homeless at dawn but the enemy of the police, that giant Victor Hugo?' That early morning, as the leaves of autumn covered Boulevard Saint-Germain, he saw an empty cigarette packet. He kicked it with the toe of his trainer and the packet began to roll, getting bigger and bigger until it arrived at the Odéon very near the statue of Danton. By then the packet was the same size as the statue. He snatched at the wind with his hand and grabbed hold of an invisible staircase. He climbed to the top and when he opened the huge packet, he found his father asleep inside, smiling.

10

Austerlitz,
Austerlitz,
You are my house and my home,
My dear station,
Austerlitz,
Austerlitz.

Back from Munich after three weeks staying with friends. I left my clothes, papers and typewriter in a locker at my home, Austerlitz, and went to lie down on a bench in the Jardin des Plantes opposite. I looked up at the cloudy sky at the 'Greatest Scriptwriter' and was overcome by the strong desire to shout 'God, I'm tired of playing this role!' at the top of my voice. I stayed in the garden until it started raining gently. Then I hurried back into the station to change my few remaining deutschmarks and burst out onto the streets of the city that I could find my way around with my eyes shut.

I went to get a drink at L'Irlandais in Place de la Contrescarpe. After two glasses of Guinness the pub quickly filled up with customers and I began to feel uneasy. Irish pubs had become fashionable in Paris, even though a pint of Guinness could cost between 38 and 45 francs. Indeed, there were so many that a special syndicate with its own magazine had been formed for Irish pub employees. I moved from L'Irlandais to the Mayflower in Rue Déscartes nearby, and didn't leave there until I got hungry. It was almost midnight and still raining. I hurried through Place du Panthéon and Rue Soufflot into Rue Victor Cousin and Place de la Sorbonne, which led into Rue des Écoles, and there I did what I usually did when passing the statue of Montaigne, which was to stop for a moment and contemplate the smile on his face and touch his shoe. Then I carried on rushing down Rue de Cluny, a side street in pitch darkness.

Though the pavement was crammed with vehicles, my eyes caught sight of a man's body lying between two cars. He was still breathing so I turned him on his back and began to clean the blood and dirt from his nose and face. A strong smell of alcohol wafted out of his mouth. I picked him up and propped him up against the hood of one of the cars as he kept repeating '*Merci, merci, monsieur*' over and over in a feeble voice.

I asked him if I should go and get an ambulance, but he replied firmly, 'No, no. No need. Thanks so much.'

He looked right and left. 'You've saved my life,' he said. 'Yes, you've saved my life, good man.' When he recovered his strength he looked into my eyes. 'Where are you from?' he asked.

I gave him a big smile but said nothing. I knew from the man's accent as soon as he spoke that he was Iranian. The Iran– Iraq War was still raging and I thought it might disturb him if I mentioned I was an Iraqi.

'From Pakistan,' I said finally.

The man laughed for a long time then said in a clear voice, 'Imagine, my dear brother, that of the twelve million pigs living in this city, God has sent a fellow Muslim to save my life. Isn't this a miracle?'

I kept smiling, and was about to say, 'I'm one of those pigs,' but thought better of spoiling his 'miracle', especially as once when I told a friend of mine, over a drink in Old Navy Café, about the charitable deeds I had done on my nocturnal excursions in the Paris streets, he had said I was a Good Samaritan and clinked glasses with me.

Although I had spent four years in Paris I had never acquired the habit of going to restaurants. I would often give lack of money as my excuse, yet this was not the real reason. I often had plenty of cash on me, but would spend it all on drink with no thought of food until I felt the pain of hunger in my stomach. I found myself heading for La Rose de Tunis to get a merguez sausage sandwich and chips, the worst thing one could possibly eat.

'Your sandwiches are dirty,' I often told the Tunisian owner.

'No one is forcing you to come here,' he would smile back.

'Where else can I go after midnight?' I used to reply.

The man would laugh. 'Not quite true,' he would say. 'You come here because you can't find a sandwich for 12 francs anywhere else in Paris.'

'Twelve francs?' I would mock.

'Have you paid more than that?' he used to ask.

'It may be only 12 francs, but don't forget that in the morning I have to buy two bottles of Perrier water to cleanse my stomach of your filthy merguez.'

'Don't ever come here again,' the restaurant owner would shout, pointing to Rue de la Harpe, 'you'll find dozens of Turkish sandwich sellers over there.'

Though the sandwiches at the Tunisian's restaurant were no good, I still preferred them to the Turkish ones (that were often called Greek). The Turks not only conducted themselves like the Mafia, but their behaviour was atrocious. For instance, a sandwich man would stand in front of you slicing and preparing the meat for your sandwich while at the same time sticking his head out into the street to wolf-whistle at a pretty girl walking past. Then he would turn to you: 'Monsieur, did you see how beautiful her mouth was? I bet she gives a good blow job.' Once when I was having a sandwich I saw a waiter nearby unashamedly rubbing his dick with both hands while watching a girl go by on the street. 'Did you see her arse?' he asked me. 'I bet she takes it from behind!' Nor was it unusual to see a Turkish sandwich seller leave the restaurant and bound upstairs, only to return smiling a few minutes later, no doubt having jerked himself off. Furthermore they would boast about it. Take this example: one lunchtime I was having a sandwich when a Vietnamese girl selling things wandered past. The restaurant worker asked her to show him what she had to offer and was eventually impressed by a gold-plated cigarette lighter. He bargained with the poor girl until he brought the price of the lighter down to five francs. When she agreed he asked, 'Can I give you a glass of Fanta or a Pepsi for it instead?' The poor girl replied that she wasn't thirsty. Less than two minutes later the guy was telling a friend of his nearby that he had got the gold lighter from a Danish girl he had fucked in one of the hotels around Notre Dame Cathedral!

Many of the so-called Greek sandwich sellers in the Latin

Quarter were like this. While – if you leave aside their love of money which is only natural in humans – the worst the waiters at La Rose de Tunis would do was blow their nose in your face and then pass you a sandwich. But we can add a note that only God knows how many thousands of merguez sausages are fried in the same oil.

★ ★ ★

In the library of the Centre Pompidou I read 'Babylon Revisited' again, and then started on *Wait Until Spring, Bandini* by John Fante, who had tasted poverty and life on the streets in his youth, and whose *Ask the Dust* I had read after my friend, the Tunisian writer Mohammed al-Qaroui, had pointed him out to me. After reading Fante I headed for the language section to continue my German lessons. I loved this language and had wanted to learn it for a long time. The lessons I read every day told amusing stories of a German family made up of Walter and Grete and their children Günter, Christel, Inge and Fritz. The truth was I relished this easy method of learning a language.

Sometimes, when the allotted time was over, which was one hour, I put my name down for another class. I copied up my notes each day and repeated the new words I had learned all the way from Place de Châtelet to Saint-Germain: *der Mantel* (coat), *der Pelz* (fur), *der Knochen* (bone), *der Friede* (peace), *der Krieg* (war), *der Gott* (God), *der Liebling* (darling/lover), *das Haustier* (pet), *das Buch* (book), *das Leben* (life), *das Eis* (ice), *die Maus* (mouse), *die Welt* (world), *die Nacht* (night).

Then I would go into Café Danton and joke with Manuel, '*Guten abend*, Manuel.' He used to smile, push his cigarette to the side, pull out an empty glass, fill it with beer and put it in front of me.

'*Ça va?*' he would ask.

'*Très bien*,' I would reply.

That evening I was drinking at the right-hand corner of the bar when the film director Jean-Luc Godard came in. He asked for a cup of coffee and began to glance around the room as though looking for someone. As Godard drank his coffee he gazed up at the ceiling and then down at the floor. Meanwhile, I signalled to Manuel to come over and whispered to him quietly, 'I hope you're not going to take any money from that man (I pointed to Godard). Tell him "On the house" and I'll pay his bill.'

Manuel smiled. '*D'accord!*'

When Godard finished his coffee he started cleaning his spectacles. He glanced at me and smiled faintly. I smiled back at him. Then he turned to Manuel, 'How much, please?'

'The bill has been paid, *monsieur*.'

'Who by?'

'It's on the house,' replied Manuel smiling.

'*Merci, monsieur*,' said Godard, and nodded, smiling too.

'Who was that man?' Manuel asked me once Godard had left.

'He is the man who saved my life,' I replied, pushing him my empty glass to fill up.

The weather was freezing, and I recalled the news that several homeless people had died on the streets of Paris. Perhaps because of this news, I decided to go and stay with Shamil, the one friend whose door I could knock on whatever the time. I went down into the metro and headed for Port de Clichy.

Shamil was not at home so I went to the Algerian café at Boulevard Bessières. After a few minutes a fair-haired girl who had been sitting in the corner rushed out of the café. She soon returned, complaining in French that 'the Tunisian prostitute beat me to it'. She looked at the barman and said, 'She's not afraid of the cold.'

When I first started coming to this quarter, I used to come out of the metro, walk along Boulevard Bessières and pass the iron railings of the girls' primary school, and I used to always see empty plastic water bottles, Evian, Vittel, Volvic and other brands, lying on the pavement and in the gutter. Every time I walked on that side of the boulevard I noticed the bottles, which always seemed recently discarded. I couldn't see the connection between the bottles and the school, until Shamil explained to me that at night the pavement by the school became a brothel for long-distance truck drivers, and that the water in the bottles was used for washing after these sexual encounters.

'Who uses it?' I asked Shamil stupidly.

'No idea. I haven't thought about it,' he said, twirling his moustache.

'Take care,' the café owner replied when I told him I was going to see if my friend had returned home yet. At that moment I saw Nadia getting out of a truck. She was crossing the boulevard towards me, waving her scarf at me, and she seemed very pleased.

'*Ça va?*' she asked, and gave me a hug. 'I've missed you.'

'Me too,' I said.

'Your friend Shamil told me you were staying in Germany for a while?'

'My friend was right, but unfortunately I didn't have enough money.'

'Money, money. Damn money. I leave my kids alone and stand in the cold, all for the sake of money.'

She took a small bottle of water out of her bag, and before drinking any asked if I was thirsty.

'There is only a little left. You drink it,' I said.

She beat her chest. 'True, we may not have money,' she said, 'but we have water. You'll find nothing on us but water. See.' She took another bottle from her bag. 'Take it with you,' she said.

Nadia was a good friend. We had drunk together many times and would go to a grocery shop owned by a Tunisian guy and buy a few bottles of beer, especially 1664, which was her favourite.

Once the vicious-looking grocer had asked me, 'Are you Nadia's new *macru*?'

I didn't understand what he meant, and for two days Nadia did not explain, but then she told me, laughing, 'He was asking you if you were my new pimp!'

One day Nadia related her own story to me and I told her, 'It is the same story, dear Nadia, for all Arab prostitutes.'

'At least I have some principles,' she objected vigorously.

She set out these principles for me, but unfortunately I have remembered only some of them. 'I'm a believer, and follow the teachings of Islam,' Nadia had declared. 'I don't have sex with Christian customers during Ramadan. For that, we came to an agreement with the French girls to hand over Turkish and Albanian drivers to us North African girls for the whole month of Ramadan.' 'I never sleep with Arabs' was another of her principles.

'Is that from a religious consideration too?' I had asked.

'Not at all. The reason is purely financial.' She began explaining why: 'The Arab customer will always pay the full price on the first day. On the second he'll pay half, and then after that he will announce he's in love with me and wants to become my lover. Once he is my lover he'll come and live with me, and once he is living with me he'll begin requesting money from me every day. And when I'm sick and can't go to work he will beat me! I know lots of girls who've suffered this scenario, so why would I want to get involved?'

Then she brought her face up close to mine. 'Look! No knife or razor marks. My whole life I've never been beaten by anyone except my ex-husband!'

★ ★ ★

Just as I went to look at Shamil's window, which was still dark, the one next to it lit up. 'Dino,' I said to myself. I looked up at the dark sky and hurried to ring Dino's doorbell.

'Who is it?' came a voice from the entry phone.

'Dino. It's me, the lost Iraqi,' I said, as he sometimes referred to me as that.

'Ha ha ha, zzzzzzz.' His laughter fused with the sound of the electric buzzer opening the outside door of the building.

Dino, who was originally from Italy, worked as a bouncer at one of the nightclubs in Neuilly-sur-Seine and also performed in some small Paris theatres – comedy sketches that he wrote himself and in which he played the role of clown. A year before he told me that when he performed his artistic clown acts at a festival in Krakow he was unexpectedly confronted in his dressing room after the show by the famous writer Umberto Eco, who had congratulated him and expressed admiration for his performance. Umberto Eco told him of his own passion for the art of the clown, and said he was preparing a book on the subject based on the works of the film director Federico Fellini, who was another person who admired the clown.

Dino told me Umberto Eco had expressed a wish that they should meet in the future.

'Did he speak to you in Italian?' I had asked at the time.

'Of course. The whole thing was very friendly.'

Dino welcomed me warmly and straight away said, 'You can have a wash, if you like.'

I told him I had washed that morning in the washroom at Austerlitz Station but he looked at me angrily. 'You can come to me or Shamil any time.'

Then he started to pour a glass of wine. 'You know I like you very much.'

After a silence, he said, 'I've come straight from Rome. Do you know who I was with?'

'Umberto Eco,' I replied quickly.

'Exactly! Who told you?'

'I guessed. You told me the story of your encounter in Krakow, don't you remember?'

'You've got a good imagination and a strong memory, you know. You don't need to be on the streets. You don't deserve all this suffering,' Dino spoke passionately. 'Are you hungry?' he asked.

I nodded an affirmative.

'I'll make you some spaghetti.'

I had got to know Dino during my visits to Shamil, who would knock on Dino's door whenever he needed an onion or some garlic or bread. We also knocked on his door if we were having a party, inviting him to join us. As the days passed we became friends. I recalled the first time I had been to Dino's place. It was in the afternoon and Dino was in the kitchen.

'What do you do for a living, Dino?'

I watched him take a small tomato. After he had hollowed it out he put it on the end of his nose. 'This is what I do,' he said, and smiled.

I devoured my spaghetti quickly.

'You still have the same bad manners,' Dino said. 'Don't eat so fast.'

After talking about the theatre and movies, about dreams and aspirations, Dino looked at me enquiringly. 'You've been homeless for a long time,' he said. 'I'm sure this must cause you a great deal of suffering. Can you tell me how you deal with your pain?'

'I postpone it,' I answered straight away. 'Yes, I always try to postpone my pain to another time.'

'How?'

'My dear Dino, I discovered early on that when a man finds himself lying in the street he has no option but to do as Scheherazade did. He must postpone the pain. The homeless guy has to be clever like Scheherazade in *One Thousand and One Nights*. He recounts his dreams and fantasies to take him away from concrete roads, public park benches, train stations, cold winter winds and his empty stomach, and then he sees the benches become feather beds and the cold winds blowing around him become warm and comforting.' I looked at Dino. 'And you, dear Dino? How do you deal with pain?'

'Pain is what drives a man to be a clown,' he said softly.

Dino started making up a clean bed for me in the sitting room. I watched him arrange the sheets and put on a new floral pillowcase.

I found him waiting for me, when I came out of the bathroom the next morning, holding a wallet in his hand, like a mother getting her child ready for school. He had made me a sandwich and handed me 50 francs, a few metro tickets and up to 33 francs worth of food vouchers.

Dino laughed when he saw me looking at the postcards hanging on the wall of the hallway, among which were a number I had sent him from the various cities I had visited.

'You know,' he said, 'François Mitterand sends postcards to his old friends from wherever he travels. He has kept up the habit since he was young.' Then, just as I was leaving the apartment, he said, 'You see, there are things in common between a man living on the streets and the President of France!'

11

'From the moment someone starts going to bars in the morning he's on the road to self-destruction,' Maurice announced. 'I have many friends who've become drifters and some who've even committed suicide, and they all used to frequent bars in the morning.'
It was a hot morning and we were walking down Rue de Seine. Suddenly Maurice stopped and pointed to a narrow street.

'That's Rue Visconti,' he said. 'Lots of people think it's named after the Italian film director but it actually takes its name from the architect Visconti who designed Napoleon's tomb at Les

Invalides.'

As we reached the intersection of Rue de Seine and Rue de Buci, packed with people and stalls selling fruit and vegetables, Maurice commented, 'Look, isn't this a marvellous scene that we're a part of? On the other hand, imagine if you were in a café right now, no doubt leaning against the bar under artificial lighting, you'd have nothing in front of you except the waiter and the boring view of bottles carefully lined up behind him. Am I right?'

'You are, Maurice,' I replied.

'What a person does in the morning determines his future.' He went on: 'Take me, for example. I start work every day in the afternoon, and so I exploit the hours of the morning practising sport.'

Listening to Maurice and nodding agreement, I noticed for the first time that smoking had ruined his teeth. At that moment I saw Marcello Mastroianni standing at one of the fruit stalls chatting with the young shopkeeper as she handed him a piece of fruit. He blew on it, put it in his mouth and ate it. I had seen the same sight many times.

'Look! It's Mastroianni,' I said to Maurice. 'Come on, let's go and say hello. I know him personally.'

'Do you really?' He looked at me in amazement.

'Yes.'

I made sure I was in front as we approached Mastroianni. '*Bonjour, monsieur,*' I said.

'*Bonjour, monsieur,*' he smiled back. '*Ça va bien?*' he asked.

I nodded to show I was well, and said shyly, '*Très bien, merci monsieur.*'

'*Passez une bonne journée!*' he said, and continued on his way.

A few moments later, back on Rue de Seine, we saw the film director Marco Ferreri coming out of the Champion supermarket and I greeted him loudly. '*Bonjour, Monsieur Ferreri.*'

Ferreri stopped for a moment and regarded me silently. Then all of a sudden he smiled as though remembering who I was –

'*Bonjour, bonjour!*' – and continued on his way.

'You know them all,' Maurice said.

'Well, we see each other nearly every day.'

Maurice coughed and spluttered for a few minutes, then said, 'It's quite normal, I suppose. You're constantly on the streets, and if you live on the streets of Paris for years on end you'll come face to face even with God himself.'

I had got to know Maurice two years earlier at the Café Au Chai de l'Abbaye. We had both been drinking at the bar and had started chatting. He had heard me talking about movies once and told me he worked as a technician for one of the French television channels.

I'd told him I dreamed of making movies, 'But at the moment I make do with watching them.'

'Have you seen *Midnight Cowboy*?' he enquired.

'Of course.'

'And *The Elephant Man*?'

'Yes'

'That's the kind of movie I love,' said Maurice.

'Have you seen *Ironweed*? ' I asked.

'Is that the movie that begins with Jack Nicholson sleeping out on the street on a cold day and meeting his old friend Meryl Streep, who's also living as a tramp?'

'Yes.'

'It's a very sad film,' said Maurice. He took some gulps of his beer. 'Yes, it's a very sad film.'

'I love that type of movie,' I told him.

That day Maurice said he was going out to buy some cigarettes. He insisted on buying some for me too, and asked what brand I smoked.

'Camel non-filter,' I said.

I was surprised when Maurice came back carrying two packets of Winston. He passed one to me, and I took it and said nothing. A few days later we met by coincidence on Pont Neuf. It was afternoon. He pointed out a small garden below on the bank of the Seine.

'I spent my teenage years down there,' he told me. 'I used to play my guitar every day under that large tree.' Before we came off the bridge he patted my shoulder and added, 'One day I'll hold a picnic in that very place and invite all my friends and let them hear how I played sixties music.'

Throughout our meetings over those two years, whenever Maurice went to look for cigarettes he insisted on buying me some too. Each time he asked me the same question, 'What brand do you smoke?'

'Camel non-filter,' I would reply, and he'd go off to the tobacconist's and return a quarter of an hour later with a packet of Winston. The last time this happened, which was about a week ago, I was determined to surprise him.

'I'm going for cigarettes. What brand do you smoke?' he asked, putting his empty glass on the bar top.

'Winston,' I answered quickly.

He looked at me, quite taken aback. 'Have you changed brands?'

The following summer, after returning to Paris having spent a month at the Hamel campsite in Trouville, I met Maurice propping up the bar in Le Conti and looking extremely sad.

'Do you know', he said, 'that when you're away from Paris sad things happen.' He told me about Alain, who sold paintings in the street. 'He committed suicide yesterday.'

'How?'

'He gassed himself,' said the kind-hearted Parisian, who could not have known that the following summer I would be lying on the grass at the L'Eau Vivre campsite in the village of Mougins, which looks out over the French Riviera, and that the campsite owner would tell me, 'You're in luck, monsieur. Right now, in the garden of the villa next door, right by your tent, Mr Clint Eastwood is playing golf with a French friend of his.'

That summer afternoon, too, I would feel in need of something to fire my chest and would head down the road leading to the market in search of a bottle of Jack Daniels. And what a surprise it would be when I met Selina, an Armenian artist and the ex-wife of Maurice. She would tell me she had come to sell her paintings on the sidewalks of the Riviera and would add, 'Oh! I forgot to tell you. Maurice died. We scattered his ashes in the Seine, near Pont Neuf, as he requested.'

Afterwards I would take my Jack Daniels and lie down on the sandy beach until the sun went down, repeating to myself, 'You're right, Maurice. Sad things do happen when I'm away from Paris.'

12

I stopped on rue Soufflot, tired and sad, and gazed at the picture of a beautiful, seductive woman advertising underwear. I noticed I was standing by the entrance to an underground car park and immediately went down the steps to the second level basement, where I spread my papers on the ground under the stairs and went to sleep. As it was crossing my mind to write on the concrete wall 'I Slept Under these Stairs on . . .' I stopped short. It just so happened it was my birthday. I laughed.

I couldn't have been asleep for more than an hour when I opened my eyes to the sound and sight of a large panting dog, its long tongue flapping against my nose; it would have pounced on me had it not been for the guard, who appeared calm, restraining it. With his head, he pointed me in the direction of the exit.

'I'm sorry. I was tired and didn't know where to go. Really, I do apologise,' I said to him, gathering up my papers and putting them back in my folder. 'They're my German language lessons.' I smiled, adding, 'Would you believe that today is my birthday?'

'*D'accord!* OK! Now, Bolero. Get out of here immediately,' said the guard, chewing his gum.

'I know you don't believe me, but today really is my birthday. I'm telling the truth.'

'I said *d'accord*, Bolero!' and he pointed to the exit a second time.

'I'm not lying when I say it's my birthday today. Why should I lie?'

'Fine, Bolero. Happy Birthday! OK! Now please leave.' He spat out his gum.

'I don't get why you keep calling me Bolero, *monsieur*,' I said as I headed for the exit.'

'You don't?'

I shook my head.

'While you were asleep, monsieur, you were playing with yourself and muttering "Bolero . . . Bolero".' He laughed as he said it.

The dog was right behind me as I climbed the stairs, and I could feel the heat of its heavy breathing on my balls until we came out onto the street.

'*Auf wiedersehen*, Bolero!' shouted the guard loudly and pointed to the advertisement of the beautiful girl wearing sexy Bolero underwear.

It was eleven o'clock in the evening when I got to Au Chai de l'Abbaye. I waited for Majid to finish talking to some customers, then said to him, 'Tomorrow I'll look for a job. Today I slept in a car park even though it's my birthday. Isn't that awful?'

Majid looked at me. He laughed and said in English, 'Happy Birthday, *monsieur*.'

'I don't want a happy birthday, Majid. I just want a drink and I'll pay the bill later.'

'*D'accord, monsieur*!' said Majid, pinching my cheek affectionately.

There was a couple sitting a little way off from me. The woman was plump and blonde, in her mid-fifties, elegantly dressed and drinking some kind of cocktail. The man, somewhat older, was wearing a white suit and a panama hat, both of which showed up his dark, friendly features. I finished my wine and went to get another glass. When I came back the man was striding up and down, a glass of whisky in his hand.

'How are you, young man?' he said to me in an Egyptian dialect, approaching my table. 'May I invite you for a whisky?' he declared dramatically. Before I could say anything, he added, 'Wine is not good after midnight.'

He roared with laughter and I joined in, feeling very happy.

I told him he had caught my attention as he reminded me of Albert Finney in John Huston's movie *Under the Volcano*. He became lost in thought and then asked the woman with him if she knew John Huston. Before she could reply, he gestured to me, 'This is Ludmilla, my wife. She's American.'

'Have you forgotten, Fouad? We watched that sad movie *The Dead* only a while ago. That was directed by John Huston. Mr Huston is from Missouri like me.'

'Yes, yes, Ludi. I remember, *habibati*,' said the man.

Fouad really did look like Albert Finney in that movie. He was drinking glass after glass of whisky, and asking me to finish up my drink and bringing me new ones all the time. I didn't need to tell him it was my birthday, as it seemed he was celebrating already. He was speaking as if he were on stage, not in a café. It was fortunate for him it was after midnight, there weren't many people there, and most of them were at the bar.

I discovered that Fouad and I shared the same ideas in spite of our difference in age. He told me how he hated talking about politics because, as he said, 'The Arab world is mired in poverty and ignorance.' Downing another whisky, he added, 'Arab decadence started after Gamal Abdel Nasser came to power in Egypt in 1952 and destroyed democracy. And since the mid-seventies the Saudis have started founding fundamentalist Islamic groups to destroy the achievements of the modern Arab world.'

I kept nodding as I drank my whiskies, saying to myself, 'This is a very good birthday party.'

'How did you leave Iraq?' asked Fouad.

I told him my life story, and that I was writing a script called *Nostalgia for the English Time*, and I was looking for an American actor called Robert de Niro to play the role of the deaf-mute baker.

I finished by telling him, 'I'm pretty sure I'll make this movie next year.'

Fouad kept nodding and drinking his whisky. 'They destroyed your life,' he said, and shook his head sadly.

'You haven't told me how you left Egypt!'

'Oh, that's another story,' he replied.

'Please tell me.'

'Not before another two whiskies, hahahaha.'

Coming back with the two glasses of whisky, he pointed to a lady standing at the bar. 'D'you see that lady with the thick dark glasses at the bar? I don't think she's an ordinary woman. I can sniff out great ladies!'

I looked at her and recognised her instantly. 'It's Anna Karina. She's a regular here.'

'Who's Anna Karina?'

'She was a Danish top model and an actress. She was married to the film director Jean-Luc Godard and acted in many of his movies. She was the most famous actress of the Nouvelle Vague.'

'She certainly looks very special!'

'Are you going to tell me your story?'

'It's so long, but I'll make it short. I was a clerk in the post office in Cairo when Ludmilla came in to send some postcards. The moment I saw her I was crazy about her. We wrote to each other

119

for five years, and then in 1975 we decided to get married. We live in Missouri.'

He raised his glass to mine and said, 'In the Arab world today, people are becoming religious fundamentalists because they all dream of getting a house in heaven. I'm sure there's going to be a housing shortage up there.'

He looked at me and added, 'But why am I trying to be a bad man? Do I not have a house in Missouri? Aren't I a happy man?' And he roared with laughter.

We were sitting drinking our whiskies, Fouad, Ludmilla and I, when I saw Robert de Niro coming into Au Chai de l'Abbaye. He looked towards the bar and walked over to speak to Majid. Majid smiled and pointed at me. De Niro came over to where I was sitting. 'Here we are!' he said. 'What's the matter with you, man? Calling people in the early hours. Getting someone to paint a portrait of me as an old man, seventy years old? What's going on? Are you mad? Who told you I wanted to be a deaf-mute baker? Who told you I'm interested in falling in love with a queen? Huh? . . . or whatsisname, that fucking Greek guy, Kir . . . Kiryakos? I don't give a damn whether he likes John Wayne or John Ford.' Then his tone changed and became quieter, and he looked at Majid and shouted, 'Majid, bring us a good bottle of wine!'

I woke up to find myself lying on a bench. A paunchy baby-faced Frenchman in a silk dressing gown was shaking me. '*Monsieur! Monsieur!* I can't sleep. You've ruined my night!'

I looked at the man and glanced all around me. On one side was Montsouris Park, and there were no other benches anywhere. '*Monsieur*,' I asked, puzzled, 'where are you sleeping? This is the only bench in the area.'

The man pointed upwards at a block of apartments. 'There. Up there. Where the light is. On the sixth floor. That's my apartment.'

I was quiet. I didn't know what to say.

'Your snoring woke me up. So loud, it was so loud . . .'

I stood up and looked at him, 'Oh, *monsieur*! I am very sorry. I'm really sorry . . . and if I had a bottle of wine now, I don't think I would disturb you any more.'

He looked at me strangely. 'What did you say you wanted?'

'A bottle of wine,' I replied.

'A bottle of wine! And what kind of cheese would you like with it? he oozed. Before I could say anything, he added, 'Don't tell me. . . you want a pillow as well!'

'No, *monsieur*! No, *monsieur*! Don't get me wrong,' I blurted out, and put my head in my hands.

'Oh, this Egyptian postman killed me with his whisky. Can you imagine, this Egyptian postman insisted on giving me whiskies all night, shouting at me "Drink, drink".'

'An Egyptian postman drinking whisky?' he said. 'Where was this? Where was this Egyptian postman?'

'I think he told me somewhere in Missouri,' I answered.

'*S'il vous plaît, monsieur*, I want to sleep. Can you leave this place? And please, don't sleep here again!'

As he walked away I could hear him muttering to himself, 'An Egyptian postman drinking whisky in Paris . . .'

13

My appointment with Faiza was for eleven in the morning in Café Bonaparte. Faiza had told me some time ago that her friend Melanie's grandmother usually spent the summer outside Paris, and she had suggested to Melanie that she persuade her grandmother to give me her apartment while she was away. 'She lives in a splendid apartment on the first floor, looking out over a wonderful garden. And where? In the Boulevard Montparnasse, near the Duroc metro station.' Faiza's words were ringing in my ears.

I was about to finish my third beer when Faiza arrived, accompanied by Melanie. Faiza ordered a hot milk and Melanie a hot chocolate. She ordered me another beer.

'You are entitled to celebrate today!' she said cheerfully.

I smiled. I felt a little shy of Melanie, whom I was meeting for the first time.

She looked at me. 'You're lucky,' she said in a friendly tone. 'I have persuaded my grandmother to give you her apartment, but she wants to see you before she leaves.'

Faiza seemed extremely happy. 'Three months is long enough for you to finish the screenplay you dream of writing,' she said. She added laughing, as she put the glass of milk to her beautiful mouth, 'You've killed us all with *Nostalgia for the English Time*.'

And we all laughed.

The next day we were on our way to her grandmother's apartment.

'I told my grandmother I have known you for four years,' said Melanie. 'You should know that. She attaches importance to long relationships.'

I nodded knowingly.

Melanie's grandmother was a sailor's widow who looked just like the actress Jessica Tandy, especially in the movie *Driving Miss Daisy*.

'I trust Melanie and respect her friendships,' said the grandmother (whom I shall call Jessica Tandy). 'The reason I asked to see you before I leave is that I don't want to be in the Alps with a phantom staying in my house.'

Then she took me by the hand and we walked a few steps to stand in front of a large map hanging in the hallway. Jessica Tandy looked at the map for a few moments, then took a long baton fastened beneath its heavy ornate frame and said, 'This is France, we are here in Paris.' She turned towards me. 'Show me where you come from!' she demanded, putting the baton into my hand.

I looked at the map and pointed to Iraq, then to Baghdad. 'My family lives here.'

Jessica Tandy laughed as she took the baton from my hand and went back to the map again. 'You come from here [Baghdad], to stay in my house here [Paris], while I am here [the Alps]. What a small world this world is,' she said, almost whispering to herself, '*Un Irakien à Paris!*' She continued laughing. Seeing that I was looking at her a little warily, she said, 'Don't be afraid, I'm not going to fall over from laughing. Sit down, sit down, I'll make you some tea!' As she made her way to the kitchen, I heard her murmuring, 'Real Arabs prefer tea to coffee, that's what my dear husband used to say.'

I looked at Melanie and said, 'Your grandmother is right, I can't stand coffee.'

She patted my bottom and said with a smile, 'In less than an hour this will be your house, there's no need to pretend!'

I looked at her hands and asked her, 'What do you do, Melanie?'

'Sculptor,' she replied.

As she handed me the keys, Jessica Tandy asked me not to go near 'that room' and pointed to a closed room at the end of the hall, looking out over the garden on the Boulevard Montparnasse side. 'It is personally very special to me,' she added, 'and I am sure you will respect my wishes.'

As we were getting ready to leave, Jessica Tandy glanced at the map. 'Anyway, the key to the room is hanging to the right of the map,' she said. 'No one knows what's going to happen!'

By the time I had gone and collected my things from the locker at Austerlitz, the beautiful sculptor with the strong hands had filled the refrigerator with various sorts of cheeses, jam, eggs, cherry tomatoes and some small bottles of Perrier, and left a note on the kitchen table: 'Try to concentrate on finishing your work. I'm confident that in the future you will live in a better apartment than this one. Here is my telephone number in case you need it. Kisses, Melanie.'

What happiness surged through me as I unpacked my little bag and put everything in its right place. I was almost in paradise. My clothes were arranged in rows in my very own wardrobe. My shaving things had finally come to rest on a glass shelf near the large gleaming mirror in front of which I would stand naked every morning. My typewriter crouched on an antique inlaid side table. As it had an Arabic keyboard, I went to Duriez and had my name printed out in large Latin characters, which I stuck on the mail box next to Jessica Tandy's name.

My name soon attracted the attention of the good Romero, a man of Spanish origin, who was the handyman for the building. Romero seemed confused.

'Are you certain this is your name?' he asked.

'Yes, *monsieur.*'

'The odd thing is that Jessica Tandy told me a young Arab man would be staying in her apartment.'

'That's me.'

'An Arab with a name like this?'

'I'm an Iraqi, not an Arab.'

'What does that mean – I'm an Iraqi, not an Arab?' the man asked.

He seemed completely at a loss. I was forced to repeat the boring facts that Iraq was made up of several ancient peoples, such as the Arabs, the Turkmen, Assyrians, Armenians, Kurds, Sabaeans and Jews.

I finished my lecture by saying, 'As you can see, Iraq is like a dish of Spanish paella.'

The man burst out laughing, and repeated over and over, 'Ha! Ha! Ha! Iraq is like a dish of paella.'

Monsieur Romero would make a point of greeting me whenever he saw me going in or out of the building. One morning he told me he had noticed that North African Arabs, when they talked to each other, 'looked as if they were having an argument, just like the Italians'. He asked me whether Iraqis and North African Arabs spoke the same language.

'Yes,' I said, and added cheerfully, 'the only difference is that Iraqis talk like Germans.'

Monsieur Romero laughed. 'You make me laugh easily!' he said.

At that moment, a blonde girl walked past us and greeted us with a '*Bonjour*'.

'*Bonjour, mademoiselle,*' we replied. The girl walked towards the entrance of the building.

'That's the new postwoman, but only for a few weeks,' said Monsieur Romero, not knowing that I was going to be driven crazy for the whole of those few weeks! She was slim, with a beautiful pale face. Her full breasts stood out under her thin, olive-green blouse. She seemed to have come straight from the swimming pool, for when she bent down to take the letters out of her bag, her orange bathing costume could be seen clinging to her bottom, leaving some moisture on her thin white trousers.

'*Bonjour, mademoiselle.*' I greeted her in a soft voice with a big smile.

'*Bonjour, monsieur,*' she answered coldly and went back to her work.

The postwoman was cold with me the next time too. I began to make excuses to start a conversation with her.

'It's strange,' I would say to her, 'I'm supposed to be receiving some important letters from America' – or on another occasion 'from Australia' or 'from Canada' – and she would shrug her shoulders and say '*Je ne sais pas*' in an offhand way.

'Mademoiselle,' I said to her once, in an attempt to interest her in the fact that I worked in the film industry, 'I've been on tenterhooks for days, expecting a letter from the Gaumont Film Production Company.'

She looked at me in astonishment. 'Monsieur,' she said, 'please, why don't you contact the company then, and ask them what has become of your letter. *Au revoir!*'

'*Au revoir, mademoiselle!*'

I fell in love with that blonde postwoman, and began to take an interest in my appearance. I shaved every morning, sprayed my body with lots of deodorant, and bought two new shirts, one black, the other red, to match the two pairs of jeans that I owned. Once, as I was trimming my moustache, I shouted at the top of my voice, 'Fuck you, Aldo Maccione! And everyone else can go to hell!' And I shaved off my moustache again.

A few weeks earlier I had been lying on a bench near the Jardin du Luxembourg, wondering where to go, and realised people were staring at me and looking all about them. I knew they were looking for the film cameras, thinking Aldo was making a movie there.

'*Bonjour, mademoiselle!*'

'*Bonjour, monsieur,*' the blonde replied, staring. She asked in a refined voice, 'Have you contacted the Gaumont Company, *monsieur?*' Her manner had completely changed.

'It's best to wait, *mademoiselle,*' I replied.

From that moment, my imagination was working overtime, inventing any story or pretext that would allow me to approach the blonde postwoman I was besotted with. Well, the upshot was that I decided to write a letter as if from the Gaumont company, addressed to myself, 'even if I had to put a blank sheet of paper in an envelope'.

I was standing at my corner of the bar in the Danton, unable to get her out of my mind, when I heard Manuel talking with a customer and mentioning the name of the American actor John Ashton. Manuel pointed to me and said to the customer, 'This monsieur is a good friend of John Ashton.' I nodded and smiled proudly in agreement.

Well, this wasn't the first time Manuel had told this story. It was autumn 1988 and my friend Nabil and I had just seen *Midnight*

Run with Robert De Niro, Charles Grodin and John Ashton. After we left the cinema we had gone straight into the Café Danton next door. How strange! After just a few moments a man stood beside us at the bar and asked for a Red Label.

Nabil whispered in my ear, 'Isn't this Marvin from the movie?'

'Yes – it's John Ashton, you're right!' I murmured.

I turned to him, 'Hello, Mr Ashton!'

'Hello,' he replied with a smile.

My friend Nabil and I told him we were poets. John Ashton shook us by the hand and we told him how much we liked his role in *Midnight Run*. At that moment a group of our Algerian friends joined us. I introduced them to John Ashton and we all began to enjoy our drinks. When the actor was about to pay and go, I told him to leave the bill with us.

'We are celebrating today,' I said, 'as the Swedish Academy has awarded the Nobel Prize for Literature to the Egyptian author Naguib Mahfouz.'

'Thank you so much,' he said, returning his wallet to his back pocket. He took out a pen and notebook. 'What was the Egyptian author's name?'

'Naguib Mahfouz, Mr Ashton,' I answered.

'Does he have any translations in English?'

'Of course.'

John Ashton had continued to come to the Danton to drink every evening that week and he always came over to see me in my corner. We would talk about Paris and the movies, and I told him I was writing a script and that I would like Robert De Niro to be the hero of the movie. He drank Red Label and smiled.

'In Iraq we prefer Black Label to Red,' I told him.

He laughed. I asked him what he was doing in Paris and he explained he was shooting a movie called *I Want to Go Home*, with Gérard Depardieu.

'Who's the director?' I asked.

'Alain Resnais.'

'He's a great director,' I said.

One evening I arrived at the Danton later than usual and Manuel shouted at me, 'Where have you been? Why are you so late?'

'What's up with you, Manuel? Don't I have the right to come to the Danton at any time that suits me?' I exclaimed.

'I'm sorry,' Manuel said, 'it's just that Monsieur John Ashton waited for you for a long time. He wanted to say goodbye before he went back to Hollywood.'

First thing next morning I went to the Duriez shop and put a blank piece of paper in an envelope. Should I write a line or two in French? It would certainly be full of mistakes. Suddenly Robert De Niro came to mind. Maybe because last night I had been remembering *Midnight Run*? The letter could be addressed to him! Why not? He was a famous and handsome actor, most girls were in love with him, and I was sure the blonde postwoman was one of them.

In the end, I wrote a letter as follows:

> *Cher M. Robert De Niro*
> *Tout va bien.*
>
>
> D. F. *Hugo*
> *Gaumont Films*

Then I put an envelope in the machine and typed Robert De Niro's name, c/o me where I was staying in Boulevard Montparnasse, Paris.

I sent the letter from the Odéon post office, then went into the Café Le Relais Odéon to order my favourite midday sandwich of *jambon et cornichons*, ham and gherkins, with a glass of beer. I sat waiting for the miracle next day.

Sure enough, the following morning the blonde postwoman

was sitting on the stairs next to the mailboxes. As soon as she saw me, she started up towards me.

'*Bonjour, monsieur!*' she said, with a broad smile.

'*Bonjour, mademoiselle,*' I replied, and went towards the mailbox. 'How are you?' I asked her.

'Fine, thank you, *monsieur*, and you?'

'Very well. Ah!' I exclaimed as I flicked through the letters addressed to Jessica Tandy, 'this is the letter we have been waiting for!'

'Excuse me, sir, can I please ask you a question?'

'Of course,' I replied, looking at her pale beautiful face. She seemed younger today.

'There's a letter for Monsieur Robert De Niro. Is that the famous American actor himself?'

I gave her a serious sort of look. 'You're a post office employee, *mademoiselle,*' I said. 'I think you should respect your customers' privacy, shouldn't you?'

'Certainly, sir, but I was only wondering,' she said, with a certain embarrassment.

'Yes, it's him, but please let's keep this between ourselves.'

'Of course, I'll respect that,' she said, with a smile. 'I'm studying architecture, and I'm just working for the post office for a few weeks.'

'Wonderful! A*u revoir, mademoiselle!*'

'*Au revoir, monsieur!*'

The Gaumont letters to Robert De Niro began to flood in every day, without any change in their contents (*Tout va bien*). With every letter, my relationship with Delfina – for that was her name – was becoming stronger and stronger. She would greet me with a kiss on the cheek and say goodbye to me with another.

One day around noon we were smoking a cigarette, leaning against the iron gateway to the apartment block. Delfina told me that Robert De Niro was her favourite actor and proceeded to talk at length about his films, nearly all of which she had seen. She then confessed that I was better than her in analysing the parts he had played. 'You're really good at plumbing the depths of his personality. And you know a lot of details about his private life as well. If I was in your position,' she added, throwing the stub of her cigarette towards the Boulevard Montparnasse, 'I'd be writing a book about him.'

Throwing away my cigarette just as she had done, I answered her in a slightly offhand way, 'But, my dear Delfina, you don't know how difficult it would be to write about a close friend like Bobby!'

'Who?' she asked, surprised.

'Bobby De Niro. We've been talking about him for days!'

'Bobby De Niro,' she said, laughing.

Delfina. I was very happy repeating her name. 'Delfina, you must meet Bobby!' The words escaped my lips spontaneously. I found myself saying, 'Yes, yes, I must introduce you to him.'

'I'm really happy to have met you!' she said, then embraced me.

'Please don't tell anyone about this,' I said, pointing to the window of the room overlooking the garden – the room that Jessica Tandy had asked me not to go into. 'He's there, in that room,' I said, shaking my head a little sadly.

Delfina said nothing for a while, then asked me, 'But why does he shut himself up in that room?'

'Sorry, I'll tell you the story later. There are some temporary difficulties. Bobby is having family problems as a result of vile rumours the American press published about his personal life. Anyway, he won't be staying cooped up here for long. Very shortly, he'll be moving to St Tropez to stay with a friend of his, a famous tennis star.'

'What a coincidence! I'm from Fréjus, near St Tropez. I'm half French and half Spanish!'

I began to examine her face. 'Apart from your name, what is Spanish about you, Delfina?' I asked.

She shrugged her shoulders innocently as if to say 'I don't

know' or 'I don't want to say'.

As I said goodbye to the fair Delfina, the thing that came to mind immediately was that I needed some francs. What would Delfina say if she went into the kitchen and saw nothing in the fridge except for some eggs, a tub of butter and a few cans of beer, and the shelves piled with tins of chickpeas, beans, lentils, onions and tomato paste and a few bottles of cheap Côte de Rhône? Was this the food of choice of Hollywood stars?

I had to contact Adams.

Flicking through the long poem I had typed up for him, Adams asked me, 'Did you like it?'

'Very much,' I told him.

'Don't just be polite, your opinion matters to me,' he said. 'You have a different sensibility.'

'Believe me, Adams, it's a great poem.'

Adams would always ask my opinion of anything I typed for him. This was partly modesty on his part, but also he looked on me, as he once told me, as a Christian on whom 'the Qur'an has not worked its linguistic eloquence'.

We were in Café Saint-Claude, which Adams favoured at that time. He had brought a new manuscript with him for me to type, describing it as 'extremely important'. 'You know that I always trust you,' he said. 'Please, please, no one else but you must look at this manuscript.' As we drank our Stella Artois, he asked me whether there were any other Arabs living with me where I was staying.

'Only Robert De Niro,' I said, joking.

Adams laughed loudly. 'You talk a lot about the movies, but you don't make any movies, just like most Arab men who talk a lot about sex without having any – and even if they do get some the poor guys remain repressed.' And as he put the manuscript in my hands, he said to me, 'I've been working on this manuscript for eighteen months. Rewriting Ibn Hisham's *Sira*, the life of Muhammad, in a modern narrative style. You know what that means?' He nodded his head as he smiled. 'It means it's not a joke!'

'You know I like you, Adams,' I replied.

From the bank next to the Madison Hotel in Boulevard Saint-Germain Adams withdrew 2,000 francs for me, then wrapped his silk scarf around his neck and left.

Two bottles of champagne in the fridge, *Newsweek* magazine on the kitchen table, the *Los Angeles Times* on the floor in the hallway and I was in the sitting room playing the piano, raising my head from time to time and glancing out through the window overlooking the beautiful garden and the entrance to the building. There was Delfina pushing open the iron gate with one smooth hand and carrying a bunch of red flowers in the other. Even the old post bag looked elegant, hanging over her shoulder.

'They're for Bobby,' she said, holding the flowers to my big nose. 'What a nice bouquet!' I replied, taking the flowers. 'Come on, Delfina, get on and deliver the letters quickly. Come and give the flowers to Bobby yourself!'

'In these dreadful old clothes?' she asked coquettishly.

I stretched out my hand and caressed her cheek, then embraced her. 'You're amazingly beautiful, Delfina.'

We exchanged shy smiles.

Delfina went to the bathroom. I immediately went and took the key to the locked room that was hanging in its place to the right of the big map of the world. I went into that room for the first time. Everything was covered with sheets. The double bed, the chairs and even the pictures hanging on the walls were all covered with sheets embroidered with pictures of boats, harbours and sailors. I spent a short time in the room, then said in a loud voice to be sure that Delfina would hear me, 'It's OK, Bobby, don't worry, nothing bad will happen. Be sure, Bobby.'

'Is there some problem with my being here?'

'No, no, not at all, Bobby's not that sort. It's my fault, Delfina, I should have told him about you coming. I forgot. Let's leave it until tomorrow.'

Then I took the bunch of flowers from her, went back again into the locked room and put them on the double bed. I took more than $150 from my pocket (I had bought the dollars the day before – these would always remain in my pocket) and shouted again on my way back to the sitting room, 'Very kind of you, Bobby. Yeah, yeah, I will. All the papers, of course.'

I was careful to keep the dollars in my hands as I stood in front of Delfina.

'Bobby gave me some money to take you to any restaurant you choose this evening.'

'How kind he is!' she said.

'We have to go to Rue Saint Benoît to buy the American papers for Bobby.'

'OK. I'm dying to meet him. I can hardly believe that Bobby De Niro and I are in the same apartment.'

'Imagine, Delfina, that the *Los Angeles Times* wrote yesterday that Bobby was in London, in Elton John's house. Isn't that rubbish?'

'Incredible story!' Delfina replied in English.

And I answered her in English, 'It is indeed!'

'Oh, I've forgotten, it's champagne time for Bobby!' I exclaimed, before we left. I went into the kitchen, put one bottle on one of Jessica Tandy's nice trays with a glass and put it beside the flowers inside the locked room.

In Rue Saint Benoit we bought *Newsweek*, the *Los Angeles Times* and the *Herald Tribune*. 'Why are you buying *Newsweek* again?' asked Delfina suddenly. 'You've got this issue at home.'

'Are you sure?'

'Of course,' she said in English.

I threw the American papers into the locked room, went into the kitchen and opened a bottle of champagne. 'There's nothing better than champagne at midday,' I said to Delfina and then started to sing 'Mona Lisa', the song that Nat King Cole sang. We sat down on the spacious sofa and I told Delfina in a soft voice that Bobby had said to me, 'Enjoy yourselves, guys!', and that I had replied 'But she's here for you, Bobby!'

Delfina put her glass on the table. 'You're very nice too,' she said, and kissed me on the mouth.

I kissed her back.

'Not today, please,' she said in a whisper when I put my hand inside her see-through trousers.

Before we finished the bottle of champagne, she said to me, '*Embrasse-moi encore*, kiss me again.' I began to kiss her and when my hand started to undo the buttons on her blouse she repeated again in a whisper, 'Not today, please.' We went on kissing for several days, but when I kissed her breasts she always said 'Not now'.

Despite the fact that my happiness was indescribable, a slight feeling of sorrow would come over me from time to time, for I was unable to tell my beautiful Delfina the story of the boy who dreamed of becoming a film director and making a movie about his deaf-mute father, the baker madly in love with the Queen of England, and searching for Robert De Niro to play the part of the baker, which I had repeated in bars, cafés, parks and streets so much that sometimes I felt that half the inhabitants of Paris must know it.

Every day Delfina and I would go out to cafés and restaurants. Whenever my money ran out, I would contact Adams for help. When I paid a bill, I would say to Delfina, 'It's dear Bobby that's paying for us'.

The evening came when I felt Delfina had become so close to me that she would say '*Je t'aime*' with her whole heart, and I would then declare my love for her as well. I decided to say to her the next morning (just as Manuel had said to me) 'Where have you been, Delfina, why are you late? Bobby waited for you for ages, he wanted to say goodbye to you before he went back to Hollywood.' Unfortunately, however, I was out of luck.

That evening, after coming out of a restaurant on Rue

Mabillon, we walked to the Café Le 10 on Rue de l'Odéon. I remember that before going into the café I pointed out to Delfina the building next to it, telling her, 'It was here at 12 Rue de l'Odéon in 1922 that the American publisher Sylvia Beach agreed with James Joyce to publish his famous novel *Ulysses*.'

At Le 10 we drank a lot of sangria, so that we returned home half-drunk and threw ourselves into bed. After I had kissed her, Delfina said '*Je t'aime*' and began to undress. 'Now I'll show you the Spanish part of me.' We laughed. We made love. I brought a bottle of Côte du Rhône and we drank it. We made love again. I remember that I was naked and was opening a bottle of champagne. I was singing 'Mona Lisa'. I could hear Delfina saying, 'Keep your voice down, please, keep your voice down, it's not nice to disturb Bobby so late at night. Please, please, keep your voice down, keep your voice down, please!'

I continued hearing Delfina's voice until I woke up in the morning to find myself alone in the bed with no sign of Delfina or her clothes. The champagne and Côte du Rhône bottles were empty and there were two empty tins of chickpeas and fava beans.

I couldn't find Delfina in the bathroom, or in the kitchen. When I saw the door to the locked room open, I felt jealous. I approached the room apprehensively, almost ready to believe that Bobby De Niro was in the house and that he was sleeping with Delfina. There was nothing there except for the sheets embroidered with pictures of boats, ports and sailors, a bunch of wilting flowers and a number of American newspapers and magazines.

That morning, Delfina left me a letter in the mailbox. It read as follows:

My dear cheat,

I am glad I discovered your trick just as my post job is finishing. When I saw you yesterday going into that ghost's room naked and coming back with a bottle of champagne (which you drank warm) I realised you were conning me. But you made me laugh, gulping down the chickpeas and fava beans so amazingly quickly. I also liked the story of your father, the deaf-mute baker, and your search for De Niro to bring his character to life in the movie you dreamed of making. I wish you luck. What else can I say? Well, I am not angry with you, Aldo Maccione!

It was signed 'Delfina' and had a PS:

When I first saw you, I didn't like you at all. With your moustache, you reminded me of a taxi driver from Barcelona who had once given me a hard time.

14

*On the Concorde bridge
the sad Assyrian found
on a certain night his lost tongue.
On the Concorde bridge
he was not alone,
he was clothed in his hunger
and his worn-out clothes,
his beard,
the pallor of his face
and his down-at-heel shoes
worn thin as his pockets.
On that same night
the ancient boy stroked his big nose and said,
My friends are no more my friends
and I am no more their friend.
On the Concorde bridge
he was not alone,
watching the Seine,
frozen with cold.*

I woke up in Austerlitz feeling very guilty. I had had a very good chance that summer of finding a solution to my situation but I had spent it on my dreams. I was determined now to find a job. But sometimes it seemed that God, who guided my steps, as I believed, did not want me to be ambushed by the routines of life.

The previous week, I had had an appointment for a job at an Italian restaurant. I had made my way to meet the owner of the restaurant, who had agreed over the telephone that I replace a friend of mine who had left his job there. It didn't bother me that I would be working as a dishwasher since most of my friends' wives considered me 'the best dishwasher in history'. As I walked along, I was thinking of the wages that would come into my pocket at the end of the month, and of renting a small room that would rescue me from the life of the streets, and from occasionally bothering my friends.

A few steps away from the restaurant with its elegant modern façade, I stopped for a brief moment, probably to straighten my clothes or my hair, which was oiled and combed back like an Italian opera singer's.

Suddenly, something like lightning spread through my body and made my feet turn away from the restaurant and point towards Saint-Germain, landing me in Café Au Chai de l'Abbaye. And there I stayed, drinking Gamay, my favourite wine. That day an American tourist had said to me, after buying me several glasses, 'The unemployed know the joys and pleasures of life, and they are the closest to God's mercy and compassion.'

But, today, I woke up and exchanged greetings with the cleaners in Austerlitz, who always treated me with kindness for when they saw me sound asleep they passed their brooms gently near my head so as not to stir up the dust. They were so gentle, those North Africans and Africans (when they wanted to be).

I got up full of energy, muttering to myself, 'How long will you go on without work . . .'

I went straight to the washroom and took a shower for 20 francs. I swore on my father's grave that I wouldn't go anywhere near Saint-Germain-des-Prés for at least three months – not until I had improved my economic situation. So, after my shower, I immediately washed and dried my clothes and stuffed them into the left luggage locker. I quickly took the metro and threw myself into Place de la République.

'Paris is not just Saint-Germain,' I said to myself.

I strolled down the long Boulevard Magenta and began to look in the agencies for temporary jobs in construction, painting and cleaning. I imagined myself painting the front of a tall building, suspended in the air and looking down at the people like midgets below me.

Sometimes I saw myself digging the streets – and at this moment the spectre of a friend who always competed with me on the streets passed before me. Standing for a few moments, he lit a cigarette and took a can of beer out of his pocket. He stood and considered it carefully.

Then I heard him say, 'Ah, life is truly beautiful.'

At other times, I saw myself cleaning the floor of one of the offices where two beautiful secretaries would be smoking cigarettes and chatting about the night before.

In the midst of my fantasies, I wasn't aware that my feet were gradually changing direction and sliding towards Boulevard Sepastopol and crossing Place du Châtelet, then the Palais de Justice, then Pont Saint-Michel, so that I found myself in Saint-Germain again, standing in the Café Le Relais Odéon with my Algerian friend Ahmad. Before I could explain my problem, Ahmad bought me a beer. He seemed to be worried.

After he had bought me another, I said to him in a shy voice, 'I'm sorry, Ahmad, I'm always broke when I meet you.'

'Screw the money, drink twenty glasses,' he said nervously, with a swift glance at my hands. He offered me a Marlboro cigarette, but then withdrew it quickly. 'I'm sorry, you don't smoke this brand of cigarettes.'

After he had lit his cigarette, he added in a frustrated tone, 'I'm tired of my wife and of Paris . . . There is nothing left but to get away from them, from both of them. That's all, I have to get away . . . Yes, I have to escape . . .'

I was gulping down my beer and looking at the smoke of his cigarette. Ahmad motioned to the waiter to bring two more beers.

'I think very highly of you,' said Ahmad, then he looked outside and added, 'They don't have your kind of cigarettes in this café.'

He smiled and handed me a 50-franc note. I took it and hurried outside to buy a packet of Dunhill, my brand of cigarettes after Maurice's death. When I came back he refused to take the change, just winked and patted his thigh, which I took to mean he had a lot of cash in his pocket.

'An Algerian never leaves his friend in a crisis,' said Ahmad.

'*Je sais*,' I said, gulping my beer.

'We've been friends for several years, and as Algerians and Iraqis we are living through very, very hard times,' said Ahmad.

'*C'est vrai*,' I replied.

Ahmad looked at me for a moment, then added uneasily, 'What's up with you?'

'*Rien.*'

'Damn you, what's with "*Rien*". I speak to you in Arabic and you answer me in French.'

'I'm very sorry, Ahmad, you're right.'

Ahmad took a cigarette and I did the same, then he quickly drained his glass. I finished my drink too, but before I could make my excuses and leave he interrupted me by ordering another.

He began to smoke like a man tormented and said, 'I'm tired of Paris, I'm tired of my wife. Yes, I must get away from them. If I stay here one more day, I will surely die. I can't, I can't stand the woman, she's evil. I swear on my father's grave and my beautiful daughter's life, I will not stay in this miserable situation. I will travel to Toulouse. I don't like Paris and I don't like my wife. In Toulouse, I will be a happier man, believe me, my friend.'

Then he took a railway ticket from his pocket and said, 'Here is the ticket, one way only!' And he looked at me. 'Don't you want to ask me why Toulouse and not somewhere else?'

'Why Toulouse and not somewhere else?'

'Because I love a woman there. The women of Toulouse are more beautiful than the women of Paris. I'm sure that what I'm saying is one hundred percent true.'

After he had finished his drink, he took out a 500-franc note and shoved it into my pocket, 'I know you love Pascal.'*

I smiled and turned to the waiter to fill up our glasses.

'It's better that you put the money away, I'll be gone soon . . .' said Ahmad, 'and I don't think this will last you till the morning. Don't you want to ask me when I will travel?'

'When will you travel?'

'Tomorrow at dawn . . . just one way. Yes, one way only. On the train I will close my eyes until it leaves the outskirts of Paris. God, I will be so happy in Toulouse. You can't imagine how happy I'll be to leave Paris. You know, I don't like Paris. I have to get away as soon as possible. I have to save myself from going mad. There is a conspiracy between Paris and my wife to destroy me.'

'Ahmad . . .'

'Yes.'

'Try to give your wife another chance.'

'Are you crazy? I thought you hated family. . . don't try to play the good guy.'

'I'm trying to say, Ahmad, go home . . . and . . .'

'Why don't you change your bad habits . . .' interrupted Ahmad, shaking his head with bitterness and pain, then he added, 'As soon as I put money in your pocket you want to send me off home so you can go and drink somewhere else!'

* The 500-franc note depicted the head of Blaise Pascal

140

'Please, don't get me wrong.'

'I know you well, you're always like this. You take advantage of our affection and friendship and as soon as we give you money, you disappear . . . Hameed was right when he said, "Pay for his drink and buy him a sandwich and don't ever give him cash".'

I ordered another drink while Ahmad remained silent, dragging deeply on his cigarette and exhaling the smoke forcefully towards the floor.

He began to shake his head, repeating, 'I don't like Paris, I don't like Paris and I don't like my wife either.'

His cigarette was in one hand and he put the other in his pocket as he made his way to the toilets. I pulled out the 500-franc note and put it on the bar. When the waiter reached out to take the money, I looked up at his face and the upside-down bottle of Jameson hanging behind him caught my eye. I asked for a glass, then another and another . . . and since it seemed Ahmad had been delayed, I went outside to buy more cigarettes.

I remember I walked into another café, but I don't remember what happened after that.

When with great difficulty I opened my eyes, I found I had been sleeping under the statue of Danton, which was sheltering me from the midday sun. I never liked to sleep in the street during the day. I felt my pockets (this is the first thing I do when I wake up) and as soon as my hand touched the coins, the image of the Serbian woman who hands me the towel in Austerlitz appeared before me.

Usually after I had slept on the street, I would walk with my head down so my eyes don't meet those of the passers-by until I was at least one square kilometre away from the area.

Walking like this, I left Boulevard Saint-Germain and went into Rue Danton, and Place Saint-Michel, then Rue de la Huchette, to walk on the Quai de Montebello on my way to Austerlitz – and there I saw Ahmad and his wife. They were each holding a hand of their little girl, who was walking between them. We were face to face, and there was no escaping it – we had to say hello. Ahmad kept playing with his little girl while his wife reproached me for not visiting them for several months, and she didn't forget to add that she always kept in hand two tins of boiled chickpeas 'or *lablabi*, as you call it in Iraq'.

Ahmad said, looking at his wife, 'He's like this. Just imagine, I haven't seen him since last summer.'

In a shy voice I said, 'What can I do? I'm working in an Italian restaurant from morning till midnight.'

When we exchanged farewells, I went up to the little girl and stroked her hair, and she said gleefully, 'Papa is taking me to McDonald's . . .'

I felt happy as I watched Ahmad and his family gradually moving away. However, in spite of the fact that I was rather hungry, I wasn't thinking of McDonald's, not because I was a fan of Burger King and especially the Double Whopper, but because I wanted to ask Ahmad about the fate of the train ticket, since like him I didn't love Paris and wanted to travel to Toulouse – one way only.

15

The waiter at the Café Au Chai de l'Abbaye, Claude, asked me to finish my drink quickly. It was a quarter past two in the morning and he had to close up the café. I walked a few paces and sat down in Place Furstenberg. This was where I 'cleared' my mind every day. Opposite me was the house in which the famous painter Delacroix had spent his last years, and which was now a museum. I started to smoke a cigarette. I thought of walking to Austerlitz, but I couldn't sleep now, I was in such a troubled mood.

'How long will the French go on repeating this tedious drama?' I shouted loudly, as if addressing the great painter.

I meant those enormous military parades that they put on every year. Thousands of soldiers, hundreds of tanks, rockets and artillery, scores of planes circling in the sky, and everywhere thronged with people, with traffic policemen closing the main roads leading to the heart of Paris. All this led to complete chaos that lasted the whole day. The television channels broadcast these parades live. We could see the same pictures on the screens of hundreds of thousands of television sets displayed in the windows of electrical shops. I love France, but I never liked this day they call 'Quatorze Juillet' when they celebrate the anniversary of the French Revolution.

I left Place Furstenberg and decided to take a stroll around Saint-Sulpice church, waiting for dawn to break so that I could go into the first café I found open. At the end of Rue Bonaparte, where it meets Rue Vieux Colombiers, I noticed an attractive woman walking in a way that caught my attention. She was wearing white shorts that allowed one to see her sturdy legs. I guessed that she was nearing fifty. As the distance between us narrowed, I thought she looked sad. Without expecting any reply, I asked her, 'Why are you sad, madame?' I was drunk, and it was nearly three in the morning.

The woman stopped. 'Yes, I am very sad, monsieur,' she said, trying to put on a little smile.

'I am very sorry, madame,' I said.

'I lost my little dog on *quatorze juillet*, monsieur,' she explained. 'Isn't that sad?' she added in a coquettish way, licking her lips and pouting.

'And I lost my country on *quatorze juillet*, madame, isn't that sad?' I said sarcastically.

She laughed and closed her eyes flirtatiously, 'And how did that happen?' she asked.

143

'It's a long story, madame.'

The woman remained silent for a moment, then said, 'Listen, would you like to have a drink with me? I know a place that stays open till dawn.'

We crossed Boulevard Saint-Germain and walked on past the church. 'I live on this boulevard,' she said. 'Isn't it wonderful for someone to live in this quarter?'

'It's just a dream, as far as I'm concerned,' I replied.

'For me too,' she said cheerfully, then added, 'Think how wonderful it would be if we were to find my dog now!'

'We'll find it, madame, believe me. I feel it,' I said.

She stopped and looked at me. 'You are kind,' she said. 'You make me feel I've found a friend. You said "We'll find it". That's very kind of you.'

I shrugged my shoulders and didn't know what to reply.

'Yes, you are kind,' she repeated.

When we went into the Café Conti I was greeted by Damien, the manager, who shook hands with me.

'It seems you are famous,' said the woman.

'Only in bars,' I replied.

She laughed loudly.

I asked for a red wine and she asked for a Kir Royale. I noticed Damien leaving the bar, and knew that he would be going to the storeroom behind it, near the toilet. I immediately made for the toilet and waited for a few moments for him to come out of the storeroom, then said, 'Damien, please, if we have to drink a lot, can I settle the bill tomorrow? I only met this woman today.'

'Certainly,' said Damien. He added, 'She's only been living in Paris for two weeks. She was in California before.'

'You know her?'

'She comes in for a drink in the evening. She lives only a few steps away from here.'

The woman said that her name was Micheline, and asked me my name, about my life and what had happened to my country.

144

I told her that I was working at the moment in a translation and printing company and that my ambition was to be a film director. About my country, I told her that on 14 July 1958 a group of wicked officers had carried out a bloody military coup that had done away with the monarchy in Iraq, and that since then the Iraqi people had been living under the rule of the loutish military.

'Are you a royalist?' she asked me.

Yes, I'm a royalist. I believe that the monarchy in my country was better for us.'

She nodded her head in an understanding way. 'I lived more than fifteen years in California. I had a big restaurant there, specialising in French cuisine. OK, it was owned by myself and my husband. I separated from him a month ago.' As she ordered another drink, she added, 'I'm a professional chef. I thought of opening a restaurant here in Paris, but I decided to test the waters first, so I took a job as a chef in a well-known restaurant behind the Palais de Justice. My customers are among the best known judges in Paris.'

After a moment's silence she asked, 'Where do you live?'

'A little while ago, I left the place I was living in near here, and I'm now living in a small studio near the press where I work. Near the Bourse de Paris.'

'A nice area, but it's a long way away from here,' she said.

We went on drinking until the café closed its doors. She invited me to continue drinking in her house, 'It's only a few steps away, come with me.'

In the morning, Micheline appeared out of the bathroom while I was still in bed. She said good morning and bent down to kiss me, so I pulled her back into bed.

'You know, I'm a royalist as well,' she said. 'I'm a chef, and chefs have to be royalists, don't they?'

'Yes,' I replied, pulling the large towel from her body.

Micheline went to work and left me to sleep. When she came

back, I was in the bathroom taking a shower, singing Charles Aznavour's song 'Dans tes bras' with vigour. She started singing with me as she took off her clothes and got under the shower.

'I know Charles Aznavour personally,' said Micheline as we ate some wonderful French food she had brought from the restaurant. 'I was the personal chef of the pop singer Lionel Richie.'

'Wow, I like Lionel Richie a lot,' I told her.

'Me too,' said Micheline. 'I was his favourite chef for several years. Once, Charles Aznavour was one of Lionel Richie's guests and I was in charge of the cooking. Lionel Richie said to me, 'Micheline, please pay even more attention to the food than usual. Charles Aznavour is our guest. He's a stickler, he puts his nose into everything in the kitchen, big or small. Please, I don't want him to complain!' And when Aznavour came, he did indeed meddle in every detail concerning the food. He's very fussy and demanding.'

'Is Lionel Richie a nice man?' I asked Micheline.

'Very,' replied Micheline enthusiastically. Then she asked me whether I had contacted the translation company to tell them I wouldn't be going in. I told her that they were used to my habits. 'Don't forget that yesterday was *quatorze juillet*,' I reminded her.

'*Quatorze juillet*, that reminds me, we should go out and look for my dog. Perhaps we'll find him where I lost him.'

'In Place Saint-Sulpice?'

'Yes, near Catherine Deneuve's house, the actress, do you know about her?'

'Who doesn't know about Catherine Deneuve?'

'True. Yesterday you said something to me about the movies.'

'I'd like to be a film director.'

'Yes, I remember that.'

We went to the police station opposite Saint-Sulpice church and Micheline handed in details of her lost dog. Then we spent the afternoon wandering around the streets near the church. We drank a few glasses of white wine in a café in Rue Lobineau.

Then she told me she had to go back home and afterwards go to work. She suggested I go with her so that she could give me a spare house key.

'I have a feeling I've begun to fall in love with you,' she said.

'Me too,' I said.

Before she left for work, we went to bed. Then Micheline took a shower and went out. I got up and put a small table by the window overlooking Boulevard Saint-Germain. I brought the bottle of bourbon and began to drink. Since the apartment was immediately above the Old Navy Café, which I was forbidden to enter as a result of an argument with the café owner, I imagined myself sitting on the upstairs floor of the café to spite him.

So far as work was concerned, I still had no steady job. There was just a small company undertaking translation and publishing work, run by a Lebanese called Jean, who needed me occasionally for typesetting a few pages in Arabic. Luckily, a week before I met Micheline, Jean had told me he had signed a contract with a French company, well known in the arms manufacturing trade, to translate some catalogues of arms that the company had sold recently to a number of Gulf states. The Arab states were making it a condition that the catalogues should be in Arabic. Jean was happy that day, inviting me to have a few drinks with him as he gave me the news of the deal. He told me that he would need me 'for two months at least', then gave me a sum of money on account.

Before Micheline came back from work, the telephone rang. There was a young Frenchman on the line who asked for Micheline and said that on *quatorze juillet* he had been in a café with his girlfriend when a small dog had come up and sat beside them. When they left the café at dawn, they had taken the dog with them 'because we realised it was lost'. Then he explained that he had seen an American telephone number on its collar. He had called the number and a man speaking English with a French accent answered and told him that the dog belonged to his former wife who was now living in Paris. Then the man had given him Micheline's telephone number.

I thanked the young man, asked for his telephone number, and told him that as soon as Micheline came back from work she would call him.

'Didn't I tell you we would find him?' I shouted at the top of my voice as I lifted her up, along with the bags she was carrying.

'Be careful, be careful, there are bottles of white wine!' said Micheline, then stopped dead in her tracks. She stared at me. 'I can smell bourbon, please don't play games with me.'

'I'm not playing games, Micheline, we've found your dog.'

'Where? Did the police get in touch?'

I shook my head and told her the story. She took the telephone number and started to dial it, while I occupied myself with emptying the bags and putting the food and wine in the fridge.

'We have to celebrate this news,' Micheline shrieked. 'It's a big celebration!'

She had satisfied herself that the news was correct, and started dancing, hugging me and pulling me towards the bed. Before taking off our clothes, she asked me to open a bottle of white wine and leave it beside the bed.

I never did like Micheline's dog. It was ugly. She kissed it all the time. From the moment it was there with us, it started to annoy me. When Micheline was at home, it would bark the whole time in protest at my being there. When Micheline went to work and it was left with me, it never opened its mouth at all. It would disappear from my sight and hide away, in God only knows what corner of the apartment. It stayed there until suddenly it would run out, come up to me, look at me in an impudent way, and begin barking in my face. At that precise moment, the door would open and Micheline would come in.

Despite the petty arguments between us, the result of differences of temperament and mood, Micheline started to feel comfortable with me and buy me clothes, especially shirts with designer labels. She particularly liked the Agnes B brand. And because I had some experience of printing and publishing, she bought a computer and a colour printer.

She said that she was going to write a book about French cooking, that we would supervise the technical production of it together, and 'you can use the computer to write your script. It's better than a typewriter'.

We never missed a chance to go to bed. Before leaving home, when we returned, after a meal, after a shower. One day, on the way back from work, she said that she was inviting me to a fancy Mexican restaurant. In the restaurant she put to me the idea that 'we should live together permanently'.

'What do you think?' she asked.

'But we *are* together, Micheline,' I replied.

'True, but so far we haven't talked about some important details.'

'Let's leave it until another time,' I said offhandedly, clinking my glass against hers.

'As you wish,' she scowled.

This 'As you wish' didn't come from her heart, though. As soon as we had left the restaurant and taken a few steps, she started to shout, 'You all take advantage of my good nature in the same way. I take you out for a first-rate supper to talk about our relationship and all you can do is answer coldly, "Let's leave it until another time". What other time? Eh? Tell me. At the moment you just want to drink and fuck, isn't that the truth, you bum?'

She opened her eyes as wide as she could and stared at me as she said 'you bum'. I looked at her in astonishment.

'Naturally,' she said, 'I asked about you. They told me that you lived on movie fantasies and slept on the streets. Despite that, I put up with you, even inviting you to one of the best restaurants.'

She continued her tirade, which was attracting the attention of some passers-by, 'You all take advantage of me in the same way. My husband cheated on me with my closest friend while all the

149

time I was working for him.'

'And you were also fucking a young Mexican boy while your husband was taking his siesta. You told me the story yourself!'

'That's none of your business,' she said, then fell silent.

We walked on a few paces. She turned to me and said, 'Give me the key to the apartment please. Come tomorrow and get your things. I'm sorry, I'm not going back home now, I'm finishing my evening entertainment.'

I gave her the key as we stood there in the middle of the street. She went to finish off her evening in the bars of Rue Princesse. I headed for my favourite place, Au Chai de l'Abbaye, where I stayed drinking until two o'clock. A few minutes before the bar closed, Micheline came in and ordered a drink. Majid and Claude were astonished to see her standing beside me without talking to me.

I put my hand in my pocket and was about to pay my bill. I hesitated for a moment and thought of paying hers, but I was afraid of her reaction. I was conscious of the fact that I was wearing a shirt she had bought me. Who could guarantee that she wouldn't demand it back in front of the customers? I was in a dilemma.

A Japanese customer, a regular, was standing at the bar. He was an eccentric fellow. He would go for days refusing to speak to any of the other customers, then on another day he would come and talk to everyone. He had a habit, when he was talking to one customer, of withdrawing in the middle of a discussion and going to talk to another.

The Japanese man went up to Micheline and asked her if she'd like a drink. They started having a cheerful conversation and Micheline's loud laughter could be heard throughout the bar. I took the opportunity to slip out. Not for a moment did I think that she would follow me and actually lure me in so that I would end up seeing in the dawn in a police station.

At first I thought of getting away from the quarter, especially as the cafés that I drank in were all closed – Danton, Le Relais Odéon, Tennessee, Atlas, Bonaparte. I was reluctant to go to the Opera or Montparnasse quarters. I went to the Café Conti. It was only a few moments before Micheline came in, with her arms around the Japanese man.

She came up to me and said calmly, 'Take this key, please. Go and collect your things. My Japanese friend and I have decided to get married, and I don't want any hassle.'

'OK,' I said and took the key, while she began to kiss her Japanese boyfriend.

'Oh, my love, my Japanese love.'

Some customers were looking at us and smiling, some of them regulars who knew that she was supposed to be my girlfriend. As the apartment was only two hundred metres away from the Conti, I went at once and began to gather my things together. The dog looked at me from its corner, trembling. I smiled at it. It carried on panting and staring at me. Before putting the bottle of Jack Daniels in the bag, I thought of having a drink. Micheline wouldn't come back before five, or so I thought. But no sooner had I started to drink than the dog began to bark and Micheline came in with her Japanese friend. She patted the dog, then flew into a rage when she saw me sitting with the glass in my hand.

'My apartment's not a bar, do you understand?' She tried to snatch the glass from my hand, so I pushed her hard towards the sofa. The dog began to bark, and I saw the Japanese man undo his flies and go into the bathroom, shutting the door behind him.

'You hit me!' she shouted.

'You're a bitch,' I told her angrily, grabbing hold of her.

She took the telephone and dialled the police. She wouldn't let me leave the apartment until the policemen had arrived and she had told them that I was a violent man and was refusing to leave.

'You're a lying bitch, Micheline, and you know it,' I said as I left with the police. The Japanese man was still in the bathroom, and the dog seemed happy in her lap.

In the car, one policeman asked me, 'Did you buy a new dog?'

I looked at him in astonishment. He said that he had seen us when we came to the station to report the loss of the dog. I told him how we had found the 'ugly' dog. The policeman laughed. Then he told me politely that they were obliged to detain me until eight in the morning. I asked him whether it was possible to stay until eleven as I wanted to sleep a little.

'I don't think so,' said the policeman, adding, 'Actually, my shift ends at nine so I won't wake you before then.'

But the policeman and I had both forgotten that it was Sunday and the bells of Saint-Sulpice church wouldn't let anyone sleep.

After that incident, Micheline began to look for me in the bars and to call my office. Two or three days later, she found me sitting in Place Furstenberg. She told me she had been drunk and stupid and that she was sorry, and she blamed herself for her tactless behaviour.

Then she repeated her account of her hard time with her former husband. 'Oh, you don't know how cruel he was to me in that foreign country!'

She lit a cigarette and went on: 'I was a foreigner like you. America wasn't my country and I was afraid my husband would throw me onto the street and I'd become exactly like you, a vagabond or a refugee.' And she added, 'What does it mean for someone to become homeless? Any one of us could become homeless at any moment.'

She concluded, with a reference to the two famous cemeteries, 'There is no stability in this life except in Montparnasse or Père Lachaise.'

I listened, nodding.

'He would come at night and throw himself onto the bed and keep on snoring until morning. Of course I knew he was sleeping with the Mexican maids in the afternoon.'

'But, Micheline, you told me about your own adventures with the Mexicans as well!'

'One adventure, with a good-looking guy,' she said teasingly.

I remember, one evening we were lying on the bed and Micheline had told me this story: 'We had a large villa about seven kilometres away from the restaurant. My husband preferred to take his siesta at the restaurant, while I would go home as soon as lunch was over. Until, that is, the young man who worked as a dishwasher told me that my husband used to stay at the restaurant in order to spend his siesta sleeping with the waitresses. I broached the subject with him and we argued about it a lot, but to no avail. I had to do the same, in the end, I'm not stupid. Especially as I knew that the dishwasher, who was a strapping young man, dreamed, like any Mexican, of sleeping with blonde women. I used to notice his glances in my direction as he worked in the kitchen.

'One day, I went up to the young man, told him I had left the car trunk open and asked him to get inside it, then shut it behind him. After work I opened the trunk and found the young man stretched out, dripping with sweat. I closed it again and headed home, where we, too, began to take a siesta every afternoon. After a bit, my husband found out, fired the young man and began to keep watch on me until he turned my life into hell.'

I agreed to go back to Micheline to get away from the hell of the street. The period I had spent with her, as a resident of Boulevard Saint-Germain, was a happy one. It helped me escape from the vagabond life I had led for nearly ten years. I had persuaded myself that the best way of staying with her was to go out every morning as if I was an employee going off to work, and to come back in the evening to spend time with her like any couple.

But this plan only worked for a few days. I began to pine for the streets and cafés again, and drinking with friends. Whenever I went to meet friends, Micheline would end up spending the evening with us. She'd search every café until she found me. Sometimes she made trouble between me and my friends, and on many occasions she said to me, 'You go home, I'll follow later.' We had several arguments, and I had to leave the apartment more than once, but then we'd make up and I'd go back.

One morning, an official holiday, the sun had been slipping through our window since the early hours of dawn. I woke up in a cheerful mood and began to caress Micheline, who was rousing slowly, responding to my caresses with a considerable appetite. Afterwards, I suggested to her that we should go spend the day at Versailles.

'Aren't we royalists, after all?' I asked her.

'Wonderful,' she said. 'To Versailles. That would be really nice.'

We made an assortment of sandwiches, and I took two bottles of Muscadet from the fridge. Then we took the train to Versailles. We wandered around among hundreds of tourists. I took lots of pictures of Micheline at the palace gate, in the fascinating palace grounds, then Micheline asked a Japanese tourist to take a picture of us together wearing sunglasses. And we found a cosy spot under a tree where we finished off the sandwiches and Muscadet and lay down.

When sunset approached, I said to Micheline, 'I'll hire a rowing boat so we can spend the sunset on the lake.' Micheline smiled and seemed very happy.

'You'll see the strength of my arms,' I added, making rowing motions.

No sooner had we got into the boat than Micheline, looking left and right, said, 'But almost everyone has gone.'

'The tourists like to look at the rooms inside the palace,' I replied.

'The place is so beautiful,' said Micheline in a gentle voice. 'Imagine, after all these years the Palace of Versailles is still like paradise. Admittedly, at the time of Louis XVI, it was far better.'

I nodded in agreement.

'You're right, I feel proud to be a royalist,' she said, massaging my outstretched feet between hers. Micheline was talking as I guided the boat towards the far end of the lake, to a place where overgrown trees touched the water, until we were in a secluded, almost completely shaded spot.

I started to look left and right, then at Micheline, smiling. She got her camera out and took a picture of me.

'Why don't you speak?' she asked.

I was smiling as I looked into her eyes for a moment, then at my own arms as they worked the oars in the water of Lake Versailles in that enticing sunset.

'Won't you say something?'

I looked left and right and pulled on the oars vigorously to steer the boat into an even more shaded area.

'Say something,' said Micheline loudly.

I didn't reply, but continued to stare at her.

'What are you thinking about? Come on, what are you thinking about? Say something, please! Tell me what's going round in your head!'

I looked into her eyes and said nothing.

She took out a cigarette and began smoking. 'But say something! Come on, what are you thinking about, come on, tell me what you're thinking about.'

'I'm thinking about Hitchcock, I'm thinking about a movie of Hitchcock's, Micheline.'

She looked at me and said in a pleading tone, 'No, that's not true. That's not what you're thinking. But you did tell me you wanted to be a film director, didn't you?' Micheline began to look left and right, while her face turned completely red. I felt that she was about to lose her power of speech completely. Finally, she said, 'Don't scare me, please, you're too nice.'

'You too,' I said to her, smiling, then asked her to light me a cigarette.

'Right away,' she said, sighing. She lit the cigarette and added, 'Now it's my turn to row.'

She began to row quickly. 'Don't you think that we'd better go back?' she said, out of breath.

I nodded agreement.

She rowed like mad – as if she were trying to escape drowning. I was smoking my cigarette and looking at her. A big smile came over her face whenever our eyes met. When we reached the jetty, Micheline became confused. 'I have to go home quickly, yes, quickly, I'm very tired,' she said.

We didn't talk at all on the train. Micheline quickly opened the door to the apartment. She made for the telephone, which she carried into the room overlooking the street. She shut the door from the inside and spoke to me through the large glass window that separated the two rooms.

'Please take your things and leave me to myself. Our relationship is over, over, over.'

'*Au revoir*, Micheline.'

I took my things and went out, without hearing any reply.

That night I wandered from café to café and carried on drinking until dawn, without Micheline appearing. She didn't appear the following day either, or the next one. I didn't see her for more than a month, and then one day I heard she had left Paris and gone off with a Moroccan dishwasher, who had been working with her, to another city where she had decided to open a restaurant of her own.

16

Riadh was right somehow when he once told me, 'When you have a wife and a home and a car you will see the real faces of those you call friends.'

When I was with Micheline some friends criticised me, 'We

didn't expect you'd end up with that cook.' Or they said, 'All these years of adventures and you end up with a woman who considers you and her dog as the same kind of thing.'

When my relation with her ended it seemed they celebrated my going back to the streets. They invited me here and there every day for a few days until I found myself alone on the street once more.

Other friends blamed me for not being clever enough. 'Even if you don't love her, you should stay with her until you have better luck, and then abandon her,' they used to tell me, without realising that I was a romantic dreamer.

But I have to admit that after those quiet days with Micheline, I started seriously wanting a place of my own. I was no longer that adventurous child who gave his kite more and more line; the kite was now in front of me smashed up.

I was feeling exactly the same as when I read Scott Fitzgerald's story 'Babylon Revisited', and I realised now it was not by accident that I had been reading it again and again. I see now in front of me Scott Fitzgerald standing at the bar of the Ritz Hotel, drinking whisky, and psychologically completely destroyed.

'The fairy tales are over, and it's not possible to postpone the pain. You have to face the punishment,' I said to myself, and decided to escape from Paris.

Jean-Claude Ming encouraged me to leave. 'Don't worry. Leave Saint Germain-des-Prés and go and live in Saint-Germain Lès Arpajon.' He laughed and added, 'Fabian's house is a very quiet place in the countryside, and I will visit you from time to time. I'm like your brother, so listen to me.' We were at the Café Saint-Claude. 'I can borrow some money for you from Madame Beatrice,' said Ming.

I had met Jean-Claude Ming for the first time a few years ago in this same bar. He had invited me for a beer without knowing me. 'I'm happy. I want to treat you. And don't think I'm gay.'

He was drinking and keeping an eye on his paintings that were hung on the railings of the Saint-Germain Church. He saw a lady stop to look at his work and ran out quickly. After a few minutes he returned. 'She was an Australian tourist and bought two drawings of Place Furstenberg.'

He looked at me. 'You see, I just made 600 francs. I can sleep a few days in a hotel with that.'

From that day we became friends, and from time to time I used to sell his paintings for him, but that's another story.

★ ★ ★

'Lucie! Lucie! Where are you? Come here, Lucie!' The neighbour, in her seventies, was calling from her garden.

'*Bonjour, madame!*' I said, holding my bag and my typewriter and standing in the front garden of Fabian's house, as we called it. The old lady went into her house without replying.

Fabian's house was a small abandoned bungalow consisting of two rooms, one big one small, and a small kitchen straight inside the front door that was full of large empty plastic containers, two jerrycans, a big tin bath, and in one corner an old fridge with a broken door that wouldn't shut.

'Lucie! Lucie! Where are you, Lucie?'

I was sorting out my things in the kitchen and could hear the neighbour shouting again. At that moment I saw a little white cat sitting inside the abandoned fridge, eyeing me warily.

'Are you Lucie?' I asked her. As I bent down to stroke her, she ran off out the door.

I went and stood outside the bungalow, looking at the huge foul-smelling back garden.

'Is Monsieur Propre★ here?'

I smiled as I remembered what the children of my friends used to call me when I stayed with them and gave their wives a help-

★ Monsieur Propre is 'Mr Clean', a cleaning product. It is also an abbreviation for 'the owner', *le propriétaire*.

158

ing hand to clean the bathroom or the kitchen: Monsieur Propre. One friend said that every time I visited them the kids would ask her afterwards if she had bought a new shower, or taps or kitchen sink because they sparkled and shone so brightly.

'So, Monsieur Propre, why don't you clean your own home, now that you have one?' I said to myself.

I went to the supermarket, walking the two kilometres, and bought food and cleaning stuff and boxes of candles. I was very lucky that there were some gypsies living only 400 metres away, and they agreed that I could take water any time from the irrigation water tap that stood near their caravans.

'Take as much water as you like, but don't touch any of our produce, and don't disturb our land,' they said.

For one week I worked really hard; I cleaned up the garden around the house, cleaned out the stinking toilet hut that stood in the middle of the back garden, where much of the foul smell was coming from, and filled in a disused well that I discovered was the other cause of the disgusting putrid stink. It seems all this earned me the old lady's respect, as she finally said to me at the end of the week, '*Bonjour, monsieur!*'

I turned round and Grandma, as I called her later, was leaning on the metal fence between our two gardens.

'*Bonjour, madame!*'

'Do you want some eggs!' she asked.

'*Merci, madame,*' I answered.

'What do you mean by "*merci*" – you want or you don't want?'

'Oh, madame, yes, I would like some eggs. You are very kind, madame.'

She brought me a handful of eggs and passed them over the fence, saying, 'They're from my chickens.' Her dog ran round the back, and, after a few seconds, was with me, playing with my feet and then going to sniff the typewriter.

'Oh, he wants to type,' she laughed. 'My animals like you.'

She told me that there had been some squatters in the house

before me. 'They were very dirty,' she said, 'and they stole some of my chickens.'

Next day, I cut back all the branches of an overgrown plum tree that were overhanging her garden and had left the ground strewn with squashed, rotten plums.

'You really are a nice boy!'

'Grandma, I am Monsieur Propre!'

She laughed, and I suggested cutting back the plum tree in her garden that was making the same mess on her garage roof. I was up the tree on a small ladder, and she was holding it still when I had to tell her, 'Sorry, Grandma, I'll be back in a minute!' I ran off and came back quickly. After three or four more minutes, the same thing. 'Oh, sorry, I have to go again.' And that happened several times.

'What's up with you, son?'

' Er. . . er. . . I'm writing a book, and each time a new idea comes to me, I have to go and write it down.'

'Why don't you put a notebook in your pocket?'

'Well, er . . . I type it directly onto the typewriter.'

Again, I had to come down quickly. 'Another idea has come to me, Grandma.'

'Have you been eating plums?' she asked me when I came back.

'Yes.'

'How many?'

'Too many!'

And she started laughing. 'That's what's making you go to the toilet all the time, son!'

I looked at her. 'I'm sorry, I was too embarrassed to tell you.'

After two or three hours daily weeding, I used to make a fire outside in the front garden. I heated water and filled the tin bath in the kitchen, and sat in it, soaping myself all over. The tin bath was exactly like the one I had sat in as a child with my mother washing me. Now I was forty years old. It was a strange moment. After my bath I cooked spaghetti over the fire – it was either spaghetti or potatoes.

And that afternoon, I put all the pages I had written till then into the fire.

I was very enthusiastic about this, telling myself, 'I will write something completely new and different. I want to start from the beginning. I want to write a book about a man who wants to write about his father and who finds in the end he is writing about himself.'

I started writing a story I was calling 'The Street Vendor and the Movies'.

One morning I woke to hear someone opening the wrought-iron gates of the front garden – that is, uncoiling the long metal chain that I had wound round the bars of the two gates to keep them shut. I looked out of the window and saw Jean-Claude Ming.

'I'm jealous! You're enjoying your holiday while I'm spending all day in Boulevard Saint-German with nobody buying my drawings.'

Ming brought with him some tins of food, some noodles and two bottles of Côtes du Rhône. He took a small radio from his pocket that he said he would leave with me.

'And because I don't want you to forget about Hollywood, here's my present to you!' he said as he opened a large bag and took out a piece of strong cardboard.

It was a cut-out of Marilyn Monroe down to her chest, with a hand attached that moved to wave to the crowds. I placed her right away over one of the many broken panes of my bedroom window. 'When Marilyn Monroe waves to you, that will mean it's windy outside,' said Ming. From that day I always opened my eyes to Marilyn Monroe.

When Ming left, the grandmother told me, 'I've seen him before. I remember him because he used to play his radio all the time.'

She was right, Ming couldn't live without the radio, he played it wherever he was, day and night. At night, he listened to comedy programmes. I used to see him sleeping and laughing, and once when I turned the radio off, thinking he was asleep, he immediately shouted, 'Leave it! I'm listening!'

'Where is he from?' asked Grandma.

'He's half-Vietnamese and half-French. His father was a French officer. He's a good artist. He sells his drawings on the streets. He doesn't have a house. He lives in hotels, and, when he doesn't sell anything, on the streets.'

Ming had been an art teacher in a secondary school in Marseilles, but always dreamed of living in Paris. When I asked him once about his family, he told me, 'They don't like to see me. They don't like my life. They think I've brought shame on them.'

It was a hot day when I opened my eyes and saw a snake on the floor looking up at me. It was nearly a metre long. I was so scared I couldn't move. I snatched an empty beer bottle that was by my head and threw it. The snake slithered off into the other room as I asked myself whether it hadn't followed me from my childhood – just the day before I had been writing a chapter about the snake I killed when I was a little boy. From that day I couldn't sleep naked. I had to wear socks and all my clothes, and cover myself with blankets in spite of the heat, exactly as in my childhood. In fact, the most difficult moment for me was when I wanted to go to the toilet in the garden, and I opened the wooden door with a stick and looked down the hole in the ground to see if the snake was hiding there. I had to go to the toilet standing up, trembling, expecting it to jump on me at any moment. This snake was tormenting me.

After two or three weeks of this, I walked one kilometre up the road to a truck repair garage, assuming that they must have a toilet. '*Pas de problème*, no problem, monsieur,' the manager replied when I told him where I lived and the story of the snake and asked whether I could use their toilet.

Once, when I was in the toilet, I heard two mechanics talking.

One said to the other, 'Can you imagine, that American drifter has left his country and come to live in our little village. Very strange, isn't it?'

I laughed to myself, 'They think I'm American. It must be because of my accent.' So I started deliberately making my accent sound more American. Once I even said to them, 'Ah, New York is a boring city. I love this village.'

I also remember hearing the manager telling some of the mechanics, 'Our friend, the American drifter, is scared to use his own toilet because there's a snake and he thinks it's going to jump up his arse!' They all started laughing, and when they saw me coming out, tried to stop themselves and pretend they were working.

I sat in the garden every day, typing my new book very enthusiastically and happily until my food ran out. No more spaghetti, no potatoes. No sugar, no bread. I finished the plums and even the sour green grapes from the vine in the garden. Then I remembered that from the window of the repair garage toilet I had seen a big field of corn. The moon was full that evening when I filled my pillowcase with some ripe corn cobs. I remembered Kevin Costner in the movie *Field of Dreams*, and I kept quiet for a while. Maybe I would hear that voice saying, 'If you build it, he will come'. Alas, I kept eating from that field until it was harvested, but I never heard any voice.

I was in the garden drinking red wine and frying minced meat with onions and garlic and spices, trying to make spaghetti the proper way. 'What a lovely smell,' Grandma said, leaning over the fence.

'I would be very happy if you joined me, Grandma.'

'What is the occasion?'

'I'll tell you later.'

She looked at the sky. 'OK, but I need to get my sweater. Do you have plates?'

'No decent ones, really.'

'I'll bring some nice plates and glasses.'

We sat round the table, which was a thick plank sawn from a massive tree trunk.

'How's your writing going?'

'Very well. I've nearly finished a story called "The Street Vendor and the Movies".'

'Very good.'

We started to eat, and she asked me where I learned to cook 'because it's delicious' and then asked me whether we ate spaghetti in my country.

'Well, Grandma, we sometimes ate macaroni.'

After a moment's silence, she said, 'You're a nice boy. May I ask what your religion is?'

I looked at her and told her, 'I'm forty years old, Grandma. I have lived a very difficult life. I have known many nice people in my life and my best friends have different religions and when I'm with any one of them I feel I share with them the same religion.'

She smiled, and I added, 'My mother used to tell me I am like a tomato.'

'Why a tomato?' she exclaimed, laughing.

'I think my mother meant that I was soft, and that I could also roll with the days.'

Again the grandmother laughed, 'But you haven't told me the reason for this feast!'

'I think God loves me, Grandma!' I said, and continued: 'For three days I didn't have anything to eat at all, and wanted to go back to Paris, but I told myself I must stay to finish my book. One day I took the spade and went to work in the garden, and after two hours of digging do you know what I found, Grandma?'

'What did you find?' she asked.

'I found some gold teeth. So I took them to Paris and sold them.'

The grandmother laughed and laughed, 'It's my dog! It's my dog who loves you very much.' She took a sip of wine and started laughing again. 'I spent such a long time looking for those teeth, which it seems my dog buried in your garden!'

A few days later I came back from my usual trip to the repair garage to find a fair-haired man in his thirties wearing big army boots sitting in my chair in the garden. He was unkempt and dirty and swigging wine from a bottle.

'It's a very clean house now!'

'Who are you?'

'I used to live here. I know Fabian.'

'But I live here now, *monsieur*. You don't have the right to come in here.'

'My name is Raymond and I'm French.'

'Well, Monsieur Raymond, you have to leave now.'

'I will go to the police, you foreigner!'

'You can do that. They know I'm living here, and I am supported by the neighbours. Even my post comes here. Please leave now.'

'OK, I will leave now, but you'll see . . .' said Raymond, as he got up and went, giving me a venomous look.

From that day, I was unable to enjoy listening to music by candlelight as I usually did, I had to turn off the radio and listen for noises outside. I lit only one candle and kept looking through the window where Marilyn Monroe was watching me and waving. I was wondering when this Raymond would come back and attack me when I heard the grandmother's dog barking and, a few moments later, the chains on the front gates rattle. I went out to find Raymond and two other guys, smoking and drinking.

'Ahhh . . . you're still awake . . .' he shouted. 'We're not going to let you sleep! See you later . . .'

They went off, and I stayed awake the rest of the night. I looked at the shovel that was near my bed in case the snake came back. Now it was for Raymond as well. As I am not a good fighter, I started imagining a fight with these guys. I struck Raymond with the shovel, and his head spun off and smashed on the ground; I hit another and split his guts open; I hit the third I don't know where. And then I stared in disbelief at the massacre. I even imagined burying them in the garden.

When I opened my eyes in the morning, I found I had fallen asleep completely uncovered. Marilyn Monroe was waving at me.

Raymond and his gang made my life in Fabian's house hell. (It could have been the subject for a book.) They started coming every night, smashing empty bottles on the concrete path and throwing them onto the roof. They threw stones at the windows. I thought they might come during the day, too, and I changed my usual typing position out in the garden so that I faced the front gates instead of having my back to the road.

I finished writing the manuscript of 'The Street Vendor and the Movies' – and used up all my money – by the beginning of October. I went to the railway station to telephone my friends.

On my way back, I was thinking that the right thing to do would be to leave Fabian's house the next day, without knowing I was to leave that same day.

I found my typewriter thrown on the floor in the kitchen, its keys smashed, with bits of broken bottle inside it and wine spilled everywhere. I looked in the bedroom; the two jerrycans of water had been poured over the bed and the blankets were torn. My posters and photos were ripped from the walls and lay trampled on the floor. Marilyn Monroe had gone from the window. My papers, my manuscript, were gone. My clothes were ripped and soaked in wine and what smelled like piss.

'You're lucky you weren't there. There were four of them. They are very dangerous men!' said Grandma when she saw me in the garden.

'Grandma, I'm just a man without a house. I'm not looking for trouble. I'm going back to Paris.'

After an hour of shock, trying to think what to do, I started looking for my manuscript, but I found nothing. I decided I had to leave that very minute.

'I have nothing now. My manuscript has gone. My Erika is gone.' This was the first time I was without my bag and type-writer.

'Lucie! Lucie!' Grandma was calling outside.

Then I heard 'Miaow! Miaow!' coming from my kitchen. 'Miaow! Miaow!'

The sound was coming from the old fridge in the corner. I looked inside and there I found the cut-out of Marilyn Monroe and my manuscript, but no Lucie. I took them quickly and left.

When I turned to look back and wave to Grandma, she was standing there with Lucie in her arms.

17

He sat with his back to the engine.
He exhaled his cigarette smoke.
He saw the smoke melting into the window,
things flashing past,
the speed of the train,
and the rain.
Oh, to how many years do his eyes bid farewell now
while his shoulders cleave the wind not knowing.

A hand touched my left shoulder and I turned to see a man in his seventies, his white hair combed back, smiling, a cigarette between his wine-stained lips. I realised he was asking me to light it for him. We exchanged smiles. He looked like my father. I wanted to talk to him to see if he could speak. I was sitting on the top deck of the train, smoking and watching the forest we were passing through. The hand touched me again on the same shoulder and I turned again to see the man, his hand stretched out holding an apple that was green and as large as a tennis ball. He gestured with his head for me to take it. I took the apple and the man smiled and left the compartment.

And when the train stopped at the next station I glanced through the window. I saw a white bird lying dead at the foot of a tree. I stared at it for a while, and started rolling the apple around in my hands until the train moved off. A few moments later I saw a white bird flying, little by little approaching my window as if it wanted to touch it. Then it flew away.

PART THREE

The Street Vendor
and the Movies

A Story of Childhood
dedicated to the memory of John Ford

*The dialogue in the following pages includes many titles of movies,
mainly by John Ford, which are in italics.*

Summer was salt,
winter was a sandwich
and I was a kid in love with the movies.
My days were short scenarios
full of dreams
I was flying, flying, flying
and didn't know that life is a long American movie.

That evening, as I left the cinema, sadness was gnawing at my little heart and my eyes were brimming with tears. I turned into a dark and narrow alleyway and kicked with my gym shoes at every stone and bit of dirt in my path, crying out in rage, 'How can the hero die? How can the hero die?'

Despite being just eight years old, I knew that this was only a 'cinematic' death, just as I knew what 'director' and 'scriptwriter' meant, because Kiryakos had taught me the ABC of the film industry, making me learn the real names of the Hollywood stars, their dates of birth and many anecdotes about their lives. He would read to me from American film magazines, which I'd leaf through for hours then ask, 'Where do you get all these magazines, Kiryakos?' And he'd smile and reply, '*Air Mail.*' I think it's fair to say that, right from the start, I learned a lot from what Kiryakos used to read me.

One afternoon, Rafiq al-Hindi, the manager of the al-Habbaniyah cinema, stopped me and asked me jokingly, 'Hey, Joey, do you know John Wayne's real name?' 'Of course I do,' I replied immediately, 'Marion Michael Morrison, and his friends call him Duke.' I didn't stop there but went on to explain how John Wayne became an actor: 'John Wayne was working in the studio as a wardrobe assistant when he was approached by the great director John Ford who put the storyline for a new movie into his hands, saying, "Hey, Morrison, read this and let me know who you think would be right for the leading role." A few days later John Wayne came back scratching his head. "Mr Ford," he said, "truly I can't think of anyone more suitable than Lloyd

171

Nolan." At that John Ford gave a sarcastic laugh and said, "What a fool you are! Truth is it's you who's going to play the part".'

Rafiq al-Hindi laughed and, raising his hand to his forehead to shield his eyes from the sun, said, 'You can come to the movies free for three days.' Before he had gone far I heard him say, 'But you didn't tell me the name of that movie.' '*Stagecoach*,' I shouted back, glancing down to look at the checks on my shirt just as Kiryakos did.

When I reached the main road, my sadness was still painful, almost taking my breath away. 'How can the hero die?' I took up a large pebble and aimed it at a street light where hundreds of bugs were fluttering around the glowing aureole; one shot and the area of shadow expanded as the bugs scattered away to other sources of light.

It didn't occur to me that it would be my mother who would make me forget the 'hero's death'. As soon as I got home she pounced on me and began attacking me mercilessly, leaving teeth marks on my arms and shoulders and screaming out, 'Son of a bitch, are you a son of the movies or my son?' Kiryakos, who was drinking tea and toying with an apple, commented, 'Joey was born, *My Darling Clementine*, to be a film-maker.' At the same time Ali, the son of Nasrat Shah, told her, 'Joey works all day and asks for nothing save the price of a movie ticket, what more can you ask of him than that?'

At that moment I looked at my mother and saw a deep feeling of self-reproach in her eyes. 'I know he helps us,' she said, 'but he's beginning to grow up and still hasn't registered at school,' and she turned to Kiryakos and Ali who were sitting in the doorway under the light of a lantern, then added sadly, 'That's what hurts me. And you both know that his father doesn't bother himself with such things.'

Kiryakos, with no thought for the neighbours sleeping on the roofs of their houses, let out a great sequence of guffaws. 'My dear sister Gorgiya, you can be as sad as you please but not about what will happen to Joey,' he told her. Then, casting a glance at the darkness of the nearby alleyway, he added, 'Your son will grow up, he'll go to Hollywood and we'll see him here on the screens of al-Habbaniyah's cinema.' Shaking his head and still playing with the apple, he turned to me and said, 'I'm certain of it, absolutely.'

I was sitting on the dirt floor spitting into the palms of my hands and wiping them over the marks my mother's teeth had left on my body, then blowing on them in an attempt to calm the burning caused by the hot weather and the sweat running from my limbs. The whole time I don't think I once took my eyes off Kiryakos's apple, green and the size of a tennis ball; I was longing to eat it, and had I done so it might have made me forget my pains.

My mother turned to me and said, 'Off you go, son. Go to the bar and grab your deaf-mute father before he spends all his weekly wages.'

'He's a working man,' said Ali.

'*Strong Boy*,' observed Kiryakos.

'But I don't see him much,' said my mother.

I could hear them talking as sadly, very sadly, I left the house.

Entering the bar amidst the noise and the smoke, I went to stand in front of my father. He was drinking with Youshiya the grocer, from whom my mother would borrow money on those mornings when she found my father's pockets empty. I didn't know what to say.

My father noticed my sadness and hugged me to his chest, ruffling the hair that was covering my forehead and eyes and asking me with a wave of his hand, 'What's up?'

Wiping away my tears, I raised my right arm, showing off my muscles, brought my right hand close to my eyes and shook it right and left, then put my palms together and rested my head against them. My father understood I was referring to the death of the hero in the film; he gave me a playful smack on the backside and started searching among the large beer bottles stacked on the table until he came across one less than half full, handing it to me and indicating that I should knock it back in one go. I gulped the lager down, looking at him as he directed a challenging gaze at me. When I finished the bottle he clapped in approval, putting his thumb in his mouth and pulling it out again quickly with a sound like the popping of a champagne cork. At that moment I completely forgot the 'hero's death' as I searched among the beer bottles and drank their contents, one after the other. My father alternated guffaws with glances of admiration as Youshiya the grocer, clearly perplexed, shifted his cunning eyes first to my father, then to me.

As the two of us left the bar we felt obliged to play our favourite game, or rather my father's favourite game, peeing as you walk. He looked around and, when he was certain there was no one about, gave the signal to begin. Each of us pulled out our dicks and began to walk and pee, the winner being whoever could pee for the longest distance while drawing a line, preferably straight. A few seconds into the race I sensed I was walking alone and, turning around, saw my father about twenty metres away. I was flooded with joy because it was the first time I had won. It also confirmed the truth of what my big brother Samson used to say about his constant victories being 'all thanks to the beer'.

However, my joy quickly turned to amazement as I saw my father, dick in hand, turning round and round in circles as he peed. I zipped up my trousers and approached slowly, gazing at the concentric rings he was drawing on the asphalt. Puzzled and turning my head from right to left, I thought at first they were just random circles, but after a few moments I found they looked something like a rose.

I gazed at him, then bunched the fingers of my left hand and brought them to my nose. I drew a deep breath and opened my eyes greedily and asked him with a smile, 'Is it a rose?'

He shook his head by way of negation as he buttoned his trousers, then drew me by the hand to the streetlight, where he stood me in such a way that my shadow fell on the asphalt like a guard to the right of the 'circles', while he stood making his shadow a guard on the left. Then he told me to imitate an animal, craning his neck, opening his mouth as wide as he could, stretching out his open hand and shaking it right and left. I understood he meant the lion that appears at the beginning of MGM films, and so we stood there like a pair of lions guarding the circles he had drawn. He asked me if I understood the *mise-en-scène* and I nodded, grabbing his left arm where a green tattoo depicted the lion and the unicorn guarding the crown of Great Britain.

I remembered all the times I had heard my mother say scornfully whenever my father annoyed her, 'Fool! In love with a woman who wouldn't employ him to clean her toilet.'

The warm June breeze erased most of the traces of the 'crown' my father had drawn, to the point that it now looked like four sardines sleeping on the asphalt.

Panting, my father slipped in next to my mother who, turned her back on him, said, '*Iman shakilly alaha, lebaiyan metan min rikhit ouwa lala.* When God takes me, I don't want to die from the stench of this deaf-mute.'

In the meantime, I found a place for myself between my sister Shamiran (the Kim Novak of Iraq, as Kiryakos called her) and my little brother Robin, and stared up at the clear sky of al-Habbaniyah. I put my hands to my chest and said humbly, 'O Lord. O Christ. I swear that all I want to be is a film-maker.' Before closing my eyes I realised I'd forgotten something, so I added, 'O Lord. O Christ. I swear I'll never eat apples.'

With that I closed my eyes and turned onto my left side. At that moment, Shamiran reached out her arm in her sleep and covered my shoulders. I smelled her sweet odour and remembered how she had once asked me, 'What do you think of my perfume, baby brother?' That day I'd drawn a deep breath which added two inches to my height and replied, 'It's great, like the movies.'

The sun hadn't yet risen when the three-fingered hand stretched out and roused me from my slumber. I rubbed my eyes with the back of my hands and smiled broadly, which surprised the three-fingered man who was standing by my head. Nasrat Shah was surprised because he knew, if his memory served him correctly (in fact he rubbed his forehead for a few seconds), that he'd woken me at daybreak more than four hundred times before, and I had never once smiled. Indeed, he was often obliged to stretch out his three fingers to hoist me from my bed and stand me on my feet, repeating, 'The sun will get hot and we'll lose the salt', and I would answer him while looking at the sky, 'But the sun isn't up yet.'

I had been in a great vineyard full of bunches of red grapes growing in a red lake. The water of the lake was boiling and sending up clouds of red vapour. Hanging from one of the vine shoots and trying to cross the lake towards dry land, I reached out with my right hand to grasp a bunch when suddenly a long shiny sword appeared, cutting through the branches which spouted hot blood, and crying out 'Ah!' I was forced to grasp another bunch with my other hand, and again the sword appeared like lightning and cut through the branches. I reached out my right hand and again the sword appeared, and so it went on until exhaustion overcame me and I began to cry. I could see the bubbles in the boiling lake rising and almost touching my skinny body.

It was at that moment that Nasrat Shah extended his three fingered left hand, removing me from the vineyard of red grapes and causing me, for the very first time, to wake with a smile on my face. And of course it didn't occur to me to ask Kiryakos about the meaning of my dream because I knew he would just say '*The Grapes of Wrath*'.

Nasrat Shah rested the wooden ladder against the wall of the house and climbed up, leaning his weight on his lame left foot, to rouse his two sons Ali and Hussein, while I went to wake my father, tapping my left wrist with my right finger: 'It's time for work'. He rubbed his forehead with his hand, feeling the effects of the night before, then aimed a sudden playful kick at my backside, his cackles shattering the peace of the dawn.

My mother opened her eyes and looked at him, tapping her finger to her forehead and blowing into her hand, 'You're a fool!'

My father renewed his cackles, bending over to kiss her head and slipping a few coins under her pillow, but she, well aware that he'd spent most of his wages in the bar, pulled the coins out and, without counting them, flung them into the air. My father gave her a kick on the backside and grabbed the water bucket, jokingly threatening to throw it over her.

'*Ishkulli alaha, ishkulli!* Take me, my Lord, take me!' she cried, burying her face in the pillow, at which my father took a handful of water from the bucket and sprinkled it over her bare legs. She looked at him angrily through her half-closed eyes, but he pretended not to notice and blew her a kiss as he left for the bakery. My father was fifty-eight, my mother thirty-three, and he played with her just as he played with us.

We followed the road that runs up by the chain of hills on the left bank of al-Habbaniyah river, then continued down towards the salt marshes. Ali looked at the sun, which had begun to send out its first rays, and said, 'We've got lots of time.'

'But your father never stops saying, "The sun will get hot, the sun will get hot",' I replied without thinking.

'You're right, Joey,' said Ali with a smile, 'and my father's also right.' Then he added, 'You're growing up, Joey, and you know now how much salt we need to keep the ice from the summer sun.'

I nodded to show I understood, then removed my gym shoes and threw them to one side. Rolling up my shirt sleeves and the bottom of my trousers, I went down to the salt marsh. My skinny legs broke the solid crust of salt lying on the surface of the water like sandy glass. I thrust my yellow sieve deep into the water and, after a few moments, drew it out, examining the water as it ran away through the holes, now white with shiny salt crystals. Hussein looked at Ali as they too made their way into the salty water and said, 'I know the secret of that little rascal's energy today.'

'What's up, Joey?' asked Ali.

I was bent over, with my sieve immersed in the water, waiting to fill it with salt. I looked at Ali, closing my left eye against the sun which had begun to appear behind the hills, and said happily, 'Your father has promised to register me at school for next year.'

'That's great, you're smart and should go to school,' said Ali.

'I know,' I said, my attention focused on my work, 'All my friends are at school except me. I want to learn to read and write so I can make films.'

'That's good,' said Hussein, then asked me jokingly, 'What year are we in, Joey?'

'One thousand nine hundred and sixty-four,' I replied happily, 'and in the year one thousand nine hundred and sixty-five I shall go to school.'

With the back of my hand I pushed my long hair away from my face and saw they were laughing. The sun was burning my sweat-drenched face, and I licked my lips and the corners of my salty mouth and spat away from the swamp.

'Hey, Joey, listen. What you said is right but you must know that you'll be going to school this year,' said Ali.

'I don't know,' I said nonchalantly. 'It was your father who told me it would be next year.'

'He was talking about the next academic year. For example, we're now in June and the school year will come to an end in a few days' time. That's followed by a three-month holiday and in September a new academic year begins, even though we're still in 1964. Got it?'

I said nothing.

Three sieves were being pushed into the depths of the swamp, drawing out the salt which little by little was piled into little crystalline hills that sparkled in the burning sunlight. From time to time, Ali, Hussein and I would exchange cheerful glances, and when Ali noticed how the salt was piling up he'd ask me to begin loading it into the sacks.

We placed the sacks on our bicycles and went down the road on foot, leaving the sun hanging in the blue sky at our backs. Drops of water trickled from the sacks onto the hot asphalt, which became white with salt crystals. Ali had a sack on the front of his bicycle, while Hussein had one sack at the front and half a sack at the rear under my control. As we drew close to the cemetery next to the river, I saw a cart being driven by an old man wearing a kaffiyeh. He seemed sad. Seated behind him was a young woman with her two children . . .

In a matter of moments the image presented itself to me, from the movie *Mother of India*, of the hero Birju entering the house of the old moneylender Sukhilala and violently taking back his mother's jewels, which the moneylender had appropriated when Birju was a child. Birju also carries off the moneylender's beautiful daughter and, putting the jewels in his cloak and the girl on a horse, off he goes. However, before he can leave the village he comes across his mother lying in wait and pointing a rifle at him. She demands he take the girl back home because 'an Indian mother cherishes moral values and doesn't approve of offending other people's honour'. But Birju cannot be convinced and with his horse goes on his way. His mother cries 'Birjuuuuuuu . . .' as she presses the trigger of the rifle (bang!). Birju returns, soaked in blood, to fall from his horse at his mother's feet. He draws the jewels from his cloak and tells her that while still a child he had sworn to restore her jewels and take revenge on the moneylender. The 'hero' falls to the ground dead and the mother weeps while the moneylender's daughter and the horse contemplate the heart-rending scene . . .

The soldier guarding the checkpoint laughed as he opened the great iron gate leading to the town. When he saw the tears on my cheeks he said sarcastically, 'Were you gathering salt or peeling onions, Joey?'

I wiped away my tears and tried to get close to the solider in order to touch his machine gun, as I had done many times before, but I was afraid the bag of salt would fall so I contented myself with looking at it.

As we moved away I heard the soldier shout out, 'I'll pass by this evening to buy a sandwich from you!'

Hussein looked at me and said, 'Don't you see that everyone knows you? Why were you crying?'

'Because I'm hungry,' I replied, pushing back my hair.

'Me too,' said Ali. 'We're going to cut your hair for you, you hedgehog,' he added, 'so you can see the blackboard properly.'

'What's a blackboard?' I asked.

'School,' said Ali.

＊ ＊ ＊

I clasped my hands and struck them against my chest, brought my index fingers together, then with my right index finger tapped the palm of my left hand, by which my father understood I was saying, 'My brothers are waiting for *sammoun* bread to eat before going to school.'

He nodded and gave me some fresh *sammoun* before turning to regulate the heat of the oven, throwing a quick glance at the trays of dough neatly arranged inside. He pulled a white handkerchief from his back trouser pocket and wiped his face and neck before putting it back, leaving a corner hanging out like a dog's left ear. With a rapid movement he pushed the long oar-like wooden pole into the maw of the oven and began extracting the trays of *sammoun*, emptying them into a wooden chest standing at the entrance to the bakery where customers were crowded around in their pyjamas and dishdashas.

I was sitting on a heap of four or five sacks of flour piled one atop the other, watching the customers. Within a few moments all that was left in the chest was one lonely *sammoun*, which my father picked up and gave to Adnan, who was responsible for cutting and weighing the dough, shouting at him because it was too small. Adnan, since he used to come to our house some afternoons to join us for tea and milk, didn't want to answer back and contented himself just smiling at my father, who was acting as if he was the municipal bread inspector or the owner of the bakery. My father became even more enraged and began pointing at the ceiling of the bakery and at the tattoo on his left arm, then crossing his wrists. Adnan understood this to mean that 'if you'd made such a mistake in an English bakery you'd have been thrown into prison' and he replied jokingly by pointing to my father's arm with its tattoo of the lion and the unicorn defending the British crown, then blowing onto his outstretched palm, meaning 'The English time is over'.

My father became crosser still and began looking about for something to hurl at his colleague, but just at the right moment Gilbert the orphan, the bakery cleaner who was my brother Samson's classmate, intervened by giving my father the thumbs up as if to say 'You're right', while Adnan remained in hiding behind the flour sacks, trying to supress his laughter.

Shamiran made cream and jam sandwiches for Teddy and Samson who went off to school, then began preparing me my favourite breakfast of onions in tomato sauce (Kiryakos had advised me to avoid meals like this because, he said, along with chickpeas and beans 'they weaken a film-maker's power of imagination'). Shamiran, however, didn't finish preparing breakfast but rushed out to the communal wash place, saying, 'Joey, don't forget to leave a little food for your brother.' I looked at Robin and saw he was sleeping like a tortoise.

My mother was at the communal wash place washing the dishes and clothes, like all the women of al-Habbaniyah, and chatting to Nasrat Shah's wife Sakina, and to Sabiha who had married three months earlier when still not quite seventeen years old. Sabiha always wore a small scarf, embroidered with roses, on her head and a tight-fitting dress, 'to excite men's lust and women's jealousy', as Zahra the oldest spinster in town would say.

'The stench of the public latrine kept us awake last night,' said Sabiha, rubbing away gently at a pair of small red cotton panties in her washbowl (I often watched her doing that).

'Razouqi has grown old,' my mother replied, 'and can't work any longer.'

'Poor Razouqi, cleaning the toilet morning, noon and evening,' said Sakina, wiping her nose with the black scarf covering her head and shoulders. 'What would Razouqi do if people ate a lot of beans and went to the toilet after midnight?' she asked.

At that moment Nikola, the army nurse at the Republican Hospital, rode past the wash place on his bicycle.

Sakina turned her kohl-rimmed eyes that were deeply set in her lean face to Sabiha's naked thighs and said, 'Cover yourself up, my girl. There are people about.'

My mother continued to gaze at the dark-skinned nurse as he slowly receded into the distance on his bicycle, and then, before she could pick up her tray laden with glasses and plates, saw Shamiran running towards them, blood dripping from one of the fingers of her left hand.

'Here we go again,' cried my mother in frustration, but Shamiran, who always knew how to evade my mother's looks, simply said, 'What can I do, Mum? I was making breakfast for my brothers when the knife cut my finger,' and she bent down to kiss her friend Sabiha who, to keep Sakina happy, had pulled her dress down over her legs.

'How many times have you cut that finger?' my mother wondered, lapsing into a perplexed silence.

Sabiha cast a conspiratorial glance at Shamiran and said, 'You'd better get straight off to the hospital before the whole hand gets infected.'

'Go to the hospital,' said my mother. 'We're in God's hands.'

It was raining the day that Shamiran cut her finger for the first time, and Sabiha was not yet married to her relative, Mohammad the junior officer. That day Shamiran, accompanied by Sabiha, had gone to the Republican Hospital where Nikola the nurse examined Shamiran's hand in a way displeasing to Sabiha, who broke in saying, 'Take the girl's hand properly, my dear, it's as if you've never held a woman's hand before.'

Nikola looked at her smiling, not hiding his admiration at her audacity. After sterilising Shamiran's hand with Mercurochrome and bandaging it he said timidly, 'I always buy my bread from her father', to which Sabiha replied as she dragged Shamiran out of the clinic, 'But we're not here to sell bread.'

After closing the door from the outside, she rejoiced, 'Poor thing, he wants to get married.'

Then they both ran out under the rain across the hospital garden, leaving Nikola behind, unable to follow them to lend them his ancient English umbrella.

A week later, he was surprised to see Shamiran reappear, by herself this time, having cut another finger. Despite the fact that she said good morning in Arabic, the nurse deliberately replied in Assyrian, '*Kedamtakh brikhta*. May your morning be blessed.'

And this time he did not forget Sabiha's advice to 'hold the girl's hand properly', in fact he went further, making her sit down on his chair and massaging her hand finger by finger. Finding the patient well disposed, he began rubbing the muscles of her arm and brought his nose close to the opening of her blouse, sniffing at her armpit like a dog.

These cures, which set Shamiran all aflame, were very much to her taste and so she began, whenever assailed by a desire to sit in front of the orphan nurse, to choose a healthy finger and cut it.

Shamiran's visits to the hospital became more frequent, and I once heard my brother Samson shouting at her, 'We'll buy you a bottle of Mercurochrome and put an end to this hospital business.'

I don't know if my big brother had heard something from his friends; quarrels between boys would often reveal a lot of secrets. For example, Mahdi once got into an argument with Jalil the Bear (so-called for his bulk) and insulted him by saying, 'You hit me, you great bear, because you daren't hit Mahmoud, who's shagging your sister every Thursday behind the secondary school fence.'

The Bear had gone there the next Thursday evening and found his sister Batoul leaning against the school fence, skirt round her waist, panties round her ankles and Mahmoud pressed up against her backside.

It was said that Jalil the Bear heard his sister say, 'Mahmoud, if only you could stick with me for life.'

That day the Bear had given his sister a massive nosebleed and broken Mahmoud's feet, preventing him from playing football for a whole month.

A similar thing had happened to me when Nasrat Shah's son Hussein tried to give me a hiding because I'd used his bicycle without his permission and punctured the back tyre, but backed down for fear of what I might say when he remembered that I had seen him one afternoon lying on top of Samar (Jane Russell, as Kiryakos used to call her) licking her breasts as her splendid long legs encircled his waist.

This is why I say that perhaps Samson, arguing with one of his friends, had heard something to the effect of 'What's your sister doing every day at the Republican Hospital?'

And the truth is that Shamiran's visits to the hospital had increased, as had Nikola's boldness. He had taken to sitting her on his bicycle and making the rounds of the streets and parks of al-Habbaniyah military camp, talking to her of marriage, then stretching out with her under the eucalyptus tree to kiss her and caress her Assyrian body with hands that smelled of Mercurochrome.

Shamiran had a light brown complexion and tender lips, which she kept moist with her pink tongue. Her graceful legs made her appear tall, and she wore her hair in a ponytail down her back tied up with a small white handkerchief. She was pretty and looked more mature than her sixteen years.

'Last summer, a young Lebanese man came with his rich businessman father and asked for her hand,' my mother used to tell the women sitting around the wash place. 'But we refused the match because she was too young, and the young man fell ill for a long time. He was an engineer,' she added, 'and a Christian, just like us.'

★ ★ ★

'Joey, I'm your brother Teddy's friend, give some to me first.'

'Joey, God spare you, the bell's about to go, give me a glass of sorbet, I love the movies just like you.'

'Joey, ask your dad, one evening I found him drunk and accompanied him home.'

The primary school pupils were crowded around my handcart shouting, and I was taking the coins from the small hands stretched out in front of me and distributing little glasses of sorbet. Nasrat Shah was standing next to me, watching my deft work. He adjusted his yellow cap (an import from Tehran) and glanced smilingly from the corner of his eye at my bulging pocket. I guess he was smiling as he remembered what he once said to my mother: 'Joey is the world's fastest street seller.' That claim was now being verified before his very eyes, which, for some reason I never understood, always took on the colour of his caps.

When the school bell rang and the pupils rushed off to their classrooms, not one of them had failed to try the sorbet, and I had even given Amer a glass for free because he had indeed, as he claimed, once accompanied my drunken father home.

After the school had closed its main gate, Nasrat Shah told me he was going to pray at al-Hussainiya. 'Listen, Joey,' he said, 'you'd better head for the girls' school, especially because the sorbet is red today.'

Nasrat Shah was absolutely right. No sooner had the girls come out of their classes than they made a beeline for the sorbet, quaffing back one or two glasses each. Some of them borrowed money from their friends and ordered another glass to make their lips red.

Sitt Madeleine was also right. One day she had said to us, 'I know you use dye to make it redder and colour the girls' lips. What you're doing is a real disgrace.'

Nasrat Shah hadn't replied to the teacher's accusation but pulled his cap down to cover his forehead and stood contemplating her backside as she walked away. 'Bitch,' he said in a low voice, 'we redden the girls' lips and cool their hearts, what more does she want?' Then shaking his head he added, 'She's in her forties and still a spinster!'

After that I pushed the handcart back towards al-Hussainiya and, while waiting for Nasrat Shah to finish his prayers, began making a new lot of sorbet. I filled the copper pot with water and emptied in two kilos of sugar, two and a half spoonfuls of green colouring, a spoonful and a half of vanilla and a lump of lemon flavouring. I then extracted half a block of ice and broke it up into small lumps with a screwdriver, distributing it round the outside of the copper pot and covering it with a thick layer of coarse salt to prevent it melting too quickly. I then began spinning the pot and little by little the green liquid inside started to freeze and turn into sorbet. I opened the little parasol to protect myself from the hot sun and began to count the money I had earned that morning. There were two dinars and 380 fils, and I was proud because I knew that such a sum would make Nasrat Shah happy.

'Hi Joey, have you sold a lot today?' It was my brother Samson.

'Yes.'

'You're a great worker,' said Samson, stroking my head.

'Do you want a glass of sorbet?' I asked him.

'You bet.'

As I handed him the glass of sorbet I noticed his books and shoes were splashed with mud. 'You didn't go to school today, did you, Samson?'

He nodded while gulping down the sorbet.

'Did you know that next academic year I'm going to register at school?'

'Great,' said Samson,

'That way you can read all the movie magazines and even the subtitles of American films.' He had finished his glass and I wanted to give him another but he told me, 'No, I don't want sorbet, what I need is 50 fils.'

I looked right and left, and up at the sky, then drew a coin from my pocket and slipped it quickly into my big brother's hand, who took it and hurried off unaware that I was longing to keep on talking to him. We rarely talked at home and sometimes a whole month would pass without us exchanging a single sentence.

Samson, a year younger than Shamiran, was tall, dark and handsome, and had an athletic build. He used to spend the whole day out of the house, and it reached a point when my mother would say of him, 'My God, this boy's never sees the house in daylight, he looks on the house as a bed, a bed to sleep in and that's all.'

Shortly afterwards I saw Nasrat Shah approaching from al-Hussainiya, limping on his left foot. 'We made two dinars and 330 fils today,' I said proffering him the coins.

'You're Tarzan, Joey,' said Nasrat Shah, putting the earnings in his pocket and adding, 'Off you go, son, get yourself something to eat and prepare yourself for the evening shift,' and he patted my head gently with his three-fingered hand.

'Mum, how long have we known Nasrat Shah's family?' asked

Samson one afternoon when he had come home for a bite of bread before heading out again.

'I don't know, we've always been together. I breastfed Fatima and Ibrahim for them, and Sakina breastfed Teddy and Joey.'

Having eaten a couple of plates of beans, I was stretched out on the concrete floor of the threshold as my mother busied herself with hanging up the washing when Shamiran appeared unexpectedly, humming to herself in Assyrian, '*Mani merreh lebayyennakh? Mani merreh bitshoqinnakh?* Who said I don't love you? Who said I'll leave you?'

At which my mother, shaking out a large towel, told her, 'You too have begun loitering around the streets, just like your brothers', and bending over to gather up another piece of washing, added, 'Clearly I'll go to my grave without knowing why you all run away from this house.'

I wanted to say to her, 'Because, dear mother, very simply, our house is not a home', but the beans had got to my blood and my whole body was in a torpor.

In the meantime, Shamiran had gone inside still singing, '*Atin khoubbi . . . atin khayey.* You are my love . . . you are my life.' Less than a minute later we heard my father's screams ring out, like the whooping of Red Indians attacking a cowboy wagon train, and Shamiran came out scowling, saying with a mixture of sadness and coquetry, 'How was I to know he was in there?'

'What's up? What did you do to him?' asked my mother.

'Nothing,' said Shamiran. 'He told me, how dare you come into my room without knocking on the door.' And wiping away a few tears, she added smirking, 'Great, next time I'll knock on the door and I hope, Dad, that you can hear my knocks.'

Then she drew close to my mother and said in a low voice, 'Mum, Dad was drinking and cleaning that silver box of his.'

This set my mother off on the litany we'd heard so often before, 'What can I do with him? We could never expect he'd forget that wretched box which almost got him killed. Let him get drunk and knock off work, then we'll see who's going to feed you. That deaf-mute! I lost my youth trailing after him while all he thought about was the English. He spent more than thirty years slaving for them like a fool, and in the end they just cheated him with a silver box that's not worth a kilo of lentils!'

She said all this with immense sadness then, wiping her nose with her left arm, she suddenly jerked some of my father's clothes off the line and threw them into the dusty road. 'Let him go to England and wash his clothes there,' she cried, and burst out laughing.

Shamiran joined her, and I too found myself seized by gales of laughter that liberated me from the effect of the beans and put an end to my nap – which anyway was a bad habit I had picked up from Nasrat Shah despite Kiryakos warning me more than once that 'napping is only good for dogs and cats'.

When his son Ali became a student at the teacher training college, Nasrat Shah built him a separate room with adobe walls next to his own house. But Ali hated the confined space and stopped using it so Ibrahim and I took it over, making it a games room and using it to make a shadow theatre.

We called it the 'movie room' and hung the walls with film posters and photos of actors: the British comic actor Norman Wisdom, Roy Rogers (the King of the Cowboys), Alan Ladd, Randolph Scott, Gary Cooper, Cary Grant, Errol Flynn, King Kong lifting up Bob Hope, Montgomery Clift, Eleanor Powell, Frankenstein, John Wayne, Tyrone Power (with a thick beard and tattered clothes, Kiryakos used to say that Samson, when he grew up, would look a lot like Tyrone), Jean Harlow with Clark Gable, Vera Miles, Lee Marvin, Katherine Hepburn lighting a cigarette for James Stewart, a number of shots of Henry Fonda, Victor Mature wearing a red fez and kissing Gene Tierney, Richard Widmark reading a newspaper on a train, Bing Crosby, Jane Russell exposing her prominent bosom while reclining on a pile of hay (Kiryakos told me that when I grew up I would discover the charms of women with long legs), John Ford wearing a woollen hat while sitting in a trench surrounded by a group of cameramen during the filming of *The Iron Horse*, John Ford wearing dark glasses and drinking tea, John Ford wearing a cap and laughing among his assistants, John Ford smoking a pipe and stroking his dog with his right hand, John Ford in Africa during the filming of *Mogambo*, John Ford as a young man standing next to his brother Francis Ford, John Ford with Harry Curry, John Ford between Vittorio De Sica and René Clair, John Ford holding a 16mm camera and wearing army fatigues during the filming of *The Battle of Midway*, a big picture of Charlie Chaplain and the boy Jackie Coonan, and a number of others.

I was five years old when Kiryakos showed me how to make a shadow theatre. I would light two candles and place them behind a sheet of paper, one at either end. Then, taking two cardboard cut-out characters, I would move them nearer and further away from the sheet of paper (the screen) making the shadows bigger and smaller, at the same time altering my tone of voice for each character:

First voice:	Your father can't hear, your father can't speak.
Child:	My father's like the movies, images, images, images.
Second voice:	My father can't see.
Child:	He conjures up images, like the movies.
First voice:	My father can see well, hear well, speak well, eat well, sleep well.
Child:	He's a policeman!

I had composed this particular sketch to get revenge on Khachik, who, in our discussions about the movies, had said to me, 'You prefer silent movies because your dad's a deaf-mute.' One day I'd stolen a bit of rope and was resolved to strangle that repulsive Armenian boy with his fat red neck, but I desisted when Ibrahim said, 'Don't forget, Joey, that your dad's doing everything he can to get a job at the bakery owned by Khachik's mother.'

What is more, I had heard my mother say to Sakina, 'I do hope that Umm Khachik accepts Kika into her electric bakery, her workers don't tire themselves out and they do get reasonable wages.' And I felt a certain remorse because Khachik's father used to give me a whole dinar at Christmas, except for last year because he'd died just a week before the festivities began.

★ ★ ★

My father came into the 'movie room', closing the door behind him and gesturing to Ibrahim to leave. He looked at me for a few moments then burst out laughing and coughing, the smell of arak issuing from his mouth. He tapped himself on the backside with the fingers of his right hand then brought them up to his nose, screwing up his lean face in disgust and pointing to the two candles and the sheet of paper. I understood he was saying 'The shadow theatre is a load of shit'. When he then went on to crush the two candles with the tip of his shoe it became clear to me that he was drunk.

The room was plunged into murky darkness until my father illuminated the scene with the flame of his lighter. That, I believe, was the moment that consolidated my relationship with him. He was standing in the corner to the right of the door, holding his 'silver box' in his raised left hand, while the lighter burned in his right, which was stretched downwards to its full extent. Little by little, he began raising the hand holding the lighter, and as it got higher the silver box began absorbing the rays and gleaming until its light reflected on the pictures hanging on the walls, and particularly on the picture of Monty Clift. My father remained standing for two or three minutes without moving, until seized by a coughing fit which caused him to remove his thumb from the lighter flint. As his wheezing mingled into the darkness of the room, I hurriedly looked for a box of matches and lit one of the candles, thinking to myself that no one in the family would believe me if I told them my father had placed his silver box in my hands, though on the condition that I wouldn't open it. I brought the box close to my mouth and breathed on it, wiping it gently with my shirt to increase the shine. When my father had stopped coughing he tapped the side of his forehead with his index finger as if to say 'Do you remember?'

'Yes, I remember,' I said to myself while nodding my head at him.

It had happened when I was five years old. Robin and I had been left alone with our father because our mother, Shamiran and Teddy had gone to hospital to visit Orahim the electrician who, having blown his nose while mending a faulty streetlight, had got an electric shock that sent him flying from a height of four metres. Thereafter, when walking down the street, Orahim (or Stewart Granger, as Kiryakos called him) would stop and kick his right foot in the air, just like a football player, then go on for another ten metres and kick the air again, and so on until reaching home or a café where he would sit down in front of the television.

My father was drinking arak, every now and again feeding us a spoonful of *jajeek*, a thick yoghurt mixed with chopped cucumber and garlic, or *lablabi*, boiled chickpeas. He told me to pick up Robin and go into the other room until he called for me. When we heard him shout out, like the whooping of Red Indians attacking a cowboy wagon train, we returned to the room and found him holding a parcel in his hand. He removed its cloth wrapping to reveal a nylon one underneath; removing that, another wrapping appeared, this time of white lace. Removing that too he finally exposed a 'silver box' engraved on one side with two animals standing on their hind legs on either side of a crown. He pointed to the other side of the box and made a movement as if signing a piece of paper, then tapped his chest with his forefinger as if to say, 'My name is written here', and he proudly placed the box on the table and gulped down a glassful of drink. Robin and I both smiled and he encircled us in his arms, kissing our faces and heads. He then kissed the box, breathing on it and rubbing it against his chest and, once satisfied with its shine, returned it to its cloth and nylon wrappings.

It was in that box that I first saw a clear reflection of my face, quite unlike the mirror we had at home, full of patches of rust that made us seem as if we had freckles. In the box I saw my face dark and soft, just like the faces of children in Indian films.

As my father took the box from me, he added another condition. He pointed to his tongue and to his eyes, then put his right index finger in his left palm and closed his fist around it ('Don't tell anyone you've seen it. It's a secret'). When we passed in front of Nasrat Shah's house, my mother looked at us disapprovingly and said to Sakina and Fatima, 'We've accepted the madness of the deaf-mute, but what does he want from the boy?'

Strange to recount, but it was as if my father had 'heard' what she said because with his hands he symbolised two breasts, sucked his little finger, put his left forefinger against his temple and breathed into his right palm, meaning, 'Your mother's a fool'.

It was in the box room – where the bed was crammed, its blankets thrown around in a muddle – that my father hid his silver box, in one of the three large wooden chests that were full of old clothes and smelled of Ceylon tea (near which Sakina had delivered me into the world).

★ ★ ★

'Audrey Hepburn' Kiryakos called her when he saw me sitting with her by the door of her aunt's house, and me telling her everything I knew about movies and about the town. She was pale and slim, and her black hair was cut at the level of her ears;

her mouth was broad and she had a delicate nose which I kissed within three days of her arrival. Nisreen had come from the north of the country a few days before and was staying with her aunt Zahra who worked in the garden of the British airbase, a post she'd held since the age of eighteen, when she took over from her brother Khidir who died of tuberculosis, leaving her on her own. Despite receiving numerous offers, Zahra had never married.

I was drinking Mission at Youshiya's shop while he was engrossed in reading a letter recently arrived from his daughter Victoria, when Aunt Zahra called me, 'Joey, come with me to the town gate because my sister's daughter Nisreen is coming today.' I agreed immediately, even before she added, 'I'll buy you two bottles of Mission as soon as we get back.'

Aunt Zahra introduced me: 'This is Joey, Kika and Gorgiya's son, who helps me out whenever I need something, he's like my own son.' She didn't add that what she mostly did was send me to buy cigarettes.

I looked at Nisreen and smiled, stretching out my hand to pick up her bulging suitcase and saying, 'They all call me "my son", Sakina, Aunt Zeinab, Aunt Zahra, even my mother. Are you going to call me "son" too?'

'You're my friend,' said Nisreen, ruffling my long hair and gazing at her aunt with a look that said, 'Clearly I'm going to be happy here'.

Next day I accompanied Nisreen to the bakery to get bread and introduce her to my father, then took her on a trip around the market to show her where she could buy tea, sugar, vegetables and meat (and cigarettes, of course). On our way back I also told her she could get everything she needed from Youshiya's grocery store, which was near the house and also accepted credit, adding, as I pushed my hair back from my forehead, 'His daughter Victoria went to Detroit three years ago'.

On our way to gather salt one day, I decided that from then on I would give none of the proceeds from selling sorbet to Samson or to anyone else. With Nisreen's arrival my daily expenditure had increased and I resolved 'to put aside' 50 fils every day before handing the earnings over to Nasrat Shah. I had to take a certain amount of care because (Kiryakos had told me) there are eyes in earth and sky constantly watching men's doings. I stood behind the handcart, looked up to heaven, then left and right, before slipping a 50-fils coin into the pocket of the black running shorts I wore under my trousers.

Yet despite all these precautions, I found myself confessing to Nasrat Shah, 'Uncle Nasrat, I've already taken my daily allowance because I needed it.'

'But why did you put it in your shorts pocket?' he asked, rubbing a piece of ice over his bald patch.

His question unnerved me and I hesitated a moment before replying, 'So I wouldn't lose it.'

'Off you go, son,' he said with a smile, 'off you go and take it easy for a little while.'

I wanted to say something but couldn't, while Nasrat Shah simply placed his three fingers against the copper pot and, humming a Persian song, began to spin it.

One day Nisreen came to Youshiya's shop to tell me her aunt would be away all afternoon, and she asked me to buy her 'a watermelon and three pieces of dough'. I went to the market where, adding my money to hers, I bought what she ordered and hurried back.

'What's this?' she asked in surprise as she saw me pile a large watermelon and five pieces of dough onto the kitchen table.

'Ah . . . You wouldn't know it, but I always get things cheap,' I said boastfully. 'The fruit and vegetable sellers, the grocers, butchers and clothes sellers, they all know me and like me.'

'You're so nice,' said Nisreen, and her breasts pressed against my chest as she planted a kiss on my cheek that almost touched my lips. I felt a prick in my heart, or something falling from it.

'Do you want me to sing you a song from the Indian movie

195

Junglee?' I asked.

She whispered a quick 'yes' and removed the warmth of her breast from mine.

I told Nisreen to lie on her back in the living room. She obliged, and I explained the rest of the scene to her.

I came out of the kitchen singing the words '*Haaya mawta junglee kahi*,' humming the music, 'tara ra ra ra ra ra ra rrrrrrr ran' and running towards the living room, dancing and singing at the same time. As I got down on my knees Nisreen began rolling in my direction (as if down a hill) before coming to a stop at my knees. I bent over her, still singing, and brought my face close to hers just like Shammi Kapoor (at that moment I discovered that Nisreen looked a lot like Saira Banu, and not like Audrey Hepburn as Kiryakos had said) and gave her three quick kisses on the nose.

'Isn't that great?' I asked her.

'Really great,' she replied, her eyes on the ceiling which, like all the houses in al-Habbaniyah, rested on intersecting wooden beams. 'Thanks, Joey, you're really nice.'

> *I'm going to begin the song,*
> *said the Assyrian boy,*
> *and when I become feverish, just shut me up.*
> *Then he began to swim in the throat of Nadhem al-Ghazali,*
> *and they made him shut him up.*
> *But Nisreen poked her head round from behind the wooden door,*
> *'For God's sake let him finish his song. He has a beautiful voice.'*
> *The little boy was happy*
> *but did Nisreen love him?*
> *She sent him to market to buy pieces of dough,*
> *red watermelon and a few olives.*
> *The boy supplemented her money with his daily earnings and said*
> * to her,*
> *'Don't you see that I got things cheap?'*

But
does Nisreen know of his throbbing heart?
In the school sprint
the boy runs
fast, fast, fast;
he sees Nisreen in a castle devoured by flames.
And he runs, runs, runs,
crossing the finishing line
to help Nisreen.
And he receives an aluminium cup
empty of wine.
But
did Nisreen see his flying heart?
And there
on the dusty square,
drums and pipes,
black rope rings
like rings of dancers
and the hard beating of their feet.
The boy's face pales
and his thin legs go weak.
Is it true that today is Nisreen's wedding day?

Kiryakos noticed that I no longer showed any interest in what was going on in the world of movies, not even in my shadow theatre. One day he saw me in front of Youshiya's shop and asked me to accompany him to the movie room, saying, 'I've got lots of fresh news from Hollywood.'

'I'll join you there in a bit,' I replied, my eyes riveted on the door of Aunt Zahra's house, but the truth is I completely forgot and Kiryakos was left waiting for a long time.

He told Ibrahim of his amazement at what had happened to me. 'I hung more than ten new pictures on the walls of the movie room and he didn't even notice. Just think of it, Ibrahim, five rare pictures from the movie *The Man Who Shot Liberty Valance*, which one of these days I hope to see.'

Ibrahim didn't know what to say. Later he told me that Kiryakos 'sat for a long time in the movie room, and I saw tears streaming from his eyes'. Kiryakos took my 'betrayal' of him and of cinema very hard.

One afternoon I was sitting alone in the movie room when a pale-looking Kiryakos appeared and announced in a tragic voice, 'Hey, Joey, I've just read a worrying piece of news.'

I straightened up on the bucket I was using as a seat and listened to him as he went on in the same tone: 'Jack's really ill, and it appears that he won't be able to finish shooting his new movie *Young Cassidy*, isn't that heartbreaking?'

I averted my gaze and said blankly, 'Nisreen told me she doesn't know John Ford.'

An instant later Kiryakos had felled me to the ground with a sudden slap. 'I'm talking about a genius and you're concerned about some silly girl,' he said angrily, then twisting his narrow face into a scornful pitying smile he added, 'You know, that foolish country girl doesn't look a bit like Audrey Hepburn,' and with that he left the room.

My mother was amazed when Kiryakos told her he didn't want to see me on his visits to our house, but Samson was quick to back him up, saying, 'You know that Joey has always brought trouble', and he hinted to her (with what words I don't know) that I had been doing shopping for Nisreen with Nasrat Shah's money (of course he didn't dare tell her that I also used to give *him* Nasrat Shah's money).

In the meantime Ibrahim, upset because we no longer played together as we used to, made the problem worse, whispering in his mother Sakina's ear, 'Nisreen doesn't only send Joey shopping but she uses him to do the housework and clean the dishes as well.'

Sakina saw it was a serious matter and said to my mother, 'Your son, whom I delivered into the world with my own hands and suckled at my own breast, is living under a spell cast on him by that gardener woman with the fondness for military boots.'

'You must be right, Sakina,' my mother replied, 'otherwise who could believe a day would go by without my son disturbing one and all with his talk of movies and actors?'

For his part my father, in his own way and using his own senses, understood what was happening between my mother, Sakina and Kiryakos. I was in the movie room eating a plate of rice and some yellow lentil soup – without meat because 'we're like Jesus, who doesn't like to eat meat', as my mother would say, although the truth was that when she got her hands on a bit of money she'd rush out to buy meat – when my father appeared, smiling. He raised his left finger, pushed his hair back, traced some squares on his chest, passed his index finger under his left eye and shook his head, meaning 'I know the tall guy who combs his hair back and wears checked shirts doesn't want to see you.' He blew a raspberry, meaning 'but you shouldn't care', then he pointed at me, tapped his finger against his chest and brought both index fingers together: 'You and I are friends.'

When he noticed I was rushing my food, he touched his breast where he kept his silver box as if to say, 'Don't rush, it's here.'

I cast a quick glance at the pictures hanging on the walls of the room, trying to think of some way to get out but could come up with nothing better than making the following sign: I brought my hands up to my nose with an expression of disgust and rubbed them together, that is 'my hands are dirty and I must wash them before touching the box'.

He nodded in agreement and I slipped out.

I ordered a bottle of Mission from Youshiya and began to wait for that musical voice to reach me from behind the wooden door.

'Joey, Joey, Joey.'

Nisreen's voice fell sweetly on my ear, blending with the sugariness of the Mission. I didn't answer but kept on drinking, relishing the echoing of my name as it issued from her lips.

'Joey, Joey.'

Finally Youshiya yelled in my ear, causing me to spill the drink down my shirt, 'Have you become deaf like your father? Can't you hear the girl's calling you?'

Smiling, I put the bottle down in front of Youshiya. He smiled too and said, 'I know you can hear her perfectly, you rascal, but you're playing hard to get. Ah, young people today . . .'

* * *

My mother and Sakina were washing clothes at the communal wash place. 'Just think, Sakina,' said my mother, 'last night Kika wanted to beat his head in, and would have if I hadn't stopped him.' She turned to me. 'What did you do to him, what did you do?'

'*Hichmindi bi-Urishlim, hichmindi*! Nothing, I swear by Jerusalem, nothing!'

'*Urishlim masmiyalukh*! May Jerusalem blind you!' was my mother's angry reply. 'By God, if I hadn't stopped him he'd have beaten your head in. Even when he woke up this morning he spat on you as you slept and said he'd break your legs if you went anywhere near the bakery or the bar.'

My mother was convinced that Nisreen had me under her spell. 'Look at him,' she said, 'his face is as yellow as turmeric.'

Sakina didn't say anything but, intent on her washing, kept glancing over at me with her deep-set eyes.

'I swear to God, Aunt Sakina, I did nothing,' I said beseeching-ly, and she turned to my mother and said, 'Kika loves no one as he loves this boy, and the boy swears he did nothing.'

'But he's not normal,' my mother insisted.

'I told you, Gorgiya, that the boy's bewitched. Blast that gardener woman with the military boots who won't give us any peace.'

'No one has the power to break the spell except you,' my mother told her in fearful and tremulous tones.

There had always been some who believed that Sakina was a genuine 'healer' possessed of supernatural powers and with a vast knowledge of medicine and its remedies, and their numbers had increased since Sakina had (under compulsion) saved her arch-enemy Zahra the gardener, or 'she of the military boots', as Sakina herself insisted on calling her. The discord between Zahra and Sakina had arisen because at some point Zahra had claimed that her grandfather had been the spiritual authority for all the Kurdish villages in northern Iraq, and that the British military engineers used to kiss his hand because he would show them exactly where to build their roads over the rugged mountain terrain.

Zahra once swore to my mother that 'the English would reach the mountain peaks by helicopter, but my grandfather would get there before them, leaning on his stick and wearing shoes made from car tyres.'

'And how,' my mother asked naively, 'did the cars get to the top of the mountains?'

To which Zahra answered cunningly, 'Don't you know, Gorgiya, that the Iranian merchants would bring their wares over the mountains to Baghdad, and that some of them had accidents on the road or were waylaid by bandits, and would have to leave their cars behind? Sakina's husband, Nasrat Shah, may be one of those who went bankrupt and chose to stay in our country.' And in some way my mother believed the story, because she'd heard Nasrat Shah say on a number of occasions, 'I wasn't born a street seller, time was when I was an important merchant.'

One afternoon in 1959 Zahra came back from work. After getting undressed and removing the military boots her late brother Khidir had bequeathed her to protect her pale and delicate feet from the thorns of the garden, she stretched out in the living room as she did every day. Her nap over, she was putting the boots back on when she felt something pricking the big toe of her left foot. Putting her hand in the boot to investigate, she pricked her finger as well and, turning the boot upside down, out fell a large scorpion. She began to scream, 'Help! I'm going to die! Ah, my foot! Ah, my hand!' Many neighbours came running but not one would lift a finger to help. In the end Sakina stepped from the crowd. She took Zahra's finger, sucked at the poison and spat it out, then she sucked the poison from her foot and spat that out too. Finally she put her own bare foot in front of the scorpion and, her eyes turned up to heaven, said, '*Ya Rahman, ya Rahim, ya Ali Bin Abi Talib, ya Rab al-Alameen.* O Merciful Compassionate Lord, O Ali Bin Abi Talib, O Lord of the Universe.' The scorpion stung her foot and immediately flipped onto its back, jolted its legs in the air for a few moments then lay still. Sakina advised Zahra, by way of a cure, to swallow the ash of her cigarettes for a whole month.

It is said that that day Kiryakos commented, 'Poor Zahra, they've opened *Tobacco Road* in her stomach.'

Despite her victory over her enemy Zahra, Sakina could not resist whispering in people's ears, 'She of the military boots brought the scorpion herself to injure one of her adversaries, because the fact is that there are neither scorpions nor rabbits in our town.' Unfortunately for Sakina, Kiryakos was on the side of justice and even prepared the draft outline of a script which went something like this: 'Zahra arrives at her workplace in the garden; she removes her cloak and places it near a tree trunk. Then, taking a large pair of shears, she begins pruning the trees and the grass, after which, with a shovel, she alters the course of the irrigation streams . . . and so on with other garden tasks. In the meantime a scorpion slips into one of the pockets of her cloak and remains trapped there. Zahra returns home, the scorpion comes out of its 'prison' and crawls towards the smell of human feet, in other words towards the boots, where it hides.'

Kiryakos added another possible scenario: 'Or perhaps Zahra

grew tired while at work and lay down on the grass, and the scorpion came and clung on to her loose cotton kaftan, the kaftan her brother Khidir left her to hide the form of her tender white body.'

Zahra was well pleased with Kiryakos's flight of fancy and decided to bring a bit of joy to his heart by saying, 'Just think, Kiryakos, isn't it strange that scorpions should appear in the military camps that were always like the Gardens of Babylon, and just a year after the English have left?'

To which Kiryakos cannot but have replied, '*How Green Was My Valley*.'

So it was that Sakina decided to break the spell that Zahra and her niece had cast on me. In doing so she killed two birds with one stone, on the one hand saving the child she had suckled and enabling him to return to work with her husband, while on the other hand (and most importantly) laying to rest the last iota of doubt as to the authenticity of her Persian spiritual powers.

'As soon as he gets back from work, bring him to me immediately, and make sure you give him nothing to eat,' she told my mother.

My mother dragged me by the hand to Nasrat Shah's house, where she made me lie on my back while awaiting Sakina's attentions. I stared at the ceiling, thinking about my empty stomach, then turned to look at the beautifully framed picture of the Imam Ali Bin Abi Talib hanging on the wall, at the bottom of which in an elegant script were the words: 'No man but Ali, no sword but Thulfiqar.' My mother lit a paraffin stove while Sakina put a piece of lead into a frying pan and placed it over the heat, then pulled up my shirt and began massaging my stomach while gazing into my eyes. My mother poured a little water into a tray, and Sakina picked up the frying pan and emptied its contents into the tray where the molten lead assumed an amorphous shape.

Sakina slapped herself on the cheeks and said, 'They fear not God. They would blind the boy. Yet where will their necks escape from Thulfiqar?'

She looked at the picture of Imam Ali and I too turned my eyes in that direction. He had a light brown complexion and a kindly face with a thick beard and honey-coloured eyes. His hands were clasped around the sword on his lap, and a green turban covered his chestnut-coloured hair.

'Close your eyes, son,' said Sakina. I did so and she stroked them with her hands and kissed them, adding, 'Be sure not to open them.'

With that she began wrapping my head in a handkerchief which I could not see but knew was black. I could smell her incense (imported from Tehran) and hear her mumbling in a low voice, '*Ya Rahman, ya Rahim, ya Ali Bin Abi Talib, ya Rab al-Alameen*'. When she had finished she said to my mother, 'Leave him like this until dawn tomorrow.'

I let out a screech and tried to get up, 'But I'm hungry! God preserve you, Aunt Sakina, I'm hungry!'

Next day I was sitting in the movie room, my mother having removed Sakina's handkerchief from my eyes, when Ibrahim came in shouting, 'They're showing a new Norman Wisdom film at the cinema today,' and began dancing around the room. He told me that Rafiq al-Hindi had given the new film the title, *Norman Wisdom in the Paratroopers*. I went up to Norman Wisdom's picture hanging on the wall, wiping the dust away and kissing it.

'*Norman the Lover!*' I cried at the top of my voice.

'*Norman the Milkman!*' cried Ibrahim.

'*Norman the Football Player!*'

'*Norman in the Doctor's Surgery!*'

And so we continued, shouting out the Arabic titles of Norman Wisdom films as chosen by Rafiq al-Hindi, the cinema manager.

Rafiq al-Hindi really was Indian. His father had come to Iraq to work as a 'babu' for the English army and then chosen to remain in the country, quite unlike Shaker al-Hindi, the fruit and vegetable seller, who had come to al-Habbaniyah from the town of Al-Bukamal on the Iraqi–Syrian border.

Shaker al-Hindi was a popular figure, short and fat with a red face, thick lips and bulging eyes. Every afternoon he would take a nap behind the cash register, the sound of his snores filling the shop. When he awoke, he would sprinkle water over his fruit and vegetables then drink a glass of milky tea, swatting the flies away from his face and lamenting that 'since the English left people have stopped eating fruit'.

Not a day would go by without Shaker picking out one of his customers to tell him the story of the English dogs. 'Many of the wives of the English officers', he used to say, 'would hang baskets around their dogs' necks and send them to me. In the basket I'd find a dinar or two and a note with the words "Good morning Mr al-Hindi". While the dog waited outside without moving, I'd fill the basket with apples, bananas, grapes, oranges, tomatoes, cucumbers, you name it, then hang it back on the dog's neck, leaving a note of my own to them: "Please enjoy your fruit and very best wishes from Mr Shaker al-Hindi".' At this point Shaker would pull out a cigarette, but before lighting it would end his tale on a bitter note. 'Those were the days, these days are cursed, cursed.'

At a certain point Shaker al-Hindi found he was no longer able to work all day and got in Ali, Nasrat Shah's son, to work for him. Soon, though, he sent him packing without giving any explanation. Some people said that Shaker al-Hindi had discovered that Ali was stealing but did not want to cause a scandal. For my part, I knew for a fact that Ali was stealing from Shaker al-Hindi, and my mother and Shamiran knew it too. My mother had noticed that for some weeks Samson hadn't asked her for any pocket money, yet she saw he was always eating fruit and consuming bottles of Seven Up. One day, to allay her doubts and put her mind at rest, she grabbed him by the ear, banged his head against the door and asked, 'Where are you getting all that money from?' I was sitting in the tin bath while Shamiran was intent on pouring water over my head when we heard Samson confessing that Ali would give him a quarter dinar note and he'd go and wait by Shaker al-Hindi's shop. As soon as he saw Ali take over he would come up and buy a kilo of cucumbers or half a kilo of apples, Ali would take the quarter dinar and give him change for a dinar or more, depending on how much money was in the till. Then later the two of them would meet and divide the 'swag'.

The arrival of a new Norman Wisdom movie would immediately turn al-Habbaniyah on its head, especially as Rafiq al-Hindi knew how to attract his public, writing under the film poster, 'Come and see Norman Wisdom and spend a hundred minutes of non-stop laughter in his company'.

For the occasion Ibrahim and I gathered the other kids together in the movie room – Jalil the Bear, Jalil the Jap (who looked Japanese), Ghalloubi the Bastard, Teddy, Mahdi, Pious, Mahmoud and Farid. Ibrahim said he would pay for Teddy, while the Bear complained his mother hadn't given him enough cash to buy a ticket, to which Mahmoud replied, 'Despite the fact you broke my feet, you old Bear, I'll make up the price of your ticket.'

Ibrahim said, 'Unfortunately we don't know anything about the film,' and I felt a sudden pang of regret. Kiryakos's image appeared in my mind – he seemed sad and emaciated. I hurried out, saying, 'Wait a moment, I'll be back with the information.'

'Where's Kiryakos?' I asked my mother. She looked at me in dismay then left Robin in the bathtub and hurried off in the direction of Nasrat Shah's house. A few minutes later Sakina appeared, distributing glasses of ginger beer. My mother told her, 'You're a real healer, Sakina, I swear by Imam Ali Bin Abi Talib that I'll dance and sing at the weddings of your sons and daughters.'

That evening I left home, heading for the cinema to do my evening shift, and passed in front of Youshiya's shop, who was surprised I didn't stop to drink a Mission. Nisreen saw me and asked me to buy some cigarettes for her aunt.

'I can't,' I told her, 'I haven't a moment to lose, I have to do some work then see the Norman Wisdom movie.'

'Just five minutes, Joey,' she pleaded.

'I'm running late,' I said, 'I can't,' and with that I went on my way, nothing in my mind except Norman Wisdom.

Youshiya reported what had befallen between me and Nisreen to my mother, who passed on a somewhat exaggerated version to Sakina: 'By the blood of Christ and the Blessed Virgin, Nisreen was begging and crying but my son told her to leave him alone because he wanted to go to work.'

Norman Wisdom was leaping into the air, a cap on his head and his mouth open in a broad grin. Under the poster Rafiq al-Hindi had written in large letters 'Norman Wisdom in the Paratroopers'. I was selling sorbet at the entrance and my customers, such was their desire to go in and see Norman, were breathing on their frozen glasses so as to gulp down the content as quickly as possible. I envied them as the bell went, as they were about to enjoy 'a hundred minutes of non-stop laughter'. But I made light of the matter because I was sure I'd see the second show. I had been promised as much by Nasrat Shah, who had gone off to sunset prayers saying, 'If I can't come, I'll send Hussein to take your place. Take it easy, you'll see the movie today.'

Nasrat Shah didn't show up and neither did Hussein, but what really got to me wasn't Nasrat Shah's delay but all those thoughtless wretches who came out of the first show laughing. I saw Ibrahim, Teddy, Ghalloubi the Bastard, the Jap, the Bear, Farid, the son of Sabir the bean seller, Mahdi, the son of Saleema who loves a scandal, Khalil, the son of Fahima the lame, and Pious who was laughing away having quite forgotten how five officers from the Dulaim tribe of al-Ramadi had carried his big sister Rosa off to the lakeside and screwed her for two solid days. I saw Zayya, son of Haroun the hospital cleaner and medicine thief, Khachik, the fat son of the equally fat Umm Khachik, and Luqman, son of

Hama, the most famous pigeon trainer in al-Habbaniyah. They were all coming out of the cinema imitating Norman Wisdom's antics and reproducing his high-pitched laughs which were like pinpricks in my heart. Of course I kept a brave face, looking at them coldly and with scant attention, but my courage was entirely due to the fact that I was convinced the three-fingered man would keep the promise he had made me.

But Nasrat Shah didn't come, and neither did Hussein. The bell went for the second showing and the management had begun switching off the external lights and closing the doors. I stood there dazed, hardly believing what was happening. In the end I tried to forget my anguish, consoling myself with the thought that I'd see the movie the following day.

I was busying myself with washing the glasses, lining them in rows and cleaning the surface of the handcart when I noticed one of the ushers had placed a wooden ladder next to the noticeboard and was removing the Norman Wisdom poster.

I ran up in alarm. 'Hey, what are you doing?' I asked.

'We're going to show another movie,' he replied.

'But there are still a lot of people who haven't seen this one.'

'That's true,' he said, letting the scraps of poster fall to the ground.

I rushed to pick up the fragments and smooth them out carefully. 'I haven't seen the movie yet. Everyone's seen it except me. It's not fair. You know that I know Norman Wisdom better than anyone else. I know everything about him,' I said beseechingly.

'All right, what year was he born?'

'On 4 February 1915, in London,' I replied without hesitation.

'That's right,' said the usher, 'and his first movie was called *The Bag Seller.*'

'No, no, that's wrong,' I cried, 'Norman's first movie was *Trouble in Store.*'

The man came down and approached the handcart. 'Don't worry, Joey,' he said taking an empty glass, filling it with sorbet and contemplating me where I was standing by the noticeboard with the bits of poster still in my hand. 'Listen, what do you say to me letting you see the movie by yourself?'

'Great!' I cried. 'May God bless you with a long life.'

'I'll let you see the movie this evening on condition you help me clean the cinema after the people have left.'

'I'll clean the cinema, the corridors, everything,' I said, taking the glass from his hand and refilling it. 'I could sweep the whole building in half an hour.'

'But there's another condition,' the man added, making me uneasy.

'What's that?'

'That you don't tell anyone, this is a secret between the two of us. Anyway, I'll also show you some clips from other movies.'

'I'll never reveal the secret, by Christ,' I replied.

'We're agreed then,' said the man.

As I drew near home with the handcart, Nasrat Shah came hurrying out to meet me, limping on his left foot, clearly worried about how I was going to react. 'Forgive me, son, I couldn't come because I was exhausted, forgive me,' he said. Then he just stood looking in amazed disbelief as I handed him the money smiling and not saying a word.

Nasrat Shah would have been ready to give me anything if he'd seen the slightest sign of anger in my face. He knew that when I got cross I just downed tools and ran off, not coming back until I chose to do so.

That evening I told my mother I was going to the bar to fetch my father and went back to the cinema.

The usher went to sort out the projector while I eagerly began sweeping up the piles of rubbish massed under the wooden seats, looking up at the screen from time to time and hoping . . . if Norman Wisdom leapt out now and took me away with him, I'd follow without hesitation, perhaps asking him to leave a note telling my father that I'd never forget our friendship . . .

Suddenly the lights went out.

'Hang on,' I cried amidst the gloom, 'don't start the film, I haven't finished sweeping yet!'

No reply.

'Hey! Put the lights on, put the lights on!'

The shadowy silence persisted and fear crept into my heart. I held on to the brush and stood there sobbing, when the usher appeared suddenly from among the seats saying, 'Don't be afraid, I'm going to show you the movie, you'll get a private show.'

'I want to go! I want to get out!' I wailed.

'Take it easy,' said the man, and he embraced me, reaching out a hand to unbutton my trousers, 'I'll give you a load of movie reels and magazine pictures.'

'I want to go! Leave me alone! Leave me alone!'

'But I told you I'm going to give you some real film reels!'

'Leave me alone!' I screamed at the top of my voice (and I remembered Birju stabbing the old moneylender Sukhilala) and, grabbing the man's hand, I sank my teeth in as hard as I could, almost as if to bite it off. He let out a screech of pain that shook the whole cinema and began kicking me as I crawled away between the seats in the direction of the exit.

'If I see you in here again, you son of a bitch, I'll kick your face in, and Kika's too, that deaf-mute father of yours!' The usher's voice reached me from the depths of the shadowy cinema.

I sat under the street lamp, undecided as to whether to go to the bar or to go straight home. I don't know how long I'd been there when dad's shadow appeared next to me; as soon as he saw the tears on my cheeks he knew that I wanted to make peace and that it was fear of his refusing me that stopped me going to the bar to see him. He put his index fingers together in a sign of friendship and hugged me to his chest, then slowly and wearily we turned for home.

★ ★ ★

The first day I went to school I was already familiar to everyone, both in class and elsewhere, because the pupils and teachers had known me for years as a street seller.

Now they simply began to consider me a pupil-cum-street seller. Also, on that first day I discovered that my name wasn't Joey and that my father's name wasn't Kika. The teacher standing by the blackboard had called out 'Shmuel Youkhanna' a number of times without receiving any reply when he came up to me and tapped me on the head with his cane, saying, 'When I call out your name, stand up and say "Yes sir!"'

The other boys fell about laughing. 'But I didn't hear my name,' I said.

'What is your name?' the teacher asked.

'Joey Kika, sir.'

The teacher laughed, tapping his left hand with his cane. 'No, son, your name at school is Shmuel Youkhanna. You can be Joey Kika when you're outside school and selling in the street.'

'Yes, sir,' I replied shyly.

'And Shmuel, don't forget to get your hair cut,' said the teacher, returning to his place near the blackboard.

I stood up and replied, 'Yes, sir', feeling a pang of anguish as I realised that I was the oldest of the pupils, and perhaps that was the reason the teacher had appointed me to be a monitor over the others.

My mother was sitting in the doorway. As was her habit, she sat me on her lap and began looking through my hair for lice. She found nothing, but nonetheless repeated the admonition she used when she did 'make a prey': 'I've told you a thousand times, be careful with the Bedouin kids, their heads are full of lice.'

'Mum!'

'Yes.'

'Who's Shmuel?' I asked her, looking at the clothes hanging on the line.

'He's a prophet.'

'Who chose the name for me?' My eyes were still fixed on the clothes flapping in the breeze that was bringing us a little cool relief on that scorching afternoon.

She answered sadly, 'The day you were born, Kiryakos came to visit and asked me if I'd chosen a name for you. I was alone, and unsure what to call you. Kiryakos picked up the Bible and opened it, then asked me what I thought of the name Shmuel. I agreed immediately.'

'Where was Dad?'

'He'd gone into hospital to have an operation.'

'Is that why you call me "ill omen" when you're cross with me?'

She stroked my face with her hand, pulling my head towards her and looking into my eyes, smiling and tearful. 'You have beautiful eyes, my son, just like the eyes of a prostitute,' she said, then wiping away her tears she got up and added, 'Take your brother Robin and go to Younan the barber, get your hair cut, then go on to Israel the photographer and have your pictures taken. Tell them your dad will be by to pay at the end of the week.'

My mother subsequently told me another story about how my name was chosen. One of our neighbours, a woman called Surma, was sterile. When my mother was pregnant with me, Surma told her, 'If it's a boy, I pray you call him Shmuel,' her own dream always having been to have a boy called Shmuel.

When we reached the photographer's I said, 'Uncle Israel, Mum sent us saying to take three pictures of us and Dad will pay you at the end of the week.'

'And so I will, by God,' said the photographer, ruffling Robin's hair and stepping into his studio.

The photographer's shop was scrupulously clean and tidy. I stood contemplating the pictures in their decorated wooden frames, some hanging on the walls, others in a glass cabinet; pictures of locals, pictures of English pilots and, to one side, a black and white picture of a beautiful woman, which I kept staring at until Israel and Robin emerged from the studio.

'Who is that woman?' I asked Israel.

He laughed. 'Come on, son, hurry up, I'm running late and it's time to go home.'

'She's very beautiful,' I said, looking into the camera lens in front of me as Israel covered his head with the black cloth. He took the picture then replied with some surprise, 'Of course she's beautiful. She's the Queen of Hollywood.'

'The Queen of Hollywood? Kiryakos didn't tell me about any Queen of Hollywood.'

'Well, Joey, you ask my friend Kiryakos about Marlene Dietrich.'

I didn't forget to ask Kiryakos about Marlene Dietrich when he came to the movie room. 'Who,' he answered dismissively, 'told you about that boring actress?'

I didn't answer.

Kiryakos was enthusiastic about my going to school. 'School is useful,' he said, 'but only for learning to read and write, especially for a genius like you.'

'What about the school certificate?'

'What certificate, Joey? Don't be silly. Jack Ford didn't have a school certificate. I learned long ago that schools don't turn out geniuses.' With that he pointed to a little box he'd brought with him. 'Do you know what's in this box?'

'What's in it?'

'Listen, Joey, I've thought about it for a long time and I believe you were right to give up the shadow theatre, because it's boring, just like that actress you mentioned to me earlier. That's why I've decided to give you this magic box that's been in my possession for more than thirty years. This box makes real movies, Joey, real movies.'

It was a square fibreboard box with a hole at either end. Through the front hole was a light bulb which had been emptied of its filaments and filled with water, while at the back was a long reel of film wound around a spool which could be turned by means of a handle.

Kiryakos put the box on top of the bucket. He told me to stay where I was, went out of the room and, producing a small mirror, held it in such a way as to reflect the sunlight onto the water-filled light bulb. An image of Henry Fonda wearing a blue scout uniform appeared on the opposite wall.

'This really is the movies,' I cried looking at Kiryakos, 'but where will we get the films from?'

'I've got loads of movies that I keep in a special place, you'll love them when you see them.' He glanced quickly at the checks decorating his shirt and added in a whisper, 'If I had a camera and a dark room I'd have filmed you and Kika.'

Kiryakos went to sit in the corner and I next to him. I noticed tears beginning to well up in his eyes, and he turned his head towards the pictures hanging on the wall and said sadly, 'I don't know why I didn't become a film-maker. Sergeant Mike told me I had the necessary skill and imagination. Listen, Joey, you must learn all about the movies, you must become a film-maker. I'm sure you can do it, that's why I'm giving you this box. You just need to grow up then everything will be easy.'

He was a sad sight to behold, and I felt it was somehow incumbent upon me to relieve his woes. 'Tell me, Kiryakos,' I said with a smile, 'how's John Ford's health? How's he doing these days?'

'He's doing just fine. He's busy preparing his new movie. It's called *Seven Women*.' Then he turned towards me with a smile: 'Next time, don't call him John Ford but Jack Ford, as his friends do.'

'My friend Jack Ford,' I said to myself.

Kiryakos always kept his promises. A week later he turned up with seven reels of film, each several minutes long. There were clips from various movies – westerns, musicals and thrillers – which Kiryakos had harmoniously spliced together.

My friends were delighted when I showed them the movies and would gather outside the movie room waiting for me to return from work. Thanks to Kiryakos's movie box I could see the Hollywood stars on the wall of my room just as if I was in a real cinema. I would reflect the sunlight onto the waterfilled light bulb and let the images of the actors project onto the screen, where I stared at their faces, absorbing their features, their clothes their hairstyles. And when the sun went down and the pictures began to fade a question would arise in my heart: 'O God, why can't the sun rise at night?'

My father loved the screenings of the new movies, and would happily spend his time with me watching them. He made it clear he was upset because I lost daylight time in working for the three-fingered cripple (his language for Nasrat Shah), and when I explained to him that I needed to work to earn a little money, he shook his head, pointing to the sky, closing his eyes and agitating his hand right and left, 'How can we make it work at night?'

★ ★ ★

Nasrat Shah had taught me how to make *amba*, mango pickle, which we would sell in the winter (and sometimes on summer nights). We made the *amba* at Nasrat Shah's house, but I would tell the customers we'd imported it from Bombay where it was produced using the finest Indian spices. One day a customer asked me to swear to him that it really was imported from India. 'By Imam Ali Bin Abi Talib, it's produced in Bombay,' I vowed, but the customer didn't believe me and insisted I swear by Christ. 'By Christ, it's produced in Bombay,' I said. Of course I was aware at the time I was committing sacrilege but I knew from my mother and my friends' mothers that angels only begin recording people's sins from the age of fourteen.

Nasrat Shah's only real competitor in the sale of *amba* sandwiches was Moussa, and Moussa was the one person to whom I admitted that we made the *amba* at home and that it was actually me who made it most of the time. I found myself forced to own up one day as I was selling *amba* in front of the cinema and saw Moussa finishing up his stock of sandwiches before us and closing up his handcart to return home. I approached him and whispered, 'Uncle Moussa, may God preserve you, leave a sandwich to one side for me before you finish everything.' Moussa laughed, refusing to take the money from my outstretched hand. 'A real boss man doesn't take money from another real boss man,' he said, then looked surprised and added, 'But, boss man Joey, isn't it strange that you should like my *amba* when it's produced in Bombay just like yours?' I saw there was nothing for it but to confess. I waited a few moments for one of his customers to move away then said in a low voice, 'Our *amba* is made at Nasrat Shah's house, Uncle Moussa.'

'So,' said Moussa smiling, 'your *amba* is produced in Buckingham Palace.'

'No, Uncle Moussa, Buckingham Palace is our house, not Nasrat Shah's!' We both laughed.

I would half fill the yellow bucket with water then add half a kilo of turmeric, five teaspoonfuls of salt, three lumps of lemon flavouring, a hundred thin slices of aubergine (which had been left to soak for two days in pepper juice), ten chunks of potato and ten crushed hot peppers, mixing all the ingredients together with my hands for ten minutes. From time to time Nasrat Shah would dip one of his three fingers into the bucket to taste the mixture (which he swore was produced in Bombay), then he'd produce a kilo jar of real *amba* imported from India and pour that into the bucket. I would continue stirring the concoction around for a while before emptying it into five or six large jars and, trusting in God, go out to earn a living.

'Joey, may God preserve you, a quarter sandwich!'

'Joey, may God preserve you, a half sandwich!'

'Shmuel, may God preserve you, a quarter sandwich!' said one, and I remember threatening him one day as we left class, 'If you call me Shmuel, you'll never taste an *amba* sandwich as long as you live.'

'All right, Joey,' he said apologetically.

A couple of minutes before the school bell went, I'd gather up my 'work tools', stow them in the handcart and enter class. Then, forty-five minutes into the lesson, the teacher would look at his watch while the other pupils turned towards me, knowing that he would nod at me to leave a couple of minutes before them so as to give me time to get behind my handcart and sell them *amba* sandwiches . . . 'Joey, a quarter sandwich! . . . Joey, a half sandwich!'

Only once did the teacher find himself obliged to upbraid me, and that in a tone that managed to avoid hurting my feelings, 'Joey . . . excuse me, Shmuel, I know your *amba* is delicious but try and stop the smell clinging to your clothes!'

★ ★ ★

My mother was aware that my father's infatuation with the movie box – or 'Kiryakos's cinema' – had turned him into a child. 'Like a little kid,' she would say, 'enthralled by the pictures Joey projects on the wall,' and she begged Kiraykos to warn Dad that Atallah, the owner of the bakery, had been complaining about him for two days. 'Kika has become very careless in his work, he's burning the bread and a lot of customers are going to the bakery of the fat Armenian woman,' he'd said. My mother also remembered something else Atallah had told her before he left: 'My son has finished his military service, he's thinking about getting married and he's looking for work.'

In her confusion she looked at Kiryakos, 'Isn't that a warning, Kiryakos?'

'People go to the fat Armenian woman's place because she has a modern bakery, not because of Kika,' Kiryakos replied.

'But can't you see that the box you brought for Joey is the cause

217

of our problems?' my mother asked. 'I don't know how we're going to live if Atallah decides to sack Kika.'

'What do you want me to do if your husband's a sensitive soul who cares for nothing in the world but pictures?' asked Kiryakos, smiling in a way calculated to arouse my mother's anger.

During lunch my father picked a fight with my mother. From his gestures I understood he was telling her, 'We agreed to send Joey out to work because Samson, Teddy and Ibrahim were going to school. Now, though, Joey's become a schoolboy too,' and he put his hands on his waist, a sign that meant, 'So what do you think? What do you have to say?'

My mother replied by tracing a number of circles around her head, hollowing out her cheeks and entwining her little fingers then releasing them, 'The thin man who wears the headscarf – Atallah – is angry and wants to fire you from your job.'

My father replied by firing off a loud raspberry ('I don't give a damn'), then pointing to his behind ('He's only worth a fart').

When Sakina tried to resolve their conflict he screamed in her face and waved his hands in the air ('This has nothing to do with you'). Sakina put a plate of rice and beans in front of me but my father jerked me away by the hand in the direction of the movie room, pointing to the sun and tapping his left wrist with his right forefinger ('Time is getting on').

Using gestures, Dad told me that he wasn't happy with my working for Nasrat Shah, and that I should have time to play like other children. Working in movies (he pointed to Kiryakos's box) was more important than working for the man with three fingers, and he sketched out a daily schedule for me if I were to give up work ('You get up in the morning and come to the bakery to get bread, you make your sandwiches and go to school where you read and play with the other boys. In the afternoon, I'll be home from the bakery and we'll make the most of the daylight to use the movie box. And when I go for my evening shift at the bakery, you can do your homework, then go to the cinema, after which you come to get me at the bar'). He put his hands on his waist, ('What do you think? What do you say?').

I smiled and tapped my head with my index finger ('Let me think about it!'). However, when I noticed he was getting a little upset I didn't give him time to suggest another programme, but ran out and adjusted the mirror, which was beginning to capture the sun's rays and reflect them towards the movie box. My father busied himself with regulating the image reflected on the walls of the room and, as I clapped my hands in amazement, he let his imagination run wild and began moving the box forwards and backwards, left and right. He pulled his white handkerchief out of the back pocket of his trousers, wiped his face and neck then put it back, leaving a corner hanging out like a dog's ear. The image projected on the wall was of Victor Mature wearing black and holding a revolver. As my father slowly turned the spool, the pictures moved and a man wearing a white shirt and black waistcoat entered throwing a revolver onto the table in front of Victor Mature. Little by little, the right side of his face was revealed and we realised it was Hank Fonda. Then with a sudden movement my father stretched his hand into the depths of the image, seized the revolver and opened fire on me. Bang! Bang! Bang! I put my hands on my stomach and fell to the ground dead, not getting up until I heard his applause. We laughed and played and laughed until the images disappeared from the walls and we realised that Teddy, Ibrahim, Pious, and Jalil the Jap were standing by the door and blocking the sunlight. My father stuck his tongue out at them irreverently, then went home.

'What did you do to your father, Joey? He went off to the bakery with his face full of joy.'

I mulled over my mother's words as I stood selling sandwiches outside the cinema, asking myself how an hour spent playing with the movie box could make my father go off to work 'with his face full of joy', and what would happen if I stopped working for Nasrat Shah and implemented the programme he had drawn up for me, or rather for us. I wanted to see him happy, of course, but without leaving Nasrat Shah. I continued serving my customers with my mind on my father and took no notice when that swine (the usher) passed in front of me, his arms theatrically outstretched to show me he was buying his sandwich from our rival Moussa. I was engrossed with thoughts of my father, never imagining for a moment that he would commit a 'crime' against Nasrat Shah that very night.

Black, everything around me was black. I was walking naked and alone, cold and thirsty, when suddenly I was covered from head to foot in black robes. As soon as I smelled the incense with which they were impregnated I let out a cry for help, 'Sakinaaaaaaa!' In a few seconds a long narrow thread of light appeared, dancing right and left before steadying at my feet, and I understood that I had to follow it as a guide. I walked and walked until the thread of light came to an end at a lake, the waters of which emitted a powerful light as if a mirror in its depths were reflecting the sun. I smiled when I saw him, sitting on the surface of the water not far from me with his round, light brown face, black beard, twinkling eyes, a green turban over his chestnut-coloured hair and in his hand a long thread of light. As I stretched out my hand to scoop up a handful of water, the man and the light disappeared together and I awoke to find myself lying in the bedroom between my sleeping brothers. My mother's gentle snores were rising from her throat, like a piece of music that brought us peace whenever we awoke from a nightmare.

My gaze ranged around the room and I was surprised to note my father's absence. Then my eyes turned to fix on the skylight in the ceiling, as I wondered to myself where he could be at this time of night. I knew that Mikhail (Mikha, as his clients called him), having closed the bar, would be sleeping beside his wife. I got out of bed to see if Dad had lain down to sleep by the front door as he did when he came home full of drink and didn't want to disturb us with the smell of booze.

The night was peaceful save for the croaking of frogs coming from the communal wash-place, the frogs that disappeared during the day, we never knew where. I stood there for a few moments, unsure what to do, then before I could go back to bed I heard a noise coming from a few metres away, near the movie room. I didn't think it could be thieves for there was only one thief in our neighbourhood and that was Hassouni, who once ventured to pilfer one of Sakina's chickens. Samson caught him and dealt out fifty strokes with the military belt my father had given him as a present to use on just such an occasion. Samson told us that Hassouni had been stretched out on the ground receiving lashes with the belt and screaming, 'I swear by Christ that I won't do it again!' But Samson continued to beat him, shouting, 'I'll flay the skin off your back like a chicken if I find you in our alleyway again, you chicken thief!'

The 'chicken thief' had taken more than a month to plan his revenge, waiting until he knew his father the butcher had decided to move to the city of Fallujah before putting the despicable plot into effect. As I was coming back from the cinema one evening, Hassouni, knowing the road I would follow, lay in wait behind the corner of the public latrine. As I passed his hiding place he leapt out and began spitting on me and thumping me. 'Tell your brother that Hassouni won't leave al-Habbaniyah until he's gutted you as my dad guts lambs.' Then he hit me on the head with a bicycle pump and, putting the hem of his dishdasha between his teeth, ran off.

That evening my mother had been taken aback to see the blood covering my face (for my part I was quite happy to have a bloody head, it made me feel like Birju) and she took me round to see Haroun, the hospital cleaner and medicine thief (father of my friend Zayya). He dressed the wound and bandaged my head, laughing, 'You're still young, Joey, you're still at an age when superficial wounds heal easily.' My mother kept on thanking him, unaware that Haroun was delighted to bandage my head because he believed he had been born to be a doctor, or at least a nurse, and not just a lowly cleaner. I don't think he considered the medicines he removed from the hospital every day, hidden in his socks and pockets (Zayya described this to us one day when he was angry with his father), as stolen. Quite the contrary, he was convinced he had turned his house into an emergency clinic.

As I stood there I remembered Hassouni the chicken thief. He had remained in al-Habbaniyah because his father had changed his mind about moving to Fallujah, and I thought perhaps he'd begun stealing again, although I knew that he and Samson had made up and that they were even planning to carry out a few thefts together. As I approached the movie room I could smell paraffin, and there, in fact, I saw my father emptying a can of paraffin over the handcart. Seeing me, he pulled out a box of matches and I rushed forward and stood in front of the handcart. He spat and looked towards me angrily, then, after a few moments, put the matches into his pocket and began trembling and coughing. I smiled at him, then began pushing the cart as fast as I could to the communal wash place. I don't know if Dad felt remorse or if he'd just sobered up but he too appeared at the wash place carrying a box of Tide soap powder, which he emptied over the handcart, and we cleaned it together. Then, despite the cold, we took off our clothes and washed them as well.

The next morning Nasrat Shah made more than ten circuits around the handcart, poking his fingers underneath his hat to scratch his bald head in wonder at its shiny green cleanness and I, walking behind him, kept repeating in his ear, 'My father was annoyed at how dirty the handcart was when we got back from the bar yesterday evening, and he suggested we clean it.' After much thought, Nasrat Shah was finally convinced by what I had told him. He said I could have two days off 'so you can show your movies to your father and let him get his fill'. Then, patting me on the head, he added, 'From now on, consider Sunday as your day off, just like the English and Shaker al-Hindi.' My father was delighted, especially because the holiday coincided with my coming top of the class in the mid-term exams.

What no one knew was that the flames my father had sought to kindle on Nasrat Shah's handcart were to break out more violently somewhere else. In our house.

★ ★ ★

One September morning Nasrat Shah came to wake me up, and I in turn went to rouse my father, tapping my left wrist ('It's time to get up'). I held out my hands and pulled him upright onto his feet, from where, without fail, he launched a kick in the direction of my backside by way of his morning exercise with which to greet the new day. I was readying the sieves and sacks while Ali was complaining to his father that 'the September sun doesn't produce salt', to which Nasrat Shah replied, 'I told you, go and you'll see'.

'By God, the September sun doesn't produce salt,' said Professor Ali, who as soon as we returned from gathering salt would wash, change into clean clothes and shoot off to the town gates to catch a bus for al-Ramadi, where he worked as a teacher.

'The sun yesterday was hotter than in August, do as I say,' insisted Nasrat Shah, closing the subject as he prepared to perform his dawn prayers on a small prayer mat. But what he didn't know was that yesterday was Wednesday and it was natural the sun should be hotter 'because God created the sun on a Wednesday', at least according to my mother.

Misery was weighing down on our tongues and our steps as we returned from the salt marshes. We had spent more than two hours plunging our sieves into the depths with nothing to show for it but a minute quantity of white crystals that melted away as soon as we put them aside.

We were returning with a heavy tread when we noticed the

flames devouring our little house. My mother's hands were on her swollen stomach and she was crying, while Kiryakos (what had he come for at that time?) and Samson were taking buckets of water from Teddy, Fatima, Ibrahim, Shamiran and a number of neighbours and emptying them onto the fire.

'Where's Robin?' I asked Shamiran as Ali and Hussein rushed off to join those fighting the fire. 'I sent him to the bakery to call Dad.'

I ran to the communal wash place, filled a bucket and passed it to Kiryakos, all the while thinking of the distress my father would feel when Robin pointed his dainty little fingers at the oven, used his delicate palms to make a pyramid shape and then put his hands on his chest ('A blaze like the one in the oven is raging in Mum's house'). Dad might pass out, imagining the flames getting closer to his 'heart' hidden in the wooden tea chest.

My mother had put the teapot on the paraffin stove then gone to do some laundry at the wash place, as she usually did. The water had all boiled away and the burning wick had done the rest. The flames grew higher and higher until they spread to the wooden window that divided the two rooms of the house, and from there to the wooden beams of the ceiling. Shamiran, sleeping in the doorway with my other brothers, was startled by an unnatural heat running through her body and awoke to find the blaze well underway.

Kiryakos stared at me as he took the bucket from my hands. He seemed tired, or he may just have been frantic from the fire-fighting. I looked at him and sensed he was deliberately opening his eyes as wide as possible, as if inviting me to plunge into them. Little by little, far away, I could see . . . Birju falling from his horse at his mother's feet, and reaching into his pocket for the jewels he'd retrieved from the moneylender Sukhilala. Kiryakos gave me a secret smile, as if the rays from his deep-set eyes had projected their images onto the movie screen in my head. I smiled at him and, taking one of the empty salt bags, I soaked it in water, put it over my head and leapt into the flames.

My mother shrieked, '*Kiryakos, khooni, bayyet qatlit brooni? Qamoodi Alaha, qamoodi bayyet qatlit brooni*? Brother Kiryakos, do you want to kill my son? Why, O God, why do you want to kill him?'

As I crossed the first room I held my breath. The steam rising from the sack over my head was burning my shoulders and neck. I stepped into the other room and began rummaging through the first tea chest, then the second, then the third. Coughing continually, I emptied the contents of each chest until my hand touched against my father's parcel. Seizing it, I ran out.

'*Shidana broonit shidana!* Fool, son of a fool,' screamed my mother as Kiryakos poured several buckets of water over me.

'Fool, son of a fool,' she said again, not knowing whether to laugh or cry. In the meantime my father, who had arrived while I was amidst the flames, was ignoring everyone else while he anxiously opened his parcel. He removed its cloth, nylon and lace wrappings, and the silver box appeared. He breathed on it and rubbed it against his chest to increase its sheen, then, pressing a little button, the lid sprang open and the melodious notes of a piano tinkled out. People came to look and saw the box contained a black and white photograph of the young Queen Elizabeth. My father laughed and laughed until everyone began laughing with him.

'Almighty God, the man is out of his mind,' said my mother, laughing and wiping away her tears.

'Buckingham Palace has finally burnt down,' said Kiryakos, laughing too.

That day Samson decided to leave school for good, my mother and Shamiran concentrated on cleaning the house, while Teddy, Robin and I had to go to classes in our gym clothes. The school administration presented us with brown winter uniforms made of some coarse material that made our bodies itch all the time.

Alone among us my father went back, back to that summer day of 1958 when he was working as a cook at the Royal Air Force base in al-Habbaniyah. At sunset that day, wearing his cook's uniform and cutting onions, or perhaps frying potatoes or braising a shank of veal, he was looking out of the kitchen window onto the garden where the officers, with their wives and children, were watching a newsreel about their young queen being projected on a screen set up in front of them.

That day the commander of the airbase had approached my father and handed him an oblong box made of solid silver, as used by kings, nobles and the rich to keep their cigarettes. With his finger the commander tapped my father on the chest and pointed to the writing engraved on the surface of the box, then at the young queen who was still waving and distributing smiles to the public.

From this my father understood that 'Your name is engraved here, and it's a gift to you from that young woman wearing a crown on her head.'

At this point I can well imagine that my father looked at the tattoo of the lion and the unicorn guarding the British crown on his left arm, then turned his head towards the kitchen window to contemplate the face of the young woman wearing the crown; and that he saw her smiling and heard – for the first time in his life – a beautiful melody that carried him far away from the kitchen, from the commander, from al-Habbaniyah, even from my mother.

★ ★ ★

The smell of plaster was still rising from the walls although two months had passed since the house had been renovated after the fire, and my mother was washing Robin in the bathtub. When she rubbed his body too hard he protested, '*Kha-cha kha-cha, yemmi, khlapakh hawin!* Please, Mum! Easy does it!'

'Holy Virgin, what have I done?' she replied angrily. 'Apart from all the disasters that assail us, the children of the deaf-mute have reached a point where they don't even like being clean.'

With that she began looking with a mixture of sadness and despair at the pictures hanging on the wall in front of her, a picture of the Virgin and Child, another of Mar Gewargis on horseback with his long spear deep in the dragon's body, and a carefully framed image of Mar Shimun which had attracted my attention ever since I was small.

One day I had asked Shamiran who he was. She was dancing around, singing, and without breaking off replied, 'It's God.'

Ever since then the word 'God' always conjured up the image of a man wearing black, with his hand resting on a lump of marble and a priestly smile emerging from the depths of a dark beard.

My mother turned to me as I was playing with my new brother John, and said, 'Put your brother to bed, fill the stove with paraffin and prime it.'

'Yes, Mum,' I replied, still playing with the baby boy Sakina had delivered late one rainy afternoon three weeks earlier. That evening Kiryakos had rushed out to get two bottles of arak while Shamiran and Fatima prepared a large amount of fried curried fish; and as we all sat together my mother had raised the question of what to call the newborn sleeping in the wicker cradle next to her. After a long silence she looked at my father, licking her right index finger and pressing it against the infant's forehead ('What should we call him?').

My father replied by shrugging his shoulders and smiling slightly shamefacedly ('I don't know').

Kiryakos, his eyes completely red, tossed back a large glass of arak and replied, 'John.'

'John?' asked my mother in a faint voice.

'John,' confirmed Kiryakos, 'after the man for whom you wept so much almost exactly this time three years ago. Have you forgotten John Kennedy, Sister Gorgiya?'

'How could I forget John Kennedy,' said my mother, throwing

a glance at the baby. 'All right, John it is. It's a lovely name. Thank you, Brother Kiryakos.'

A few days later, however, as we were sitting together in the movie room, Kiryakos asked me, 'Did you see how I fooled your mum into naming your little brother after our friend John Ford?' 'But we like John Kennedy too,' I replied. 'Of course, of course,' said Kiryakos, 'but we mustn't forget, Joey, that we are film-makers and that John Ford is dearer to us than John Kennedy.'

I put John to bed and was beginning to fill and prime the stove when my mother (who had become irritable since the fire) screamed out again, 'Take your clothes off and get yourself ready!' I began to undress slowly, hiding my private parts with my hands and looking up at the Virgin and Child who were gazing down at me.

'Mum,' I said, 'may God preserve you, let's move the bathtub into the other room.'

She pulled me by the hand towards the tub, smiling as if she understood what I meant, then poured water over my head and began scrubbing at my body, saying, 'When all of you grow up I hope you'll know the meaning of shame but, alas, who can promise me you'll be at my side then? All of you want to leave. Kiryakos has planted Hollywood in your head, Samson wants to go to Australia when he's finished his military service, Teddy to Detroit like Youshiya's daughter, and even little Robin has begun talking about flying. And as for your father, he'd have had no objection – if only he'd known how – to throwing me out into the street and going to join the English.'

'But Kiryakos told me that Dad refused to go with the English,' I said defensively.

'Stand up! You stink like the dead yet you hate the idea of getting washed,' said my mother. 'Kiryakos is a poor fool, he can say what he likes, but if your father had had the slightest inkling that the English wanted to take him with them, he'd have gone to England on foot. Instead they just made fun of him with a cigarette case that's not worth a penny . . . maybe, God knows, Shaker al-Hindi the greengrocer would take it in return for a couple of kilos of apples.'

'I don't like apples, Mum.'

'It was just an example, son. Apples, onions and English silver all have the same value.'

'Long ago there was an Assyrian bear who lived in the mountains near one of the villages of Nineveh. In October the peasant women would climb to the heights of the surrounding mountains to pick walnuts, and every day the bear would watch them. As the days went by he was attracted to an Assyrian peasant girl called Nazo. She was tall and dark with long red hair, green eyes and pink lips, a real beauty, and the bear would spend long nights thinking of her. His heart filled with joy whenever he saw her walking among the trees, picking walnuts and singing, and he would hide nearby to listen to her sweet voice.

> *I will wait for you, my love.*
> *Don't believe what they say.*
> *I am yours and*
> *I'm waiting for you.*

'One day the bear noticed that Nazo no longer came out with the other peasant women, even though the trees were still full of walnuts. He thought and thought about it until one evening, hearing the sound of drums and pipes, he emerged from his cave and looked down into the valley to see hundreds of lanterns burning all over the village, and the people dancing, drinking wine and making merry. At first the poor bear believed the lanterns were there for the 'Feast of the Cross', then, having thought for a while, he remembered that he'd joined the villagers when they celebrated the Feast of the Cross (which fell every year on 14 September), and even that he'd drunk too much and not

gone hunting the following day, remaining in his cave to sing
Nazo's favourite song.

> *I will wait for you, my love.*
> *Don't believe what they say.*
> *I am yours and*
> *I'm waiting for you.*

'The bear was sad, so sad, when he discovered the people were
celebrating Nazo's marriage to Awikam, son of the village doctor,
but then he put on his best clothes, donned a red tie, combed his
hair back just as Kiryakos does and went down to the village.
There he walked among the people and drank a glass of red wine
before creeping stealthily into Nazo's room, where she was
combing her long red hair. He rolled her up in a large rug and
carried her off to the mountains. 'Nazo lived with the bear for
more than a year before giving birth to a baby girl whose top half
looked like Nazo and whose bottom half looked like the bear.
Every time the bear went out hunting he rolled a great stone over
the entrance to the cave, but with time he mellowed and decided to leave the cave open. 'One evening at sunset, the bear
returned home from hunting, whistling and singing happily, and
carrying two deer. No sooner had he approached the cave than
he heard his baby daughter crying and knew that Nazo had run
away to the village. The bear picked up the weeping child and
began to weep himself, and, looking towards the valley, he shouted at the top of his voice, "*Nazo, tatta waq waq! Nazo, tatta waq*
waq! Nazo, tatta waq waq! Nazo, the baby's crying! Nazo, the baby's
crying! Nazo, the baby's crying!"'

'What did the bear do then?' Robin asked my mother.
'He's crying and shouting still. That's enough. Go to sleep. It's
getting on for midnight. Quickly now, go to sleep.'
But Mum fell asleep before us. Within five minutes we heard

her snores, at times breaking off, at others taking on high operatic tones. For us, it was the music of safety. When we awoke from our nightmares and heard our mother's operatic snoring we knew all was well with the world and went back to sleep.

Little by little, as we looked at our mother's eyes fixed on the ceiling and concentrated on the sounds issuing from her open mouth, our eyelids would tire and droop, the lantern and my mother's snores would fade away and each of us was lost in the maze of his dreams.

★ ★ ★

Just like in the American and English movies in which the hero or heroine would buy vegetables or come out of the grocer's carrying a brown paper bag in their arms, so Kiryakos, when he came to visit, would always bring a large brown paper bag full of fruit. He was in his forties, tall and thin, and wore his shiny greasy hair combed back. He would come in the morning to have breakfast with us, then disappear only to emerge again at teatime. Sometimes he'd come to dinner, then disappear again for the night. He claimed he owned a house, though no one had ever seen it.

I was the person closest to Kiryakos. He used to carry me in his arms while I was still a little baby, and later, when I was around five, he began taking me to the pictures. He'd wanted to become a film-maker, but unfortunately that wish was never fulfilled.

I had always wanted to know more about his private life, but I don't think I'd ever have had the courage to intrude if it hadn't been for my mother's constant repetitions of 'poor Kiryakos, he's an orphan'. So one day as we were sitting under the pomegranate tree and Kiryakos was reading me bits of movie news, I interrupted him. 'Kiryakos, is it true you're an orphan?'

He contemplated his red and blue checked shirt, put a cigarette in his mouth and said, 'Yes, Joey, I'm an orphan. Your dad's also an orphan, and so is your mother. Her mother gave birth to her then died an hour later.' Then, with a smile on his face, he added, 'Most of the inhabitants of al-Habbaniyah are orphans.'

'And how did you become an orphan?' I asked without hesitation.

He reached out his left hand to push back the hair covering my forehead and said, 'I was happy once. I had a father, a mother and a sister called Virginia who was three years older than me. She loved to draw and hoped to become an artist, while I was interested in theology. I still feel a little embarrassed when I remember that I wanted to become a priest. We lived in the north, in Irbil.'

That was the first time I'd heard such information from or about Kiryakos. My mother was always telling me, 'You ask a lot a of questions, Joey. That's not good in a little boy of your age but, ah, what can we do if Kiryakos encourages you?'

Kiryakos looked at me and said in English, 'Satisfied?'

'What does "satisfied" mean?' I asked.

'Are you content with what I told you?'

'I don't know,' I said smiling, then added, 'But why are you an orphan?'

'You're a little devil,' said Kiryakos. 'All right, I'll tell you the whole story of the film.

'In the summer of 1933 I was twelve years old. One night as we were doing our homework by the light of a lantern we heard a knock at the door, just like in the films, Joey. I got up to open it, but my father beat me to it and no sooner had he opened the door than five or six masked men pushed their way into the house. I saw one of them drive a knife into my father's neck and throw him to the ground; others stabbed my mother in the chest. I fled into the back of the house where Virginia was sitting and tried to get her out by the rear window overlooking the street, but she refused to leave, and wanted to go and see what was happening to our parents. I was trembling with fear, then I saw two of the masked men approach us with their daggers and, just as I'd seen the knife buried in my mother's chest, I saw the same thing happen to Virginia. I don't know how I managed to get to the window and throw myself out to flee through the steep narrow lanes. It was a night of horror. Dozens of masked men burst into the houses of the Assyrians and massacred the inhabitants. I saw the bodies of women and children, old men and youths cast onto the doorways of their homes or into the road, dozens of severed heads lying on street corners like motionless footballs. Women were screaming as their killers chased them with knives, cleavers and heavy cudgels. I kept on running. At a certain point I noticed I was being followed by a military jeep, which then came alongside me. Panting and trembling, I heard the driver of the jeep address me in English, and I understood from his gestures that he was telling me to climb in. I did so and we took off down the mountain tracks. For two days after that I lost the power of speech and, despite Mike's efforts, refused to eat anything.'

'Who is Mike?'

'Mike, or Michael, was the name of the driver of the jeep who rescued me. Sergeant Mike continued looking after me and trying to calm me down. He would speak to me in English, sometimes using a few Arabic words in an Iraqi dialect. After I'd spent a week at his house in Mosul he told me that the English had known that armed Kurds were about to slaughter the Assyrians but could do nothing about it. Later we learned that soldiers from the Iraqi army had assisted in the massacre, which became known as the "Simele Massacre", and that our King Ghazi had approved it.'

'What does "massacre" mean, Kiryakos?'

'It's like what the slaughterman does with the lamb.'

'But Mother says we like the king,' I said.

'They say he was afraid of the armed forces. There was a Kurdish officer, a villain called Bakr Sidqi, who was in charge of the army. He intended to attack the royal palace if the king opposed the Kurds' decision to slaughter the Assyrians.'

'And why should the Kurds want to slaughter us? Most of my friends are Kurds.'

'Poor Kurds. They claim northern Iraq as their own country. They call it "Kurdistan" and don't want any other peoples to live there.'

'What are "peoples", Kiryakos?'

'Peoples are human beings, Assyrians, Arabs, Kurds, Persians, Turkmen, Jews, Armenians, they're all peoples, in other words human groups that live in Iraq.'

Before I could ask Kiryakos another question, he said to me, 'Listen, Joey, I only told you of the massacres perpetrated by the Kurds against the Assyrians so that you'd know how I became an orphan, just as thousands of other Assyrians did. It's past, don't think about it at all. I can say now that if the Assyrians had been strong enough they would have massacred the Kurds, just as the Arabs massacred the Kurds, because in the end we're all victims of backwardness.'

'What does "backwardness" mean?'

'When people think like sheep, then they're backward!'

'Where did you go after you became an orphan, when you were still so young?'

'Mike worked as a film projectionist at the Royal Air Force base in al-Habbaniyah, showing movies to the officers and their families, and when he learned that I was now an orphan without family or relatives he asked me to go with him to al-Habbaniyah and work as his assistant. You don't know how happy I was, Joey, when I thought of projecting those movies. I forgot the massacre, I forgot my parents and my sister, I forgot everything. I went movie mad. Mike wouldn't let me visit my old house after things had calmed down, not even for an hour. "Listen, Kirk," he said to me (that's what Mike and the other English officers called me), "it's all over, and there's nothing as bad as seeing mass graves, it's even worse than scenes of war itself. I advise you to turn your back on the past once and for all."

'I listened to his advice and came to al-Habbaniyah. The journey lasted three days, and Mike never stopped talking about a film director called John Ford. He loved him. In fact, right from the start Mike called me *Strong Boy*, just as I do now with you. He gave me a number of his checked shirts, some of which I still have today. Poor Mike, he wanted to become a film director but unfortunately that wish was never fulfilled. His intention was to go to Hollywood and meet John Ford, and he used to tell me that when he arrived there he'd march into the studio and tell John Ford, "Listen up, Jack, I've come from al-Habbaniyah, which is in the middle of nowhere, to work with you."

'Just think, Joey, to this day I don't know why Mike didn't travel to Hollywood, after all he was Irish just like John Ford.'

Kiryakos glanced sadly down at his blue and red checked shirt and lit a cigarette.

'One morning,' he said, 'after I'd spent a few years with Mike at the airbase, I went to his room to wake him up, only to find him lying on the floor with three or four empty brandy bottles scattered around him. I tried to pick him up but couldn't, he was so heavy. When I noticed that he wasn't moving at all I rushed off to find Doctor Raymond, but it was too late. Mike had departed this life after a heart attack.'

'What does "departed this life" mean?' I asked.

'It means he died. Mike died having taught me everything about the projector and how to splice worn-out film reels. Soon after, the airbase offices issued an order whereby I took his place and inherited all his things. And when I learned to drive I received the jeep, the same jeep that had rescued me from the massacre! Can you believe that, Joey?'

After a brief silence Kiryakos began laughing, shaking his head and staring at the ground.

'Once,' he said, 'Mike told me that had I been in America I would certainly have become the hero of *Stagecoach* in place of

Marion Michael Morrison, the young man who later became known as John Wayne. Can you believe it, Joey, that I could be John Wayne? Just imagine that. There were more than twenty pilots and officers in the airbase who told me that if John Ford had seen me before making *Young Mr Lincoln*, he would have given the part of the hero to me instead of Hank Fonda. But I think Mike was right and that I look more like John Wayne.'

'Why didn't you go to Hollywood, Kiryakos?'

'In 1947 I read that Mr John Ford had finished filming *The Fugitive* and that he was preparing two new movies, *Fort Apache* and *Three Godfathers*. I got ready to travel to London within two or three days, and from there to America. But I didn't go because of your father.'

'My father!'

'Your father came to me and told me that he had met an Assyrian family who had emigrated from northern Iraq to Turkey, but having encountered problems there had returned to Iraq, finally settling in al-Habbaniyah. He said he wanted me to be best man at his wedding. I went with him and discovered to my surprise that the prospective bride was a girl of thirteen who was refusing to get married to your father. Her stepmother was insisting the wedding go ahead in any way possible, and I saw her slapping the bride and threatening to throw her out of the house if she refused to marry your father. Yet the girl still refused the match. Your father went crazy and began drinking more and more, making a lot of mistakes in his job until I was afraid the English would fire him. So I decided to give up my journey temporarily until I could resolve your father's problems. He was a close friend of mine. After two weeks of toing and froing the wedding took place and that little orphan girl became your mother.'

'But couldn't you have made your journey after Dad got married?'

'Firstly, there are opportunities that only come around once.

Secondly, a surprise happened, a wonderful surprise that flung me into a torrid love story and made me forget all about that journey.'

'What happened?'

'Martha Longwood's arrival in al-Habbaniyah changed all my ideas, and drove me more and more to drink. She was the most beautiful English woman around. Truly, Joey, I really want to tell you all about my love story, despite the fact the English gave me the nickname *The Secret Man*. Major Longwood called me and told me he had a routine air mission, and could I go to the airstrip to meet his wife and take her home. I was sitting in the jeep avoiding the heat of the sun and watching the plane settling on the runway. There were about fourteen passengers, women, officers and enlisted men. People came up to meet them and they quickly dispersed. Then the most beautiful lady came up to me, accompanied by a little girl of about five. 'Mrs Longwood?' I asked.

' "Yes, and this is Jackie,' she answered, pointing to the child.

' "Jackie is a beautiful name," I said. "It's the title of a movie by John Ford."

' "Is that so?" she asked flirtatiously, removing her hat.

' "Yes. Mr Ford directed the movie *Jackie* in 1921, which is the year I was born."

'She opened her eyes wide and asked me, "And what did Mr Ford direct in the year 1911?" I knew she was referring to the year she was born and, feeling a little ashamed, I replied, "Nothing, unfortunately, because Mr Ford only began making movies in 1917." '

'Did Mrs Longwood love you?' I asked Kiryakos.

'She worshipped me, Joey. What a paradox it was. Just imagine, she never knew that I cancelled my travel plans as soon as I set eyes on her, and she never returned to London after coming to al-Habbaniyah, saying, "I'll stay here for you, Kirk".'

When I asked Kiryakos how their love affair began he looked

at me and said, '*Hearts of Oak*', then broke a branch from the pomegranate tree and began hitting the surface of the stream flowing at our feet.

I was fascinated by the love story of Kiryakos and Martha and remained enraptured by it for days. But when I told some of the details to Nasrat Shah he began laughing.

'What movie was Kiryakos – pardon me, Kirk – talking about?' he asked, and began laughing again, playing with a coin he was holding in his hand.

'No, Uncle Nasrat,' I said, 'Kiryakos was talking about a real story that happened to him with an English lady.'

'What a mighty imagination he has. What English lady would go around with an impotent man?'

'What does "impotent" mean, Uncle Nasrat?'

'It means that our brother Kiryakos can't sleep with women,' he said, then added sorrowfully, 'but there's no need to talk about that painful subject.'

I subsequently discovered that Nasrat Shah belittled Kiryakos's love story with the English lady to get his revenge because Kiryakos had previously scoffed at a love story Nasrat Shah had had with a beautiful young woman, or 'the peerless one' as Nasrat Shah himself used to recount.

Nasrat Shah would tell his story as follows: 'You all know that I was once a merchant and that I used to visit nightclubs. One day I fell in love with a woman called Masouma. She was enchantingly beautiful, and a real artist who could sing effortlessly, and without any accent, in Arabic, English and Persian. No one knew anything about her. For a while an English officer competed with me for Masouma's affections, but I soon saw him off. I brought a sharp knife and placed it on the table in view of the entire nightclub clientele, then shouted in my rival's face, "Listen, you English officer, I won't let anyone, whoever it may be, share my love for this beautiful lady. In front of you I'm now going to cut off this finger of my left hand, and if you really love her, you'll do the same."

'Then I cut off the little finger of my left hand. The English officer seized the knife and an instant later threw his own finger down in front of me. Without pausing to think, I put my ring finger under the knife, pressed my right hand down on the blade, and off the finger came. At that, I saw the English officer's face turn pale. He was no fool and knew that if he remained there for long he'd lose all his fingers, so he put his hat on his head and left the nightclub, defeated. That day Masouma loved me, and her bed became my bed.'

Kiryakos would fall about laughing whenever he heard this story told by one or other of the inhabitants of al-Habbaniyah. 'Nasrat Shah may not watch movies much, but he truly has an outstanding imagination,' he said, then explained, 'Nasrat Shah used to work in the English army bakery. One day the poor guy was tired and, closing the iron door of the oven with his right hand, he didn't notice that his left hand was near the opening. The door slammed shut and cut off two of his fingers. I saw them with my own eyes burning in the oven like sausages.'

★ ★ ★

I packed a sandwich in among my books for school. It was made with yellow Kraft cheese which came in a blue tin that had 'Made in Australia' written on it, and whenever I saw the phrase I would hear my mother's voice saying, 'Children, you have cousins who live there, in a city called Sydney.' It was a very cold morning, luckily for me a Sunday and my day off work, which meant I could stay in the warmth of the classroom and leave Nasrat Shah to stand behind the handcart, rubbing his eight fingers in the cold.

I was surprised to come across a group of soldiers running through the streets on my way to school, their leader calling out and the others chanting in unison behind him, '*Haifa fain? Haifa baladi! Akka fain? Akka baladi!* Where is Haifa? Haifa's my home! Where is Acre? Acre's my home!'

When I got to school, I found the pupils were all talking about the soldiers and imitating their movements, and they didn't come and gather round me, as they usually did on a Sunday, to hear the latest gossip from Kiryakos about the new American movies. They were amazed by what they had seen, and the teacher was obliged to rap his cane on the blackboard again and again to silence the chattering in class.

'They're Egyptian soldiers,' he explained, 'and they've come to train at the al-Habbaniyah camp in preparation for the war in Palestine.' When he saw that we didn't understand what he was talking about he added, putting down the book in his hand, 'You're still too young to comprehend such things. Now, open your maths books.'

So the pupils postponed their zeal for imitating the soldiers until break. After school I found myself in a long column of boys roaming through the streets and chanting *'Haifa fain? Haifa baladi! Akka fain? Akka baladi!'* We crossed the street by the market, passed in front of the cinema (I saw a poster of Rock Hudson, my mother loved Rock Hudson), came up to the communal wash place, then headed for the old mosque near the secondary school. I was running towards the town gates and chanting with such enthusiasm that I failed to realise the column behind me had dispersed when we'd reached the mosque, the pupils had all gone home, and I was running alone, just like crazy Abbas, who would roam the city streets night and day with a lit lantern.

I was running along and repeating the 'chorus', my eyes on the asphalt of the street watching my gasping shadow. Suddenly I saw another shadow merge into mine and, as I raised my head, a young man riding a bicycle hit me straight on, the front of his bike catching me full in the mouth and throwing me off the road where I landed flat next to a large garbage container. For a few moments the cyclist stared at me, trembling. So terrible was the scene that he almost lost his nerve and would have fled on his bike had it not been for the sight of the blood and broken teeth in my mouth almost choking me. So he took me on his bike and headed for the Republican Hospital.

Along the way he kept repeating in a shaky voice, 'Almighty God, the fault is yours, son. Couldn't you find anywhere better than the street to practise your sports? As God is my witness, it's your fault . . . Ah, you're too young to know the meaning of chemistry and physics and how they make a man's head spin.'

When the effects of the anaesthetic had worn off and I woke up, the doctor had extracted most of my teeth from the roots and filled my mouth with cotton wool. He led me out of the clinic, where I found my mother, my father and Shamiran listening to Nikola the nurse, who was telling them, 'If you see he's in pain, please bring him to me so I can examine him. He's like my little brother. There's no cause to worry, his adult teeth will soon grow through.'

My father was nodding in agreement without understanding what the nurse was saying because the gestures he was using were not to be found in my father's dictionary. On our way home my mother said, while gazing at the cinema (at the picture of Rock Hudson, of course), 'Criminal! Does he think my son has no future, to pulverise him like that?'

'But, Mum, if he was a real criminal, why did he take Joey to hospital?' answered Shamiran, her right arm round my shoulders.

'And why didn't he wait in the hospital?' my mother asked angrily.

But the poor student – or 'criminal', to use my mother's expression – hadn't escaped. There was a pick-up parked in front of our house, and a tall man wearing a white dishdasha and holding a black *agal* was talking to Kiryakos, Nasrat Shah and Sakina. From time to time he raised the agal and seemed to beat the ground. As we got closer we saw the 'criminal' lying there, his body writhing under the lashes of the *agal*.

'This dog is here before you, Hajja,' the tall man told my mother, panting. 'He's my son, do with him as you wish.' Then with a sudden movement he raised his agal and began beating his son again, crying, 'Get up, you animal! Get up and kiss the Hajja's hands and perhaps she'll forgive you.' The poor guy got up and, not knowing what part of his body to rub, threw himself on my mother's hands and began kissing them.

'That's enough, Hajj,' said my mother in a low voice, 'what's done is done.'

'The fool should have kept his eyes open,' said the man preparing to raise the *agal* once more, but Kiryakos held his arm before it could fall on the boy's body saying, 'That's enough, Hajj. The matter is closed.'

At that, the man went to his car and produced a scrawny lamb which he put into my hands. 'Accept this animal from me, son, perhaps it'll relieve some of your pain.'

Later Kiryakos expressed the view that 'the accident that befell Joey was due to those foreigners who appeared so suddenly, they brought the misfortune'. Then, looking at Nasrat Shah, he added, 'They'll probably bring their families over from Africa and settle them here in our homes.'

'They're from Egypt, not from Africa,' said Professor Ali.

'That's right, Ali ... excuse me (we were sitting in Nasrat Shah's house and clearly Kiryakos had noticed the picture of Imam Ali hanging in front of him and felt it wasn't right to address Nasrat Shah's son simply as Ali) ... excuse me, what I want to say, Professor Ali, is that Egypt is in Africa.'

Kiryakos, having pushed away the dish of rice ('commoners' food', in his opinion), began picking the little balls of *kofta* from his plate and putting them inside a piece of bread to make a sandwich.

'But do you really believe they'll bring their families, Mr Kiryakos?' Nasrat Shah asked him.

'Anything's possible, Uncle Nasrat Shah. These days the radio and the newspapers never stop talking about what they call "Arab nationalism", and how all the Arab states together form a single homeland, as is shown by our one language and our shared religion and history. So what's to prevent these foreigners from appropriating our houses on the basis of these ethnic links?'

'You're exaggerating, Mr Kiryakos,' said Nasrat Ali in Persian.

'Thank you, Sister Sakina,' said Kiryakos, taking a slice of watermelon from her hand. Then, turning to me, he added with a smile, '*The World Moves On.*'

I nodded in agreement, my mouth full of cotton wool, and my father also made a gesture with his head, as if he too understood what Kiryakos was saying.

★ ★ ★

With the appearance of the soldiers, Egyptian movies began to be screened in the town. One evening at sunset, a van belonging to the municipal authorities pulled up in the middle of the main square near al-Hussainiya and began showing two Egyptian movies in the open air, one after the other. Most people stretched out on the ground to watch, entranced by the actors who spoke Arabic, though with a rather strange accent, an accent that then became widespread among the young people because it rolled off the tongue easily and had a pleasing resonant ring. Having noted the demand for this new entertainment, Rafiq al-Hindi, the cinema manager, didn't hesitate to bring huge numbers of Egyptian movies in from Baghdad, especially singing-based films, because the actors (Abdel Halim Hafez, Muharram Fouad, Farid al-Atrash, Mohammad Abdel Wahab, Mohammad Fawzi, Leila Murad and Karem Mahmoud) were already known as singers, thanks to the radio.

These movies found their way into people's hearts and little by little left their mark on our daily lives as we began vying with one another to memorise long clips of dialogue and bring them into our conversations. Ghalloubi the Bastard went even further, saying that to use the Egyptian dialect among ourselves was ridiculous and that the real measure of mastery of the 'language' was to put it into practice.

'And how can we do that?' asked Jalil the Jap.

Ghalloubi pulled his trousers up to his belly button and, smiling like someone with an ace up his sleeve, said, 'We'll talk to the soldiers.'

'The soldiers!' said Ibrahim.

'Do you think they'll be kind to us?' I asked in my turn.

'Let me give it a try,' answered Ghalloubi proudly, putting an end to our chatter.

That afternoon, Ghalloubi plucked up the courage to stop an Egyptian solider who was walking down the street alone and greet him in Egyptian dialect. 'How are you, sir?'

The Egyptian answered politely. 'Just fine, and how are you?'

'The solider talked to me exactly like in the Egyptian movies,' Ghalloubi told us afterwards, laughing. He also said that at the end of their conversation the soldier had asked him, 'What do you say if I come by *bukra* and take you for a spin in the *arabiyya*?'

'*Bukra*,' we told Ghalloubi, 'means tomorrow, but what does *arabiyya* mean?'

'It means car,' he said, pulling his trousers up to his belly button.

Envy ate away at the boys' hearts that day as they discussed Ghalloubi's adventure with the Egyptian soldier, and the next afternoon they were all to be found hanging around the street corners near the military camp awaiting the appearance of the soldiers who, thanks to Ghalloubi, had been transformed overnight from a group of isolated strangers into creatures who had assumed the semblance and allure of Egyptian movie stars. 'Relations' between the soldiers and the town's children quickly consolidated, despite Kiryakos grumbling to the boys' parents about the danger of 'the soldiers' influence over the children's minds.'

Kiryakos didn't add 'and over our daughters' honour' because no one was yet aware that the Egyptian soldiers had infiltrated (nobody knew how) the girls of al-Habbaniyah and had instantly occupied their hearts and their bodies. These love affairs would have remained a secret had it not been for the courage shown by Jacqueline, which made Ghalloubi's daring seem like a childish prank that paled into insignificance.

It was one afternoon, a time when the streets and alleyways were crowded with people coming and going to the cafés and markets, that Jacqueline chose to announce before the eyes of the world her love affair with an Egyptian officer. He opened the door of the military jeep and she got out, adjusting her short tight skirt. The man was short, fat and bald. Dozens of people craned their necks, their eyes absorbing the scene in amazement as Jacqueline stood there smiling and exchanging farewells with her officer, unconcerned by the looks of the curious bystanders. As he turned to climb back into his jeep Jacqueline reached out her right hand and stroked him with her fingertips, brushing away the dust clinging to the six stars on his powerful shoulders. That scene was enough to get tongues wagging and digging up Jacqueline's past.

'*A Woman's Fool*,' said Kiryakos smiling, when he heard the news of Jacqueline getting out of the Egyptian officer's car.

Jacqueline was tall and slim with an oval face, large breasts, and well-turned slender legs. Faced with her 'astonishing beauty' Kiryakos had been completely unable to find a comparison with the stars of Hollywood and didn't therefore give her a stage name. Jacqueline lived with her widowed mother and her brother Nelson, whom most of the men in the town were friendly with, not only because of his sister's beauty but also because he knew so many girls.

'What can we do about Jacqueline,' Youshiya the grocer would ask everyone without hesitation, 'if Nelson himself chases honest girls? Thank God I'll soon be joining my daughter Victoria in Detroit, and won't have to hear any more of these tales of corruption.'

He continued repeating his comments to his customers until finally they reached Nelson's ears, who felt obliged to defend himself, saying, 'Why can't that measly grocer forget the past? His daughter has lived in America for three years, and I don't think anyone there knows the story of the grocer who came home one day to find his daughter raising her legs in front of Nelson.'

During dinner, Kiryakos told us that Father Raphael had been to visit Jacqueline to talk to her. 'And what did Jacqueline say?' my mother asked.

'*The Whole Town's Talking*,' answered Kiryakos, cackling out loud. We laughed with him, my mother beating herself on the breast to release the mouthful that had lodged in her throat. 'Tell us, Kiryakos, what did the father say?'

'He told her, "Listen Jacqueline, my daughter, no doubt you remember when you came to church three years ago and said you wanted to travel to Lebanon because the son of Dadisho the shoemaker was going to send for you from Chicago. We helped you get to Beirut, but five months later you came back without saying a word. You know people talked a lot, saying you were on intimate terms with a man from Lebanon without being married. And here you are doing exactly the same thing with a man from Egypt." '

'And what did Jacqueline say?' my mother asked again.

'She said that he was a Coptic officer, in other words an Egyptian Christian, that his name was Imad Butrus, that he'd promised to marry her as soon as possible, and that she would go with him to Egypt.'

My mother extracted her left breast and put the nipple to the lips of my baby brother John, then, looking questioningly at Shamiran, asked, 'What did the father say?'

'What do you expect him to say?' answered Kiryakos, pushing

back his shiny oily hair.

Bending his head to examine his shirt, he added, 'Of course he congratulated her, and then advised her to be a little more prudent until the Copt actually came and proposed to her.'

Then he turned to me. 'Hey, Joey, come with me to the bar so we can drink a beer with our friend Kika.'

'Poor Jacqueline,' cried Shamiran, her face flushed. My mother looked at her in amazement as Shamiran went on with increasing fervour, 'Yes, poor Jacqueline, if the shoemaker's son had kept his promises none of this would have happened. As it was, she waited 164 days for him in Beirut, but the swine, instead of sending for her sent her a letter saying he'd married some American girl. The shoemaker's son is a rotten coward.'

She leapt up, wiping her tears away. 'Son of a bitch,' she screamed and marched into the other room.

None of us said a word.

★ ★ ★

One day, before people had forgotten the story of Jacqueline, Qassim appeared waving a pair of lace panties and a white sheet, both stained with red patches, and marched round the streets and alleys near Samar's house crying at the top of his voice, 'Look, people, look! Look at the blood and look at it well! This is Samar's underwear, these are her sheets, but where is the honour the whore claims to have? Yesterday it was Jacqueline, today Samar. O God, what's happening to this beautiful town, the town I love and for which I left my own town, my family, my friends, my job? You all know how much I loved this whore! But as of today, having seen what I've seen, it's over, it's all finished. Please listen well, I want to proclaim the truth, the whole truth. Having thought about it all afternoon, I said to myself, "Qassim, you're a fine and upright man, go and talk to Samar one last time, perhaps she'll be pleased to accept you as her husband." And when I saw Samar's

247

mother at the market and her little brothers playing football in the square, I resolved to go to her house and tell her of my honorable intentions. Two hours I waited outside her door, not daring to go in, because I was raised to respect the houses and property of others. And after two hours waiting like a dog ... O God, what did I see? My heart was rent with pain and I swear I cried like a woman when I saw three Egyptian soldiers coming out of Samar's house. How I wished my eyes hadn't seen it. As my anger boiled over I burst into the house and saw the terrible, shameful scene. I saw the whore stretched out naked on her bed. I would have strangled her if I hadn't pulled back at the last moment, for I'm an emotional and kind-hearted man. But, I told myself, duty dictates I must expose her to you all, so I stole her bloodstained underwear and sheets that you might see them with your own eyes and decide how to deal with the evil whore.'

Then Qassim began crying and, wiping away his tears, said, 'Oh, the shame, the shame! From today you'll not see my face again.' And with that he disappeared.

After that, it was Samar's turn to make the rounds of the houses, one after the other, denying everything Qassim had said, tears flowing from her eyes. 'Believe me, Aunt Fahima, no stranger came into our house!' And, 'I swear to you all that I've never been with a man in my life!'

She also came to my mother. 'Believe me, Aunt Gorgiya, Aunt Sakina, I'm innocent. That lying bastard sneaked into our house through a back window, stole my underwear and stained it with blood. I swear I'm innocent, I'm honourable. You know that Qassim asked me to marry him a number of times and I always refused. Isn't that cause enough for him to want revenge on me? Believe me, I'm an honourable girl. As God and His Prophet are my witnesses, no Egyptian has ever entered our house.'

Nasrat Shah's daughter Fatima said she'd come across Samar beating her breast and saying, 'No one believes you, Samar, the pig's plan worked well.'

And Kiryakos claimed he'd seen her looking pale and sad, and that she 'reminded me of the actress Margo Graham, walking along tired and pallid in a scene from the movie *The Informer.*'

With the disappearance of Qassim, people's gossip began to throw some light on the darker corners of his character. It was said that he had come from al-Ramadi for the first time four years before, when he was twenty-two years old, and that like many young men from the surrounding towns and villages, he looked upon al-Habbaniyah as a paradise amidst the harsh strictures of clan and Bedouin life. He liked the town and its people and began visiting once a month, then once a week, but once his eye had fallen on Samar he began visiting every day. People said that since Qassim had fallen for Samar he'd started bringing many gifts for her and her family; but Samar herself had never cared for him. When Samar's father Qamindar died, Qassim bought two sacks of rice and beans which were cooked and distributed to people on the night of the funeral.

Qassim was unconcerned by Samar's refusals and kept on asking for her hand again and again. The problem was that Samar couldn't hide her dislike of him. More than once she'd screamed in his face, 'Qassim, don't you get it? I don't love you!'

Qassim thought she might change her mind one day, but that didn't happen. On the contrary, relations became even more strained. Once Samar shouted at him in front of a crowd of people at the communal wash place, 'Almighty God! If you were the only man on the face of the earth, I wouldn't let you touch me! I hate you! Understand?'

That day, Qassim had seized her hand and said, 'There's not a man in town who hasn't stroked your body. Be a good girl, we've had enough scandal.'

All to no avail did Samar yell back, 'Leave me alone, you wretch, I hate you!' She even felt obliged to lift up her skirt and point between her thighs, shouting, 'This is mine, and I'm free to do with it as I please. Understand? Now listen, and listen well.

Only an hour ago, just one hour ago, I gave this body to a man I love. That's right, to a man I love!'

'I know him,' answered Qassim, holding back his emotions.

'Of course you know him,' said Samar, readjusting her skirt and hiding her lilac (some said yellow) panties from people's view. 'How could you not know him when he was the one who gave you such a good beating, and you stretched out on the ground like a woman, crying and screaming "Enough! Enough!".'

At that Qassim completely lost control, went red in the face and pounced on her, thumping and kicking, 'You whore! If your baby brothers and your poor mother can't teach you, then Qassim knows how to put you back on the straight and narrow.'

* * *

After Jacqueline's and Samar's affairs with the soldiers, the police commissioner went to the military headquarters, where he submitted a strongly worded protest at the behavior of 'our brothers, the Egyptian soldiers'. That same afternoon he visited the citizens and assured them that the soldiers would not come into town except on Fridays, and that 'their movements will be closely watched by my men'. A warrant was also sent to al-Ramadi demanding the arrest of Qassim for assaulting Samar Qamindar. The police commissioner took these steps to calm the people, although he said that what had happened to Samar was different from what had happened to Jacqueline because, 'you all know that the daughters of our Christian brothers imitate English girls in the way they dress and in their dealings with men'.

'If what Shaker al-Hindi said is true, I'm going to throw a huge party,' said Kiryakos, sitting down with a bulging paper bag on his lap which, given the mention of Shaker al-Hindi's name, I assumed to be full of apples.

'And what did Shaker al-Hindi say?' Sakina asked.

'Something to bring joy to your heart, Sakina. Please let this remain between us, but he told me that the police commissioner told him that the foreigners . . .'

'The Egyptians,' Sakina interrupted.

'The Africans, Sakina,' replied Kiryakos hurriedly. 'Those foreigners are going to leave after holding a parade next week . . . Ah, finally they're going to leave.'

'A parade?' asked Ali.

'Yes. God knows exactly what they mean by parade,' muttered Kiryakos, casting a glance at the black and red checks of his shirt. Then he extracted an apple and presented it to me saying happily, 'Take it, *Strong Boy*.'

'I don't like apples,' I answered.

'Take it,' said Kiryakos again. 'I don't want it. I don't like apples . . . I don't like apples,' I replied, getting up and heading for the movie room.

The soldiers fanned out through the streets and alleyways of town, wearing camouflage gear and carrying Kalashnikovs. At around ten o'clock I was selling *amba* sandwiches with Nasrat Shah when we heard announcements being made from municipal authority vehicles approaching the school.

'His Excellency the President of the Republic will be arriving shortly to inaugurate the new mosque,' they said, and called on people to gather between the main entrance to the town and the al-Habbaniyah bridge 'in order to greet the illustrious guest'.

That 'shortly' lasted more than five hours. We were still waiting on the bridge that afternoon when the president's plane appeared in the distance, then passed over our heads on its way to the landing strip at the airbase.

'What a beautiful plane. I really really love planes,' said Robin, squinting against the glare of the sky.

'It really is a beauty,' I replied looking at him. 'What would you do, Robin, if we gave you the president's plane?'

'What would I do?' asked Robin in surprise. 'I'd take Samson to Sydney, Teddy to Detroit, and you and Uncle Kiryakos to

Hollywood. Then I'd fly away on my own.'

'Where to?'

'I don't know. I'd just stay in the sky.' There followed a few moments of silence amidst the clamour and uproar of the crowds, then Robin added suddenly, 'I'd go to Canada!'

'Canada?' I asked him.

He nodded. 'Yes, to Canada. It's white, I've seen pictures.'

'Do you like the colour white?'

He nodded again and began contemplating the president's plane, which was slowly banking over the airstrip.

A few days later the plane exploded and the president's body was blown to bits. Robin fell ill and didn't go to school for more than ten days, grief-stricken not for the president but for the plane he loved so much, for he'd never heard of a plane exploding before. As I was helping him with the lessons he'd missed in his absence, he shouted at me, 'You don't love me! Why didn't you tell me that planes explode?'

'I'm not God, to know when it would explode,' I said, turning towards the picture of Mar Shimun hanging on the wall.

'Swear to God that you didn't know that planes explode.'

'By the head of Mar Shimun I never heard of a plane exploding,' I swore, knowing full well I'd heard of hundreds of exploding planes.

Robin didn't believe me. Then, by chance, I learned something from a customer who happened to notice, as I was handing him a sandwich, that I was looking at the newspaper he was carrying. He showed it to me and said, 'It's a picture of the helicopter that exploded with the president on board.' That evening I rushed home and told Robin that the president had been on a helicopter, not a plane. Next morning Robin was better, and as he accompanied me to school he waved his hand through the air like a plane while making the noise of the engine with his mouth.

Sitting in the movie room, I told myself that when I grew up I wouldn't, under any circumstances, travel to Hollywood by air.

Then, in order to dispel the ghost of the president's plane, I panned my gaze over the pictures on the walls, my eyes lingering over images from the movie *Four Sons*, and in particular the one in which the grieving mother Margaret Mann uses both hands to hold a letter telling her of the death of one of her sons at the front, while the postman Albert Gran stands by the window overlooking the garden. I felt even sadder as I contemplated another picture, of a soldier pressing himself to the ground behind a barricade, awaiting death, the last of his troop.

I was still thinking of death when my father came in clapping his hands, whistling and making the following gestures: he lifted his right palm to his right temple, pointed to his dick then moved his right index finger over his left index finger as if cutting it off. He stretched out his right hand in front of him and shook it right and left, producing strange and wonderful noises with his mouth, concluding with a loud raspberry. I understood he was saying, 'The soldiers with the circumcised dicks, whom we see gossiping in the cinema, have gone.'

★ ★ ★

When I saw Father Raphael, Youshiya and Nikola the nurse all approaching our house together, I ran up to them and Father Raphael stretched out his hand for me to kiss. Once inside, it was Youshiya – a 'clever devil', as my mother called him – who spoke first.

He dwelt at length on Nikola's character saying, 'He's our friend, he's an Assyrian like you, and he's an orphan, which means, Sister Gorgiya, that he will be one of yours. You know me well, and if I wasn't certain of his morals I wouldn't have come with him. I won't conceal that he's about to move to Baghdad, because he was promoted last week and made a sergeant.'

A few moments of silence followed, then Youshiya looked at Father Raphael who in turn looked at my mother and said, 'Yes,

Sister Gorgiya, what Youshiya says is right. Mr Nikola is a fine upstanding man and I believe that your consent will be in all our best interests. Brother Nikola tells me that were it not for the order calling him to Baghdad, he would have waited for the girl to grow up a bit more.'

At this point Youshiya interrupted him with a laugh. 'We all know, Sister Gorgiya, that you married our friend Kika when you were just thirteen years old (my mother gave a smile as if to say 'I curse that day'), yet you have a large family and all your children are well and blessed.'

My mother's gaze ranged over all of us, coming to a halt on my father. She gestured to him as if putting a ring on the little finger of her left hand. Father Raphael nodded his head as a sign of satisfaction and, knowing my father to be a faithful Christian, traced a sign of the cross in the air, looked up at the ceiling, pointed to Nikola, then nodded again ('May God be witness to Nikola's morals'). My father tapped himself on the chest, passed his left hand over his cheeks and stroked his lower lip ('Speak to the beautiful girl').

'As you wish, Mother,' said Shamiran with a shy smile, at which Youshiya leapt up like a fox, kissing my mother's hands and saying over and again, 'I was sure of your kind hearts!'

Then he turned to Nikola and added, 'Hey, get up, kiss your family's hands, and off you go to get us some kebabs and three bottles of arak.'

The wedding took place just two weeks later in the garden of the social club. My father was happy, knocking back one glass after the other and tripping in and out among the dancers to the strains of Assyrian folk music. When the music changed and a slow western number was put on, Nikola dragged my mother by the hand to make her dance with my father, but he refused. 'We wanted poverty,' my mother said laughing, 'but poverty didn't want us.'

We often questioned the strangeness of our parents' relationship. On one occasion, Samson asked our mother, 'How did Dad become deaf and dumb?'

Mum was clearly in a good mood that day and she replied proudly, 'Ah, children, your father was a pilot and his plane was struck by a shell that left him deaf and dumb.' We would have believed her had it not been that in times of anger she'd say, 'Ah, curse the day they made me marry that deaf-mute!'

And we'd say to her, 'But, Mum, he was a pilot!', to which she'd give the anguished reply, 'Pilot! Him? What kind of pilot comes out of his mother's belly a deaf-mute!'

When my father saw that the rings of dancers were breaking up, and that each man was dancing with his wife, he circulated among them until he found a pretty girl, dragged her onto the floor and began dancing with her. Little by little the other dancers left the floor to my father and his 'friend', and stood around watching them.

I remember well how a fine rain began falling at sunset, and how the guests ran indoors and began watching the dance floor from the balconies, windows, kitchen and bathroom of the club-house. They saw how my father had pushed his partner away and was dancing alone in the rain, which had become a lot heavier. He wasn't with us, but instead was dancing to the notes of a melody that only he could hear, a melody that transported him to a royal ballroom where, wearing a tuxedo among the princes and princesses, he waltzed with his friend Elizabeth. He kept on danc-ing like that until my mother went out in the rain to wake him from his reverie, kissing him and pulling him inside the club-house. 'You madman, who's going to feed your children if you fall ill?'

My mother was sad that Shamiran, her eldest child, had left home for good. 'The only girl has gone, Sakina, and I'm left with five boys,' she said, to which Sakina answered, 'Don't be sad, Sister Gorgiya, they'll soon grow up and be a help to you.'

★ ★ ★

My father insisted I accompany him to the river to go fishing. I agreed and we went into the old orchards, leaping from one stream to another, looking for worms to use as bait. On the bank of one of the streams we came across a black typewriter with an Arabic typeface. I also knew the English alphabet so was able to spell out the maker's name: C.A.R.P.E.N.T.E.R. I was delighted with our find, and so was my father, who gestured to me that we need not take it home immediately, and that he knew a safe place where we could hide our 'treasure' so we could pick it up after fishing. Grudgingly I agreed, and Dad leapt off across two or three streams, disappeared for a few moments behind a large thorn bush, then returned smiling.

The hook was dangling in the water and we were waiting for it to start bobbing again when I imagined the Carpenter floating across the surface of the water, drifting towards the other side of the river. I indicated to my father that we should go home but he just laughed. Putting his hand in his breast pocket, he produced a page cut from an English magazine and pointed to the picture of a blond-haired woman, making the following gestures: he shook his fist back and forth a number of times, tapped himself on the chest with his left forefinger (meaning he was having an affair with her), then laughed boastfully.

I closed my eyes and shook my head, trying to banish Mum's words from my mind, 'Children, God is unjust to no one, He knows why He cut off your father's tongue.'

A few moments passed, then Dad pointed to the little fish in the plastic bag next to me, then to my dick and to the length of his own fishing rod, finally making a gesture as if peeling a banana. And I understood he meant, 'Your dick is now like a sardine, but when it grows it'll be like a banana.' We both laughed.

Returning from the river, the Carpenter was no longer in its hiding place. Seeing the tears welling in my eyes, my father reached out suddenly with his left hand and grasped one of the branches of the thorn bush, the blood oozing out from between his fingers. I felt a prick in my heart, or something falling from it, and, taking off my blue shirt, I tied it round his hand, smiling.

The image of the typewriter remained in my mind constantly. I was selling *amba* sandwiches in front of the cinema and thinking of the Carpenter, my sufferings made even worse by what Kiryakos had told me.

'A long time ago I read that a typewriter has a special magic that touches the innermost essence of the person using it, and that it is better for artists to type their works themselves, because in that way they discover how much handwriting can betray.'

He was also of the opinion that 'typewriters, apart from improving the appearance and legibility of a work, give it a seriousness and dignity evident from the very first lines,' and added prophetically, 'I don't believe that the typewriter that appeared before you on the bank of the stream in the old orchards could have disappeared so easily. That was just the beginning of the story, and the typewriter will appear again sooner or later.'

Two or three days after the 'theft' of the Carpenter, Kiryakos told me, 'An artist without a typewriter is like a driver without a car.' We all knew that Kiryakos had been a driver in his youth.

The day came when Youshiya the grocer decided to close up his little shop and emigrate to Detroit to join his daughter Victoria. One afternoon he called me over. 'Come here, you young rascal, you cowboy. I've put aside a full crate of Mission for you, along with another ten bottles for your friend Nisreen.'

I gathered up Nisreen's share and went to knock on the door of Aunt Zahra's house. Nisreen opened the door and smiled, accepting Youshiya's gift and leading the way to the kitchen. I was placing the bottles on the table when my eye fell on the Carpenter, lying on the floor to my left.

'Ah . . .'

'What's up?' asked Nisreen.

'Nothing, nothing,' I said heading out, the image of the Carpenter before my eyes.

'If you're ready to do anything to make her happy,' I told myself, 'then let the Carpenter be a pledge of your love for her.' Yet, how – and the thought worried me for days afterwards – did the Carpenter get from under the thorn bush into Nisreen's aunt's kitchen?

* * *

One day I was selling sorbet in front of the girls' school when some of the pupils began screaming, 'A snake! A snake! A snake!' It was a very long snake, about a metre and a half, but I thought it looked scared. I picked up a stone and aimed at its head and after a few blows it lay quite still. Then, with a courage that came from I know not where, I took the snake by the tail and waved it in front of the girls who began chanting, 'Joey killed the snake! Joey killed the snake!'

Had it not been for the school caretaker, who took the snake from me and threw it into the rubbish, I might have stripped off my shirt like Hercules and put my hands into the beast's jaws to split it in two.

When I told my mother how I'd killed the snake and saved the girls, she began slapping me on the cheeks with both hands and shouting, 'Madman, son of a madman! Have you ever seen anyone in their right mind kill a snake in the month of May? Why did you have to do that? Why didn't someone else kill it, hey? Don't you know that snakes have vengeful souls?'

When she'd calmed down a little she explained. 'Son, if you'd killed the snake at the end of the summer, then perhaps over the winter its offspring and husband would have forgotten their wish for revenge. But as you killed it in May, its family will use the whole summer to plot their revenge on you.'

'What are you saying, Mum?' I replied in tears.

'Almighty God, those movies haven't left a shred of sense in your head! You've become worse than your father. Listen, as of tonight you sleep inside and you make sure you close the door. Got it?'

'Yes, Mum,' I said, trembling.

My mother then told me the story of her grandfather and his seven sons. 'My grandfather', she said, 'used to keep a snake in the house. One day, one of his sons plucked up the courage to examine the crack between the wall and the ceiling, which had been the snake's home for many years. Finding two eggs, he took them and began playing with them with his friends in the street. That night the snake came down from its "house" and slithered between the boys, who were sleeping one next to the other, until it identified the one that had stolen the eggs. Then it dug its fangs into his right foot until his head exploded and he died.'

After hearing that story I couldn't stop thinking about death. I would inspect the handcart before reaching out to touch anything, look around in all directions before walking down a dark street and, at night, despite the great heat, I'd wrap myself up in a blanket and close the door, not forgetting to stuff something into the gap underneath. And I wouldn't do my homework by lantern light, afraid it might lead the snake's relatives or children to my hiding place. This lasted a number of days.

Even though Nasrat Shah assured me that what my mother had told me was a kind of fairy tale, I was still scared.

'Read the Surat al-Nas ten times before going to sleep and neither man nor jinn will come anywhere near you,' said Sakina.

I took her advice and began reading the sura ten times a night before going to sleep; and when I was in doubt, as I sometimes was, as to whether I'd read it nine times or ten, I'd read it through another five times just to be sure.

★ ★ ★

Two days before the school exams began, my father and I went to the cinema to see the Indian movie *Do Badan*. It was a very sad movie, and whenever the hero or heroine sang my father rested his head on my shoulder and hummed, 'Hmmmm mm ahahahah ha ha hu hu hu hu hu hu mmmmm hah hahahah mmm mm mmmmmmm hahammmmham himmm.' Before the end he whispered something in my ear and left. I knew he was going to the bar.

A few moments after my father had left, someone sitting in the seat behind me began tossing pumpkin seed shells over my head and shoulders. I brushed them off while continuing to watch the movie, but the person behind me kept on. When I turned around I saw it was Khachik, the Armenian boy, eating seeds and gazing at the screen. Suddenly, emboldened by the fact that he was sitting near one of the employees of his mother's bakery, he spat out some shells right in my face. I stood on my seat and threw myself at him, pummelling his fat red face with my fists and reaching out to strangle him. I would have killed him if the cinema management hadn't stopped the film and switched the lights on. I looked up to see the usher coming towards me, and I knew he'd take the opportunity to get his revenge so I slipped away, fleeing from the cinema to the bar, where I explained to my father what had happened.

Within a few minutes, a policeman appeared, dragging me away by my shirt collar and saying, 'What did you do to the son of the fine Armenian lady? Tell me, you little brat! Come with me to the station so I can show you how to be a hero!'

My father took a beer bottle and emptied it in one draught, then cackled out loud. 'Is he telling himself that all his efforts to get a job at Umm Khachik's bakery have gone up in smoke?' I asked myself.

I gripped the iron bars in the door of the police station cell and looked out over the shadowy garden. Within an hour my mother and Kiryakos turned up, pleading with the police chief to let me go because I had exams at school over the following two days. But he told them that he would keep me in at least for one night 'so he doesn't do it again'. Before they left, of course, Kiryakos said with a smile, '*The Prisoner of Shark Island*.'

The croaking of the frogs in the garden broke the peace of the night. Alone in the cell, I spent some time examining the cracks in the walls, then more time looking out over the garden. Bit by bit the ghost of the snake began to appear before me. I stood in the middle of the dark cell, looking around in all directions and stamping my feet on the floor in the hope of crushing the beast, but I wasn't able to and I began shouting, 'Help, I want to get out! There's a snake chasing me! I don't want to die! God preserve you, let me out of here!' But no one took any notice and, finally, sleep overcame me.

When I opened my eyes the following morning, I found myself lying under a blanket in the corner of the cell. In the opposite corner was Qassim, smoking a cigarette.

'Good morning, Mr Joey,' said Qassim, his voice hoarse and sad.

I leapt up in terror and began hunting through the folds of the blanket, but Qassim just smiled. 'Don't worry, you didn't stop talking about the snake all night, but it came and went.' He put a fresh cigarette in his mouth and asked, 'Hey, Joey, have you seen Samar?'

'Yes,' I said, 'I see her every day. She's very kind.'

'I'm going to marry her and resolve everything.'

'But how can you marry her when you saw the Egyptian soldiers in her bed?'

'No, Joey, no. That story was made up.'

'What does "made up" mean?'

'That it's not true.'

'But you saw her clothes stained with blood.'

'It wasn't blood, just red ink.'

'Red ink?'

'Yep, red ink,' he said calmly, lighting another cigarette and continuing. 'Once, when their house was empty, I got in by the back

261

window and emptied a bottle of red ink I'd brought with me from al-Ramadi over her clothes and her bed.'

'Are you going to tell this to the police?'

'Of course. I'd already told a lot of people before I came here to hand myself in.'

'Are they going to put you in prison?'

'I don't care about prison. All I ask is that they put me here, in this prison, and not in al-Ramadi.'

'So you can be near Samar?' I asked smiling.

'You're a smart boy, Joey,' he said with a laugh.

When the police chief appeared he grabbed me by my left ear and said, 'We're going to release you now so you can go and sit your school exams. But the next time we'll put you in the electric chair; you know we've got one. Understood?'

'But it was Khachik who attacked me,' I told him.

'I don't want to hear another word,' he replied. 'Off you go now, go home.'

Just a few days later I nearly ended up in prison again when Mahdi's mother Saleema lodged a complaint against me at the police station, and I had to swear my innocence to the police chief. This is what happened: I was with my friends on the football field near the old orchards when I had the brainwave of making a 'movie' in the open air. I appointed myself as scriptwriter and director and began handing out roles to the boys, each being given one to suit his character.

Ibrahim was the hero, Ghalloubi the villain, Albert the sheriff, and Mahdi (who was only eight) the heroine. I supervised the preparation of the script: the villain was to kidnap the heroine and make off with her into the orchards; then the hero would appear astride a horse searching for the villain and, when the two of them came to blows, the sheriff would intervene.

Once we'd agreed the script, I yelled 'Action!' at the top of my voice and they all dashed off towards the orchards pretending to be cowboys on horseback.

Half an hour later, the hero and the sheriff came back alone saying they'd looked for the villain and the heroine but had been unable to find them. At that moment Gladys, a thirteen-yearold girl we all found irritating, appeared out of nowhere and helped us in our search for the heroine and the villain. Making our way through trees and over streams, we eventually found Ghalloubi lying on top of Mahdi and kissing his chest, exactly as we used to see in the cowboy movies (it wasn't a scene I'd written in my script). Gladys ran off and told Mahdi's mother what she had seen and soon a furious Saleema appeared, wielding a knife.

She grabbed her son and began shouting and screaming, 'God is great! God is great! Gorgiya's son has brought shame upon us. By God, but I'll kill my own son with this knife, I'll kill him now in front of you all, just watch, watch!'

When no one lifted a finger she went on, 'If you can't raise your own son, that jailbird, then send him to a reformatory . . . I'll kill my son, by God, I swear I'll kill him!' At this point some people came out to calm Saleema down, but she wouldn't leave our house until she saw my mother pounce on me and sink her teeth into my chest. All the while, the sheriff, the villain and the hero were standing on the roof contemplating the fate of their 'director'. (Later Ghalloubi told me that when he saw my mother sink her teeth into my chest it reminded him of Dracula. I didn't lose my temper but I did tell him that my mother had a kind heart.)

Despite the fact that Saleema wouldn't withdraw her complaint, the police chief didn't throw me in jail. This was for two reasons: first, because Kiryakos explained the details and rules of the 'game' to him, saying that 'Joey drew up a script for all the kids to follow, and he isn't responsible for what they did outside the script'; and second, because the chief was well aware that Saleema's own moral record wasn't unstained, indeed half the city knew that she often wandered the streets at night with nothing but a black abaya over her completely naked body.

I was lying in bed gazing up at the sky and asking God (who

appeared to me like Mar Shimun with his black clothes and soft beard) to make my dream of being a great movie director come true.

'Stop moving!' mumbled Teddy, digging me in the stomach.

So I turned to the Surat al-Nas and read it through ten times, or perhaps thirteen times, or maybe more; and before falling asleep, in order to confuse the snake that was chasing me, I rested my right foot between Teddy's feet and slipped my left foot between Robin's.

I hadn't noticed that my mother had heard my Qur'anic recitation, until I heard her saying to me, as if talking to herself, 'One of these days I'm afraid you'll renounce your own faith.'

* * *

As we made our way to the old orchards, Ghalloubi the Bastard told me that Razouqi, the public lavatory attendant, had given Albert the Ape (so called because he was hairy) a good drubbing, while Jalil the Jap and Jalil the Bear had managed to escape. According to Ghalloubi, they had been spying through the gaps around the water pipes that connect the public lavatory (on the inside) to the communal wash place (on the outside) in order to get a look at the women's thighs, in particular Sabiha's open legs, as they bent over to do their washing. They were all pulling on their dicks when Razouqi pounced on them, managing to get hold of the Ape and give him a sound beating with his rubber boots.

'Sabiha knew what we were doing,' said the Ape.

When I asked him how he knew such a thing, he replied that he'd heard Sakina ask Sabiha why she didn't wear a long dress, 'but Sabiha just kept on washing and singing, in fact she deliberately moved her thighs further and further apart, and we could see her panties, which were pink that afternoon.'

The Ape went on and on about Sabiha's thighs until Ghalloubi pointed suddenly to his dick. 'Let's see who's got the biggest!' he said laughing.

'My dick's the biggest,' replied the Ape.

'But you're not circumcised,' said Jalil the Jap.

'No,' said the Ape, 'but in matters like this, girls think only of size.'

I looked at my own dick and found it small and uncircumcised. I wasn't bothered about not being circumcised because, as my father would gesticulate, men with 'cut dicks' are 'a dirty bunch', but I felt reassured when I looked at the Bear's dick and found it was small too.

'Here under this thorn bush, Samson and I found an Arabic typewriter,' cried the Bastard all of a sudden.

'And where is it now?' I asked, screwing up my eyes against the sunlight filtering through the trees.

'Your brother gave me 50 fils and took it himself.'

But Ghalloubi – born in the same month and year as me – didn't stop there. He went on, innocently shooting an arrow into my little heart, 'Samson and Nisreen often spend the afternoon here in the gardens, among the trees.'

They all went away and I remained alone, until the trees were lost in the shadows and I made my way home by the light of the moon reflected in the streams. I was sad, and mulled over thoughts of blood vengeance, but how could I take revenge on Samson, my own elder brother? Besides, people were forever talking about the war, it was late summer, 1967, and my mother never stopped staring at Samson, who was waiting to be called up for military service and might be sent to the Syrian or Jordanian front.

One day in October as I was returning from school, I found reason to refute Kiryakos' maxim that 'a man who truly loves the movies must forget all memories that smack of revenge'. I was walking along, my books under my arm, when from afar I saw the black rope rings, the circles of dancers with their feet beating hard against the ground, the drums and pipes, and the dust rising from the sandy ground like steam. 'It's a wedding,' I muttered to myself, heading towards the men who were distributing plates of rice and beans. I ate two helpings, watching the bridegroom's mother show people the bloodstained cloth.

'It's a wedding, we have to go and eat with them,' I told Kiryakos, who was standing by himself. He smiled, then cackled out loud, bending his head to throw a quick glance at the blue, yellow and red checks of his shirt, 'Ha ha ha! What it is is a massacre. Ha ha ha!'

As if she had heard Kiryakos' remarks, the bridegroom's mother began shouting at the top of her voice and shaking the bloodstained cloth.

'Don't eat too much. Aunt Zahra has brought us a large dish of *kibbeh* and *kofta* for Nisreen's wedding,' said my mother, settling into a seat near Kiryakos.

'Whose wedding?' I asked, dumbfounded.

'Your friend Nisreen's wedding. Had you forgotten her?'

I felt my head spinning and a numbness creep down to my feet. I went home crying.

Wiping away my tears with the back of my hand, I decided to take my revenge. As soon as my father came home from the bakery I went up to him and outlined the shape of a box with my hands, then tapped on it with all ten fingers. He understood I was talking about the Carpenter typewriter and shook his left hand ('Where is it?'). I put my left finger under my eye then pointed at Aunt Zahra's house.

I brought a wooden ladder from Nasrat Shah's place and rested it against the back wall of Aunt Zahra's. I went up first, my father behind me, both of us glancing in the direction of the dancers, the dust rising from their feet like steam. Having reached the roof, we pulled the ladder up behind us and let it down into the garden on the other side. Entering Aunt Zahra's house, I found the typewriter still in its place, on the floor of the kitchen to my left. I picked it up and climbed to the top of the ladder, where my father took it off me. He handled the typewriter just as he used to handle me when I was a baby. Before climbing down from the roof we again looked over towards the dancers and the crowds (what a wonderful view it was).

I remembered how Kiryakos had explained to me that for scenes such as this, the best position for the camera was an over-the-shoulder shot towards the centre of the action. The camera would then tilt up and zoom in on the chosen image, the blood-stained cloth, for example, the bridegroom emerging from the bridal chamber, or his mother's tongue moving up and down in her mouth as she ululated. Then it would pan across to another part of the scene.

At home, to the rhythm of the drums and pipes wafting in from outside, I began tapping on the keys of the Carpenter while my father drank arak. From time to time he would breathe on his silver box, then polish it against his shirt, the silver surface reflecting now my face, now the letters of the typewriter.

★ ★ ★

The summer of 1968 was the last for our town of al-Habbaniyah. Shamiran left for Baghdad with her husband Nikola, Youshiya emigrated to Detroit and Samson left to do his military service. Nisreen's story also came to an end. That summer too, we heard the sound of gunfire at the airbase, after which a decree was issued ordering people to stay indoors for three days. Subsequently we heard there had been a military coup in Baghdad and that a group of Baathist officers had taken power.

Three months after the coup, a military delegation visited the city to inform the people that 'the revolutionary government has decided to evacuate all civilian inhabitants from al-Habbaniyah, which will be used exclusively as a military base'.

When some of the citizens were bold enough to ask why, the

officers replied, 'Al-Habbaniyah is a strategically important location in the struggle against imperialism and Zionism and their agents in the area who are working to destroy Iraq.'

But the truth is that the expulsion orders only affected Assyrian, Kurdish and Turkmen families, and those dubbed 'of Persian origin'. It was said that the new military regime considered such people 'leftovers of British colonialism'.

'O God, where will we go? Where will we go?' Most of the women of al-Habbaniyah were weeping and moaning, slapping their faces in despair.

'Take care of the child you're carrying in your belly,' Sakina warned my mother, but she continued to slap herself on the cheeks. 'Sakina, where will I take the children of the deaf-mute?'

Even the poor chief of police, when some of the women gathered outside the station, appeared with a sad expression on his face, saying, 'If the matter were in my hands, you could stay here another thousand years, but I'm like you, sisters. I've been ordered to go into retirement. I advise you to leave your houses as quickly as possible, because the new government will implement its orders mercilessly.'

Just two days before leaving al-Habbaniyah, my mother gave birth to a little girl, Mary. And despite the circumstances and the tragic times we were living through, Kiryakos began playing with the baby, calling her '*Mary of Scotland*'. My mother still hadn't recovered from the birth when the soldiers came and ordered us to leave our little house immediately. A few hours later it was bulldozed to the ground before our eyes.

Kiryakos was the only person who followed what was going on in the capital. He claimed to have read terrible news in the papers prophesying that 'Iraq is going to change definitively. The new government believes in a chauvinistic form of Arab nationalism. And it's true, they look upon us as leftovers of British colonialism.'

'What does "English leftovers" mean?' I asked Kiryakos. 'Aren't we Iraqis?'

'Of course, we're the origin of this country. We're exactly like the Red Indians in America.'

'If we're like the Red Indians, then how is it that you like John Ford, who always makes cowboy movies?' I asked on impulse.

'That's a very important question,' Kiryakos replied. 'Most of John Ford's movies are very respectful towards the Red Indians, and he always tries to be fair in his presentation of them. He knew their language and was friends with certain Indian tribal chiefs. They wouldn't let anyone film their holy sites – such as places of worship or the burial grounds of their spiritual leaders – except John Ford.'

That day, Kiryakos disappeared, and no one saw him again.

Fortunately we owned no furniture of any kind. We put our few items of bedding and clothing onto a small wooden cart and my father, Teddy and I began pushing it, while Mum carried the babies. That evening at sunset we sat at the crossroads of the main highway near the chain of hills overlooking al-Habbaniyah. To the left, the road led to Fallujah and Baghdad, to the right to al-Khalidiyah and al-Ramadi. As we had no idea where to go, my mother spread a blanket on the ground and put out some bread, tomatoes and cucumbers, which we wolfed down eagerly as if we were on a picnic.

In the end, Teddy and Robin went off with the other families to Baghdad to stay with our sister Shamiran, while my mother decided to lodge temporarily in al-Khalidiyah. We fixed our cart to the back of a large pick-up which Nasrat Shah had hired to transport his own family to al-Ramadi. When we reached al-Khalidiyah, Nasrat Shah asked my mother if they could take me with them.

God, how I weep with regret when I remember what a traitor I must have seemed in my mother's eyes as I leapt for joy at the prospect of going with Nasrat Shah's family.

Where, O Lord, is the gift of forgetfulness?

★ ★ ★

The pupils in the classroom were surprised to find a Christian with a very strange name in their midst (I don't know if there had been any Christians living in al-Ramadi before).

The teacher had introduced me graciously, saying, 'This is Shmuel, your new classmate, he's from an Assyrian family and is a son of our great country.'

I remember how he talked about the greatness of Iraq, its variety of peoples, its religious and ethnic differences, and its invincible unity. The teacher was extremely kind, and I later learned that he was a stranger to the area like me. We were in the west of the country and he was from the south.

The teacher had hardly finished introducing me to my companions when someone behind me hit me on the back of the head with a ruler. Despite the pain, I didn't turn round. The teacher was busy writing on the blackboard and the pain had still not diminished when I was struck again.

'Sir, someone's hitting me on the head,' I said, rising to my feet.

'Liar! Liar, son of a liar!' said a voice behind me.

I turned around to see a pupil of about fourteen with a dark, vicious-looking face, reclining in his seat, holding a metal ruler in his hand.

'Mohammad, leave the class immediately!' said the teacher. Mohammad got up and left carrying his ruler and his books, pausing at the door of the classroom to throw an angry look in my direction, shaking his fist and biting his lip. Without asking the teacher's permission, two other pupils followed him out while I remained in my seat, terrified.

I was making my way home along the shade of the graveyard wall to avoid the heat of the sun when I heard a voice calling me. 'Wait, I want a word with you.'

Mohammad and two of his gang were approaching me but,

before saying a word, he suddenly head-butted me in the face and his two friends began kicking me in the stomach. I was bent over to protect my face (Kiryakos had told me that anyone who wants to work in movies must have a handsome face) while the blood flowed from my mouth and nose. As the blows rained down on me I said to myself, 'My God, I've never seen violence like this except in movies.'

'That's the first lesson, you miserable creep, just so you know that the teacher's not going to help you in any way,' said Mohammad as he moved away with his two mates.

Nasrat Shah refused to believe that I had been the victim. Sakina was bandaging the cut over my left eyebrow (which was to leave a permanent mark) as he kept on insisting, 'They wouldn't have attacked you if you hadn't provoked them in some way.'

'I didn't do anything! Believe me!'

'The boys from tribes don't attack people without a reason,' replied Nasrat Shah, placing his 'prayer stone' on the prayer mat and beginning his devotions.

Going to school became like a ritual punishment, as Mohammad and his gang wouldn't leave me alone and looked for any excuse to assault me. On one occasion Mohammad ordered me to play table tennis with him. We played and I lost.

'You're a coward, you could have won but you're just a sissy,' said Mohammad, flinging his paddle onto the table.

Nasrat Shah's house stood facing one of the long sides of the rectangular graveyard. It was a twenty-five-minute walk along the dusty lanes behind the cemetery for me to reach the main road, and from there another five minutes to the town centre. After many hours of boredom at school (thinking up ways to avoid 'the gang'), I'd return home to spend a couple of hours playing with the Carpenter and leafing through movie posters and pictures of American movie stars. Later, I'd head back to the town centre to take Nasrat Shah's place selling sandwiches in front of the cinema.

One day Sakina asked me, 'Why don't you take the path through the graveyard? It'll get you into the town centre in just five minutes.'

'The path through the graveyard?' I asked.

'Why not?' said Sakina.

'I'm afraid of walking among the graves.'

Smiling, Sakina pulled over a chair and climbed up to get a green bag resting on top of the radio which was fixed high up on the wall. She extracted a Qur'an from the bag and began leafing though the pages, stopping at a certain point and calling me over. 'Come here. You know how to read. Copy out this verse in your own handwriting and, when you step into the graveyard, read it and keep on reading it until you're on the other side, and no harm will come to you.'

I got a piece of paper and a pen, and began writing:

> *God! There is no God save Him, the Living, the Eternal. Neither slumber nor sleep overtaketh Him. Unto Him belongeth whatsoever is in the heavens and whatsoever is in the earth. Who is he that intercedeth with Him save by His leave? He knoweth that which is in front of them and that which is behind them, while they encompass nothing of His knowledge save what He will. His Throne includeth the heavens and the earth, and He is never weary of preserving them. He is the sublime, the Tremendous.**

'Have you finished?' asked Sakina.

'Yes.'

'Almighty God speaks the truth,' said Sakina.

I paused in front of the opening in the graveyard wall and stepped through, left foot forward, into the burial ground, beginning my recitation of the *Ayat al-Kursi* (Verse of the Throne) and threading my way between the graves. Within five minutes I

* Pickthall, Mohammed Marmaduke. *The Meaning of the Glorious Quran*, Hyderbad-Deccan: Government Central Press, 1938. Sura 2, verse 255, online edition.

found myself on the main road. I was delighted with the experience and began repeating it every day until I'd learned the verse by heart. Every night before going to sleep I read the Surat al-Nas ten times or more, not forgetting to supplement it with a prayer for the protection of my parents. Since my arrival in al-Ramadi, I had also begun adding another prayer, asking God to deliver me from the evil of my enemies at school, and it would often happen that I'd forget my old prayer, asking the Lord to help me become a film-maker.

God must clearly have accepted my supplications because one day as I was walking among the graves my eye fell on the headstone of a small grave (about 40 inches long) upon which was written:

> *O you who read this inscription*
> *Weep for my youth*
> *Yesterday was I alive*
> *And today under the dust*

I liked the inscription on the headstone and, saddened that the deceased had been so young, sat down to gaze sadly at the grave and reread the words. At that moment I saw Mohammad and his gang coming in my direction. I was gripped by fear but remained sitting where I was.

'What are you doing here?' shouted Mohammad, kicking me repeatedly, though not very hard, on the back.

'What harm does it do you if I like this grave?' I said getting up and brushing the dust off my trousers, my eyes darting between Mohammad and his friends, anticipating a punch from one side, a kick from the other. 'God have mercy on him, he was only a boy,' I added.

Mohammad dropped his fist, then with a sudden movement he thumped his two companions on the chest, shouting at them angrily, 'Get back, you cowards!'

'This is my brother's grave,' he said after a few moments silence.

'May God have mercy on him . . . how old was he?' I asked in a sad voice.

'He was fifteen,' answered Mohammad. Then he kissed the grave, got to his feet and, giving me a pat on the right shoulder as if he were an old man (he was in fact two years older than me), said with a sad smile, 'His blood will not have been spilt in vain. That, my friend, is a promise and a vow I must keep.'

'A thousand blessings on his grave,' I said once more. He patted my shoulder again and said, 'Please, pardon and forgive me for what I did to you. I'm sorry. I swear to you on the grave of the departed that I'm sorry.'

As Mohammad moved away I remained where I was, contemplating the dust clinging to his dishdasha, and I felt a prick in my heart, or something falling from it.

Next day the teacher was surprised to see Mohammad sitting next to me at the same desk. He came up to us smiling, and Mohammad said, pointing to me, 'Shmuel is one of the deceased's best friends.'

The teacher and pupils were all well aware that when Mohammad spoke of the deceased, he meant the occupant of the grave, that sacred figure who had fallen victim to the internecine feuds of the clans.

After that no one dared come near me. Even Mohammad himself became timid and could not look me in the eye. I remember how he asked me to play table tennis, and when he came out the loser he told me, 'See, I knew you were a great player!'

We laughed and, together, hand in hand, headed for the classroom.

★ ★ ★

After three years living with Nasrat Shah's family in al-Ramadi, I asked to return to my own family. Nasrat Shah nodded in agreement, somewhat against his will (I know he loved me as one of his own children) and Sakina was also sad.

Entering the graveyard, I began reciting the 'Verse of the Throne' until I reached 'my grave', where I sat down, reading the inscription over and over again until the sun began to set. I looked at the Carpenter (the most beautiful thing I owned) and pulled out the sheet of paper with the 'Verse of the Throne' written in my own hand. I put the paper into the roller of the Carpenter, then placed the typewriter on top of the grave and ran off to catch the bus for al-Khalidiyah.

It was night when I arrived in al-Khalidiyah. Before coming across my family's place I had to knock on the doors of many houses asking, 'Do you know where the poor Assyrian family lives, that came here from al-Habbaniyah three years ago?' When finally I knocked on the right door, I heard my father cry out, like the whooping of Red Indians attacking a wagon train. From my bag I took out a poster of Norman Wisdom leaping into the air, a cap on his head and his mouth open in a broad grin, and slipped it under the door.

The door was opened immediately.

EPILOGUE

★ In October 1978 I finished my compulsory military service, and immediately began the procedure for obtaining a passport. It was not easy, but in the end I got it, and in January 1979 I left Iraq with only a few dollars. Everyone said it was madness, but later I felt I was lucky and that divine providence was behind me, as just a month after I left, Khomeini came to power in Iran and in April declared the Islamic Republic, while in July, Saddam Hussein's military coup saw him become President of Iraq; military skirmishes began on the Iraqi-Iranian border, the Iraqi government recalled all reserve soldiers, among them my fellow servicemen, who were thrown into the fire of war from 1980, with the few who remained alive being released only in late 1988 after the war ended.

★ When war broke out between Iraq and Iran in 1980, Samson was sent to the front again and was wounded. Teddy was also called up and wounded. Robin, too, did more than six years of military service in the war until he was paralysed. He still loves aeroplanes and dreams of studying aeronautical engineering.

★ As for Shamiran, two of her three children were sent to war. Later she was informed that Sargon had been killed and her other son, Ashur, was missing. After four years she learned Ashur was a prisoner in Iran, and after ten years he came home, telling his mother that he and many other prisoners had spent all their time constructing buildings and palatial homes for the Iranian mullahs.

⋆ Kiryakos remained faithful to John Ford to the end. After his disappearance from al-Habbaniyah we subsequently discovered he had been arrested by the Baath security services on suspicion of 'spying for the West'. When he was released three years later he laughed and said he had written a letter of complaint to the head of the security services demanding the return of his personal archive of movie pictures. His friends advised him, 'Kiryakos, you should be glad you're still alive, forget the pictures.' But Kiryakos responded with his customary laugh, 'I know they won't give me back the pictures, I just wanted to put some titles of John Ford movies in their files!'

Kiryakos had worded his letter as follows:

> *I demand you return my personal archive of movie stills. The photographs have absolutely no bearing on the strategic security of our country, being pictures from the movies of an American director called John Ford, whose real name was Sean Aloysius O'Fearna, born on 1 February 1895 in the American State of Maine, and died on 31 August 1973 in the American State of California. The pictures I wish returned are from the following movies:* Cheyenne Autumn, Donovan's Reef, How the West was Won, Two Rode Together, Sergeant Rutledge, The Horse Soldiers, The Last Hurrah, The Rising of the Moon, The Wings of Eagles, The Searchers, Mister Roberts, The Quiet Man, The Tornado, Wild Women, The Scarlet Drop, A Fight for Love, Rio Grande, Drums along the Mohawk, Wee Willie Winkie, The Plough and the Stars, Arrowsmith, The Lost Patrol, She Wore a Yellow Ribbon, They Were Expendable *and others.*

Kiryakos died while I was in Beirut. He was sixty years old.

★ After leaving al-Ramadi, I never saw Nasrat Shah again. He too died while I was in Beirut.

★ As for Qassim and Samar, one day while doing my military service, it was the summer of 1976, I was in a jeep with another soldier travelling along a desert road a few kilometres from al-Ramadi. It was a very hot afternoon and I asked the driver to stop so we could buy a cold drink from the only shop on the road. The storekeeper was bent over busy at some task or other and there was a woman with two children sitting at the back of the shop. 'Two bottles of cold Sinalco, please,' I asked the shopkeeper, who was still bent over. He turned around and it was Qassim. He stared at me in amazement, then tears began streaming from his eyes. 'Joey, it's Joey!' he cried, hugging me hard. And the surprise continued as he cried out, 'Samar, come here, Samar. It's Joey; Kika and Gorgiya's son.' And Jane Russell appeared with her two small daughters, pregnant with her third child.

ACKNOWLEDGEMENTS

I would like to take this opportunity to thank my wife Margaret Obank who encouraged me to write this book. I would also like to acknowledge my gratitude to the Künstlerdorf in Schöppingen, Germany, where I spent four months working on my book. I am grateful for the support and encouragement of my friends Fadhil al-Azzawi and Anton Shammas. Also, I must thank Paul Starkey, Issa Boullata and William Hutchins for their help in the translation.

GLOSSARY

agal: the black cord that fastens around a keffiyeh to hold it in place.

al-Hussainiya: a mosque for Shia Muslims

Bonsoir, cher monsieur! Ça va bien?: Good evening, dear sir! How are you?

boukha: a traditional Tunisian liquor made from figs

Ce n'est pas loin de l'église de la Madeleine: It's not far from the church of Mary Magdalene

C'est trop tard, c'est trop tard!: It's too late, it's too late!

Depuis toujours: forever

ful: boiled and mashed fava beans

habibati: Arabic word for 'my love'

Imam Ali Bin Abi Talib: son-in-law and cousin of the Prophet Mohammad, and the fourth Caliph (656 C.E until his assassination in 661 C.E). Shia Muslims regard him as the first and rightful Imam after Mohammad.

kibbeh: oval-shaped balls of bulgur wheat, sometimes of cracked rice, filled with a meat and spice mixture

kofta: spiced balls of lamb or beef mixed with chopped onions and herbs

lahmajoon: a flat baked bread-dough pocket filled with spiced minced meat

Mar Gewargis: Saint George

Mar Shimun: Saint Shimun, Patriarch of the Assyrian Church of the East, who was assassinated

Mission: a brand of soft drink

Nadhem al-Ghazali: famous Iraqi singer (1921–1963)

pacha: a traditional Iraqi dish made from sheep's head, trotters and stomach, all boiled slowly and served with bread in a broth

Passez une bonne journée: Have a nice day

Sinalco: a brand of soft drink

Sitt: Arabic term of address for a woman such as Mrs, Ma'am, Madame

Surat al-Nas: the Chapter of Mankind is the final sura of the Qur'an

Thulfiqar: the name of Ali Bin Abi Talib's sword

zaatar manaqish: baked flat circles of bread dough sprinkled with a mixture of olive oil and zaatar (a thyme and sumac spice blend)

ABOUT THE TRANSLATORS

Christina Phillips is a Lecturer in Arabic Literature at the University of Exeter. She began translating Arabic fiction as a PhD student at the School of Oriental and African Studies, London. Her translations include *Morning and Evening Talk* (2008) by Nobel Prize Winner Naguib Mahfouz and *Like A Summer Never to be Repeated* (2009) by Mohamed Berrada.

Piers Amodia translates from Arabic, Italian and Spanish into English. He spent eight years in the merchant navy before going to Edinburgh University to study Arabic. He lived briefly in Cairo teaching Italian before moving to Rome where he works as a translator for the Vatican.

Lightning Source UK Ltd.
Milton Keynes UK
UKHW021237080322
399751UK00008B/2055